MIDNIGHT'S MASTER

MIDNIGHT'S MASTER

CYNTHIA EDEN

KENSINGTON BOOKS

www.kensingtonbooks.com

KENSINGTON BOOKS are published by

Kensington Publishing Corp.
119 West 40th Street
New York, NY 10018

All Kensington titles, imprints, and distributed lines are available at special quantity discounts for bulk purchases for sales promotion, premiums, fund-raising, educational or institutional use.

Special book excerpts or customized printings can also be created to fit specific needs. For details, write or phone the office of the Kensington Special Sales Manager: Kensington Publishing Corp., 119 West 40th Street, New York, NY, 10018. Attn. Special Sales Department. Phone: 1-800-221-2647.

Kensington and the K logo Reg. U.S. Pat. & TM Off.

ISBN-13: 978-0-7582-3427-8
ISBN-10: 0-7582-3427-9
First Kensington Trade Edition: July 2009
First Kensington Mass Market Edition: September 2015

10 9 8 7 6 5 4 3 2 1

Printed in the United States of America

Chapter 1

Having a breakdown in the middle of a live broadcast was really not a very good thing for a reporter's career.

Holly Storm's fingers tightened their already white-knuckled grip around the microphone. Her breath came too hard and way too fast as she fought to hold on to her control.

"Holly . . ." The reed-thin voice of her producer.

Shit. Her career was about to hit the toilet. She dragged her gaze away from the body—away from the body that she *knew* didn't belong to a human—and glanced back toward the round lens of the camera. "Uh . . . I'm . . . H-Holly Storm, reporting to you live from the scene of—" *A freaking slaughter.* "A brutal . . . murder." Yeah, brutal was a good word choice considering the way the poor guy had been sliced to ribbons.

Get a grip, girl. She couldn't afford a meltdown right now.

After a hard swallow, she finally managed to suck in a full breath. Holly cleared her throat, then spoke in that calm, cool voice she'd perfected back in her college communication classes so long ago. "Police aren't talking . . ." At least not to her. But then, the two detectives on the scene—Colin Gyth and Todd Brooks—weren't exactly on her "friends" list. "But this reporter can't help but wonder just what sort of *monster* is loose on our Atlanta streets."

There was a growl to her right. Her gaze darted over, just for a moment, and she met the bright stare of Detective Gyth.

Screw him. Her chin lifted. "Reporting live from a downtown scene of death, this is Holly Storm, signing off."

The camera lens watched her for a silent moment. Then . . .

"Christ, Holly, you think that was a little dramatic?" Ben Blake muttered, lowering the camera from his shoulder. His Braves hat, the one the guy always wore, rain or shine, night or day, rested high on his head. A line of stubble lined his jaw.

"Dramatic's good," she told him, aware that while her voice was cool, her heart thundered hard enough to shake her chest. "Drama gets folks to forget about their crappy days and pay attention to the news."

"Are you okay?" The quieter, and no longer panicked, voice of her producer asked. "Not everyone is cut out for these kinds of stories."

Her shoulders, already straight, stiffened even more. No way was she about to be yanked off *this* story. Her last encounter with the *Other*—the supernaturals who walked the streets acting like humans and hiding behind magic— had left her with singed hair, a body full of bruises, and the acid of fear on her tongue.

But she wasn't the running-and-hiding type. Okay, fact one: Monsters existed. Fact two: Those monsters scared the hell out of her. Fact three: If she wanted to work in this town, and she did, then Holly was gonna have to learn how to live with the darker beings that stalked the streets.

"I'm fine, Mac." McArthur Phillips was a news veteran. Once an anchor for News Flash Five, the sixty-three-year-old had turned his attention to bossing folks around in his producer gig. Not that Mac looked sixty-three. The guy worked out four times a week to keep his body in top "anchor" form and his black hair was only now starting to gray.

From what Holly could tell, Mac was one of those guys who generally spoke softly, but could rip the flesh off anyone who got in his way with just a few careful words. Probably a leftover trait from his army days. She knew the guy had served back in Vietnam. She'd heard more than a few of his stories before.

"Don't lie to me." Still soft, but with a hard rasp beneath the words. "You looked pale as death for a minute there. A reporter fainting on camera—"

"Would be a major ratings score," Ben cut in, tugging his hat down a bit as a smile curved his thin lips.

Holly glared at him. "Right, because I *want* to be known as the Fainting Flash Five girl." Asshole. She liked Ben, really did, but sometimes he could piss her off.

Holly's nose wrinkled. Oh, dammit, she could smell the blood.

"Well, if you're not goin' to faint, then get your ass over to those cops and find out just what the hell is goin' on," Mac growled.

Her back teeth locked. The cops had already said there would be no interviews. At least, no "official" ones. *A girl had to try.* Holly shoved her microphone toward Ben. "Be back in ten." And hopefully, she'd be back with a story.

Holly turned on her heel. Zeroed her sights on the detectives. They were talking to a uniformed cop. Faces intent. She slipped under the yellow police tape, then crept toward them, hoping to overhear—

"Ms. Storm, just what the hell do you think you're

doin'?" Colin Gyth demanded, blue eyes glittering down at her. His arms were crossed over his rather impressively muscled chest. "This is a *crime* scene." He grabbed her arm and hauled her back toward the tape, ignoring her outraged yelp. "If we wanted reporters screwing up the evidence, there wouldn't be a damn barrier set up."

A flimsy barrier. He pushed her under the tape, shook his head, and frowned down at her. "Hell, woman, didn't you learn your lesson the last time?"

Learn her lesson? What was she, a two-year-old? "What I learned," she pitched her voice low, knowing others couldn't overhear this, "is that this town has a lot of deadly secrets." She pointed toward the body. "Looks like you've got someone hunting demons."

His eyes widened. *"What?"*

Uh, oh. The detective hadn't known—

He was under the tape and beside her in less than two seconds. For a big guy, he could sure move fast. "What did you just say?"

Holly licked her lips. The detective was intimidating as hell with those dark features and the glinting edge of teeth that looked a bit too sharp and—

"She said the victim wasn't human." The cold, slightly mocking voice had every nerve in Holly's body tensing. No, shit, not—

She and Colin turned together and met the coal-black stare of Niol Lapen. It was just after dusk, and the dark shadows gathered around him, wrapping over the tall, muscled length of his body.

He strolled toward them, power evident in his every rippling move. His face, a face that Holly figured most women would find attractive—not *her,* of course, but most women—showed no hint of emotion. But then, she'd rarely known Niol to bother much with emotions.

Midnight-black hair swept back from his high fore-head. The guy really had perfect features, aesthetically speaking anyway. High cheeks, square jaw, long, straight nose, and lips that were—

Not for me. Holly jerked her gaze back up to his black eyes and away from the lips that she was not the least bit interested in. She needed to focus on his eyes—because it was the eyes that told the true nature of the man. Or, in Niol's case, the true nature of the demon.

Because Niol Lapen was a demon. Probably the strongest and most dangerous demon she'd ever met, and she wasn't going to forget that fact.

Or the fact that she was pretty sure he'd killed a man the last time they'd met.

His gaze swept past her. Holly followed his stare and saw that the body had been covered with a sheet. About time.

"How did you get here so fast, Ms. Storm?" Niol's voice, harder now, dark and demanding.

Her eyebrows shot up. Just what was the demon implying? "I was covering a story two blocks over. I followed the sirens." Okay, probably not her classiest moment, but she'd landed an exclusive.

And stumbled onto a scene that would give her nightmares for a week.

Not now. She couldn't let this get personal now.

But dammit, why *him*? He'd been a good guy, harmless. He hadn't deserved terror and death in a dirty alley, behind a strip club for God's sake.

"Fuck that." Colin stepped toward Niol. "You knew the victim?"

"Um." Neither agreement not denial.

Colin's hands clenched. "Don't play with me, Niol. If you'd seen the way the poor bastard was slashed—"

"I did."

Colin stiffened. "You didn't—"

Niol laughed, a rough, dry sound, and his gaze returned to Holly. "I didn't kill him. One of *her* kind did."

What? Her kind? What was he—

"Come with me. *Now.*" Colin pointed at her. "And as for you, Ms. Storm, stay away from my crime scene."

Niol's gaze raked over her, for just the briefest moment, darting from her head to her strappy black shoes, and Holly shivered. *Dangerous.*

But, dammit, *sexy.*

Focus. "You can't just shut out the press, you know, detective. The public has a right to know—"

Niol shook his head. "Still playing that song, Holly?" Holly, *not* Ms. Storm any longer. And his voice was different too. Husky. Rough. The voice a man would use in bed. Goose bumps rose on her uncovered arms.

"I don't know—"

"You *knew* he was a demon." His lips twisted and those soulless black eyes bored into her. "He was one of your sources, wasn't he?"

No way was she going to answer that question, even if the dark demon before her was right. Carl Bronx had been one of her sources. She'd talked with him more than a dozen times. He'd been young, a little over twenty-one, with a ready smile and a dimple in his chin.

No. She *would* not think about him. Thinking about him and realizing that sweet Carl was the guy who'd gotten sliced to bits, well, that had almost caused her on-camera breakdown.

Niol stepped toward her and brushed the back of his hand over her chilled arm. "You're not as hard as you pretend to be," he whispered. "Pity." His breath stirred the hair near her cheek.

Holly blinked back the tears that stupidly filled her eyes because even though the sheet was over him, in her mind, she could still see Carl's bloody body.

Niol shook his head. "You're out of your league. Go home, Holly. Back to your safe world." He stepped back. "Leave the demons and the death to me."

The guy couldn't have given her a more clear dismissal.

Holly watched Niol turn and stride with Colin toward a patrol car.

Oh, yeah, that had been a rather nice "Fuck off."

Unfortunately for the demon, she wasn't the fucking-off type.

"Didn't get the story, huh?" Ben asked, coming to stand at her side.

Holly didn't take her gaze off the strong lines of Niol's body. He leaned against the blue-and-white patrol car, his arms loose at his sides. "Not yet."

"The cops will release a statement later, no big deal—"

"It is." Carl had been important. One of the good guys—uh, demons. He hadn't deserved an ending like this. Hell, *no one* deserved a death like this.

Carl had trusted her with his secrets.

She wasn't going to slink away from his case. Sure, she knew the routine—don't let the stories get personal. Every reporter's mantra.

But it was too late. This kill, it *was* personal.

She wasn't about to back off.

Niol and Colin were talking, lips moving fast, but the words were far too soft for her to hear. After a moment, Niol inclined his head and marched away from the detective. Colin looked furious, his face tight and his body stiff.

Holly knew she wasn't going to be getting any help from the cop.

Niol headed toward the waiting shadows.

But the demon . . .

He was a whole other story.

Her breath hitched as a spike of excitement had her blood heating.

"Holly . . ." Ben's voice was high-pitched—a sure sign the man was getting worried. "What are you thinking?"

"I'm thinking I'm getting this story." She tossed him a hard smile, one that she knew showed a lot of teeth. "One way or another." Even if she had to walk into the devil's den.

Actually, that idea didn't sound bad at all.

Time to go into the darkness and see what secrets she could find.

After all, she was a reporter—a reporter who always got her story.

The pretty redhead walked into his hell as if she owned the place.

Chin up, slim shoulders back, one hand cocked on her hip. Oh, yeah, *serious* attitude.

But, as he watched her, Niol Lapen couldn't help but wonder . . . when he got closer to the lady, would he see fear lurking in her too-green eyes?

Because he knew that she'd been afraid of him before. The last time she'd crossed the threshold into the bar that some thought of as Paradise and others knew as hell, there had been fear in Holly Storm's gaze.

Not that she'd let the fear stop her.

And he'd always rather enjoyed fear in his prey.

Niol had decided months ago that the reporter would make wonderful prey.

He propped his elbows on the bar and kept his gaze on the woman who was slowly strolling across Paradise Found. She'd changed her clothes. The dressy top and the dark pants were gone. Now she wore a short dress, black, one that emphasized the pale silk of her skin, one that flashed the tempting swell of her perfect breasts and kissed the tops of her thighs.

Um. He'd like to do that. Like to kiss and lick those long legs. He could all too easily imagine the feel of that smooth skin against his lips and tongue.

His eyes narrowed. The lady knew how to dress. A point in her favor.

She also knew how to find trouble. Another point for Holly.

"Hell." The disgust came from the bartender behind him. It was the kind of disgust Niol normally felt for reporters, but not for Holly. "What's *she* doing here?" Marc demanded.

Niol never took his gaze off Holly. Her right hand clutched a small black bag—*bet she's got some kind of recorder in there*—and her high heels clicked across the floor. He could hear every move she made. The bar, his second home, was packed—a good thing. Yet his senses—damn strong senses seeing as how he was a level-ten demon— were wholly focused on her.

If he tried, he bet he'd even be able to smell her. That light, rich scent of lavender from her lotion.

"Want me to kick her ass out, boss?" Marc asked, and the soft clink of a glass sounded.

A smile curved Niol's lips. "That's not exactly what I want to happen to the lady's ass." No, he had other plans for Holly . . . and her gorgeous ass.

It had been too long since he'd taken a lover. At least a month. But he'd been dealing with killers and death. A guy could get distracted.

And now there was this other bastard on the streets. *If another demon died . . .*

He lifted his drink. Drained the shot glass in one quick gulp. The hot burn of the liquid slid down his throat. "Don't worry about the reporter, Marc." Though he was a pretty recent hire at the bar, Marc still knew the score. He also knew that cops and reporters normally weren't too welcome in Paradise. "I'll take care of her." Very good care of her.

Holly Storm. She was the newest reporter at News

Flash Five. Smart. Resourceful. A real looker, too. Plump lips. Small nose. High, glass-sharp cheekbones.

Oh, yeah, the reporter was sexy.

She was also trouble because she knew far, *far* too much about his private world of demons and darkness.

Most humans didn't know that the monsters they feared in their dreams—the vampires, werewolves, everything that made the night go bump—were all real. Humans were too worried about their nine-to-five jobs, too busy worrying about getting robbed by the guy in line next to them at the grocery store or getting carjacked at the red light on the wrong side of town. They never stopped and actually *looked* at the world around them.

Because if the humans would just jerk off their damn blinders, they'd see they had a whole hell of a lot more to fear on this Earth than they imagined, and that some nightmares could be very, very real.

Holly had first lost her blinders months ago. For a time, she'd even planned to air her discovery on her precious news station.

Of course, her plans had changed when he'd brought the fires of hell to her feet. Rather literally.

At that moment, her gaze locked on his. Her eyes widened, just a bit. The taking-my-time walk became faster as she tried to hurry to him and—

And a vampire stepped in her path.

Niol's fingers drummed on the bar. The undead asshole had just blocked his view. He'd give him five seconds to move, then—

Holly stepped around the vamp, her jaw locked. Her full lips—painted red, Niol's favorite color—pressed into a line. Ah, so the reporter wasn't in the mood for—

The vamp touched her. Grabbed her arm. Then jerked her up against his chest.

Niol stilled and a hot rush of power and fury flooded

through his body. Even as the floor began to tremble, he was storming across the room.

"Holly." His voice cut through the music and the shrill voices and the fake laughs.

The vamp, skin drained of color, eyes sunken, craned his head toward him. "Oh, shit." He shoved Holly aside.

She stumbled, just a moment, on her two-inch heels. "Nice, you jerk—"

The vampire bared his fangs at her and growled.

Holly's jaw dropped. Then she swayed on those heels. Niol reached out a hand and snagged her wrist, a wrist that was too thin, catching her just before she fell.

Her stare held his.

Oh, yeah, the fear was there. Hiding behind the "don't-give-a-damn" mask. Fear . . . and a helpless curiosity.

Humans, always so curious. Always wanting to know what lurked in the darkness around them.

And then, when they found out—running away in fear.

"She's a reporter, André," Niol murmured, and allowed his fingers to stroke over her pounding pulse. Already fast, the beat of her pulse began to race even more. "She's not the prey you want." *Because she's mine.*

"Reporter?" The too-sharp teeth disappeared. "Thought you didn't let *their* kind in here."

Holly sucked in a sharp breath. She tried to yank her hand away from Niol. Tried, failed. She grunted, a sound that shouldn't have been sexy but was, and turned her stare on the vampire. "It's a public place, jerkoff. From the looks of things, *all* kinds get in here. Even the dead ones."

"*Un*dead." André sniffed.

"Right." She tugged her hand again. Niol tightened his hold. "Listen, buddy, you—"

The vamp's lips peeled back, revealing teeth no human should see, unless the human was about to become a meal.

Reluctantly, Niol dropped Holly's hand. Then he stepped forward, deliberately putting his body between Holly and the vamp. "Is there a problem here, André?"

The vamp was tall—big damn deal. *He* was taller. And the last time he'd been afraid of a vamp . . . well, he'd never been afraid of the fanged freaks.

André swallowed, and seemed to shrink a bit. "I-I just . . ." He licked his lips, a quick, nervous move. "Reporters can't be here. Too risky, you know that, you know—"

Okay, the guy's voice was getting too high, and two panther shifters at a nearby table were starting to look nervous. "She's not your problem. Forget her."

"Ah, *she's* here." Holly tapped on his back. "And getting more pissed by the minute." Another insistent tap, right in the middle of his back.

André's already beady eyes narrowed. The brief flash of fear gave way to anger. "Throw her out, Niol. You want the vamps to keep comin', you *throw that bitch out.*"

The tapping stopped, and, because the vampire had raised his shrill-ass voice again, the nearby paranormals—because, generally, the folks who came in his bar were far, far from normal—stilled.

Niol shook his head slowly. "I think you're forgetting a few things, *vamp.*" He gathered the black swell of power that pulsed just beneath his skin. Felt the surge of dark magic and—

The vamp flew across the bar, slamming into the stage with a scream. The lead guitarist swore, then jumped back, cradling his guitar with both hands like the precious baby he thought it was.

The sudden silence was deafening.

Niol motioned toward the bar. "Get me another drink, Marc." He glanced at the slowly rising vampire. "Did I tell you to get up?" It barely took any effort to slam the bastard into the stage wall this time. Just a stray thought, really.

Ah, but power was a wonderful thing.

Sometimes, it was damn good to be a demon. And even better to be a level-ten, and the baddest asshole in the room.

He stalked forward. Enjoyed for a moment the way the crowd jumped away from him.

The vampire began to shake. *Perfect*.

Niol stopped a foot before the fallen André. "First," he growled, "don't ever, *ever* fucking tell me what to do in *my* bar again."

A fast nod.

"Second . . ." His hands clenched into fists as he fought to rein in the magic blasting through him. The power . . . oh, but it was tempting. And so easy to use.

Too easy.

One more thought, just one, focused and hard, and he could have the vamp dead at his feet.

"Use too much, you'll lose yourself." An old warning. One that had come too late for him. He'd been twenty-five before he met another demon who even came close to him in power and that guy's warning—well, it had been long overdue.

Niol knew he'd been one of the Lost for years.

The first time he'd killed, he'd been Lost.

"Second," he repeated, his voice cold, clear, and cutting like a knife in the quiet. "If you think I give a damn about the vampires coming to *my* place . . ." His mouth hitched into a half-grin, but Niol knew no amusement would show in the darkness of his eyes. "Then you're dead wrong, vampire."

"S-sorry, Niol, I—"

He laughed. Then turned his back on the cringing vampire. "Thomas." The guard he always kept close. "Throw that vamp's ass out."

When Thomas stepped forward, the squeal of a guitar ripped through the bar. And the dancing and the drinking and the mating games of the *Other* began with a fierce rumble of sound.

Niol's gaze searched for his prey and he found Holly watching him. All eyes and red hair and lips that begged for his mouth. He strode toward her, conscious of covert stares still on them. He could show no weakness. Never could.

I'm not weak.

He was the strongest demon in Atlanta. He sure wasn't going to give the paranormals any cause to start doubting his power.

His kind turned on the weak.

When he stopped before her, the scent of lavender flooded his nostrils.

She looked up at him. The human was small, to him anyway, barely reaching his shoulders so that he towered over her.

She was the weak one. All of her kind were.

Humans. So easy to wound. To kill.

He lifted his hand. Stroked her cheek. Damn, but she was soft. Leaning close, Niol told her, "Sweetheart, I warned you before about coming to my Paradise."

There was no doubt others overheard his words. With so many shifters skulking around the joint, a *whisper* would have been overheard. Shifters and their annoyingly superior senses.

"Wh-what do you mean?" The question came, husky and soft. Ah, but he liked her voice. He could all too easily imagine that voice, whispering to him as they lay amid a tangle of sheets.

Or maybe screaming in his ear as she came.

He cupped her chin in his hand. A nice chin. Softly rounded. And those lips . . . the bottom was fuller than the top. Just a bit. So red. Her mouth was slightly parted, open.

Waiting.

She stepped back, shaking her head. "I don't know what you *think* you're doing, Niol—"

He stared down at her. "Yes, you do." He caught her arms, wrapping his fingers around her and jerking Holly against him. "I told you, the last time you came into *my* bar . . ."

Her eyes widened. "Niol . . ."

Oh, yeah, he liked the way she said his name. She breathed it, tasted it.

His lips lowered toward hers. "If you want to walk in Paradise, baby, then you're gonna have to play with the devil."

"No, I—"

He kissed her. Hard. Deep. Niol drove his tongue right past those plump lips and took her mouth the way the beast inside him demanded.

She tasted like wine, and the more he sampled, the more he wanted.

His hold on her tightened. Her breasts crushed against him, and the tight peaks of her nipples stabbed into his chest.

His cock twitched, full and heavy with arousal—hell, he'd been hard since the moment Holly strolled into the bar.

His tongue met hers. Thrust. Took. When she moaned low in her throat, he pulled her closer against him.

Her mouth widened, letting him inside even more. Ah, yes, that was just what he—

She wrenched her head away from his. Her breath panted. Her mouth glistened.

He wanted more. Niol licked his lips, tasted her.

How long would it take to get her out of the dress? He bet he could take her into his office, have her naked and moaning in less than two minutes.

"Take your hands off me." Bright spots of color stained her ivory cheeks. She swallowed. Once, twice. "I'm here to talk to you about Carl and—"

He dropped his hands. *Too many ears and eyes in this place.* "If you're not here to fuck, Holly, then don't waste my time."

Her mouth dropped open. *"What?"*

He almost smiled. Almost.

But he had an image to maintain.

And, because of the little reporter, an aching hard-on.

"Humans who come into Paradise know the rules. They either come to *play*,"—and the blond human in the booth to the left looked like she was having one hell of a time *playing* with her vampire—"or they come to be prey." Simple enough.

Green eyes narrowed. "A man is dead, Niol. I want your help!"

He raised his hand. Snapped his fingers.

Her head jerked. "You didn't just—"

Thomas, who'd returned from his little errand with the vamp, marched to his side. "Boss?"

Niol did let his lips curve now. It was just too much fun. Ah, but the reporter's cheeks were such a lovely red. "Thomas, do me a favor . . ." A brief pause. He could feel the eyes and ears on him. He glanced toward Holly, allowed himself one last look at that tempting body, then ordered, "Throw her pretty ass out."

Chapter 2

She'd had worse nights. Not many, thankfully, but a few. Holly glared at the back of the building, because, of course, she hadn't been escorted out the front of Paradise Found. No, while the vamp had at least been thrown out the front of the bar, the NBA reject had tossed *her* out the back door and into the alley with the stench from hell.

"Get lost, lady," the bouncer ordered, pointing one thick finger toward the waiting darkness. "You won't be warned again." His face—scary, downright ugly—tightened.

Oh, right, because being thrown out like garbage was some kind of warning. "Tell Niol this isn't over!" She shouted, even as the jerk began to swing the door closed. "I'm not going to disappear! I'm not—"

The door slammed shut.

"Talking to anyone," she finished, then snarled in disgust.

Dammit. Why couldn't Niol cut her some slack? The black-eyed bastard *owed* her. Hadn't she kept her mouth shut about what she'd seen him do?

She spun around, and her gaze jerked helplessly down the alley.

Right there. She'd been standing right there and she'd seen Niol literally fry a man. The flames had been so hot. The breath of the fire had scorched her skin.

The bastard who'd died had been a murderer. A sick, twisted psycho who had planned to kill *her*. She hadn't shed any tears over his death.

But she'd had more than a few nightmares.

And now she was back here. Back at what could have been the scene of her murder.

She took a few slow steps forward. In the dim light, she could just barely make out the scorch marks at the end of the alley.

No, she hadn't shed any tears for the dead man.

But she also hadn't taken her story live, either. She hadn't blasted the truth about the killer—the fact that he was a demon, a powerful supernatural—into the homes of thousands of people.

Because after what she'd seen that terrible night, Holly knew that the world wasn't ready for the truth yet.

Monsters are real.

Oh, yeah, they were real. Strong. Dangerous. Evil.

And scary as all hell.

She stopped at the edge of the black markings. The markings that were all that remained of a demon's life.

So many monsters . . . Her hands clenched.

Some of them, like Carl, weren't bad. Some were almost . . . normal. Just trying to get by in the big, too-cold world.

Living, as best they could, until the darkness struck them down.

Holly bent, the cold air of the night brushing against her. It was late spring, should have been warmer, but a cold blast was hitting the city.

Her fingers touched the rough pavement, and her nails scraped over the black lines.

He'd been in my head. He took my control away. Made me into a puppet. Even though she'd tried so hard to fight. At night, she could still feel the whispers of her fear.

She'd been so afraid. So sure that she was staring at death.

Was that how Carl had felt? Before he'd been gutted by—

A rustle of sound reached her ears. Soft. Like clothes, fabric brushing against the hard stone walls that all but surrounded her.

In an instant, Holly was on her feet, heart racing so hard the thudding filled her ears. She whirled around, searching the alley with narrowed eyes as she squinted to see in the darkness. "Who's there?" Chill bumps were on her arms, but whether they were from the increasing cold of the air or the sudden fear that pumped through her, she didn't know.

No one answered her call, and she licked her lips.

Not alone. She knew it, with every single fiber of her being.

Someone, or some*thing*, was in that alley with her. Watching from the too concealing darkness. Her instincts screamed for her to *run*. To get the hell out of there as fast as she could . . .

But she'd come to Paradise, such as it was, for a reason.

So she didn't run. Just stood straighter.

"I know you're there." The air now felt strangely still against her. She took one step forward and hoped that she looked a lot more confident than she felt.

She hated this stinking alley. It scared her, made her realize just how vulnerable she was.

So why the hell are you standing here in the dark, when you know something's watching you?

Her lungs ached as she drew in a deep breath. She'd lured more than her share of sources out of the shadows before. Faced down muggers. Crack-high kids. But this—

Someone watched.

This was different.

Okay, time to run like crazy. Forget dignity, she'd lost that back in the bar.

"Holly!"

The growl of her name had her choking back a startled scream. Jesus. Now she was turning back around, *like a spinning top,* as she jerked to face the mouth of the alley once more. A man stood waiting there, arms thrust deep into the pockets of his long, black coat.

Niol.

She was almost glad to see him.

Ah, screw that. Holly took off toward him, pretty much at a run.

She *was* damn glad to see the jerk.

Sometimes, the devil you knew was a hell of a lot better than the monster in the dark.

As she hurried toward him, she saw his dark gaze lift and sweep behind her. He seemed to stiffen.

"Niol, what—"

"Get in the car, Holly."

She saw his black SUV then, idling near the corner. Tendrils of exhaust escaped from the back of the vehicle, drifting up into the night.

Since she'd taken a cab down to Paradise, and she really wasn't feeling the urge to call and wait outside on the street for another one to arrive and pick her up, Holly decided to follow the snapped order.

But she couldn't help glancing back over her shoulder, one more time.

Only shadows stared back at her from the depths of the alley.

Shadows and the memory of death.

* * *

He could smell the woman. A sweet scent, light, rising over the decay and vermin of the alley.

For a moment, he'd been so close to her. Close enough to touch. To slide his fingers over her skin.

Close enough to rip that perfect porcelain skin right open.

The slam of a door echoed in the night. Then another. Tires squealed as the demon bastard drove away.

Taking the woman with him.

Interesting.

Niol had a taste for humans. He loved to play with the mortal women. And the immortal ones.

He and the demon had that pleasure in common.

A whistle escaped the man's lips as he strolled from the darkness. He'd been waiting there, biding his time, when the redhead had literally been thrown into his path.

Sometimes, fate could be brilliant.

He stepped over the charred cement and his whistle became louder.

Such a nice night. Pity he'd already made his kill. It really would have been the perfect night for a slaughter.

Ah, well, perhaps it was time he found new prey.

"What the hell were you doing?" Niol demanded, his fingers tightening around the leather steering wheel. "Do you have some kind of death wish or something?"

"*What?* Look, buddy, *you* are the one who so kindly had me tossed into the alley. It's not like I wanted to be there and—"

"You weren't alone." The words came from between clenched teeth.

"I was—" She broke off, gasping, and he felt the hot weight of her stare land on him. "How do you know that?"

He turned the wheel hard to the right and heard the harsh squeal of tires. "Hell, lady, have you forgotten what I am?" After his last demonstration, in that same pit-forsaken alley, she shouldn't have forgotten any damn thing.

"Demon." A breath of sound.

Niol nodded. Demon through the skin, through the blood, all the way to the core of his bones.

No, he wasn't some pointy-tailed, horned, red freak who'd escaped from the depths of hell. Generally demons weren't like that, though most folks, when they closed their eyes at night, sure pictured them as such.

His kind weren't servants of the devil. So, okay, yeah, some had certainly chosen to walk on the trail of the damned, and he'd more than danced on the dark side a few times.

Demons, such as his brethren, were more than human. Stronger, faster, gifted with powers that normal men and women could only dream of in their wild fantasies. Some whispers said that demons came from the Fallen, those angels who'd had the bad luck to get their lily asses tossed out of heaven. Niol wasn't real sure about the origin of his race, and, normally, he didn't give a shit where he'd come from.

He lived. He breathed. He had enough power to knock down a city block. Those were generally the only facts that mattered to him.

The streets were slick with a light coating of rain. The tires flew across the pavement, sending water splashing.

"You know about a demon's power, don't you, Holly?" He knew the reporter had been digging into the lives of the demons in the city. She'd learned about demons when she'd made the mistake of taking a killer on as a source a few months back. The woman had fed Holly information about the *Other* world, and, in the end, the lady had almost led to the reporter's death.

A near slaughter should have given Holly pause. She should have kept her cute little nose with its faint sprinkle of freckles out of demon business. But, no, she'd been poking and digging, and, from the look of that bloody scene he'd witnessed earlier that day, she was still getting the wrong folks to be her sources.

And still walking straight into trouble.

Just like she'd walked into his bar.

"I know . . . some things."

Niol glanced at her from the corner of his eye. Streetlights flickered over her, revealing, then concealing, the elegant lines of her face.

Her voice was hesitant, but not afraid. The woman *should* have been afraid.

"I know," she continued, voice soft but steady, "that the power varies for demons. Some are weak—"

"Like your friend Carl." Dammit. He'd known Carl. Had seen the young demon on the streets, in Paradise. Barely a level-three, Carl hadn't been a threat to anyone.

So there had been no need to slice and dice the poor bastard. If he hadn't known better, he would have thought a shifter's razor-sharp claws had gotten ahold of the kid.

"And some demons . . ." Speculation coated the words, "are much stronger." A deliberate pause, then, "Like you."

Niol braked at a red light. Turned his head toward her. "Yes, love, like me."

In the demon world, there was a basic power scale. The generally accepted levels were from one to ten. Any demon with powers of one to three, well, that demon was barely stronger than a human. Gifted psychically, of course, as were all demons, but no real danger to society.

Fours, fives, sixes, and sevens—they had enough power to be a damn nuisance. They could start fires. Control the winds. Even push lightly into the minds of humans, delving just deep enough to pick up thoughts and dreams.

But it was the higher-end demons that humans, if they only knew, would really fear. Level-eights, or L8s, level-nines, and—

"Just how strong are you, Niol?"

The light turned green. He spared her a brief smile, one that he knew was cold and a little cruel. He stomped the gas. "Strong enough."

A level-ten. Higher, really, but he wasn't the type to brag.

Level-tens had gotten a reputation . . . back in the day. They'd been the ones to first make the mortals use words like "possession." Because level-tens didn't just have the ability to pick up a stray thought or two from humans, no, L10s could *control* humans. Completely.

"I'm not afraid of you." Calm. Cool. But he heard her fingernails scraping over the leather of his passenger-side door.

A demon had slipped into her mind before. No, not slipped—stormed. Forced his way inside and left her helpless.

The SUV began to shake.

"N-Niol?"

He sucked in a sharp breath. The shaking eased. Niol swung the steering wheel to the right and pulled to a stop in front of Holly's tidy house.

A flick of his wrist and the car's engine died. He didn't face her again, not yet.

He let her lie hang in the air between them.

One moment, two and—

"I can hear your heart, you know," he said softly, as his fingers tapped out a matching rhythm on the steering wheel. The beat became faster.

"Shifters have the enhanced senses," Holly said. "Demons just have the scary eyes."

Scary eyes. He turned toward her. They were parked

close to a bright streetlight. She'd easily be able to see his eyes.

The darkness of his stare.

Most demons cloaked their true eye color with glamour, even the lower-level ones. They hid the black irises. The scleras. They tried to fit in and not scare the good humans.

Fuck that. Niol didn't really care if the sight of his true eyes made folks nervous. The way he figured it, if folks didn't like his eyes, they didn't have to look at him.

And, well, hell, he liked scaring people. Was that such a bad thing?

"I can hear your heart," he repeated softly and let his eyes drift over her face, down her neck, to the spot where her pulse beat so frantically against her skin. "My senses aren't as good as those animals'." He'd never had much use for the shifters. "But my senses are one hell of a lot stronger than a human's." And that was how he'd known that someone else was in the alley with her. He'd smelled the stale scent of sweat. Heard the brush of a shoe against the side of a garbage can.

And known that Holly Storm was being hunted.

His back teeth locked. If anyone, *anyone,* was going to hunt the curvy redhead, it would be him.

He lifted his eyes to meet hers, licked his lips, and realized he wanted another taste.

The sample he'd had at Paradise had not been nearly enough to satisfy him. Not by a long shot.

His fingers rose to trace the line of her cheek. Such soft skin. Silky. Delicate.

He leaned toward her and damn if the woman didn't inch toward him, too.

Not what he'd expected.

But then, the lady had been keeping him guessing from the beginning.

His fingers slid down her cheek. Feathered over her lips. Her mouth parted and her breath rasped over his fingertips.

Their eyes were still locked. "Holly Storm," he whispered, "you want me."

She flinched, but made no move to back away.

His cock pushed hard against the back of his zipper. Her fragrance, perfume, woman, that lavender scent he was coming to crave, had his nostrils flaring.

"You want me," he continued, voice lowering, "but you're scared as hell of me."

He waited for another lie. Waited to hear it fall from her lips.

Instead, she smiled at him. Flashed a dimple in her right cheek, and had his heart thumping into his chest. "Course I'm scared, Niol." With a snap, her slender fingers unhooked her seatbelt. But she didn't try to leave the car. Instead, she closed the distance between them, until only an inch separated their mouths. "Knowing what you are, I'd be a fool if I wasn't 'scared as hell.'"

Her lips trembled as she spoke the words, but her voice was steady.

Of course, she feared him. She'd seen him kill. Destroy. She'd seen—

Her hand rose. Touched *his* cheek.

His cock jerked.

"And I do want you." Her lips brushed over his, just the faintest of touches.

Dammit. Not nearly enough. Not—

She pulled away from him, fumbled with the door handle. "But wanting isn't enough for me." The door opened with a squeak, sending the chilled night air flooding the interior of the vehicle. Holly pushed to her feet, flashing thigh, fucking gorgeous thigh, right at him.

Oh, he wanted a bite. A very, very big bite of her.

Growling, he nearly ripped open his door as he fought

to get out of the SUV. By the time he rounded the front of the vehicle, Holly was hurrying up her sidewalk.

"Holly."

She froze. The wind lifted her hair.

"You came to me." A reminder she shouldn't need.

Her head turned. Her gaze met his. "Not for sex."

A damn disappointment.

Holly's chin lifted. Stubborn. "You know why I came to Paradise."

Niol's hands fisted. "You need to stay out of *Other* business." Before she got herself hurt.

Killed.

The rest of the demons out there wouldn't play as nicely with her as he had.

And the vamps wouldn't hesitate to bite.

Then he'd have to stake the bastards.

"I'm not the only killer in the darkness, love. You need to watch your step." A fair warning.

She swallowed. "Tell me, did you . . . know him?"

The kid. The fool demon who'd been too soft. Niol didn't answer. "*You* did," he said instead and wondered just how close Holly had come to her source.

Her shoulders squared. "Carl was a good man—"

"Demon."

"—he didn't deserve to die that way."

"Most folks don't deserve the way they die." Simple fact. He'd seen rapists die gently in their sleep. Seen kindly grandmothers get shot down in the streets. Life wasn't fair and neither was death.

"I'm not going to forget about him." Shadows were all around her. Darkness waiting.

"Then don't." Blunt. Hard. "Report his death. Talk about what a good *man* he was, remember him when you're curled up at night and trying not to think about just what is out there on the streets." He exhaled on sigh. "But don't, *don't* go digging into his murder."

Her head tilted to the left. The streetlight shot over her cheekbone, leaving a hollow of shadow. "Sounds like an order."

Because it had been.

"But I'm not one of your little bar minions. I don't take orders from you."

That was going to be a problem.

"I could make you, you know." The words slipped out, but they were true. It would take only a minute's concentration. He could slip into her mind, force her compliance, and—

"Been there, done that." Rage shook her words, trembled her body. "If you want to try that method on me, then go ahead. But I think you'll find I'm not such easy prey—*this time.*"

The memory of her, the memory of the night an incubus had trapped her mind and tried to steal her life, flashed between them.

Niol knew he was a bastard. He'd never denied it. But for an instant, he almost felt . . .

Shame.

Fuck.

The woman was messing with *his* head.

"Don't make me force the issue." Because he wouldn't have her blood on his hands. Damn. Why did he even care? He should be shoving his way into her mind, blocking out the memory of the dead demon. But she made him hesitate.

She'd caught his attention months ago. Hell, he'd been drawn to her the first time he flipped on the television and seen her face staring back at him. Holly had been broadcasting about some pileup on Peachtree, and all he'd been able to think about was the fire of her hair.

Stupid.

Horny.

That was him.

He'd taken a redhead that night. Picked up one of the humans who *wanted* to play at his bar. He'd taken her, closed his eyes, and imagined the reporter from News Flash Five.

Insanity. Yes, it ran in his family.

He hadn't been able to stop thinking about her, fantasizing about her. He'd even taken to watching the news—

And he *hated* the local news. Yet he liked to watch her.

"Don't make you?" She repeated and he saw her breasts—nice, firm breasts—heave as she sucked in a breath. "Why don't you just try to force me to—"

In an instant, he'd closed the distance between them. His fingers locked around her arms, tight. Too strong. He jerked her up against him and glared down at her. "This is no game." Even after all that had happened, she still didn't understand how vulnerable she was.

She could die so easily.

Just as Gillian had died. His half sister had been a demon, with a demon's power, but even she hadn't been strong enough to fight the killers that hunted in the night.

"I'm not going to back off this story." Holly's lips tightened. No hint of the dimple showed now. Pity. "I *am* going to find out who killed Carl. I came to Paradise, to you, because I thought you'd want to help me."

"You thought wrong." Then, because it might just be his last chance and because, well, he wanted to taste her again, with the lights of the stars shining above them, he kissed her.

Holly's lips were parted, her mouth open as she prepared to berate him, and, oh, but the sweet human tasted good.

His tongue stroked into her mouth. Taking, demanding a response from her.

And the lady sure gave him one.

Her mouth widened. Her tongue snaked out to meet his. The explosion of hunger hit him then, like a fighter's punch in his gut, and his already erect cock stiffened even more.

Her breasts pressed against him. He could feel her tight nipples nudging against his shirt. Her hands were on his arms, wrapping around his biceps, squeezing.

Not fighting. No, Holly wasn't pushing against him, not trying to break loose—

She was trying to get closer.

Just as he was.

Her mouth fit him. Her lips, soft, full, felt right against his. Her tongue . . . ah, the lady knew how to use her tongue. Knew how to stroke. How to torment.

How to drive him even wilder.

Maybe the human did want to play. Absolutely-damn-perfect—

Holly tore away from him, wrenching out of his arms and stumbling back. "No." Her wide eyes watched him.

With hunger.

With horror.

Ah, now that look wasn't anything new. He'd seen it more than his share of times.

Yet he still found himself stiffening.

He didn't like for *her* to look at him that way.

She lifted a hand to her lips, as if to wipe away his taste, and Niol's eyes narrowed.

"You think . . ." Holly began slowly, then stopped and swallowed. "You think you can threaten to fuck my mind . . . then try and fuck *me*?"

He didn't speak. What would he have said?

"No. I'm not one of your demon-wannabe sluts, Niol. I don't want to jump you in the dark so that I can have the thrill of saying I screwed a monster."

Hit. The reporter obviously understood more than she'd pretended about the human women who came to his bar.

"I don't want to play—"

"Yes, Holly, you do." Her heart still pounded too fast, her nipples were still pebbled, and her cheeks were flushed—all from hunger.

Need. For him.

"I'm *not* going to play." Her hand dropped. "I'm going to do my job—and find out what happened to Carl. With or without your help."

He stared at her. Such a shame. They would have been good together. The sex, well, it would have been pretty phenomenal. All that fire she had—oh, yeah, *phe-nomenal.*

Pity.

Niol shook his head. "Sorry, love, it's going to be 'without.' " Then he did the only thing he could do.

He turned around and walked away from her.

As he stalked toward the SUV, he felt her eyes on him.

His hand lifted, reached for the door.

"Niol."

Oh, but the woman's voice could get to him. It was the soft huskiness when she said his name. Like a stroke right over his cock.

But he didn't look at her. Niol opened the door.

"You have to care." Her voice sharpened. "You play the bastard, but Carl was little more than a kid, and one of *yours*. You have to care—"

The laughter escaped then. He just couldn't help it. He stepped back and glanced over at her. "Have you forgotten so soon, sweet? The incubus who took you that night, he was one of *my* kind, too—and I burned him," *the fire had been so beautiful,* "from the inside out."

She flinched.

His lips were twisted in a smile that he knew could chill. "I kill my kind." The incubus hadn't been the first, and he wouldn't be the last. "I don't go out on a crusade to save them . . . or any humans who are dumb enough to get involved in a world they can't understand."

"You're a cold bastard, Niol."

So he'd been told.

"I'm not going to walk away. I'll find out what happened—"

He climbed into the SUV. He couldn't spend any more time with her. Not out in the open.

You never knew who watched in this city.

He had spies, but so did the other powerful SBs who fought for control of Atlanta.

SBs . . . supernatural beings, or, as Holly would probably have said, supernatural bastards.

He didn't look at her as he cranked the engine and drove away. Didn't look back. Long ago, he'd learned not to look back.

Poor Holly Storm. He'd tried to warn her. Now, she was going to find death.

Or death would find her.

Chapter 3

So she'd struck out with the demon. Not the biggest surprise in the world.

The next day, Holly stood on a street corner in what was so not the best part of the city. She'd hoped to score big by forming a partnership with one of the most respected—okay, *feared*—demons in Atlanta. Sure would have helped out her investigation. But since Niol had made it abundantly clear he only wanted her for sex, he wasn't an option.

Although the thought of sex with Niol had been playing through her mind and her dreams for weeks.

Dammit. Sexy. Scary. She'd really never been attracted to bad boys. Not her type. Her ex-fiancé was a professor at Mellrune University. She liked smart men. The sophisticated guys.

The guys who made her feel safe.

Or, they did until, like Zack, they started screwing around on her with students.

Asshole.

What a jerk he'd—

"You shouldn't be here."

The husky words, coming from right behind her, made Holly jump.

She turned and came face-to-face with a man, the top of his head and most of his body covered by a long cloak. His face, whiter than the snow she saw too rarely, was swollen, his lips blood red.

"Sam." She exhaled in relief. "Thanks for meeting me. I need to ask—"

But he shook his head. "You don't need to ask me a damn thing." His gaze jerked to the left, then to the right. "What you *need* to do is lose my number."

Her mouth dropped. "What? Sam, we have an arrangement—"

"Not anymore." He huffed out a breath and a plume of smoke appeared before him. The icy blast was continuing. The station weather guy had told her it would stay cold for at least the next five days. Having the inside scoop really didn't help her much, though.

Holly pulled her coat closer to her body.

"Forget me, Storm. Forget my name, forget anything I ever told you."

Not what she needed to hear right then. Anger began to warm her. "He got to you, didn't he?"

Sam's thick lips trembled. "Who? *Who?*"

She blinked. Okay, the guy had always been a little intense.

But she'd discovered that most demons were.

"Niol." Damn. If he wouldn't help her, the least he could do was stay out of her way. "He told you not to talk to me, didn't he?" Sam had been giving her info about the demon world for the last four weeks. Ever since she'd found him passed out against the wall of a basement when she'd been doing her meth lab investigation piece.

High as hell, he hadn't been able to control his glamour. His eyes had flashed night black at her, and she'd known the truth about him.

She'd been helping him to get straight. Helping him to kick his addiction because she knew just how dangerous such an addiction could be. She had the personal experience and the memory of her brother's screams to remind her.

"*Niol's* involved? Fuck, I'm out of here." He turned to go.

"No!" Holly grabbed his arm. "Wait! If Niol didn't tell you to stonewall me, then who—"

But he shook her off. "Watch your pretty ass, Storm. Hell's coming to town." Then he was gone, running across the street and disappearing into the cracks that passed for alleys.

Her shoulders slumped. Strike freaking two.

Now what?

She walked into the street, rubbing the back of her neck where she could feel the muscles tightening. This part of town was deserted—always was. One day, the city officials would take over, change things, and—

The roar of an engine reached her ears.

Her head shot up.

And she saw a white van flying straight toward her.

Aw, hell.

Holly scrambled back.

Too late.

The van's wheels turned—came straight for her. Aimed for her.

Christ!

She couldn't move fast enough. Her high heel slipped beneath her, twisting and cracking. She couldn't—

The van clipped her, catching her right hip and sending Holly hurtling back into the air. She hit the cement, hard, and exhaust burned her nostrils.

Her vision grayed. The last thing she saw before the full, sweet darkness swept over her was the back of the van, speeding away and leaving her broken in the street.

* * *

"*Jesus,* Holly, what the hell happened to you?"

Holly glanced up and grimaced at Ben as she dumped her purse on the station floor. "A van." She'd been in the ER for the last four hours. Been checked by three doctors, and they'd all wanted to keep her there in the lovely confines of Reed Infirmary for a much longer stay.

But, other than the bleeding, the bruises, and the general fury that she had going on, she was fine and did *not* need to stay overnight in a hospital.

His blue eyes wide, he began, "Babe, there is no way you can go on the air looking—"

She growled and Ben very wisely decided to shut up.

Holly pointed to the production assistant who was staring at her ripped skirt. "You." His eyes bulged. "Hook me up with a microphone." She glanced back at Ben. "Because I'm going live."

"No, Mac said Susan's doing the story about the restaurant food poisoning—"

Another growl. Then she stormed past him. She caught the eye of the cameraman working the evening news show. The assistant hurried behind her, struggling to attach a microphone.

Holly didn't bother sitting at the second "desk"—the backup that waited just beyond the main anchors. She stood, wanting the camera to catch all of her.

In the background, she heard Mac talking, heard the clear order of "switch to Holly in five, four . . ."

"What the hell?" Susan Patrick's snarl. The blonde shoved her way toward the camera, glaring at Holly. "*I'm* on the air—"

"Hold your story, Sue. The burgers can wait." Mac pointed to Holly. "She's our lead."

Mac always knew when a good story was close. When a reporter had dried blood on her clothes, it meant a *very* good story was close.

". . . three, two, one . . ."

The camera lens fixed on her. Holly lifted her bruised chin. She could still taste her own blood on her tongue. "I'm Holly Storm, coming to you live tonight with a plea for your help."

Niol stilled in front of the television. The glass of water he'd been lifting to his mouth froze.

Holly stared back at him. A long, angry red scratch slid down her cheek. The camera slowly pulled back, and Niol caught sight of her full body. The ripped clothes. The blood.

A slow fury began to burn within him.

"Earlier today, I was the victim of a hit-and-run."

The glass shattered.

"A white van, no plates, hit me on Biltmore Street just before twelve today."

Niol shook his hand, sending water and glass shards flying.

"If anyone out there has information about this crime, call the police station—"

Niol grabbed the remote. Muted the sound. Stared at Holly.

So weak.

Biltmore Street. Home of hookers, drug dealers, and gangbangers. What the hell had Holly been doing there?

And what would he have done if she'd died there?

Fuck.

He reached across his desk. Picked up his phone. His call was answered on the second ring.

"I want protection." He didn't bother identifying himself. Not necessary.

A swift inhalation of air. "For yourself, sir?"

He almost laughed. Almost, but he could still see the bruises on Holly's skin. "For Holly Storm."

Niol had said that he'd leave her, that she'd be on her own.

It looked like Holly wasn't the only liar in town.

Someone would fucking pay for hurting her.

Sam Miters had been clean for exactly four weeks, two days, and sixteen hours.

At first, he'd been counting the minutes. When little Holly Storm had held his hand in that shithole and watched him vomit his guts out, he'd counted the minutes then.

The early days were a blur. He remembered coming to a few times and seeing her. Looking like some kind of avenging angel—an angel with the fires of hell around her head. Beautiful Holly Storm.

She'd seen him through hell, all right. Offered him a second chance.

But she didn't know what his life was like. Didn't understand.

His gift . . . such as it was . . . let him see the darkness in humans. Only the darkness. He heard their painful dreams in whispers. Heard them long to kill. To torture.

He never heard the whispers from the good people in the world. He'd never so much as caught a hint of Holly's thoughts.

It was the killers. The twisted souls lost long ago—*they* spoke to him.

And they would never fucking shut up.

Being clean just made their voices louder.

One voice, one deep voice, had slipped into his head a few days ago and the damn voice had kept him awake since then, shuddering with disgust.

The things the voice wanted—Sam choked, tasting bile. No, he couldn't think of them. He'd tried to pretend the voice didn't exist, that someone wasn't out there, hunting—

Then that kid had turned up dead.

He rapped the back of his head into the brick wall of the alley. No, no, he couldn't do this anymore, couldn't—

"I can make it stop."

His breath caught. Because, this time, the voice hadn't come from inside him. He looked up, body shaking, and met the stare of a stranger.

The man smiled. "Chased any dragons lately, friend?"

Chasing the white dragon. Sam's breath caught. *Meth.* Sweet white beauty. He shook his head even as his heart seemed to jump into his throat. He swallowed, trying to ease a mouth gone bone dry. He'd been so good. Stayed clean.

For what? So that a fucking psycho could crawl into his head and he couldn't get the bastard out?

He kept hearing the words, over and over.

Cut them. Slice them. Blood on the ground. The impure will die.

Cut them. Slice them. Blood on the ground.

"I've got something you might like. Something that will make you feel real good."

He never felt good. Not even when the meth pumped in his blood.

But the voices quieted with the drug's help. Such beautiful silence. "Wh-where is it?"

The man shook his head. "Ah, now that's not the way it works. First, you've got to pay."

Cut them.

Sam's whole body trembled.

The man bent, reached into a black bag at his feet, and pulled out a glass pipe. A whimper slipped past Sam's lips. He liked to use the pipe. Liked to grip the cold glass in his hands and inhale his bitch of a lady.

His gaze locked helplessly on the pipe. He licked his lips. Just once. He could take a hit this one time, stop the voice—

Slice them.

And he'd be fine. He wouldn't get trapped by the meth again. It would just be one time.

One time.

He took a step forward, hands already up to reach for the pipe. "I-I don't have much cash . . ."

Another smile, one that seemed too cold. The man's eyes glinted like chips of ice. "I don't want your money."

He needed that pipe. "What?"

The pipe was shoved back into the bag. "Information. All I want from you, Sam, is information."

Sam blinked. How did the guy know his name?

"Tell me what I want to know, and I'll take you on a ride you'll never forget."

Blood on the ground.

He slammed his hands over his ears, but he could still hear the voice.

The man walked toward him, the black bag now thrown over one shoulder. He caught Sam's hands and tugged them down. "Hurting, are you?"

A fast nod.

"I'll make the pain stop. Just tell me what I need to know."

Another fast nod. He would have traded anything right then.

The fucking voice had to stop.

"The reporter . . . Holly Storm . . . what did you tell her today?"

Holly. She'd helped him—

The stranger's eyes caught his, held him in that grip of ice. "What did you tell her?"

"N-nothing." True. "Not working . . . w-with her anymore." He didn't want her to know about the voices. Something was wrong with him, had to be, or he wouldn't hear the killers.

Like to like. That was the way of the supernatural world.

No, no, he wasn't a killer. He wasn't—

"But she came to you because she wanted something, right?"

He tried to think. His mind was a blur of death, hunger, and fear.

He had to get his dragon.

Holly's voice trickled through his mind. He'd been desperate to get away from her, wanting only to run and hide.

"What did Holly Storm say to you?"

His lips shook. "Niol!" The word burst from him. "She thought he—he knew about the kid's death—" Hadn't she thought that? Yeah, yeah, she'd mentioned Niol, he knew she had.

Those frozen eyes narrowed. "Did she?"

Sam's control snapped. He grabbed the man's shirt, balled it beneath his fingers. "Give me the drug!" He meant for his voice to be a roar. It came out like a whimper.

Cut them.

"Of course . . ." The man's gaze flickered behind Sam for a moment, toward the darkened street. "Come with me."

He would have followed him to hell.

Sam stumbled behind the man as they tracked behind the buildings. Twisting and turning, snaking into the secret parts of the city.

Then they were at a door. A black door, heavy, behind yet another building, with the scent of garbage and smoke heavy in the air.

The stranger pushed open the door. "Go inside. I'll give you what you need . . ."

He ran inside. A lab—maybe there was a whole damn lab waiting for him.

A small, bare bulb hung from the ceiling, glinting, casting light over the shadows. Something crackled beneath his feet.

He glanced down. *What the hell?*

Looked like plastic. Spread all over the floor, all the way to that table—

Slice them.

The hair on his nape rose.

Sam swallowed. No, this wasn't right. He turned toward the stranger and felt the hot cut of a knife against his flesh.

He fell back, a scream on his lips.

Too late, he realized he wasn't staring at a man.

"Don't worry, Sam, I'll make the voices stop." The knife, coated red with his blood, rose again. "I'll make them stop . . . forever."

"No!" Sam lurched forward to fight the bastard.

The knife came at him again.

When Holly stepped inside her house hours later, she was tired, sore, and desperate for bed.

She kicked the door shut behind her, flipped on the lights—

And found Niol standing in her living room.

"Ah!" She stumbled back, slamming her elbows into the wooden door.

He raised a brow.

Holly glared and fought to suck in a deep breath. She really, *really* hadn't needed this shit tonight. "What the . . ." another deep breath, "hell are you doing in my home?" Her gaze shot to the left and she glared at her damn ineffective security system. A system that was even now beeping because she hadn't punched in her code.

Niol didn't speak, but he walked toward her. A tall, dark, threat.

She swallowed and met his black gaze.

He kept coming toward her. Her breath hitched.

You know what he's done.

A killer.

But he saved me.

Surely he hadn't come to her house to—

He stopped before her. Close enough to touch. He leaned forward. Put one hand beside her head, palm flat against the door. The other hand rose—

And his fingers punched in her security code.

The beeping ceased.

Holly exhaled. *Nice.* "Breaking and entering . . . that's against the law, Niol."

He shrugged. Then he took hold of her chin, lifting her face toward the light. Toward him. His mouth tightened and he said, "You look like hell, love."

Just the compliment she needed.

"And you look like a criminal who *has just broken into my home.*" A sexy criminal, yeah, dressed in black as he was—as he always was. Tight black shirt. Low-slung jeans. Tousled hair that looked like a woman's fingers had just raked through it, and they probably had.

Another shrug. "I needed to see you." He inched ever closer, so close that his chest brushed hers. "I watched you on the news tonight."

A lick of what was *not* excitement curled in her belly.

The black stare drifted over her face. "You looked like hell then, too."

Her breath shot out on a growl. "A demon criminal who knows how to compliment. Just what I was dreaming of—"

He kissed her. Drove his tongue past her lips and tasted her. The muscled length of his body pushed against her, his legs nudging hers apart. The length of his cock, long and heavy with arousal, pressed through his jeans, and the feel of his erection had her gasping into his mouth.

Gasping not with horror, as she probably should have been.

But with pleasure.

Dammit, she wanted him. Jerk, criminal—she wanted *him*.

Her fingers locked around his shoulders. Holly needed him closer. She wanted to feel every hard inch of his flesh against hers.

The kiss became harder, deeper. The man kissed oh so well. He knew just how to move his mouth, how to slide his tongue, and how to demand a response that she was only too ready to give.

The fingers that held her chin slid down her throat. Over the pulse that raced too fast. Callused fingertips, rough, but gentle on her.

She hadn't expected gentleness from him.

Then again, she hadn't expected to want the demon so much, either.

When his mouth lifted from hers, she had to bite back the cry of protest that rose within her.

His eyes, still so mysteriously dark, now glinted with an undeniable hunger. "Decided you wanted to play, did you?"

Heat burned in her cheeks at his words, but she never looked away from his stare. Her nipples were tight, rubbing against his chest, and, with his enhanced demon senses, she suspected the guy could even . . . smell . . . her arousal.

No need to play the innocent. She hadn't been innocent for years. "You know I want you, Niol." Hell, most women did. The guy spelled sex and danger. A wild combination, one designed to push a girl to the edge of reason.

The adrenaline thrill of the darkness. The sensual thrill of the man.

Right, like she was the first girl to fall prey to him.

Not the first, and, dammit, not the last, she'd bet.

The hands she'd curled around his shoulders slid down to his chest and pushed. "But I know better than to take everything I want."

He didn't move for a beat of time, ignoring the press of her fingers. Standing there, trapped within his embrace, with the heat of his body all around her, Holly realized just how strong Niol was.

And how helpless he could make a woman.

She licked her lips, tasted him—a rich flavor of man and sex—and waited.

The right side of his mouth hitched into what really wasn't a smile and he stepped back, taking his warmth with him.

Holly became aware of the aches and pains in her body then.

She'd forgotten about the pain when he touched her, and only thought of him.

Holly slipped around him. She paced toward her couch. The bed she'd longed for now seemed very far away. Glancing back over her shoulder, she found his gaze on her. Hooded. Watchful. "Niol . . ." Her brows lifted. "Why are you here?"

"You were . . . hurt." Stilted. Almost uncertain, and he wasn't a guy given to uncertainty.

So he'd broken into her house? "How did you know my security code?" She'd thought she was safe here. On the good side of town. With respectable neighbors. A state-of-the-art alarm—

"I know a lot of things about you." Assessing now, his gaze drifted over her. His nostrils flared, just a bit. "How's the wrist?"

"How's the—" Her mouth snapped closed. *And how
had he known that?* Her shirt had long sleeves and completely covered both wrists.

She'd twisted her right wrist when she fell—a futile attempt to break her fall—but other than sporting a really
lovely purple and black bruise pattern that looked like a
tattoo bracelet, she was . . ."I'm *fine*. Bruises, cuts, but no
major damage, okay?"

One gliding step forward. "You won't be fine next
time."

She turned around to fully face him. "What do you
know?" *Next time.* She didn't want to think she'd ever tangle with a two-ton vehicle again.

"Come on, Holly, do you really think this was just
some random accident?"

For a moment, the image of the van flashed before her
eyes. She saw the gleaming hood, the tinted windows—
and the van, aiming right for her. Swerving, not to miss
her, but to hit her. "No," her voice was soft. "I don't."

"You were working the case." Not a question. "Following up on that dead kid." A rumble rolled from his throat.
Animalistic. Dark. "I told you to drop this—"

"*I* told *you* I was doing my job, with or without your
help." Her hands fisted on her hips and she ignored the
twinge that shot from her right wrist. "I got the impres-
sion that you didn't give a damn what happened to me."

He stalked toward her. "Oh, I care—" Niol reached for
her.

The doorbell rang. The peal echoed, breaking through
Niol's words.

His eyes narrowed. "You expecting someone?"

Not this late. "No." She stepped forward.

He grabbed her hand. "Wait."

The door shook as a furious fist pounded against the
frame.

Niol's fingers tightened around her. "I'll get it."

"No, don't—"

But he was already striding back across the room. Curling his fingers around the doorknob. Holly hurried after him, aware of a tension in her gut, one that had nothing to do with her mixed-up sexual hunger for Niol. One that felt a lot like the heavy pull of fear.

The door frame shook again.

Niol wrenched open the door—

"What the hell are you doing here?"

The stunned question came from the last man she'd expected to find at her door.

Holly pushed to Niol's side. Police Detective Colin Gyth and his partner, Todd Brooks, stood waiting, both glaring at Niol.

Niol didn't bother answering Gyth. He just crossed his arms over his chest and gazed back, as calm as you please, at the detectives.

Holly cleared her throat and tried to figure out why two of the city's best detectives were outside her home in the middle of the night.

Maybe Niol had tripped her alarm after all, maybe—

"Ms. Storm." Detective Brooks finally tore his stare from Niol and cast a frown of concern toward her. "Are you all right?"

He'd been on the scene after the hit-and-run. He'd had the same worried look in his brown eyes then, too.

Holly cleared her throat. "I'm, ah, fine. There must be some sort of—of mistake." She reached for Niol's hand and curled her fingers over his. The demon was gonna owe her. "My alarm just—"

"We're not here about an alarm." Worry wasn't in Colin's crystal-blue stare. Suspicion was.

"Oh." Holly tried to ease her hand away from Niol and realized that she wasn't about to escape his now steely grip. "Then just why are you here, detectives?"

Gyth glared at Niol. "We need to talk alone, Ms. Storm—"

Niol gave a husky laugh, then said, "Not gonna happen, shifter."

Shifter. Holly almost choked. Talk about not being subtle.

Gyth's glare burned even hotter.

"Say whatever you need to, then get the hell out of here." Niol lifted Holly's hand. Kissed the top of her knuckles. "You're interrupting."

Brooks swore. "Thought you'd have better taste, Storm."

Gyth grunted. "Yeah, well, *demon* . . ." *Uh, oh, looked like the gloves were off.* The shifter detective pushed back his coat, exposing the badge that was hooked to his belt and revealing the butt of his gun. "Murder has a way of *interrupting* things."

"Murder?" Holly stood straighter. "Is this about Carl? Have you found out who attacked him?"

"We're not here about Bronx." From Brooks. A pause, then, "Ms. Storm, do you know why Sam Miters would have been in possession of your business card?"

Sam. Holly's face iced over, then prickles of heat seemed to burst from her flesh. She knew the score and the foreboding that swept over her at the cop's question had her swaying. "Yes, I-I know. He's a—" Source. Informant. Friend. Holly exhaled, aware that Niol had slanted her a quick, searching glance. She cleared her throat and met Brooks's stare. "What's happened to him?" But she knew, dammit, she knew even before Gyth said—

"Why don't you come downtown with us? We're gonna need you to identify the body . . ."

Chapter 4

Cops weren't exactly his friends. Never had been. Maybe because they looked at him and saw him for what he was.

A killer.

Niol tightened his grip on Holly's arm as they headed toward the morgue. The scent of death was too strong down here, stopping up his nostrils with the cloying odor.

Holly was stiff beside him, her movements like those of a robot. She'd trembled when that shifter ass Gyth had told her about the body. One long, rolling tremble from head to toe. She'd said the poor bastard's name, "*Sam,*" with a kind of wild despair.

Then she'd gotten control of herself—fast. Probably too damn fast. Now he saw a woman with a taut body. Expressionless face. Ice-cold hands.

He knew the name the cops had tossed out, of course. Sam Miters. Demon, level-seven. Niol made a habit of knowing all the demons in his city. Just for the sake of good business.

Unstable as all hell and an addict—old Sam had been an accident waiting to happen.

"*You* don't need to come inside the viewing room," Gyth said.

Niol grunted. The detective didn't *want* him inside, but he didn't give a damn.

Another demon had fallen on his streets. Niol wanted to see the body.

"I-I want him with me." Holly's voice, cool and hollow.

The lady was shaken. Two murders and an attempt on her own life, all within two short days. Yes, she had reason to be nervous.

Should have listened to me. Now hell's coming down on her.

She looked up at him with those glittering green eyes. So green. Humans thought eyes were the window to the soul. They were wrong. As usual. Eyes lied.

Hers were lying now. She was trying to look strong and in control, when he knew she was close to breaking apart.

His left hand lifted and shoved open the door. "Let's get this shit over with." Before Holly broke.

And why do I care?

She was just another human.

Just. Another. Hu—

He heard the soft sigh of her breath. The little hitch that gave away her fear as she stepped forward.

The body was on the table in the middle of the room. Covered by a thin, white sheet. Niol could see two feet hanging off the slab, pale toes peeking over the edge of the sheet.

Tagged and bagged.

A woman with coal-black hair and skin of dark cream stepped forward. Niol recognized her immediately—Dr. Nathalia Smith. The medical examiner. She'd been in the papers after the Night Butcher case.

Smart, tough, and in the know about the *Other*.

Her gaze was on Holly, not him. Gyth crowded in behind him, and that jerkoff Brooks crossed to the good doctor's side.

"Are you the next of kin?" Smith asked.

Holly shook her head. "A friend."

Not really, as far as Niol knew. Old Sam hadn't exactly been the friend type.

Smith's stare turned to him. "And you are—"

"Forget him," Brooks told her. "Just forget you ever saw him."

"Not likely." Her eyes were locked on his and Niol saw the shock on her face. The horror in her gaze. Her dark stare wasn't full of lies—what she felt, it was right there for him to see. And that was a stare he recognized.

He smiled at her.

Her jaw clenched and she gave a jerky nod. Then her hands rose to the sheet and she eased it down, exposing the—

"God!" Holly jerked away from him and stumbled back, ramming into Gyth. "What the hell happened to him?" She covered her mouth with the back of her hand.

Gyth caught her shoulders, wrapping his fingers around her flesh and pulling her against him.

Niol tensed and the air thickened around him. *Shifter had better back off, no one else touched her, no one—*

Gyth caught his stare, and, smart bastard, read the warning in Niol's eyes. He lifted his hands, palms up, and stepped away from Holly.

Niol glided toward Holly. He wanted to wrap her in his arms and—

Comfort her?

What the hell?

"What happened to him?" Holly repeated, her voice stronger and her eyes helplessly returning to the body. "His face, it's been—"

Carved up. Cut with perfect precision. Long, slim slices.

Smith yanked the sheet back over him. "So you can identify the victim."

A nod. "It's Sam."

Or what was left of him.

Niol's nostrils twitched. He tried to shove the stench of blood and bleach out of his system as he focused on the body. There had to be something there, a scent left by the killer—

From the corner of his eye, he saw Holly sway.

He was on her in less than a second. Grabbing her, pulling her tightly against his chest.

And she fit, dammit. Her body matched his perfectly, and she felt *right*.

Even when she shuddered. "I've got to get out of here."

Unlike him, she wasn't used to dead bodies. Not enough dead bodies at her crime scenes.

If she intended to keep working the case, though, she'd get used to them. Fast.

He pushed her toward the door. They'd seen the body. Holly had completed the whole good-citizen routine. No sense wasting more time.

The door flew open with the force of Holly's shove. She stumbled ahead of him. Poor human. She'd had one hell of day. Hit-and-run. Dead body.

Him.

The light shone on the tiled floor. "Thanks, Niol," she muttered and some of the real Holly stared back at him from her green eyes. "I never thought I'd say this but I needed you in—"

"Not so fast, Ms. Storm." The shifter's voice. Quiet. Hard.

Niol glanced back at him. He had questions for the shifter, questions he'd rather not ask in front of a reporter.

Because while he wanted Holly like hell on fire—and he sure knew about hell—Niol didn't trust her.

He didn't trust anyone.

And that was why he was still alive.

Well, one of the reasons.

The human, Brooks, stepped out beside Gyth. "We're gonna need to see you for a while in Interrogation." A pause. "Both of you."

Fuck.

They separated them. Stupid human manipulation. As if being apart would make them turn on each other. Spill secrets.

They had no secrets to spill.

The shifter stayed with him. Locked eyes on him and just stared.

Niol stared back.

After ten minutes, the cop spoke. "You killin' your own kind again, demon?"

A shrug. He was sprawled in the chair, legs out in front of him, shoulders slumped.

Where was Holly? She'd handle herself; he knew she'd be fine. Once she shook off the horror of that dead body, Holly Storm would snap back to action.

But he wanted her close by. The better to watch and protect.

"Sam Miters was a demon, wasn't he?" Gyth's arms were crossed over his chest. Niol figured the guy was supposed to be intimidating, but he was just annoying.

Niol raised his brows. "Did the Monster Doctor tell you that?" The Monster Doctor, Dr. Emily Drake, the psychologist in town who treated all the *Other* with their myriad of problems. She could tell a paranormal with just one look. The lady could even recognize the power of the dead ones.

Handy little trick. One he'd like to have.

As it stood in the paranormal world, generally, like recognized like. He could stare right through the glamour that disguised most of his kind and find the demon beneath the skin. He knew witches felt the power surge when their kin were close. Shifters—they could smell their brethren, *damn strong senses.*

But Emily Drake, a human, she could discover all their secrets in less than a few seconds' time.

And the fact that she was sleeping with the detective, well, that meant he had pretty much immediate access to Emily's wonderfully interesting mind—and her powers.

"Don't concern yourself with Emily," Gyth growled.

Ah. Some real emotion from the detective. He was a possessive bastard, but most wolf shifters were. Possessive, and often psychotic.

"Why'd you do it? Why him? Did he piss you off?"

Niol sighed. He really didn't have time for this crap. He needed to get Holly and get her home. Then he had to start hunting a killer. "Don't look to me for this one." His hands weren't clean of blood, but, this time, the crime wasn't his.

"Then who?" Gyth grabbed the chair across from Niol. Twisted it around and straddled it. "That first night, *you* knew the kid, and I think you knew who killed him, too."

The detective was getting warmer, but still damn off track.

"Tell me, Niol, *tell me.* What the hell is going on in this city? Why am I stumbling over dead demons? And why are you sniffing around Storm?"

Because I want to sniff her. Sniff her, kiss her, take her. But that was none of the detective's business.

"Don't look to me," Niol said again and rose. This interrogation was over. He didn't have to put up with this shit.

"Then who?" A snarl.

"The humans, shifter. This time, the killer's one of them." He'd bet on it.

A human, killing demons.

The world just wasn't safe anymore.

"Why'd Sam have your card?"

Holly blinked and tried to shove the image of Sam's ravaged face out of her mind.

But she knew she'd be seeing that image in her nightmares for months.

Christ. *Sam.* "He—he was one of my sources." No sense lying. She rubbed her eyes. Dammit, she *hurt*. Her body ached, her heart felt like it had been ripped out, and she wanted to get out of the cramped interrogation room with the flickering light that made her temples throb and just go back to the safety of her house.

"What kind of information was Sam feeding you?"

Her fingers dug into her forehead and she didn't look at Todd Brooks. The guy was human, like her, but he was also very heavily involved in the demon world.

The guy's girlfriend was a succubus, so yeah, in Holly's book, that qualified as *involved*.

"Ms. Storm?" The groan of a chair's legs as he yanked back the chair next to her and sat close, crowding her.

She hated being crowded.

"Just what kind of information was Sam giving you?"

Her hand dropped and she met his stare. That deceptively warm, I'll-be-your-friend, come-on-trust-me brown stare. The good cop, to Colin Gyth's badass. *Right.* Holly almost snorted. Both cops knew the game, and they'd do anything to catch their prey.

And now they thought she was that prey. "Sam was a demon." She didn't glance toward the shining mirror on the right wall. She knew somebody had to be behind that glass, watching her. Holly just hoped it was someone who knew the score, and not some paper pusher who was gonna try to get her committed to Reed Infirmary's Psych ward in the next hour. "He was teaching me about his world." Feeding her bits of information, one tiny crumb at a time.

He swore, then muttered, "Couldn't you leave 'em alone? They nearly killed you before—"

"Not they." Her jaw was clenched and she gritted the words. "*He.* One man." Not all demons were killers; she'd learned that. Just as she'd learned all humans, even those who wore badges, weren't to be trusted.

Just seven months ago, her cheating ex-fiancé had sure hammered that lesson home.

Holly drew in a deep breath and tried to calm her racing heart. Todd wanted her to lose her cool. The guy thought she was involved in the murders, and, okay, she could even see where he was coming from. She'd been on the scene of the first crime, she'd known the guy was a demon—she'd known *him*. Carl had been one of her sources, just like Sam. Wouldn't take a genius to connect the lines back to her.

But she hadn't killed them. "Sam wasn't a bad guy, okay? He was getting clean." She sure knew how hard that had been. She'd watched her brother fight that battle, and fail. "He was harmless, he was—"

"Butchered."

Holly flinched. She didn't need that visual. Really didn't. *I'm so sorry, Sam.* Until that last meeting, they'd always gotten along so well.

Until that last meeting . . .

Her heart didn't slow down. It sped up as realization dawned.

Sam had been desperate to get her away from him. *Because he'd known he was a target?* And the hit-and-run right after she'd left him—no damn way would she buy that as a coincidence.

"When was the last time you saw Sam Miters alive?"

A quick swipe of her tongue over her lips. "Um, lunch." Was that yesterday? She glanced at her watch. Nearing six A.M. "Yesterday."

"And did he seem . . . agitated to you?"

Sweat coated her palms as she met his measuring stare. "Yeah, you could say that."

"What exactly did *he* say in that meeting?"

Watch your pretty ass, Storm. Hell's coming to town.

Her gaze held his.

Sam had known. He'd known that a killer was loose on the streets. But had he realized he'd be the next victim?

"What. Did. He. Say?" Voice harder now. More demanding. Good cop starting to disintegrate into bad. Her shoulders rolled in a shrug. *Where was Niol?* And why had Gyth wanted to question him? Did he think Niol was involved?

Then she remembered what Sam had muttered when she'd asked if Niol had warned him away from her.

"Niol's involved? Fuck, I'm out of here."

Oh, shit. Just what had she stumbled into?

"Storm."

She blinked and realized Brooks was glaring at her. Time to answer the cop, or partially answer him, anyway. "He told me our arrangement was over. That I should lose his number." Her wrist and arm were throbbing again. She could really use an aspirin. Nothing stronger because she never took pain pills or anything that might make her—

"And how did you respond?" His fingers tapped out a quiet rhythm on the table.

I asked if Niol had scared him. "He left. I got hit by a van." A shrug that made her arm ache more. "End of story." Not really. The real end had come when Sam got sliced to pieces.

Not the way he should have gone. Not right—for him or Carl.

"You've got two dead sources, Storm." *Storm*. He always called her by that name. Whatever. She always thought of him as Brooks. Not exactly on a good, first-name basis. "Two dead, demon sources."

Yeah, and she *knew* it looked bad. "I didn't kill them."

His brows rose. "I never said you did."

Well, good. But why the hell was she in Interrogation when—

"But your new boyfriend . . ." A hard exhalation of air. "Now he's another story." His lips curved down. "You're in over your head, lady. You don't know just how danger-ous your new lover is."

Yes, she did. "I was there that night, detective." A re-minder the guy didn't need. She knew he hadn't forgotten one instance of that horror-filled night at Paradise Found. She sure hadn't. "I saw Niol. I saw *everything*." More than the detective had realized. His attention had been splintered. He'd been dealing with the approaching cops, trying to protect his succubus lover, and making sure the killer was down.

But her eyes had been on Niol. She'd seen *him*. She knew exactly how dangerous he was.

Niol didn't need to rip and claw a man to shreds. He could use a stray thought to kill.

Level-ten demon. There wasn't a more powerful being in the *Other* world.

She wasn't going to pretend Niol was some kind of good guy. A demon with a pure heart. She knew what he was.

And wanted him anyway.

Talk about being screwed up.

"Niol's got quite a temper," Brooks murmured. "Maybe

that temper got out of control. Maybe he didn't like other demons being near you, so he eliminated the competition."

Bullshit. If she and Niol were involved sexually, she doubted he would have considered a kid and a recovering drug addict to be much competition. Holly shook her head. "Niol didn't even know I was working with them. And you've got the wrong idea, Niol and I—we—"

The door to the interrogation room opened with a squeak. Easily, softly. Niol stood in the doorway, arms hanging loosely at his sides. "It's time to leave, Holly."

She blinked. "Ah—"

"What the hell?" Brooks shot to his feet. "Get out of here, asshole! I'm questioning her—"

"Not anymore." Niol's gaze raked over Holly. "You all right?"

Was that a thread of concern in his voice? Holly pushed back from the table, rising on legs that should have been steadier, but—

It had been one hell of a night. "Yeah, yeah, I'm fine."

She tried to walk around Brooks, but his hand caught her wrist. "We're not finished."

A growl. And one that didn't come from the shifter standing just behind Niol.

No, it came from Niol. "You don't want to do that," he said, and the words were dark and rumbling.

The air around her suddenly felt thicker, colder—and then Todd's hand was gone. Almost . . . wrenched away.

The cop swore and stumbled away from her. "I'm not in the mood for your tricks, Niol!"

"And I'm not in the mood to deal with your shit." He crossed the cramped space and took Holly's hand. "We gave you half an hour. Answered your questions like the damn good citizens we are—now we're leaving."

A muscle flexed along his jaw. His voice was controlled, but Holly realized Niol was seriously pissed.

"Yeah, he's got quite a temper," Todd said again and tossed a calculating glance her way. "You sure that you want to leave with him, Storm?"

Niol's fingers caressed the skin over her wrist. A light, gentle touch. One he didn't even seem to be aware of making.

Her pulse jumped under that touch, a hard spike.

Niol turned to meet her stare.

Such dark eyes. A perfect black.

Was his soul like that, too? Was she making a huge mistake?

"I didn't kill Carl or Sam." The words were too loud, as if they were directed at the cops, but Niol's eyes were for her only. "Holly knows that."

"You've killed in the past," Gyth said, stalking into the room.

Niol finally looked away from her. "Prove it."

"Fuck."

Holly saw the shark's smile on the demon's face. "Now get out of my way—and *stay* out of my way."

For a moment, Gyth's eyes seemed to brighten, taking on a wild glow, but he clenched his jaw and stepped aside.

Niol and Holly headed for the door.

"Screw him, but don't trust him." The warning from Gyth had her stopping a foot away from the exit. "You're not up to playing his games."

The detective didn't know her very well. She gave him a hard grin, her own version of a shark's smile. "Yes, I am." She was tired of the warnings. The bullshit. She knew what she was dealing with when it came to Niol, and she knew that *he* was the one she needed to help her solve this mess.

Keeping her head up, she walked out of that too-tight room and down the halls of the station, with her demon at her side.

* * *

"That went piss poor." Captain Danny McNeal eased back in his seat and glared at his two best detectives. He'd watched the interrogations and knew that as far as the case was concerned, they'd just gotten jack and shit.

"The woman would have talked," Collin said. "If the demon hadn't gotten to her—"

"No." Danny was certain of this. "You're not giving her enough credit." That woman was good at keeping secrets—he'd seen it in her eyes.

Why was she with the demon?

A soft knock sounded at his door, and then, almost instantly, the knob turned and Nathalia Smith strode into the room.

He tried not to look at her legs. Long, long legs. The skirt she'd worn today had been driving him crazy—ever since she'd given him that come-and-get-me smile as she pulled it *on* this morning, right after they'd gotten out of his shower.

But that smile wasn't on her face now. Her plump lips, sin sexy, were turned down and her eyes had narrowed to near slits. "We've got a problem," she announced, lifting a file.

Two problems, the way Danny saw it. Two dead bodies.

Colin and Todd glanced toward her.

"Some things are missing."

"Things?" Danny repeated softly, really not liking where this was going. Nathalia, well, *Smith* to the rest of the PD, took care of the stiffs. She was the best ME he'd ever met. The best-looking, too, but that was just a perk. The woman had a freaking genius-level IQ.

She'd also been through hell recently, courtesy of a sick fuck who'd terrorized the city, but she was clawing her way back to normalcy.

Or, what amounted to normalcy in this world.

He took the folder from her, leafed through the pages, and knew that his blood pressure was rising even before the pounding began in his temples. "Shit. Tell me you're not sayin'—"

"The killer did a brutal job on them—Miters doesn't have a heart anymore, and Bronx is missing a kidney."

"What?" The shock was from Todd. Understandable. Like Nathalia, he was a human. Still capable of being shocked, even though he was mated to a demon.

"Why the hell would someone take organs?" The disgust, that came from Colin. Colin was a damn fine detective. His shifter senses made him a state-of-the-art hunter, and few prey ever escaped him.

"Because we've got another sick freak on the streets," Danny growled, and knew it was the absolute truth. Hell, just great. Someone was slicing demons, stealing body parts, and a reporter was right in the middle of the whole stinking mess.

His luck was always fuck poor.

And this was the last story that he wanted to see headlining the evening news.

"Who knows this?" There were leaks in his department, leaks in *every* department. And Niol had too many contacts. His demons were everywhere, even in the Atlanta PD.

Those demons—they kept the peace, upheld the law, and kept Niol fully informed at all times.

"I came straight to you," Nathalia said softly.

His shoulders eased, just a bit. He lifted his hand and pointed at his detectives. "This won't stay quiet for long." Maybe a few days, if they were lucky. "When the media gets wind of this—"

"They'll have the whole city scared shitless," Colin finished.

Todd rose to his feet. "Not necessarily a bad thing. Not with some asshole out there slicing up his kills."

What the hell had happened to his city? In the last few years, the crimes had just become more violent. The killers more sadistic.

Maybe there were too many *Other* these days. Too many monsters with too much power.

Humans had forgotten to fear the creatures in the darkness and that was a mistake.

Because those monsters . . . they were in the mood to play and kill.

"Get Emily in on this," he ordered. Emily Drake, the psychologist with the power to touch the minds of *Other*. The only woman who could profile a paranormal killer.

Oh, yeah, they sure as shit needed Emily on this one.

"Get her in here, and find this bastard."

Before he killed again . . . and the story made the lead on the evening news.

Holly wasn't talking to him. She didn't speak during the ride back to her house. Didn't open her mouth when he walked her to the front door of her place.

Women and the silent treatment—what a deadly weapon.

Niol sighed and waited for her to unlock the door. The sun was up, getting ready to drift across the sky. He could see the shadows of the bruises on her flesh and anger hummed within him.

The door swung open and Holly glanced back at him. "Niol . . ."

Ah, finally. She spoke. He could tell by her expression that Holly was seconds away from telling him to get lost.

He'd do just that, after he had *his* turn to speak. He crowded against her, pretty much forcing Holly to either step back or get real close and intimate with him.

He wouldn't have minded the close and intimate part, not at all, but Holly moved back.

With a shove of his foot, he slammed the door. "We need to get some things settled between us."

Her eyes widened. "Us? I didn't think there was an 'us.' I thought there was just you telling me to stay the hell out of demon business."

The rules had changed.

He reached for her.

She flinched back.

Oh, hell, no. "I didn't kill those two men," he gritted. Those cops—they'd planted the fear in her mind. He'd have to remember to pay them back for that.

"Why were you—why were you at the scene of Carl's death?"

Because Carl had called him and asked him for a meeting. If he'd arrived earlier, he might have been able to save the kid.

Instead of finding all that blood.

"I've killed, Holly. You know that." And not just that psychotic incubus who'd attacked her in that alley. "I've never claimed to be one of the good guys." He wasn't like Gyth or Brooks, out keeping the peace and locking up the bad guys. Not his style of justice. "But I don't kill innocents."

Her lips twisted into a ghost of a smile. No dimple, dammit. "Oh, Niol, I know you're not good. I've known that from the beginning."

But she'd walked into his lair anyway. Smelling of fear and sin. Tempting him.

"I don't trust you," she told him.

Good. "I wasn't on that street to hurt Carl," Niol said. Time for some truth. "I was there to help him."

"How?"

"Someone was after him. Carl wanted protection." He could still hear the kid's voice. *H-he's following me, Niol. Hunting me.*

"Wait! You *knew* Carl was in trouble? Did you tell Gyth? If someone was stalking him—"

"Two demons are dead." Flat, cold. "This isn't police business, it's *my* business."

"Because, what? You're judge, jury, and executioner for the demons in this city? Come on, you—"

"Yes, I am." His voice cut across the tumble of her words.

And seemed to stop her cold.

"Niol . . ." Holly shook her head. "Don't try to give me any warnings about stepping back from this case, okay? I get it—these are your pissing grounds, but they were *my* friends. They trusted me. I'm not going to drop this case until I find out who killed them."

He knew that. He also knew that it was too late for Holly to back off. "You're the link, love." A link he'd use.

She swallowed, but didn't reply, and he knew she already understood.

Two dead sources.

One hit-and-run.

He would have needed to be blind not to have made the connection. "The killer's got you in his sights, Holly."

She didn't deny it.

"The question is . . . *why*?" She wasn't a demon, but maybe, just maybe, she'd learned something about the demon world that should have remained secret.

"You're telling me one of the *Other* is hunting me now?" Her breath came too fast. "Great. What? Do I have a vampire on my trail? A crazy-ass shifter? A—"

"Human."

Silence.

Then, "Run that by me again."

"Carl told me a human was dogging his steps." If only he'd gotten the bastard's name . . . but Carl had been sliced to pieces before he could give away that information. "This time, the killer is one of *yours*."

"Hell."

Hmm . . . who said monsters were just demons and shifters? Humans had monsters living and breathing in their bodies. Sometimes, the humans were worse than the *Other*.

Much, much worse.

Holly turned away from him and began to pace the length of her den. He could almost hear the wheels turning in her head. *Turning, turning—*

She spun around and pinned him with a fierce look.

And grinding to a halt.

"I don't want to be jerked around by you anymore." The hum of anger vibrated beneath the words. "You should have told me this from the beginning."

Maybe, but he wasn't big on trust, either. "I think the hit-and-run was a warning." Niol figured there was no other way to look at it. If the killer had wanted Holly to die yesterday, well, she would have been found carved up with Sam.

His hands fisted and a vase shattered to his left.

"*What?* Jesus, Niol, what are you doing?" Holly ran back to his side and bent to pick up the shards of glass. "Nice. This was a gift from—"

He grabbed her hands, heedless of the glass. Niol pulled her to her feet, kept her close. His nostrils flared as her scent teased him.

If Holly had been the one in that morgue . . .

"Niol?" Her gaze searched his.

He swallowed back the rage. "You still want to team up on this thing?" Because she couldn't hunt the killer on her own, not when she would be walking in both worlds.

Human and *Other.*

A grim nod. "You know I do. I don't have your contacts."

But she had some. For a human, she'd done a good job of slipping into the realm hidden by darkness.

Besides, if he was right, they didn't really need to explore too much in the demon realm.

"You want in my world. I want in yours."

"What are you proposing?"

Her skin felt so soft beneath his fingers. Delicate. He could hurt her, if he wasn't careful.

But he'd be careful with Holly Storm. Very, very careful. He'd gain her confidence, and in time he'd get . . . her.

She'd been a fire in his blood for too long. Time to get rid of the gnawing hunger and past time to stop a killer.

Luckily, he had the perfect plan for meeting both goals.

He lowered his head. Brought his mouth inches away from hers. "Tell me, Holly, are you in the mood for a new lover?"

Her breath hissed out.

"I'll take that as a yes. The cops already think we're together." They could keep thinking that. It would be the perfect cover. "You can talk to the demons this way, find out if any of them know anything about Sam or Carl." No demon in Atlanta would dare to touch her once he'd staked his claim.

"And what do you get from the arrangement?" Husky. Dammit. Sexy.

He got more fantasies. More hard-ons. And maybe, just maybe, the fuck he'd been dreaming of for all these long months.

If he played the game right, he'd also catch a killer. "I get enough." That was all he'd say, for now.

His eyes lingered on her mouth. She had a great mouth. He loved her bottom lip. Niol wanted to kiss her. To taste the lips so close to his.

And he was more than used to doing exactly as he wanted.

So he took her mouth.

A deep, long kiss. Lips and tongue. Craving. Hunger.

Her lips were warm and soft, and her response—*fuck*.

She kissed him with fury. With wild need.

Nothing tentative about her.

His cock, already semiaroused, swelled against the front of his jeans.

He wanted her naked. The bed was close. He could take her into the bedroom. Strip her, and make the fantasy he'd been suggesting into a reality.

It would be so easy.

Holly pushed against him, her nails biting into his chest.

Maybe not.

His head raised. He could still taste her sweetness on his tongue.

"What is it that you want from me, Niol?"

Everything.

"I want to stop the killer, same as you." He forced his hands to free her and he stepped back. He'd been careful not to jar her. He didn't want to hurt her.

She must have felt his cock straining against her when they'd kissed. The woman knew she'd gotten him turned on and ready.

But he'd pulled back.

For now. "So what's it gonna be, love? Do you want to hunt with me?"

"Yes." Instant. "But we do this together, you got me, demon? No more secrets, no more lies. *Together.*"

He wasn't going to make any promises. His life was all about secrets and lies.

"Then welcome to the wild side, Holly." She'd better get ready for one rough ride.

Chapter 5

Breaking and entering generally wasn't Holly's idea of a good time. Sure, when she'd been eighteen, she'd once had a boyfriend who'd been fresh out of juvie and he'd taught her some lock tricks, but she hadn't exactly planned on spending her grown-up nights breaking the law.

But it wasn't like she had much choice right then.

"Tell me again," Niol said softly, "just what the hell we're doing here."

Here was on the steps of a small brick house on the outskirts of Atlanta. A house Holly had visited once before, with Carl Bronx.

"Carl's parents owned this place." Her gaze swept the street. "They moved a few years back, left it to him. He had a place downtown, but he liked to stay here sometimes."

She'd thought of the house on Sycamore right before her evening news broadcast and realized that while the police had undoubtedly already searched Carl's studio apartment, they might not have had a chance to get into this place.

Or maybe they didn't even know about it yet.

Holly drew in a deep breath. She felt better, her muscles not as stiff and sore. Already, many of her bruises and scratches had healed. Her wrist didn't even hurt anymore. She was feeling pretty damn good.

Lucky for her, she'd always been a fast healer.

She'd slept most of the day away. Slept, and had nightmares about Sam. Yet every time she'd woken, a cry on her lips, the heavy weight of sleep had pulled her back into the dark world of blood and fear.

She couldn't escape the dead, not even in her sleep.

After her broadcast, she'd called Niol and told him that she needed his help. Because if she was about to go snooping into a dead man's house, well, with the crazy shit happening in this town, she wanted backup.

And what better backup could she get than her all-powerful demon?

He'd picked her up, followed her directions, and now stood with her on the stone steps of the house. Holly flipped up the welcome mat, hoping to find a spare key.

"Love, if you want inside, all you have to do is ask . . ." Soft.

She shivered. From the cold, had to be. The night air carried a definite chill.

Sure, it was the cold. And *not* because the guy's voice was sexy.

Her hands rose to her hips. "I'm asking, demon."

He glanced at the door. Narrowed his eyes. She felt that strange thickness in the air again. She'd felt it at the station and at the house, right before her mother's vase had shattered.

A soft *click* sounded and the door swung open.

"Nice." She said, and this time, meant it. Demons could be handy. Holly strode forward—

And Niol's grip on her shoulder had her jerking to a halt.

She glanced at him, brows lowered.

"Powerful demon." He pointed to his chest. "Human." Hers.

Growling, she inched back, and let the big, bad demon stride inside first. If there was a nutjob in there with a really big, really sharp knife, she wasn't going to argue with the merits of having a level-ten powerhouse take the first steps inside.

Her mother hadn't raised a fool.

The house was tomb quiet and the air tasted a bit stale. Niol flipped on the lights, exposing the worn furniture, the old TV.

"So, are your spider senses doing a tingle?" She asked him, glancing at the shadowed rooms to the left and right.

He raised a brow and stared back at her.

Holly tried not to notice just how strong his jaw looked and just how dark his hair was.

His eyes—they didn't disconcert her anymore. Midnight pools, swimming with secrets and emotions. Staring into those eyes—too tempting.

"My spider senses?" He repeated.

She motioned with one hand toward the rest of the house. "That super hearing and vision you've got." Not shifter level, but so much better than her own. "Is this place safe?"

"Safe enough."

That was good enough for her. Her shoulders relaxed. "Then let's hurry. I want to search this house, fast, before that shifter cop or his good buddy pull up." A clue. One small lead, that was all she'd need to find.

Searching Carl's place in the city would be a waste of

time. Anything important, Gyth would have already bagged and tagged it, and the shifter wasn't the sharing sort.

But maybe, just maybe, Carl had brought some information *here*. If he'd really been worried, as Niol had said, maybe he would have come someplace where he felt safe and—

Niol walked away and began pushing through some papers on the kitchen table. "Wait!" She reached into her back pocket and tossed him a pair of latex gloves.

He caught the gloves and gave her a what-the-hell look.

"The cops will find this place eventually. We don't want to leave prints behind."

He gave a faint "hmmmm," then said, "Love, this isn't your first break-in, is it?"

Holly wasn't going to answer that one. Pulling on her own set of gloves, she glanced around the den and spotted an old desk nestled in the corner.

"Just what are we looking for?" Niol called.

"Anything that doesn't belong."

She thought she heard him swear.

Holly jerked open the top drawer. Pushed aside some bills. Opened the second—

And found a brown envelope with Carl's name scrawled across the front.

Her fingers were rock steady when she reached for the envelope. She pulled out a photo, one that had her heart thumping into her chest, then she saw the note.

"Niol."

He was at her side in an instant.

Not steady anymore, her fingers shook when she lifted the photo. A shot of her and Carl, sitting on a park bench, heads bent close as they talked. "The note—the note was with the picture."

He reached for the note. "Fuck."

The impure will die.

Niol balled the note up in his fist. "Now do you believe me? One of your precious humans is out there, *slaughtering* demons."

Holly couldn't deny that it sure looked that way. *The impure.* But how had the killer known? Christ, had *she* given away Carl's secret?

Sam's?

Beside her, Niol stiffened. "We've got to go." He grabbed the envelope and stuffed the note and photo back inside. Then he shoved the envelope into his coat pocket.

"What are you doing? You can't—"

"Oh, right, cause the lady who wanted to break and enter is suddenly getting morals on me."

Her lips parted.

"I've got friends at the department, okay? I'll get a fingerprint check on it—any damn thing we need, I'll get. Now, *come on.*" His fingers locked around her arm and he hauled her toward the door.

Then they were outside, the air biting into her skin. Their feet thudded over the steps and—

"What the hell are you people doin' here?" A gruff voice demanded, and an old man, shoulders hunched, stepped from the shadows near the side of the house, armed with a shotgun.

Oh, shit.

Niol pushed her behind him. *"Lower the weapon."* His voice shook with fury.

The man's mouth fell open and the barrel of the gun immediately dropped toward the ground.

Glancing over his shoulder, Niol said, "Stay behind me, for every step, got it?"

If the guy wanted to get between her and a bullet, she wasn't gonna argue right then. Holly nodded.

He turned back to the guy. "Don't move." Power vibrated in his voice.

The guy didn't so much as blink. Distaste had Holly's mouth drying up. Compulsion. *Control.* She knew exactly what Niol was doing to the man who stared blankly forward, eyes wide and frightened, but body still.

She'd been like him, once. Trapped by a demon's power. Helpless. A puppet.

"Niol . . ."

"He can't remember us." Softer. "When the cops find this place, we can't risk him telling them about us."

She knew that, dammit, but it still didn't make what he was doing right. "Don't hurt him."

A faint nod. "You don't see us. You *never* saw us." Dark, insidious, his voice flowed in the night.

The man didn't move.

They started walking, moving slowly down the remaining steps and toward the car.

The old man watched them, gun still lowered.

Holly jumped in the passenger side. Niol slammed the door behind her, then turned back to face the guy once more. "Go home," he ordered. "Sleep, and forget you even came outside tonight."

The guy turned on his heel, marched back into the thicket of bushes, and vanished.

She exhaled.

Niol climbed in beside her. Didn't speak.

Neither did she.

He gunned the motor and they got the hell out of there.

Fuck.

Niol braked in front of the television station. Holly sat next to him, stiff as a statue. She hadn't looked at him, not once, since they'd left the house on Sycamore.

"I didn't hurt him." Not physically. Sure, he'd slammed his power straight into the old man's mind and stolen his will—okay, that probably counted as mental hurt, but there hadn't been a choice.

He'd been fucking furious when he realized the shot-gun was aimed at Holly. Instinct had taken over and he hadn't hesitated to use his power.

Hell, before her, he'd *never* hesitated. "We couldn't let him just leave, not after he'd seen us—" He'd heard the guy's footfalls. A neighbor, coming to check on the house. Probably nervous because he'd caught sight of Niol's SUV. He'd tried to get out of there before the guy saw 'em, but . . .

Too late.

"I know." Hollow. Her fingers wrapped around the door handle.

Dammit. He could practically feel the ice in the air. "There wasn't a choice."

"I know."

Again with the voice that could have belonged to a ghost. Not to Holly. Not to in-your-face, tough-as-nails Holly. His knuckles whitened around the steering wheel. "I'm not like that bastard."

The bastard who'd shoved into her mind and turned her body against her. The sick fuck who'd tried to kill her while Niol watched.

"You don't know what it's like." Finally, *finally,* she looked at him. "When someone else takes control . . ."

No, because no one else was strong enough to get in-side his head.

She has.

The whisper came from deep within—and Niol ig-nored it. He wanted to grab her and force her to—

Trust him.

Not gonna happen. "You want out?" And he wasn't

talking about the vehicle. If the lady was going to turn tail and run when things started to get a bit rough, she didn't need to be partnering with him.

His life was generally *always* rough.

Maybe she wasn't as tough as he'd thought.

Her eyes narrowed. The fear began to fade as the anger sparked.

Nice.

"You know what I want."

Justice, for the two demons she'd known and lost.

"And you know how I have to play the game," he said. If she wanted to play by human rules, she could go hook up with the cop, Brooks.

Her teeth snapped together. "This *isn't* a game, Niol! We're talking about lives, here, okay? Sorry that I'm not cold and unfeeling like—" She broke off, choking back her words.

But he knew what she'd been going to say.

You.

Holly shook her head. "People matter to me." Spoken fiercely. "I'm gonna get emotional. I'm gonna get pissed. And, yeah, I'm even gonna get scared." She unhooked her seat belt and leaned toward him. "But be clear on this. What I'm *not* gonna do is give up. Got me?"

Not yet. But, hopefully, very, very soon.

She was fucking beautiful with her eyes blazing, her cheeks stained crimson, and her breath heaving.

A woman of strength. Because he'd learned as a child that the ones in this world who were really strong, they knew how to fear—and how to keep going even when that fear rose like a howling beast inside.

Slowly, he unfurled his fingers from the steering wheel. She was close to him, the confines of his SUV and the darkness around them shielding the two of them in intimacy.

The back of his hand brushed over her cheek. Felt the heat beneath her skin.

She didn't flinch, but her pupils flared, just a bit.

Not fear.

Time for the woman to know just what waited for her. "Before this is done, I will have you, love." Wild and naked in his bed. Flesh touching. Pleasure ripping them apart.

He waited for her denial. She'd told him people didn't always get what they wanted. Screw that. He wasn't most people, and he wanted her with a driving lust that he hadn't felt before.

Not even for the succubus who'd nearly taken his heart years before.

And he'd killed for her.

There wasn't anything easy, good, or noble about him. Holly knew that—she'd seen the hell he could bring.

But she'd chosen to stay with him and if she kept coming so close, kept putting that sweet flesh near him and tempting him—

His control would shatter.

"Maybe." And she crept even closer, as if not sensing the danger when he knew the air was pulsing with power barely held in check.

Her fingers moved to his thigh. Her palm pressed against his jean clad leg.

His cock surged to the ready and more-than-willing position.

She licked her lips. A quick swipe of her pink tongue. "And maybe, I'll have you."

Blood pounded in his ears. *Too much temptation.* She should know that demons—they weren't so good on that whole temptation-resisting bit. That part of history was right.

His arms locked around her and he took her mouth. Those soft lips. That sexy tongue of hers.

He kissed her like he was desperate, like he was wild—because he was.

And she met him head-on.

Holly was the one to scramble over him, breaking her lips from his to swear softly when her leg hit the gearshift. Then she crouched over him. Legs beside his, back above the steering wheel and the crotch of her pants rubbing right over his swollen cock.

Sex in a car, not his style—but he wasn't about to complain. With her, he'd take what he could get. His fingers pushed under the edge of her shirt, then rose to smooth over the silken flesh of her back.

He loved her skin. So silky and soft—and that light scent of lavender covered her.

He loved touching her flesh. And he wanted to feel more of it. More of her.

His tongue thrust into her mouth. Taking and seducing even as his fingers trailed around her sides and pressed against the lacy edge of her bra.

He wanted the bra off.

Wanted the shirt off.

Her hips rocked against his.

Niol shuddered. So close to paradise.

Her head lifted, mouth leaving his, dammit.

"Niol . . ."

When a woman said a man's name like that, with need and hunger and lust—all coming out in a husky murmur that was more moan than anything else—she could break him.

Break him.

He cupped her breasts through the thin material of her bra. The tight nipples stabbed into his palms. He wanted her breasts in his mouth. Needed them there. Needed to taste her. To suck her and make her moan his name again.

And again.

Her head tipped back, exposing the pale line of her throat. He had to taste her there. His tongue laved her flesh. Her pulse jerked when his mouth pressed against her. The edge of his teeth scored her, and his fingertips slipped under that scrap of lace—

A knock sounded on the driver's window.

He kept touching her. Kept using his tongue and teeth and—

"Oh, dammit!" Holly wrenched away from him, falling back into the passenger seat. The windows were fogged up—huh, he hadn't done that in over seventeen years.

Another knock, harder this time.

Someone out there had just ruined the best five minutes of his week—

And they were really, really pissing him off.

He jerked the key, wrenching it forward and starting the SUV again. A rough flick of his fingers had the window rolling down. A guy in a security uniform peered into the vehicle, shining a flashlight.

"This isn't freaking Make-out Boulevard, man! This is a private parking area for News Flash and—uh, Ms. Storm? That you?"

Holly coughed and shoved back a rather large clump of her hair. "Hi, uh, Steve."

The flashlight shone right into her eyes.

She held up her hand, wincing.

Niol's eyes narrowed and the flashlight fell to the ground with a clatter.

"My, um, boyfriend was just dropping me off so I could get my car."

Boyfriend was really too tame a term. He would have much preferred lover. But they'd get to that later.

The guard's timing sucked, but at least their cover was

being firmly established. Now the guard wouldn't question his arrival at the station.

Because the guy—Steve—he was a demon. Niol could see right past the glamour and to the real man. He wouldn't have been able to use his compulsion power on Steve. Now, well, it didn't matter.

Niol smiled at the guy. "Couldn't leave without a kiss."

The guy grunted, then gave a low whistle. "*Niol*. Shit . . . didn't expect to see you."

Ah, everywhere he went in the city, folks seemed to know him. Sometimes that was good.

"Ms. Storm, you should get out, *now*."

Sometimes it wasn't.

Niol raised a brow. "Do we have a problem here?"

The guard swallowed and his Adam's apple bobbed. "N-no."

"Good."

Holly shoved open her door. She stalked around the front of the SUV. The beams of the headlights bounced off her pants.

"Thanks for checking on me, Steve. I'm gonna be heading home now."

Steve inched back.

Holly paused. "Niol, I'll see you later."

Oh, she definitely would.

After giving a nod, she turned away and marched toward her waiting car.

"She's human." A whisper from Steve as he bent to grab his flashlight.

Niol lifted his brows. "Does it matter?"

The guy's jaw worked, then he said, "Holly Storm—she's decent, okay? She's not like those other pricks who just like to see themselves on TV."

Well, well. A warning after all.

"Don't worry about Holly. I'll take care of her."

The guard shoved his flashlight back into the holder on his waist. "That's what I'm afraid of . . ."

Then he was gone.

And Holly's taillights flickered as she cranked her car.

Niol reached for his phone. Hit speed dial. His contact answered on the second ring. "Everything in place?" He asked as Holly's sporty little red car reversed and headed for the exit.

"Yes, sir."

She braked for a moment, then turned left.

"Make sure she gets home, then keep a guard on her until dawn."

No need for Holly to know about the security. She'd never realize the men were there, unless something happened and she needed them.

Niol didn't believe in taking chances. Not anymore.

He shifted gears, shoving the SUV into reverse. It wasn't even one a.m. yet. The night was still young.

Plenty of time for more hunting.

This time, he'd be going straight to the darkest side of town. The side where demons huddled in smoky rooms, black eyes glassy as they let the drugs run in their blood.

Sam hadn't been the only one to seek oblivion.

Addiction—it was the true devil for demons.

He didn't want Holly in those rooms.

Best to hunt alone.

Fucking demon.

He crouched behind the fence when the black SUV swept by him.

He *knew* what Holly had been doing in that SUV with that bastard demon, and Niol Lapen was most definitely a demon.

Impure.

His fingers tightened around the camera in his hand.

Who would have thought that Holly would have such a taste for evil? And he'd believed he knew her so well.

That bitch would get what she deserved in the end.

So would Niol.

Man had been created in God's image. Demons belonged only in hell.

And that's exactly where he'd send them. One at a time . . .

Piece by piece, if need be.

Chapter 6

Holly was hot for the demon, no denying it. And she hadn't been hot for a guy since . . . Zack.

Not that she'd ever actually been *hot* for Dr. Zachariah Hall, but she'd been interested.

Interested enough to get engaged. Stupid, stupid mistake.

Her gaze darted down to her left hand and to the bare ring finger that stared back at her.

Oh, yeah, stupid.

She'd thrown that ring back at him that last, fateful night. When she'd found him kneeling between the spread legs of one of his female grad students—right in his office.

Prick.

Her teeth ground together. Niol wasn't like Zack. Not. One. Bit.

Zack had seemed so safe and steady.

When he was really a lying asshole.

There was no way Niol would ever be called *safe*—and she sure liked that, she—

"Uh, Holly?"

She blinked, and found Mac staring at her, a deep furrow between his now-bushy eyebrows. He'd plucked like a fiend when he was on-air. But no more . . .

"Hon, you all right? I've been calling your name for the last two minutes."

And she'd been busy with lust and a pity party. Holly straightened behind her desk. "Sorry. Thinking about a story."

"Ah . . ." Sounded kinda like a bear's growl. "Good girl." His fingers curled around her open door. "That what you wanted to see me about?"

She pushed against her chair, letting the wheels rock back and forth just a bit. "Yeah, yeah, it was." Holly motioned to the seat across from her. "Mac, I've got a lead."

"Then you've got me." He crossed the room and threw himself into the chair. "Talk."

"Carl Bronx—"

"The guy who almost made you pass out on camera?"

He would remember that.

"Carl was one of my sources."

Another bear's growl.

"And the guy the cops found yesterday—Sam Miters—he was, too."

No growl this time, just silence.

Holly exhaled. That beady stare he was aiming at her had made governors break.

"What the hell are you involved in?"

She bit her lip. *Demon business.* Did Mac know? The guy was sharp, the sharpest she'd ever met. Surely he'd realized what was happening around him. She wanted to ask him—

"Are you in trouble?" Quieter.

"I don't—I was at the station, okay? I wasn't there when he—" Was carved up. *No.* "The cops pulled me in to identify Sam's body." She would *not* think about that scene again. It was bad enough that the images kept slipping into her dreams.

"Do they think you're a suspect?"

Fair question. "Maybe."

More intense staring.

She would not squirm. "Their deaths are linked, Mac, no getting around it. Someone's out there, hunting these men—and no matter what the cops think, *it's not me*." Or Niol. "I want to run this story, see if I can—"

"Scare someone," he finished, rubbing his chin.

"Yes."

"You scare the wrong person, you might just find yourself in a killer's sights."

I know. "These men deserve justice."

"That's for the cops." Now his fingertips tapped on the arm of the chair. The guy moved a lot when he was in his deep-think mode.

"They're looking in the wrong place for this guy. The trail's gonna get cold. I want to go on the air."

"With what? We've already covered the killings—"

But they hadn't covered the link between the two men. They hadn't been able to talk about the vicious attacks, the mutilation. "Just let me run with this. Schedule me a slot and let me run." Her voice wasn't desperate. Okay, maybe it was.

He exhaled. "The cops haven't talked to the media yet."

No, and they weren't planning to have a chat fest. She knew the PD wanted to bury this story, and it was an easy bury. Not like the high-profile killings that had plagued the city months before.

A shiver slid over her.

The office down the hall waited, empty and silent, because of those killings. The door always stayed shut. Just walking past that locked door gave her the creeps.

"Get 'em to give you a statement, on camera, and you can run any damn place you want with this story."

A smile broke her lips. "Thanks, Mac!" Sure, getting the interview would be a bitch, but she'd played nice with the cops—now it was their turn to play nice with her. "You won't regret this—"

"Better not."

A knock on the door frame.

Her head tilted. "Kim? What is it?"

One of the interns stood in the doorway, a manila envelope in her hand. Pretty, tall, slim, and only twenty-two, Kim was one that Holly knew had an eye out for her future.

"This was dropped off at the front desk for you." She stepped forward, the envelope outstretched. "I don't even remember when it was delivered—sorry, Holly. I think it might have gotten misplaced. It was under some papers . . ."

Holly took the envelope. "It's all right." Why was her stomach knotting? Her fingers trembling just the faintest bit?

Because there wasn't a return address on the envelope. Just her name, scrawled across the front in big, loopy letters—a script she'd seen before.

Her index finger slid under the top flap and jerked back. She felt the sting of a paper cut, saw the well of blood, but kept ripping anyway.

Then the picture fell into her hands.

Niol, sitting in his SUV, watching her walk in front of the headlights.

A piece of paper fluttered onto her desk.

The impure will die.

"Holly?" Mac jumped to his feet. "What's wrong?"

She was supposed to go live in less than an hour.

Can't.

Holly grabbed the photo and slip of paper—and shoved them back into the envelope. Her index finger pulsed. "I've got to leave, Mac."

Kim was in the doorway now, shifting from her left foot to her right. Her black hair fluttered around her shoulders. "Everything okay, Ms. Storm?" Her blue eyes were wide.

No. "Get me the security tapes from today. Have them waiting on me when I get back. I want to know *exactly* who left this envelope." If the bastard's face was on the tape, she'd have him.

The impure will die.

Whoever the sick freak was, he knew just *what* Niol was.

"Holly?" Mac demanded again.

But she was already grabbing her bag and brushing past him. "Mac, I swear, I wouldn't do this if—" *It wasn't a matter of life and death.* "Run the footage from yesterday's interview—okay? It'll cover my time."

"What the hell?"

"I-I have to go." She fumbled for her cell phone. Dialed the number Niol had given her. Listened to the relentless ring.

Die.

"I have to go . . ." She repeated even as the voice mail picked up. Then she was running into the hallway and muttering into the phone, "Niol, when you get this message—watch your ass! You'd better—"

The damn thing disconnected.

Her heels rapped against the tiled floor. She shuddered when she passed the locked door on the left.

And Holly realized she couldn't get to her demon fast enough.

* * *

There was a line leading into the club, a long snaking line full of men and women, some folks dressed up, some in tattered jeans. It was Friday night, and though it was still way early by party standards—not even ten—it looked like folks were ready for a wild ride in Paradise.

Holly passed the line and headed straight for the doors—

And was brought up short by a giant with tattoos swirling over his body.

"And just where do you think you're goin', princess?" His hand landed heavily on her shoulder. Behind her, she heard muttering, and caught a woman's voice loud and sharp, yelling, "That bitch knows there's a line!"

She ignored the crowd and focused on the bouncer. Really, really big bouncer. The muscles of his arms were so big they looked like they were in danger of bursting. And, Jesus, what was the guy? Like seven foot?

Holly rolled her shoulders, dislodging his hand. The giant raised a brow and pointed toward the end of that long, long line. "At the end, princess."

No way. "I need to see Niol."

The lines around the guy's eyes tightened, just a bit. "You and everyone else."

She rocked on her heels. "Don't you guys have a list or something? Check it. Niol gave me a pass in here, any-time I want." Okay, not really, but he *should* have. The cover story had been his idea and surely the guy had bothered to tell his muscle that his girlfriend would be dropping by—

"Oh, we've got a list." A smaller man with greasy black hair sidled up to him. His nostrils flared, and he said, "Tell us your name and—"

"Holly Storm—and I don't have time for this shit. I need to see Niol, and I need to see him *now.*" Big and mean and small and greasy weren't going to intimidate her.

No, someone else had already done the intimidating job, and she wasn't stopping until she made sure that freak bastard hadn't gotten to Niol.

The bouncers shared a brief glance, then the giant opened the door. "Sorry, Ms. Storm. I hadn't seen you here before—didn't realize you were . . . you."

She wasn't particularly surprised he hadn't recognized her from the news—most folks didn't. Maybe it was the fact that she didn't have a microphone in her hand that threw 'em off, or maybe the bouncers weren't the news-watching types.

Holly managed a nod and stepped forward. So Niol *had* told his goons to give her free rein. Nice.

"Oh, *what the hell*?"

Holly ignored the woman's shriek behind her as she stormed inside. The crowd was just as thick inside the double doors. Bodies packed tight. Music blaring.

Where was Niol?

His office was in the far back. She shoved her way through the men and women, humans and *Other*. Holly ignored the occasional flash of fang and the scrape of claws, moving as quickly as she could. Her heart seemed to pound in fast rhythm with the band.

Then she was at the door marked PRIVATE. Raising her hand and pounding. "Niol? Niol!"

No answer.

Dammit.

She wrenched the doorknob. Locked.

Holly spun around. Laughter filled her ears. Drunken, desperate, and wickedly amused.

All kinds were in Paradise.

But where was the club's owner? If that prick had gotten him—

Her back teeth clenched. Holly's gaze swept the place, but she didn't see a handsome demon with black eyes staring back at her with a twisted grin.

Holly elbowed her way to the bar. Slammed her hands down on the cold marble countertop. "Niol."

The bartender glanced up from the drink he'd been mixing. A tall guy, not like the giant, maybe a few inches over six feet. Red hair. Brown eyes. She'd seen him before— he'd glared at her the last time she'd been there. *Right before Niol had let his pet guard throw me out.*

Nice memory. One she didn't have time for right then.

"I'm Holly Storm—" She stopped and tried to raise her voice over the roar of noise. "I—"

"I know who you are." He sent the glass sliding along the bar top and down to the waiting hand of a man in a long back overcoat. A guy with fangs, of course.

The guy winked at her.

Holly shook her head and turned back to the bartender. "I have to find Niol. *Now.*" Okay, so she did sound like a demanding bitch right then, but, hell, she was *scared.* Yeah, Niol was strong, but he wasn't invincible. And if he wound up like Carl and Sam . . .

No.

The bartender's lips thinned.

"I can't get him on his phone. He's not here." She leaned over the bar. "I need to see him."

His gaze raked her. "Never cared much for reporters."

Her nails scraped across the marble. "And I don't care much for asshole bartenders." Serious understatement considering her history. "So I guess that makes us even. But the guys at the front knew about me. Niol had told them to let me in, and I'm betting he told you that I had the all clear in this place, too."

Silence. The band had stopped playing. The crowd wasn't talking. Holly glanced over her shoulder. Saw a woman with long blond hair and a tight black dress take the stage.

The succubus. The cop's girlfriend.

Holly turned away, hunching her shoulders.

"I don't buy the story." The bartender picked up a shot glass and started cleaning it with a white cloth. "No way Niol falls for a reporter, not with his secrets."

"Niol trusts me."

"Lady, Niol doesn't trust *anyone.* That's why he's the badass in town and all the other demons are just his minions." He glanced up at the stage, almost helplessly, as Cara began to sing, her voice husky, bluesy.

Wasting time.

"He's in danger," she blurted. "I have to make certain he's okay."

"He's always in danger. That's the way the game goes." Not overly concerned. His gaze drifted back to her. "You think you can save him?"

"I can try." *Prick.* Five more seconds, just five, and she was going over that bar.

His lips hitched in a half-smile. One that showed a hint of his own fangs.

Great.

He crossed to the register. Picked up a pen and scribbled a note on a stray scrap of paper. Then he came back to her, walking slow, taking his sweet-ass time.

He lifted the paper. "I'm Marc."

She was about to start snarling.

"If Niol wants to fire someone for giving you this, tell him to fire me." He'd tucked the paper between his thumb and index finger.

Holly reached for it.

"Ah-ah." He pulled back his hand. "Got to warn you about the house rules at this place."

Holly considered smacking him.

"Only go to play . . . or to be prey."

She snatched the note from him. "Heard that warning before." Niol's rule for Paradise. "Didn't keep me out of this joint, won't keep me out of the next place, either."

Holly pushed away from the bar, her eyes on the address. Montlith Court. That was a pretty ritzy street.

Laughter from Marc. "You're gonna be in for one hell of a night, lady. One hell of a night."

The house on Montlith stood, tall and elegant, behind a big stone gate. The home lay nestled between two houses that were each easily bigger than the News Flash Five station.

She hadn't been sure what address Marc would give her.

Holly certainly hadn't expected Easy Street.

She parked her car a bit down the road. Then she stalked up to the gate. Guards were stationed there. Uniformed guards with perfectly pressed pants and shirts, gleaming shoes, and wide-brimmed hats.

They waved a car in as she approached. The gates slid open and Holly thought about trying to sneak in—

"Freeze!"

Only to realize that a guy holding a taser had it aimed right at her.

She froze. "I'm here to meet a friend." Her head tilted just slightly toward the house. She could see it so clearly now, a huge antebellum mansion with white columns, elaborate steps.

Somebody had too much money.

The guy with the taser walked forward—and sniffed her.

"Human." The whisper was so light she almost didn't catch it.

One of the other guards, a guy who was at least ten feet away, gave a nod.

The back of her neck began to tingle.

"Why you here?"

Gruff, and dammit, hadn't she just told the guy why she was trekking up to Scarlett's house? "I need to meet—"

"*Why?*" The intensity in the guy's eyes and voice was just . . . creepy.

She remembered Marc's warning. Oh, hell, what was this, some kind of secret password shit? "Uh, to play?"

The taser dropped. "Then have fun."

Doubt it.

"Maybe they won't use you up too much."

And maybe she wouldn't come back with a camera crew and broadcast that asshole's face all over Atlanta.

"The party's waitin'," he murmured. "Hope you like blood."

Not particularly.

Holly.

Niol tensed, his gaze on the gleaming red hair of the woman who strode toward the house.

He'd know that hair—*know her*—anywhere.

Shit.

What the hell was his reporter doing at the biggest blood party in Atlanta?

A human like her—she'd be a meal before she even made it past the foyer.

Then he'd have to stake a vampire. Or maybe ten.

Dammit. He'd come to the house for information, to see what dark whispers were circulating about the dead demons.

This wasn't a place for a human.

Not one like her.

His hands fisted as he watched her through the third-floor window. *Leave.* The word whispered through his mind, but he didn't use the compulsion.

He could, it would be so easy. She was close enough to control. He could push, and she'd turn around, walk that sexy ass away and—

No.

He wouldn't do that, not to her.

The woman was making him weak.

Time to fucking get her out of his system.

If the vamps didn't get to her first.

Niol stalked toward the stairs.

When the front door of the mansion opened, the stench of blood hit her like a slap in the face.

Oh, damn. No denying it now, she was at a freaking blood party.

Holly tried not to gape as she crept over the threshold. She'd heard about blood parties, of course.

Carl had told her about them and said that if she was smart, she'd make absolutely sure she never attended a blood fest.

Because the humans were the dinner at the parties.

A vampire stood just inside the entranceway, his fangs embedded in a woman's throat. Her eyes were wide open, staring at Holly. The vamp was gulping, sucking, drinking as fast and greedily as he could.

The woman smiled.

Shit.

Holly stumbled past them, only to see a female vampire with two men on the staircase. One guy sat at her feet, kind of like he was worshipping her. Another, with black hair and freakishly pale skin, stood on the step above her. Her red fingernails were on the sitting man's neck. Her mouth had locked onto the wrist of the too-pale one and Holly could see the lady's throat working as she swallowed.

Shit, shit, shit.

A big part of her wanted to turn tail and run right then. She'd seen vamps drinking at Paradise before, but this was different. Everywhere she turned, they were feeding.

And fucking.

She could hear them. The cries of passion and pleasure. The moans.

She was in way over her head.

Stumbling, she rammed her elbow into a man's back. He spun around and locked pitch-black eyes on her. Not black like Niol's, every part of Niol's eyes were dark.

This was different. Only the guy's irises were black. *Hunting mode.* A vamp's irises flashed dark when he hunted or when he screwed.

"I-I'm looking for Niol." Coming in alone probably hadn't been the best idea, but she'd had little choice. The house looked like a freaking photo spread in *Southern Times*—it shouldn't have been a cover for a bloodbath.

"Haven't seen him," the vampire said, his gaze sliding over her. "Shame on him, for leaving you all alone at such a good party." Then he smiled.

Uh, oh. She knew that smile. Vamp or human, she recognized a predatory glance.

"Why don't we go someplace quiet . . ." He took her hand, brought it to his lips, and kissed her palm. "To talk."

Right. What, was "talk" some kind of euphemism for sucking her blood? "I don't think I'm up for *talking* with you." The whole blood thing was not her style.

She was too much of a fainter and her weak stomach sure wouldn't let her indulge—that was one of the reasons she'd nearly slammed onto the floor in the ME's office.

His hold on her wrist tightened and the smile dimmed a bit. "Then let's just—"

"Take your damn hand off her, Carter."

Holly didn't wait for the vampire to free her. She yanked her hand away from him and spun to face Niol.

Alive.

Safe.

She couldn't remember the last time she'd been so happy to see someone.

So she kissed him.

Holly threw her arms around his neck, yanked his head down, and crushed her mouth against his.

His lips met hers with a voracious hunger. Mouth, tongue. Taking, driving her wild and feeding the desire that burned right below the surface.

Niol's hands clamped on her hips, dragging her body tightly against his. The bulge of his arousal pushed at her, the length long and hard.

Her sex moistened, the inner muscles clenching as yearning swept through her.

Niol lifted his head. Swiped his tongue across his lips as if he wanted to take every last drop of her taste.

The silence hit her then. Heavy, overwhelming.

Glancing to the right, she saw that the vamps on the stairs were watching them. Two men—demons—walked out of another room, and their eyes narrowed on her and Niol.

No, on *her*.

"*She's the reporter,*" one of them snarled.

Oh, finally, someone recognized her. Not recognized at the bar, not at the gate—but *now*. She'd always had shitty luck.

"She's mine." Niol snarled right back, his arms still chaining her against him. "You got a fucking problem with that?"

The demons backed up a step.

Smart guys.

But the female vampire on the stairs gave a hard laugh

and sauntered down three steps. "Maybe I do. Depends on just why *she's* here." A smile that should have been beautiful—because the woman's face was freaking gorgeous with glass-cutting cheekbones, red, red lips, a dainty nose, and a curving jaw—lifted her mouth. But the smile, it was just cruel . . . and a bit creepy.

Maybe because of the fangs.

Or the blood. The blood staining her teeth—yeah, that could be causing the creepiness.

"Why are you here, News Flash Five reporter? Are we your scoop for the night?"

The air seemed even thicker. Maybe it was. Maybe Niol was using his powers and he was about to send the black-haired bitch flying back up the stairs so she could finish her meals.

And then all hell would break loose because Niol was seriously outnumbered. She didn't think that even he could take down a whole house full of vampires and demons.

Maybe, but . . .

She didn't want to take the chance.

Holly let her gaze drift slowly back to Niol. She had the feeling the vamps were just waiting for the opportunity to pounce.

The demons, too.

His black eyes met hers. Burning with intensity. "Holly . . ."

She heard the warning in his voice.

Her arms were still around his neck. She stared into his eyes, kept her body nestled against his and said simply, "I want to play."

His lips parted in surprise.

Hard laughter echoed around her.

But then the vamps started talking again, the demons slunk away, and the blood party kicked back into action.

Niol kissed her. Another one of those deep, toe-curling kisses that made her wish they weren't surrounded by the stench of blood and monsters that they really, really couldn't trust.

Because right then, she just wanted to be alone with him.

She was glad he was safe.

And when the hell had Niol started to matter so much to her?

The powerful beat of his heart drummed against her. The warmth of his body bored into hers. And his mouth . . .

That tongue . . .

"Let's get out of here." He growled the words as he tore his mouth from hers.

Holly nodded, more than happy to ditch the vamps.

Niol kept a tight grip on her wrist as he led her through the house. She passed gleaming chandeliers, fireplaces that were big enough to walk in, and half-dressed demons.

Then they were outside, stepping onto a stone walkway, one lined with rosebushes. A few party stragglers were outside, but they'd left the noise behind.

He drew her into the shadows, wrapping his arms around her shoulders and pulling her against his chest. His head lowered and Niol's breath stirred the hair near her ear.

"Most of 'em like to stay in the house. It's safer there, fewer prying eyes."

His voice was a whisper, one that shouldn't have been seductive. It was too dark, too sinister, but goose bumps rose on her arms and it sure wasn't because he scared her.

If anyone glanced their way, she knew they'd look like a couple stealing away into the night. Bodies too close. His wicked mouth at her ear.

For just a second, Holly could have sworn that she felt the warm touch of his tongue sliding over the shell of her ear.

Her knees did a quick tremble. "Niol . . ."

"Why are you here?" Another dark whisper. "And who the hell sent you to this place?"

She drew in deep breath, caught the scent of the flowers, fresh and clean from the late evening rain.

And the dank stench of blood.

Vampires.

Holly turned more fully against him. Her breasts teased the muscled expanse of his chest. Niol wasn't dressed in the fancy garb some of the vampires had worn. No silk jacket and pants.

Just his standard black T-shirt. Faded jeans.

A T-shirt that was stretched taut by his defined chest, his wide shoulders, the rippling muscles of his arms.

And those jeans . . .

Later.

Holly rose onto her tiptoes and let her lips skim his jaw. "Marc told me—I made him, but that doesn't matter." Not at all. She swallowed. "The picture at Carl's . . ." Her voice was as soft as she could make it, a breath of sound. The vampires weren't close, but she sure didn't want to chance them overhearing her. "I got one like it today, delivered to the station."

She glanced over his shoulder as she spoke, her gaze resting on the plump, bloodred petals of a rose. The roses were twisting beneath an old-fashioned gaslight. Strange to see them blooming, far too early in the season. *Magic.* She cleared her throat and said, "I got a picture, of you and me . . . and a note."

The roses shriveled before her eyes. Darkened to a sickly brown, then fell to the ground, petals raining down. Magic—Niol's magic.

Holly jerked her head back and stared, wide-eyed, up at Niol. His face was a hard mask, his black eyes glittering. "What did the note say?"

"The impure will die."

Her hair lifted in a breeze that hadn't been there a minute ago. "I think you're next on the bastard's list, Niol." The guy had all but drawn a bull's-eye on Niol's face. "I had to find you, to make sure—"

She stopped.

One black brow rose. "To make sure—what?"

"That you were safe."

The brow lowered and a crinkle appeared on his forehead. "Worried about me?"

In too deep. "Yes." Stark. She caught the surprise that flickered over his face. What? Hadn't anyone ever worried about the man before? "No matter how strong you are, you can still be hurt . . . or killed."

She didn't want to think about that. Holly's fingernails dug into his arms. "The bastard's watching us, Niol. And I'm not going to let you become his next slaughter."

A ghost of a smile feathered his lips. "Deadly."

"Right, that freak is, and I'm not—"

"Not him. You."

She didn't know what to say. Deadly—not exactly a word many had used to describe her.

"I like that in a woman."

He would.

"And if our . . . friend . . . was watching us before, when he took that picture—"

"It was from last night, in the parking lot of News Flash Five." He'd been so close to them, *too* close.

His hold on her hardened. "If that sick fuck was watching us then . . ." His stare bored into hers. "What makes you think he's not watching us now?"

Holly's breath stuttered out as her heart slammed into her chest.

Hell, yes, he could be watching. Could have been watching her the whole time.

And, if so, she'd just led the freak straight to Niol.

Chapter 7

Holly's face bleached of color and Niol swore.

"You think he followed me?" She sounded horrified.

No point lying. "Maybe." Or maybe the bastard had been following *him*. "Either way, the guy's letting us know the game's on."

"And that you're his next target."

Or she was.

No, no that wouldn't make any sense. The *impure* reference in the letters had to be talking about the demon blood.

No humans had turned up carved to ribbons. Only his kind.

So, yes, looked like his ticket was up next.

Let the fucker just come and try to kill him.

"The flowers are all dying," she murmured, her lips curving down. "Stop it, Niol. They were the best thing about this place."

He hadn't even realized he'd been letting his power leak out. Instantly, he slammed down the gates of his control.

Niol dropped his hands and stepped even farther back into the darkness. He could see the withered petals in the flickering light.

Dead.

He was good at killing.

But once something was dead, there was no way to bring it back.

His gaze locked helplessly on Holly.

Once something was dead . . .

No.

Holly might not be impure, but someone had already tried to kill her once this week. No way was he gonna let her be at risk.

She'd been in the picture, too. Maybe the killer had decided that Holly had been slumming with the demons too much. Maybe she was impure in his twisted head, too.

Maybe he just needed to find the bastard and do some slicing of his own.

She touched his cheek.

Niol nearly flinched.

It wasn't a sexual touch, though, hell, yes, he sure liked those from her. The woman's mouth was the best temptation he'd had in well, years.

"It's okay," she whispered. "They're just flowers."

Even as she said the words, he saw the memory flicker in her eyes. Another night. Another place. Another rush of his power.

But it hadn't been blackened flowers at their feet.

It had been a man's charred body.

The bastard had been planning to kill Holly. There hadn't been a choice.

Her hand didn't fall away, and he was expecting her to wrench back. But she didn't. The memories were there, the full knowledge of just what he could do.

What he'd done.

"I never thanked you, did I?" She asked quietly. "You and Cara saved my life that night."

And took another. "You don't have to thank me."

"I-I think I do."

"Don't make me into a hero." That he'd never be.

"I won't make that mistake." Did her lips curl just a bit? For a second, he could have sworn that dimple winked at him. "But you're not a hardass villain, either."

Wasn't he? Sometimes, even he wasn't sure. He caught her hand, and, for a moment, held her tight. Then said, "We need to go. If that asshole is watching us, we're not safe here." There was only one place he'd feel was safe enough for Holly.

His house.

His bed.

She glanced over her shoulder, back up at the monster of a house. "Do we have to go back in there?"

"No." He tugged on her wrist. "I know another way out. Come on." Time to get the hell out of there.

Before their new friend showed up.

They left her car at the party. Niol figured he'd call one of his men later, get 'em to pick it up, drive it around town to throw off any watchers, and then bring it back to his place.

Holly rode with Niol back to his home. When they first climbed into the car, she'd asked, "Where are we heading?"

"My place," had been his growled response.

Her slow smile had nearly stopped his heart, and then she'd whispered, "Good."

Niol didn't make a habit of bringing women into his home. Not his real home, anyway. He had an apartment over Paradise Found that he used for his lovers, but his home, that was different.

Sanctuary.

But he wanted Holly in his realm.

They drove to the outskirts of the city. He'd bought the land years ago, commissioned an architect, and built the house exactly the way he'd planned so long ago.

Years ago . . . when he'd been a dirt-poor kid all but shoving his nose against the windows of the fancy houses in D.C.

A fucking lifetime ago.

Holly whistled when she saw his house.

He drove past the thick wall surrounding his home, pushing a button to send the electronic gates closing behind him. The house waited down the lane, windows gleaming, lights shining from within.

Not as big as the antebellum, his place was a two-story brick home, with a wraparound balcony and a gleaming swimming pool. It sat on fifteen acres, plenty of privacy. The whole area had been wired for security. Cameras. Guards who knew how to watch, but not be seen. Motion sensors.

They'd be safe here. *She* would be safe.

"Didn't expect this." Holly's index finger tapped on the glass. "Didn't really take this for your style."

He killed the ignition. "And what is my style?"

Her head turned slowly toward him and she seemed to really think about that. "Dark. Private—"

Niol had to laugh. "This is private, love. Trust me, no one will bother us out here."

"No, that's not what I meant. The windows—" she broke off, shaking her head. There were over fifty windows in the house. He knew, he'd watched each one being installed. "There aren't any shutters, like you want the light to come inside."

You want the light to come inside. Niol stiffened and decided it was time to drop the damn topic of his house. He shoved open his door, then headed around the SUV.

But Holly was already out. "Niol . . ."

"I brought you here because it's safer. No one will get within five miles of this place without us knowing instantly."

"Good to know."

He bounded up the steps, with her on his heels. "There are guest rooms—" Niol pushed open the door and urged her inside. Once over the threshold, she turned back to look at him with those deep green eyes.

"I won't be using one," she said simply, and reached for the hem of her shirt. She jerked it up and tossed the garment onto the floor.

All the moisture in his mouth disappeared.

"I'll be in your room."

In his bed.

He couldn't take his eyes off her breasts. Full and tempting. Thrusting against the light pink silk of her bra. Oh, damn. "Love . . ." He barely managed to punch in the alarm code. "We aren't going to make it to the bed."

Maybe the sofa. Maybe the floor. Or maybe right there against the wall—he was going to take her.

Fuck waiting.

He'd waited long enough. Holly was ready, willing, and his cock was so hard that the brush of denim against him hurt.

Niol took a step toward her. Her head tipped back.

He took her mouth. Drove his tongue deep and hard into that wet sweetness even as his fingers jerked the hook of her bra free. He threw the silk down and groaned when her tight nipples stabbed into his chest.

Not good enough.

Niol ripped his mouth away, stared down at her breasts—

Pink nipples. Like suck-me candy.

—and then his mouth locked on her left breast. Sucking. Kissing. Licking. Tasting and taking as much as he could.

Her moans filled his ears. The scent of her arousal flooded his nostrils.

And he knew there was so much more to taste.

Her nipple pressed against his tongue, a ripe berry, one that he wanted to savor all night long.

Savor.

Take.

He drew her breast into his mouth. Laved her with his tongue. Her hips rocked against him. Her hands slid down his body and locked onto his hips. Hot hands, hands that seemed to burn him through his clothes.

He licked his way to the other breast. Swirled his tongue over her nipple. Heard her breath catch.

Then he used his teeth to lightly score her flesh.

Holly shuddered. *"Niol."*

Her hands pushed between their bodies. Fumbling, she managed to loosen his belt, unsnap the jeans, and jerk down—

"Ah, easy, love." He lifted his mouth, licked his lips, and still tasted sweet nipple. "I'm damn close . . ."

Since he hadn't worn underwear since he was sixteen, his cock sprang into her hands, and the lady knew exactly how to touch. Soft fingers, firm grip, perfect pump.

Damn.

He was going to come in her hand, when he wanted to be buried as deep as he could go in her wet sex.

He caught the edge of her skirt. Shoved it up so that he could grip the smooth column of her thigh.

Silky skin. He wanted those legs wrapped around him and clenching tight.

His fingers rose. Brushed against the edge of her panties.

Holly's grip tightened around him. *"Niol."*

He glanced down at his cock. Saw the thick, straining head coated with a gleaming drop of pre-cum. Her fingers, so pale, with her short nails, held him carefully.

And worked him so well.

But not as well as her sex.

Or, her mouth . . . that sweet, red mouth . . .

"Let me."

Her husky plea had his eyes jerking to hers and he could too easily read the intent. "If that mouth of yours gets on me, I'm done." One lick, two, and he'd come against her tongue.

No, not this time.

He ripped the panties away.

His fingers brushed over her creamy sex, plump with arousal, so slick she made him shake.

Her legs shifted, thighs widening her stance, granting him more tempting access to that pink flesh. Niol stroked the button of her desire, dragging his thumb over her clit, and loved the moan that tore from her mouth. He parted her nether lips and pushed one finger deep into that tender opening.

So damn tight.

Perfect.

The bed would definitely have to wait.

His finger slid back. Thrust deep. Withdrew.

Two fingers worked inside her and Holly's head fell back. Her skin flushed with sweet color, those nipples driving him wild—

"Niol!" A demand.

One he wasn't about to ignore.

A final plunge of his fingers—she was going to feel *incredible*—and he kissed her again. Drove his tongue deep into her mouth, and, oh, shit, she was sucking his tongue, tightening her lips around him and—

His control exploded.

He had a condom in his wallet—he had it out and on in a flash. Then his hands were on Holly, locking around her waist, and he lifted her up against the wall.

She felt so light.

For just a moment, he hesitated. Rough and wild might not be her way. She was human, but not like the other human lovers he'd had who *wanted* the rush that came from screwing a monster. She might need more time, more care, more—

Her nails dug into his shoulders. "If you don't take me, I might have to hurt you."

He laughed as a real jolt of surprise rocked him.

Her legs wrapped around his hips and the laughter died. Her creamy opening rubbed against his cock. A slight adjustment, then—

Then he shoved into her, so deep that her sheath rippled around the full length of his cock. So deep that his balls slammed against her.

So deep that it was *fucking perfect.*

Her mouth brushed over his neck. Those lips locked on him, her tongue laved the skin.

Then she bit him.

His cock swelled even more within her.

Insane.

Not like this—this wasn't the way he—

Niol withdrew, then plunged deep as a frantic rhythm swept over him. Faster, faster, harder. He couldn't get enough. Her straining sex was the best fit he'd ever had. Her breasts tormented him and the woman's scent—

His teeth snapped together and a groan built in his throat.

Un-fucking-believable.

She was pinned against the wall. Held tight by his weight and the steely grip of his hands. Every thrust and withdrawal sent his cock sliding against her sensitive flesh.

Her eyes squeezed shut. "Oh, Jesus, Niol, this is—"

Her sex convulsed around him as her climax broke over her.

Her lips parted on a soundless scream.

He kept thrusting. Kept driving his cock into her, desperate for his own pleasure, and the milking of her core around him just made him that much wilder.

"Niol . . ." A whisper of satisfaction.

He erupted. His spine tightened and he shoved deep once more as the tide of pleasure crashed over him.

Fucking. Insane.

His forehead fell against hers and he let the pleasure crest.

That was what I've been waiting for.

The lady had been more than worth the wait.

The bitch was gone and so was the fucking demon.

She'd driven like a maniac after leaving Paradise Found, and she'd lost him. Had she known he was behind her? Watching her every move?

He'd been so careful, laying back and watching her leave the news station, then trailing two cars behind her when she rushed to that godforsaken bar.

Holly Storm. He had such plans for her—had, since the very beginning.

She'd gotten past him.

He almost admired that. Would have, if it hadn't pissed him off so much.

He picked up his cell. Punched in a fast number. The phone rang once, twice, then . . . "Is she there?" Back at her house, letting that freak touch her?

"No."

Shit.

His place. And he'd already checked out Niol's security setup. No way was he going to get in there.

No need. He'd get the demon to come to *him.*

Demons. Who the hell would have thought those bastards were real?

Abominations, that's what they were.

Dark, twisted. *Evil.*

They deserved to get sent right back to hell.

He was just the man to send them there.

After he had his fun with them, of course. After he learned just how much pain they could tolerate. After he learned their secrets and how to harness their power.

Killing demons was so much easier than he'd anticipated.

Maybe Niol would be a challenge.

Maybe not.

He'd bet that when he sliced the bastard open, the tough guy would start to beg, just like the others.

His lips curved. Begging . . . and blood. Such a perfect combination.

"She was in the bar tonight," Cara Maloan said, as she drew her fingernail down her lover's chest.

Todd Brooks sucked in a sharp breath and caught her hand. "Who?" His eyes had that hot, dark look she liked so much. The look that said he was crazy to have her.

She loved that look—from him.

Only him.

Cara licked her lips. She wanted to strip off her clothes and taste her lover, but a worry nagged in her mind, and she just couldn't shut off the strange fear. "Holly Storm. She came to Paradise right before I went onstage."

Todd grunted. "That's because she's screwing Niol."

She blinked, then frowned. "What? Are you sure?" Niol went for human lovers. Hell, Niol went for vamps, witches, demons . . .

But Holly Storm was—different. "Niol doesn't like reporters." He'd told her that dozens of times. The guy had even called them parasites a few times, and he didn't even call the vamps that.

"He seems to like her." He pressed a kiss to her shoulder.

Cara pushed him back, forcing Todd down against the pillows with only the weight of her hand against his chest. "You're trying to distract me."

"I'm trying to make love to you." He smiled, but she saw the shadows and secrets in his eyes. "There's a difference."

Her lips firmed. *Just get it out there.* "This is about those demons who've been killed, isn't it?" He was shutting her out because it was a case, one that might hit too close to home for her.

After all, she was a demon, too.

"I can't tell you that, Cara."

"You just did." A shiver slid over her. "What the hell is going on? Is someone really hunting demons in this city?" That was the rumor she'd heard at Paradise. It'd come from Marc, with a warning to watch her back and to stay away from any . . . humans.

Dammit. "Do I need to be worried?"

His jaw clenched. "I'd never let anything happen to you."

Understanding dawned. "Is that why you've had that charmer cop tailing me for the last two days?"

"Hell. Tagged him, did you?"

A nod.

"I love you," Todd told her quietly as he lifted her hand from his chest and brought her fingers to his lips. "And I might be an asshole sometimes—"

She snorted at that.

"—but your safety comes first with me, *always.*"

So he'd given her a bodyguard. "*Tell* me next time." Kinda cute, really, that he thought she needed a bodyguard. Todd was still so new to this game. He forgot how strong she could be.

How deadly in her own right.

Especially if she was fighting a human.

For a moment, his face turned stark. "I hope to hell there's never a next time like this."

She wondered just what he'd witnessed at his crime scenes. Wondered about the calls that had come and taken him from her bed.

Her cop. Always trying to be a hero.

A girl could easily lose her heart to a guy like him—she sure had.

"Is Niol in danger?" She couldn't keep the worry out of her voice. She and Niol went back too far for her to pretend about him.

Todd's lip curled. "I pity the bastard who makes the mistake of going after him."

She thought about that for a moment. Remembered the stench of burning flesh.

Then gave a small nod.

Something she'd learned over the years—Niol was one hard bastard to kill and one very fine predator.

Niol was, quite possibly, the best lover she'd ever had.

Oh, screw that. Holly opened her eyes and gazed up at the ceiling. He was one *hell* of a lot better than the other five guys she'd been with in her thirty-one years.

Fan-damn-tastic.

She licked her lips, realized they were desert dry, just like her mouth, and swallowed before she said, "When can we do that again?"

Though, not necessarily against the wall, because her back and ass were hurting a bit, but . . .

That had been one wild ride.

His head raised from her shoulder.

He smiled at her. A smile that made her heart do a weird little flutter.

The darkness in his eyes, it almost seemed to lighten, just for a moment.

And the cock inside her stiffened.

Her sex shivered.

I'd like more.

But Niol was pulling back and Holly couldn't control the moan that slipped from her lips at the slow glide of his flesh. *Good.*

Niol eased her legs down and lowered her body to the floor. A chill skated over her.

A flicker of doubt had her swallowing. Maybe the fantastic sex hadn't been so great for him. The guy'd had a stream of lovers in his life, she knew that.

Rumor was he'd lost his heart years ago to a succubus. Wasn't like she could really compete with a sex demon in the buck-naked category and—

"Shower or bed?"

The words were a rumble, thick with lust and sensual demand.

The worrying voice in her head faded to a whisper. Holly blinked. "I—ah—"

His jaw clenched. "Bed."

Niol's hand lifted and he pointed toward the stairs. "First room on the right." He glanced down at his body. "I'll ditch the condom, then meet you there." His mouth took hers. A deep, toe-curling kiss.

When she turned to walk away from him moments later, her legs weren't quite steady. She held onto the banister as tightly as she could. Her thighs trembled and her sex throbbed, the flesh swollen and . . . hungry.

Still hungry for him.

Once hadn't been nearly enough. Good thing they had the rest of the night and that he seemed as wild for the sex between them as she was.

"Fucking gorgeous."

The snarl stopped her near the top of the stairs. She

glanced back down. Niol gazed up at her, completely naked now. *So much tanned flesh.* The condom was gone and his cock stood fully erect. His eyes were on her, his face a tight mask.

Then he licked his lips and she almost did a header off the stairs.

Niol smiled and began to stalk her.

A whip of fire fueled her blood.

He was coming up the stairs, fast.

Two at a time. Three.

He'd be on her in seconds.

In her.

She sprinted for the top, adrenaline kicking through her.

At the landing, she glanced to the left. The room was dark, lit only by the stars and moonlight that shone through the massive windows.

She could see the bed. A tall four-poster.

Holly kicked out of her high heels. Shimmied out of her skirt and—

Strong arms locked around her from behind. Pulled her against a rock-hard chest, imprisoning her in a steely grip. His cock nudged against her ass.

His fingers took her breasts. Curling around the nipples, squeezing, caressing.

Her breath choked out and her head sagged against him.

Niol growled and locked his mouth onto the column of her throat.

Heat flooded her core. Holly's legs shifted restlessly. That bed was so close . . .

One hand slid over the curve of her stomach.

She stopped breathing.

His fingers, so perfectly broad and strong, trailed down her abdomen. Pushed through the red curls that shielded her sex.

There was no tender searching this time. No play. No fondles.

Her legs parted.

His fingers, two, drove knuckle-deep inside her.

Holly gasped his name and strained against him.

In. Out. The fingers plunged in a wild rhythm.

His teeth scored her neck.

Oh, damn, oh, damn, oh, damn . . .

She was going to come again. Holly could feel it. The tight, clenching buildup. The aching rush of blood in her muscles. So close—

Niol wrenched his fingers away. "Get on the bed." Guttural. An order.

Please—like she was gonna argue when another mind-blowing orgasm was seconds away.

"On your back, get—"

Now, she'd argue. "On yours, demon." She shook her head, sending her hair rocking against her face as she climbed onto the bed and waited.

His gaze held hers. So black and deep.

Not evil. Not cold.

How had she ever thought that?

Such fire in the darkness. Such need.

He jerked open the nightstand drawer. When she heard a faint rip, Holly knew he was suiting up with another condom.

A man with serious stamina—what a perfect dream.

The bed squeaked beneath his weight. Holly slid away from him, on her knees now as she waited for him to follow *her* order.

His taunting smile was a white flash that made her heart pound too fast, but he stretched out, folding his hands behind his head. "You want me?"

Hell, yes.

"Then take me."

A taunt. A challenge.

She'd always loved a good challenge.

Holly straddled him, positioning her wet folds right over the bulging length of male flesh. Her nails raked over his chest. Teased his nipples.

She arched her hips, rubbing lightly. Not taking him in, not yet.

Enjoying the game too much.

Her head bent and her tongue swiped over his left nipple. The nubbin was hard and erect and when her tongue touched him, she heard the harsh inhalation of his breath.

"*In . . . side.*"

Another order.

One the clenching of her sex wanted her to follow.

But . . . not yet.

She turned her attention to his other nipple and rocked her hips again.

He moved in a blur, hands flying down, almost bruising as they curled around her hips. "No play, love." His lips peeled back from his teeth. "Not . . . this time. Too fucking *hungry.*"

Even after the first—

Oh, wow.

His cock pushed into her opening. Squeezed just inside.

The heavy, too-tight feeling rushed over her again, but she was more than ready and after a brief moment, the full length of his erection slipped right inside, seeming to drive all the way to her womb.

He lifted her with his grip, slid that cock out, then pushed her down in a relentless drive.

Again and again.

Holly didn't need his urging. She shoved down on him as hard and fast as she could, the climax again tantalizingly close.

The slick slide of their bodies pushed them toward a wild release.

Deeper.

Faster.

Harder.

Her hands were on his chest, pushing down with her weight as her hips rose and fell and she rode him with all her power.

His eyes were closed, jaw clenched.

Never, not like this, not like—

When she came, she breathed his name and she shattered. The starlight disappeared for a moment. Darkness seemed to surround her and the thudding drumbeat of her heart echoed in her ears.

He shot up beneath her, rocking her body. Holly blinked and saw his face.

Tense. Savage.

His hips hammered at her, and the long length of his shaft jerked inside her sex.

Niol's eyes widened with his release and she saw the pleasure flood his features.

Then he kissed her.

She was lost.

Dammit, *lost*.

And in the worst trouble of her life.

Chapter 8

When Holly woke the next morning, sunlight blazed through the windows, too bright and hard, and she blinked, trying to adjust her eyes to the sight and remember where she was because this was *not* her room and—

And a tongue licked over her sex.

Holy mother of—

She shoved up on her elbows as memories of the night before flooded back through her mind.

Niol.

Sex downstairs.

Sex upstairs.

More sex.

Oh, yeah.

His black head was between her thighs. One strong hand held each leg spread. Open wide.

He was tasting her. Licking. Taking his time. Sucking. Stroking with that clever tongue.

He growled against her core and the vibration had the back of her knees tingling.

His tongue thrust inside her.

Damn.

She climaxed. A hot, hard explosion that broke through her body.

Her eyes were on him as she came. His head lifted. He licked his lips, taking the last of her essence into his mouth. That wicked tongue—

His eyes widened as he stared at her and she could only shudder.

What a hell of a way to start the day.

So much better than her clock radio.

And that hadn't even given her any bad memories. Hadn't made her think of—

No. She wouldn't go there. Not now.

As the contractions of her inner muscles faded, she reached for him. The guy was more than ready to go, definitely aroused and turnabout was more than fair—

"What the fucking hell?" Niol's eyes narrowed to chips of black ice. He shot up the bed, grabbing her arms and glaring down at her.

Holly's mouth dropped open. Tender lover to pissed demon in two seconds flat. "Niol, what are you—" His fingers dug into her arms. "You're hurting me!" And he was. A too tight, too hard grip.

His hold eased, just a fraction, but the look on his face became even darker. Uglier. "What kind of game are you playing?"

Was the man insane? Holly could only shake her head. Her body still vibrated with pleasure. Her thighs trembled and Niol looked at her like he hated her.

Great sex. Best night of pleasure ever.

Now the morning from hell in a split-second change.

Was this what life with a demon was like?

"Answer me. I see you now."

Uh, he should have seen her the entire time. Her chin came up. "Take your hands off me." She wasn't sure what was happening, but she was getting . . . scared.

Her heart wasn't racing from passion anymore. No,

that pumping came from fear. Because the air in the room had thickened again. The lamp on the nightstand was shaking as if—

The lamp exploded, sending shards of glass flying in the room.

Holly yelped and jerked away from Niol.

"I see you," he said again, a muscle jerking along his jaw.

"Yeah? Well, big damn deal." She jumped from the bed, yanking the sheet up and wrapping it around her body. Being naked was all fine and dandy until your lover had a freak-out after some oral sex.

She could pick 'em. "I see you, too, asshole." Every muscled, naked, furious inch of him.

No, uh-uh, not gonna get distracted. The guy was flipping out—and she needed to *get out*.

She turned, storming for the door.

"You're a demon." Soft.

Her jaw dropped. No way. No. Way. Holly glanced over her shoulder. "What is your problem? You know I'm—"

"I saw your eyes when you came, *love*." Not a term of endearment then. More of a sneer. "Can't hide anymore." The mirror near the closet shattered.

She shook her head. "That's impossible." Not the broken shards of glass. His accusation. "I'm human."

"Fucking lie."

And she realized that sex with a demon could be very, very dangerous.

Niol bounded across the room and locked his arms around her.

He was losing control.

Niol knew it. He could barely hear Holly's voice, telling him he was crazy, that he was screwing up what could have been something great—

All he heard was the thundering beat of his heart and the roar of fury that came from his soul.

Demons had souls. Demons could love.

Demons could hurt.

Her eyes were grass green now, but he'd seen that flash of black when her face went slack with ecstasy.

Total darkness. Iris. Sclera. *Everything.*

Demon eyes.

The way his always looked.

The way a demon's eyes looked without glamour.

A climax was a weak moment for a demon. Power fluctuated then. A glamour could slip, for a few precious moments.

As hers had slipped.

She'd played me. All along. From that first night.

No helpless human. Not by a long shot.

For a demon to be able to hide her true self from *him,* she had to be very powerful.

He, of all people, sure knew how dangerous a powerful demon could be.

What if it was a setup? Everything? Carl? Sam? What if she'd been trying to get close, so that I could be her next victim?

Shit.

He hadn't been this angry, this fucking furious since—

Since he'd been twelve and his mom had dumped his ass on his grandmother's doorstep. She'd been terrified of him, his power, and desperate to get away from her only child.

He'd begged. He'd pleaded. But she'd left him with a brown paper bag full of his clothes and the taste of salt on his tongue.

She'd driven away and never looked back.

"Niol." Holly's sharp voice jerked him from the past.

He blinked and stopped seeing the flash of red tail-lights disappearing over an old, broken road and saw

Holly, face pale, lips red, as she stared up at him, a faint line between her brows.

"Let. Me. Go."

No. Not until he found out what she—

Holly kicked him in the shin.

Swearing, he dropped his hold. What kind of attack was that? A demon wouldn't—

"You're twisted." With a quick, snakelike move, she tightened the sheet around her, toga-style. "I thought we had—screw that." She sucked in a deep breath. "I don't know what kind of crazy shit you're talking about, but I do know you just ruined the best sex I've ever had."

The best sex I've ever had.

Her words calmed the fury.

It'd been the best he'd had, too.

And he'd sure had plenty of comparative experience.

But nothing like being with Holly. The pleasure had ripped through him—no, seemed to rip him apart.

And that's why it had hurt so much when he'd learned the truth.

He'd had her body, thought he'd touched more in the darkness of the night.

Only to find out everything was a lie.

A trap.

"You're good, I'll give you that." She'd slipped right under his guard, and he'd never even suspected.

"And you're crazy." Her gaze darted around the room. "Shit. Where are my clothes?"

Scattered.

"Why are you pretending? The game's over."

Her glittering stare shot back to his. "I'm not playing a game with you, jerkoff. I'm walking out on you. There's a difference."

She found her skirt. Yanked it up under the toga. Discovered her shirt near the door. He'd brought it up for her at some point in the night, trying to be a *gentleman*. Fuck that from now on.

Swearing, Holly pulled the shirt over her head, not bothering with a bra, and finally let the sheet drop.

Then she looked at him and shook her head. "I thought finding my fiancé with his face between a grad student's legs had been hard. Hell, Niol, you've just ripped me apart."

Tears gleamed in her eyes for a moment.

The taste of salt on my tongue.

She grabbed her shoes and flew out of the room.

And it felt like someone had punched him in the chest.

Niol took an instinctive step forward, wanting to go after her.

A lying demon.

Just like me.

No, no, Holly wasn't like him. He'd been watching her too carefully, seen the way she interacted with others.

His teeth ground together.

He'd also seen the flash of her eyes.

Niol heard the thud of her footsteps pounding down the stairs.

Hell. As fast as he could, Niol jerked on a pair of jeans.

Then, no choice—he took off after her. The lady was fast. She was yanking open the front door, *his* car keys in her fist, when he caught her.

He slammed the door shut with the palm of his hand, caging her between the door and his body.

Her smell, that rush of lavender and the warm scent of woman, teased his nostrils.

Her back was straight, shoulders tense, and the soft locks of her hair brushed against his cheek.

For just a second, he closed his eyes and inhaled.

The memory of her in that pit of an alley flashed before him. Terrified eyes. Pale face.

Helpless.

Trapped.

The demon bastard had controlled her, nearly killed her.

Niol's eyes flew open. That didn't make a lick of sense. One demon couldn't control another, especially not one as powerful as—

Holly turned, her body brushing against his, and her eyes stared up at him.

So green . . .

And lost.

I'll be damned. Understanding dawned and had him rocking back on his heels. "You don't know."

Because no way, *no way,* could he have been that wrong about her.

He was *never* wrong about people. He could sense evil and deception—that was part of his nature.

He hadn't sensed a lie from her. Still didn't.

One demon couldn't control another.

Not a full-blooded demon, anyway. But a hybrid— those rules didn't apply with a hybrid demon.

The line was back between her brows. "Know what?" Holly licked her lips. "Niol, stop jerking me around. I've got enough crap to deal with—"

His mouth crashed onto hers. A deep, hard, I'm-taking-you kiss that—

Holly shoved him back a good foot.

Because he let her, not because she had any enhanced strength.

"I'm not the kind of girl who likes it when a guy plays asshole one minute and lover the next." Her lip curled in disgust—no dimple—as her eyes narrowed. "Even when the sex is good."

She doesn't know.

Niol realized he had to tread very, very carefully now.

If he hadn't been so pissed earlier, he would have realized—

The woman had been thrown into his world months before, a lamb to the slaughter.

Some reactions just couldn't be faked.

He'd remember her fear in that alley until he took his last breath.

"I'm sorry, Holly." The words were rusty and felt funny on his tongue. Because it was the first time he'd ever apologized.

Judging by the look on her face, she knew it, too. "Uh, run that by me again."

"I. Am. Sorry." He wouldn't plead. Wouldn't beg. Had sworn years ago never to do either again.

"Sorry you called me a demon? Well, you should be—"

"Not for that."

Her lips parted.

"You *are* a demon, love. But the crazy thing is . . . I don't think you even know it."

She rubbed her hand over her eyes and growled. "I'm not a demon—"

He caught her hand, pulled it gently down, and kept a loose grip around her wrist. "Yes, you are."

A startled laugh burst from her lips. "You're actually serious. You believe—"

"I'll prove it to you. Just give me some time." An investigation of her background, her family history, would take a few days—maybe less, depending on who he hired and how much money he tossed around, but Niol knew he would find the proof.

He just had to look hard enough.

"I *can't* be a demon, I think I would know—"

"I thought so, too," he murmured.

"My parents would have told me, don't you think? But they didn't because they're not demons. They're perfectly normal people—" A shadow drifted over her face. "My dad was, anyway, but he had a heart attack and—" Her chin lifted. "He was an accountant, for goodness sake! And my mom, she's an engineer at the car plant in—"

"Maybe she doesn't know." Maybe neither of her parents had known the truth.

Adoption, one possibility. Or maybe somewhere far back in the family tree, one of Holly's relatives had been tempted by a demon in disguise. "Make no mistake, I *know* what I saw upstairs." When he'd had her naked and open to him and he'd been seconds away from thrusting into that slick pink flesh.

Then he'd met her stare and the world had stopped.

And started again in a red haze of fury.

"You're wrong." A whisper. "*I'd* know."

He brought her hand to his lips. He'd screwed up with her, lost valuable ground, and he wasn't sure how to repair the damage he'd done.

The idea of Holly betraying him—

It had shattered his control and let the fury rage.

"No, love," now, spoken as the endearment it was, "you wouldn't."

And that was the whole damn problem.

Holly paced her office hours later, Niol's words still spinning in her head.

A demon. The guy actually thought she was a demon.

Insane.

Ridiculous.

Wasn't it?

But Niol wasn't the joking type and the fury she'd glimpsed in his eyes had been all too real.

Because he thought I'd played him.

Shit. Holly stumbled to a stop. It just wasn't possible.

Holy Christ . . . what if it were true?

From the beginning, she'd been so fascinated by the idea of demons, drawn, almost helplessly, back to Paradise Found.

Back to the demons.

Because she was one?

No. Not. Possible.

Her hand slammed onto her desk. She was grade-A human, through and through.

No matter what Niol *thought* he'd seen.

Someone rapped on her door.

Holly sucked in a cleansing breath and turned around. "Kim, do you have those tapes—"

Kim wasn't standing in her doorway. She'd expected the intern, with the security tapes from the previous morning.

But the pretty brunette wasn't staring back at her.

"What the hell are you doing here?" Holly snapped, her body jerking as if she'd been shocked.

And, yeah, she was pretty damn shocked.

Because seeing Dr. Zachariah Hall, blond hair perfectly slicked back, golden tan gleaming, blue eyes smiling at her—stunned her. He was the last person she'd expected—or wanted—to see.

The lips that had been tilted in a warm grin sagged a bit. "Holly . . . you aren't still angry, are you?"

She growled. Finding her fiancé half-naked with his grad student hadn't been one of her best moments. Or his. Jerk. "Uh, yeah, I am. And probably will be for the next, oh, twenty years." Why the hell was the guy there? He'd tried calling her a few times after the breakup. She'd ignored him. Then, blessedly, he'd gone away.

Back to his classes and the nimble grad girls who would do anything for that A.

The smile was totally gone now. "I made a mistake. A one-time mistake."

One time her ass. She snorted. "One time, twenty

times," which she believed more than the "one time" story. "You're done in my book."

He stepped toward her and closed the door behind him.

Her mouth dropped. "Uh, Zack, I'm not in the mood to talk to you—" *Ever.*

"I'm sorry I hurt you." The words sounded sincere. His eyes looked sincere.

The apology was completely different from Niol's. Very smooth and slick. Not at all awkward. Didn't sound like the words had been dragged from him.

But she didn't buy it, not for a minute.

And what about Niol's apology?

Later.

"I'm sorry I wasted four months of my life on you. Guess we're even." Okay, that sounded like something a really cold bitch would say.

So call her cold.

And she'd always been a bit proud of being a bitch.

The faint lines around his eyes hardened. He wasn't wearing his glasses today. Usually he saved those for his classes. She knew he thought they made him look scholarly, and he was all about the smart professor look.

Dr. Zachariah Hall was an associate professor in the biology department at Mellrune University in Atlanta. He spent his days lecturing to bleary-eyed students or writing really lame research papers.

And screwing students, too.

When she'd first met him, Holly had mistakenly believed the guy was a class act. Smart. Honest. Gentlemanly.

The wild spark she'd always longed for hadn't ignited between them, but she'd figured she'd be able to live quite happily without that spark.

So she'd accepted his proposal over a lobster dinner one night, then found him having a hands-on experience with his student two months later.

Extra credit?

"I was scared, Holly." Again, sounded sincere. Maybe it was. "I fell for you, hard and fast. I didn't know what was happening to me, so I—"

She rolled her eyes. "So you decided to go down on another woman? Got you." She did not have time for this drama. "Look, I don't want to hear your explanations. I just don't—" *Care anymore.*

Her breath caught.

Wow. That was true. She didn't care. She rolled her shoulders and felt as if she'd just dropped a huge weight. "That was months ago, Zack. I've moved on and I hope you have, too." Now she got to be the sincere one.

Less bitch. More—ah, what was she more of?

His perfectly chiseled jaw clenched. "You're seeing someone else?"

Was she still seeing Niol? Even after his accusation? *What if it were true?*

"I—"

Another knock at the door.

"Come in!" She would have welcomed just about anyone then, as long as she didn't have to be in the room alone with good old Zack anymore.

Kim poked her head inside, and she was smiling. "You got a delivery."

Not another one. Her stomach knotted.

The door swung open. The red roses spilled from the vase Kim carried, their lush scent tickling Holly's nose.

She blinked. "Did you see who—"

"Oh, yeah." Kim didn't even seem to notice Zack. "Susie was at the front desk, but I caught a glimpse of him before the guy left. Real sexy, black hair, sunglasses—"

Zack cleared his throat.

Kim jumped. Okay, so she *hadn't* noticed him.

Holly hurried forward and took the flowers. "Thanks,

Kim." The vase felt slightly chilled against her hands.
Niol must have brought it right over from the florist's.

Kim gave a little wave and ducked out of the room.

Holly carried the vase to her desk. There was a small
white envelope nestled in between the bloodred flowers.
Her fingers shook a bit when she reached for it.

She'd always been a sucker for red roses.

She opened the tiny envelope, pulled out the card.

"So there *is* somebody else."

A bold black scrawl on the crisp card.

*I'm a bastard, but you know that. But you don't
know what's inside of you—waiting to come out.
I do.
Let me show you, love.*

Her fingers clenched around the card.

Demon.

Niol wouldn't make a mistake like that. Everything
she knew, every whisper of gossip she'd greedily caught
all pointed to Niol being the strongest demon in the city.

He'd *know* if he was having sex with another of his
kind.

I see you now.

Her eyes closed. Denial, yeah, option one.

But what if . . . *what if*?

He'd be able to show her a whole new world. A world
she'd been desperate to see from the beginning, like a kid
with her nose shoved up against a shop window.

"Glad you've found somebody." Gritted. *Not* sincere.
"I-I won't take up any more of your time."

She looked up just as Zack stormed out.

Holly had his flowers and his note, the next step would
be hers. She could bid his ass good-bye or she could step

up to the plate and learn what secrets *she* kept, locked inside.

"I want a background investigation done on Holly Storm," he told the man before him. A short, dark-haired charmer. Charmers were always the best at ferreting out information from the unsuspecting. And Giles . . . the guy was damn good. An investigator for the *Other*, he made a fine living by bending and breaking the law whenever he could.

Giles narrowed his gray-gold eyes. "Why's that name familiar to me?"

They were in Giles's office, a freakishly clean business in the middle of downtown Atlanta.

"She's a reporter for News Flash Five." And so much more.

"You wanna know if the lady likes to play in the darkness?"

I'm here to play. "I already know that." His fingers flattened on the desktop. "I want to know about her family, her lovers. I want to know about anything *unusual* that's ever happened in Holly's entire life. And I want to know *yesterday.*"

Because a new fear had begun to haunt him after he'd dropped off Holly's flowers and then taken his time strolling around the station. No one had stopped him. Old Steve had sure given him a wide berth.

Holly was like him, Niol knew it. Even if she didn't.

The impure will die.

Giles cocked his head. "It's gonna cost you."

"What else is new?"

"What am I looking for here, man? Point me to what you want—"

"Skeletons." Demon skeletons. "Something tells me the lady has more than a few in her family tree." They just had to knock 'em loose.

* * *

Holly was running late for her appointment. Again, dammit. If she wasn't more careful, she'd start to get a bad reputation.

But before she'd left the station, she'd needed to follow up on the security tapes.

The follow-up had lead nowhere because the tapes were *gone*.

Not erased. Not unusable. Gone.

The guys at the security station had been rattled. The station owner had been alerted.

Someone was playing a game with News Flash Five.

With her.

More cameras would be installed. More guards hired. After the last bloodbath at the station, the higher-ups weren't taking any chances.

So now, she was running fifteen minutes late for an appointment that she did *not* want to miss. The elevator chimed then the doors slid open and Holly hit the hall at a run.

A few moments later, she shoved open a gleaming wooden door, perfectly polished. Holly ignored the gold lettering and hurried inside, where she caught sight of the witch behind the desk.

And Vanessa really was a witch, or, at least Holly was about 90 percent sure she was. She'd caught the woman reading spell books the last time she'd been in the office and Holly was pretty sure she'd seen the redhead levitating her pen once or twice.

"Uh, sorry I'm late." She hoped that didn't merit being turned into a frog or something. With the *Other*, you just never knew. "Is . . . Dr. Drake still available?"

Vanessa raised her brow. "This is the second time—"

She winced. "I know. Sorry."

The witch smiled. "Try not to make a habit of it, okay? She's waiting on you."

Holly exhaled. Great. Because she sure needed to talk to the Monster Doctor today. She hurried toward the doc's inner sanctum.

"At least you don't have a damn snake with you . . ."

Vanessa's mutter had her hesitating with her hand over the knob. She glanced back. "Er, right."

The door opened.

Dr. Emily Drake, known in the darker circles of Atlanta as the Monster Doctor, stood in the doorway. Her black hair was pulled back into her usual perfect bun. Her pretty features were calm, her green eyes curious behind the lenses of her glasses.

Looked like any other woman you'd meet in the city.

But Dr. Drake wasn't any other woman. She had very, very special talents.

The lady only treated paranormal patients. Word on the street held that she could immediately sense any *Other*.

And she was heavily empathic.

No hiding from this therapist. Nope, no denial would ever work with her.

The doctor glanced at her watch. "Running behind, are we?"

"Seriously, you don't want to hear about my day." Demon heritage. Ex-fiancé from hell. Possible murderer/stalker.

Emily laughed and shut the door. "Oh, come on now, Holly, you know that's what I'm here for—listening." She motioned toward the couch and walked back to her desk. A small notebook lay in the middle of the wooden surface.

Holly crossed the room. *The couch.* Just looking at it made her nervous, and this was her sixth visit to the doctor's office.

She'd originally come to see Dr. Drake because she'd been . . . desperate.

Carl had been the first to mention Emily's name. The

first to talk about just how the Monster Doctor had helped him.

She'd thought that maybe Emily could help her, too.

Holly hadn't wanted to be helpless anymore. The world was full of beasts, predators—she got that. Both human and *Other.*

She never wanted to be as weak as she'd been in that alley. Not again. There had to be some way for her to protect her mind from those attacks. Some way . . .

And if anyone would know a way, Holly had figured it would be Dr. Drake.

So their sessions had started. Half-therapy, half-mindshielding.

The weird thing—both parts were working.

Which was one of the reasons she hadn't flipped out when she saw old Zack. Without Dr. Drake's help, she would have tried to rip the guy a new one.

"I-I need to ask you some things." Holly sat on the edge of the couch, feeling awkward. The first time she'd come into the office, she'd felt the same tension, but she'd bluffed her way through the forty-five minutes.

I know about the Other. She'd said that confidently. *You don't have to pretend with me.*

Emily hadn't spoken.

I know, and I'm here because I want to learn how to protect myself.

Emily had known about what happened in that godforsaken alley. Her lover, Detective Colin Gyth, had been on the scene within moments. Holly didn't think there were many, if any, secrets between the cop and the good doctor.

The first time she'd come face-to-face with Emily, the knowledge of that dark night had been in the Monster Doctor's eyes.

Emily had agreed to take her on as a patient. She'd started teaching her how to visualize shields for her mind—and to actually make those damn things work through a focused concentration that sometimes left Holly's head aching and her heart racing.

And . . . more had developed in the sessions. Holly had found herself talking about Zack. Her parents.

Her brother.

Christ, the first time she'd talked about Peter, she'd bawled for an hour.

"You can ask me anything," Emily said as she picked up her pen. "But keep in mind I'll have my turn to ask questions, too."

She always did. Sneaky questions that seemed easy enough to answer on the surface but were really designed to rip the scabs off all the old wounds Holly had locked inside.

She pulled in a deep breath of air. "Why—why did you originally agree to see me? You knew that I was a reporter, I could have just been scamming you—trying to get a story—"

"You're not like that." Instant response.

Those empathic powers? "You sure of that?"

A nod.

"*Why* did you see me?" Holly repeated. The answer was very, very important.

"You need me." One shoulder lifted, then fell. "I don't make a habit of turning away people who need me."

Hell, yes, she'd needed the doctor's help—so she would never be helpless again. But . . . "I'm not like the other patients you treat." She'd only seen a few of them, passed them briefly in the hallway. *Not the chatting type.*

All of the others were paranormals, while she was—was—

Emily's eyes narrowed behind her glasses. "I'm not sure I'm following you, Holly."

"You treat *Other,* okay? And I'm not. I'm just—" Human.

Right?

Silence.

Then Emily put her pen down and licked her lips. "I think I'm a bit confused."

Join the club.

"Holly, despite what you may have heard, I do treat some human patients."

Freaking relief. Her hand pushed against her chest. "Right, right, of course—"

A slow shake of Dr. Drake's dark head. "But, um, you know you're not human, don't you?"

Good thing she was sitting down. Emily had the distinct feeling her knees would have done a Jell-O routine and she would have wound up on the floor. "Run that by me again?" A squeak that wasn't her normal voice.

Emily snatched up her pen and scribbled a quick note. "You didn't know . . ."

"I *still* don't know." Okay, so Niol had told her. Dr. Drake *was* telling her, but—but—

Christ.

But how the hell could she have gone through her entire life without knowing she was *Other*?

"You don't have much power, I'd probably label you as a one or two on the demon scale . . ."

Demon scale.

"But I knew from the first moment I met you, Holly, that you were *Other*."

That hard thump—it wasn't her heart. It was her world falling off its axis.

Chapter 9

Holly walked down the hallway in Mistro Tower, putting one foot doggedly in front of the other as Dr. Drake's words rang in her head.

Haven't you ever noticed that you heal faster than normal?

Okay, yeah, she had—but she'd chalked it up to being a *fast healer.* All of the bruises and most of the cuts from the hit-and-run were almost gone now, and, yeah, in hindsight, she could see that was a bit, uh, *too* fast.

Haven't you ever been aware of a thickening in the air around you? As if pressure is pushing on you?

Just when she'd been around Niol. But she'd thought that was *his* power.

Not hers.

Certain powerful instances or stressful situations may trigger the latent powers in you. An adrenaline surge—that could ratchet up the strength you have . . .

Maybe Niol brought out the inner demon in her.

Your parents—surely they knew. Didn't they say anything to you?

Not a word about being a demon. Just the *stay out of*

trouble and God, whatever you do, don't take Peter's path.

Peter. Her steps faltered. Had he been—

Her cell phone chimed. Fumbling, she yanked it out of her purse. "Storm—"

"Get down to the warehouse district." Niol's voice. Hard. Furious. "The bastard's killed again."

No. Not another slaughtered victim. "How do you know? Niol—"

"Sources, love. I've got 'em, too."

The call ended with a click.

Another dead demon.

Swallowing, she punched in the speed-dial button she'd assigned for her cameraman.

Ben met her at the scene. It would have been hard to miss the place—it was the only building in the old warehouse sector that was surrounded by cops, swirling blue lights, and yellow police tape.

Strangely, though, no other reporters were on scene. Yet, anyway.

A long whistle from her side. "What the hell did you find, Holly?" Ben asked.

Death.

She caught sight of Gyth's dark head as he stalked toward one of the cruisers. Her eyes narrowed. "Ben, start filming the scene." Straightening her shoulders, she headed for that parked car.

"Where you goin'?"

She glanced back.

The brim of his cap shielded his eyes. "Oh, no, Holly, that guy is *not* gonna talk to you. Hell, even *I* know he hates you."

"Hate is a very strong word," she muttered. Her palms

were sweating. Her back itching. Gyth looked up right then and instantly his gaze zeroed in on her.

Maybe it wasn't too strong.

"Get the scene," she repeated. "I'll get the cop." Or try.

Or maybe just get her ass escorted off the property.

But what did she have to lose?

This was *her* story. Would be, until the freak was locked away . . . or dead.

Gyth changed course and headed for her.

She kept moving slowly but determinedly toward him.

"Holly Storm." The setting sun darkened his hair even more. "Why the hell am I not surprised to see you here?"

She lifted an eyebrow. " 'Cause I'm good at my job?"

"Oh, I'll give you that." His lips twisted. "But I think maybe you've just got one fine connection to this killer."

She pounced and ignored the suspicion. "So this scene *is* related." Niol had been right. Cagey demon.

No response from Gyth.

"Come on, detective. Give me *something*. This makes kill number three." She had no proof, but he didn't know that.

"Actually, it's number one." He exhaled and shook his head. "Looks like she was the first."

What?

It took her a minute to process the fact that the guy was actually talking to her about the case. "You're saying the woman in there was the guy's first victim?" If she'd been the first, then she would have been in that place for days, her body slowly decaying . . .

Holly swallowed.

"Looks that way." He cast her a speculative glance. "You're gonna have to be the one to tell me for sure."

"I don't follow—"

He caught her arm. "I need you to see the victim."

Oh, hell, not again.

She dug in her heels. "I'm here to cover the story, not to—to—"

"He wants to know if she's one of us, Holly," Niol said, his voice like rough silk as he walked from the covering of a nearby building.

Holly didn't jump at his approach—not this time— because she'd known he was there. From the minute she'd climbed out of her car, she'd known.

Because he wouldn't have sent her to this scene alone.

Am I starting to trust the guy?

Sure looked that way.

Talk about twisted—she had to be the only person in the state who trusted Niol Lapen.

Gyth swore. "I'm guessing it's not a fucking coincidence you're both here?"

Niol caught Holly's hand. Kissed the back of her palm. "Where she goes, I go."

His tongue swiped over her flesh and her heart jumped.

"Bullshit." Gyth looked disgusted as his mouth curled into a sneer. "And I'm not buying this whole lover crap— Wait!" His gaze flew between them. "One of *us*?"

Holly decided the best course of action right then was to keep her mouth shut. She was too new at the whole being-a-demon thing.

"Shit." He rubbed the bridge of his nose.

Two guys in blue uniforms wheeled out a gurney. On top of it, a black body bag was zipped up tight.

Her mouth dried up. *A woman.* Looked like the killer wasn't being choosy about gender. Odd, that.

Did she know her, too?

"Hold it." Gyth's words were directed at the attendants pushing the gurney. Then, softer, for her ears only, he said, "Tell the jerkoff with the camera to cut or he's gonna be losing his precious equipment."

She believed him. Holly raised her hand and motioned toward Ben. "That's enough. Cut for now."

He lowered the camera with a scowl.

Gyth took her elbow and urged her toward the body bag. Since Niol still had her other hand, he followed right along, too.

"Open it," Gyth's snarled command.

The attendant's fingers jerked as he hurried to unzip the bag.

The smell hit her first. Thick, cloying, clogging up her nostrils.

"Gyth, what the hell, this isn't protocol—"

Her eyes darted to the left. Found a scowling uniformed cop she'd never seen before.

"Take it up with the captain," Gyth said, never looking away from the body.

Her gaze snaked back down.

She saw the blond hair first. Tangled, matted with blood. Then the face. Bloated. Blackened in spots.

And she caught sight of the yawning second grin that tore across the woman's throat.

Holly turned away. "I-I don't know her." Not another source. Just a poor woman who'd been slaughtered.

"I do."

She glanced at Niol.

"Name's Julia Powers. She worked in Paradise for a while last year. Stopped waitressing right around the time she hooked up with her boyfriend."

"And her boyfriend would be?" Gyth pressed.

"He *was* Carl Bronx." Niol's lips thinned. "And she was one of mine, too."

Demon.

Gyth's jaw clenched and he motioned to the attendant. The zipper was hauled back up with a hiss.

"Tell me, detective . . ." A long pause from Niol as he waited for the attendants to move past.

That woman—God, what had she endured?

The gurney's wheels squeaked as they loaded her up.

Niol cocked his head and studied the detective. "Did he take something from her, too?"

Take something? *From the body?* Holly's palm pressed against her stomach. Oh, hell. She didn't know where Niol had gotten his information, but the look on Gyth's face told her that he was dead-on.

"How the hell do you know about that?"

Sources. The answer whispered through her mind.

"I told your partner once, there is something you guys don't realize. Your police force has more demons than you can count."

She could believe that.

"Someone in my department is coming to you with information?" Gyth's eyes glittered with fury, way too bright.

"Someone in *your* department is scared shitless because he . . . or she . . . knows there's a sick fuck slicing up demons and taking bits away."

Holly didn't even want to think about what "bits" the killer was removing. "Why did it take so long to find her?" Holly asked, her voice coming out way more controlled than she expected. "You guys were spot on the scene with the other victims—"

"Because we got a tip-off with them." Gyth's voice wasn't controlled, not one bit. "Bastard called nine-one-one. Told us where to find the bodies."

He'd wanted discovery.

Holly glanced at the black bag. *But not for her.* "Something's different about her." The possibilities had her heart racing. Maybe the killer had been sloppy—she'd learned long ago from an FBI operative she'd interviewed that killers were often damn sloppy with their first kills. Too nervous, too excited, too wired.

The wild thrill led to mistakes.

Mistakes that weren't found later, when the killer struck again.

Gyth grunted. "She's a woman, the other two vics were men." He shook his head. "Wasn't expecting a woman."

But he *had* been expecting to find another demon.

He huffed out a breath. "Vagrant found her. First, the uniforms thought he was crazy or high when he ran to 'em, talking about a smiling dead woman."

Throat, slashed, from ear to ear.

Holly shoved the image away and turned to Niol. "Still think we're dealing with a human killer?"

A nod.

A grunt from Gyth. "The crime scene guys are gonna be scraping over the scene all night. Maybe they'll find something—"

"You don't think we're suspects anymore," Holly blurted, because he was sharing too much and not looking at her and Niol with that heavy stare of suspicion.

Holly drew in a deep breath, and caught the rancid scent of decay that still lingered in the air.

That woman—

Carl's girlfriend. *Julia.*

The name clicked.

She remembered a day in the park, eating a stale sandwich and watching Carl toss some bread to the birds. "*Gotta leave soon. Meeting my girlfriend for dinner.*"

They'd never meet again.

"*Are you serious about her?*" She'd asked him, smiling.

"*Don't know,*" he'd told her. "*How do you tell if it's love? Or just really good sex?*"

They'd laughed, but she'd seen something in his eyes, and for a moment, she'd been envious.

But Carl and his Julia wouldn't have a chance at love anymore. Dammit.

"Brooks thinks Niol is good for the killings . . ." Gyth spoke slowly.

"No," Niol said, "the bastard *wishes* I were good for

them. There's nothing he'd like more than to throw my ass in jail."

No response.

"But he knows I didn't do it, and so do you." A car door slammed behind them. "This . . . isn't my style."

No, flames and fury—that was more his style.

Punishing the damned, not killing the innocent.

Niol wasn't perfect, she knew that, but there were some lines Holly knew he wouldn't cross.

Well, damn . . . looked like the trust had come through even when she hadn't expected it.

Now when had that happened?

During the night of wild sex?

Or when he'd ripped her world apart and told her the truth about herself?

A truth she still didn't understand.

"What the hell is *he* doing here?" Todd Brooks demanded as he stalked forward. "Coming to gloat over another of his kills?"

Holly turned to glare at the detective, more than ready to rip him a new one—

He slammed into the ground. Just seemed to freeze, then he fell facefirst into the hard earth.

"Fuck," Gyth muttered. "Not again, Niol."

Her breath caught and she looked at Niol from the corner of her eye. An almost smile teased his lips.

Brooks pushed himself up to his knees. Shot a look that could have melted steel at Niol. "I fucking hate you, man."

Niol did laugh at that.

Brooks rose to his feet and brushed off his hands, then his knees.

Jesus—did that count as assaulting an officer?

The human detective didn't speak again until he was toe-to-toe with Niol. "You like screwing around with humans, huh?"

"Cara obviously does," Niol murmured, and it took the words a moment to register for Holly.

Cara. The succubus. The guy's lover.

Brooks's fist lifted—

And Gyth stepped in front of Niol. "He's playing with you, Todd. You know that's the shit he likes."

The rage had the cop's face flushing. "He wants to play, then I'll damn well play."

Enough of this male crap. Holly cleared her throat. All three of the guys looked at her. "Niol, stop being a jack-ass."

He blinked.

Gyth's eyes narrowed.

Brooks slowly lowered his fist. "You're *still* with him?"

"Um." And planning to stay for a while, jackass or no. "Look, Detective Brooks, Niol isn't responsible for these kills. Gyth knows it and I think you do, too." The crimes just didn't fit Niol's MO.

"Now, we've got a serious problem on our hands," she continued. "Some freak is picking off demons." Yeah, and she was one, so that made her want to shake. "He's hiding in the shadows, getting off on slicing up his kills, and probably loving like hell that you think the chief suspect *is* a demon."

Gyth and Brooks shared a hard look. *Ah, hit something there.*

"These crimes are linked, and we all know it." Julia hadn't been her source like the others, but the dots were still connected. "This bastard is after me and Niol and I—"

"What?" The detectives roared at once.

Niol crossed his arms over his powerful chest and just watched.

"He's after us." Holly knew that with one hundred percent certainty. "The freak left a message for me at the station—a photo of me and Niol with the warning that that *'The im-pure will die.'* "

"Why the hell didn't you tell us this sooner?" Gyth demanded, stepping back to glower at Niol. "Where's the note? Where's—"

"Your captain has it," Niol inserted smoothly. "It was delivered to McNeal an hour ago."

Gyth's mouth snapped closed.

Even Holly hadn't seen that one coming.

"He's after *you*?" Brooks shook his head. "What, does he have a death wish?"

"Perhaps." Niol didn't seem concerned. "If so, I'll do my best to make his wish come true."

"No wonder McNeal told me to shift my attention," Gyth muttered. "Didn't have time to explain, got the call about the body—"

And then he'd found her and Niol on the scene. "He's jonesing for another demon kill," Holly said. "The bastard sent a similar picture to Carl—and we know what happened to him." *Don't think about it. Keep your chin up. Voice calm. Don't break down. Not now.*

Niol pressed closer to her, seeming to surround her with his warmth.

How had he known?

"And where's that picture?" Brooks asked quietly. He sounded as if he didn't want to hear the answer.

"Your captain will have it . . . soon." Niol's voice was as slow and easy as a southern summer day.

A dead body. Furious cops. Could nothing shake the guy?

"I'm going live with this story," she told them all, aware that the words came tumbling out a bit too fast.

"The hell you—"

"There's no way—"

She raised her hand. "I'm going live."

Niol nodded. "Good idea."

"Hell, you *would* say that." Brooks shook his head. "The last thing we want is for the city to panic."

"People need to be warned." She was adamant on this. "They have a right to know what's happening—"

"You really think folks can handle this shit?" Gyth demanded. "Do you know what they'll do to—"

Holly exhaled. "I'm not going to broadcast any *Other* business, Detective Gyth." Her intent to tell the world about demons had died long ago. "Just let the city know that a predator is hunting so folks will be on guard—and so they'll watch things much, much more carefully." People on alert tended to notice things the unwary never would. And maybe, just maybe, they'd get lucky and catch the bastard.

"She doesn't need you, either of you," Niol all but purred, "to run her story."

No, I don't. "I got scene shots for tonight. The body bag." She didn't flinch when she said it, just sounded like a cold bitch. That was hard, but she did it. "And now I know what 'bits' you guys have been holding back from the press."

Gyth's shoulders stiffed. "You can't broadcast that—"

Holly had no intention of airing those gory details. The freak would like that too much. No, she needed to air just enough to piss him off . . . and to make him nervous enough to screw up. "Give me an interview, on air, about this killer. You can lead me, tell me what you want the public to know, and I'll keep *that* information quiet for the time being." Deals—the way of the world.

Gyth's jaw worked, but it was Brooks who answered. "Five minutes?"

Ah, now he'd promised her an interview before . . . only to never deliver. "Five minutes—*now*." She wouldn't be put off again.

The shifter's lips curved. "Looks like you're goin' live, pretty boy."

Brooks muttered something back to him, something that sounded a lot like "fuck off."

Her heart began to drum in the fast, steady rhythm she always got right before a shoot. "Then, detective, looks like we are, indeed, going live."

It was the first time Niol had been close enough to watch her work. At the scene of Carl's death, he'd arrived right after the camera lowered, and he'd been too preoccupied with blood and death and vengeance to pay much attention to the news van.

A bright light shone onto Holly. She gripped a microphone in her right hand. The cameraman had his equipment hoisted onto his shoulder and the round lens zoomed in on Holly's tense face and the face of Todd Brooks.

She let the guy lead, as she'd promised, allowing him to make some general statements about the crimes and the connections between the victims.

"At this time, the Atlanta PD strongly suspects that the person who murdered Carl Bronx and the perpetrator who killed Sam Miters is, in fact, one and the same."

Brooks didn't mention Julia Powers. Niol had heard the cop and Holly talk about the woman a few moments before the camera went live. Holly had said she wouldn't air the other woman's story, not until family members were notified.

He'd been surprised by that. Holly wasn't like most reporters, and he'd sure seen his share of them over the years. She wasn't just after a story, not worrying about who she hurt or screwed to get the scoop.

No, she . . . cared.

Dangerous, that, because the lady might not realize it, but she was opening herself up to a whole world of pain.

Still, she *had* gotten herself an exclusive.

And now she may have also gotten the full attention of a killer, one who already seemed to have a hard-on for her.

"You really think this was smart?" The cop shifter's voice was whisper-soft and came from right beside him.

Niol didn't bother glancing his way. He liked his current view. Holly looked damn sexy under the bright light, her face pale perfection, her eyes so deep and green. That mouth . . .

"You're making her a target."

He knew that, but . . . "I'm the one the bastard wants." Demons didn't come much more "impure" than he did.

"You're probably right on that."

Not the typical reassuring cop answer, but then, Gyth wasn't a typical cop.

He also wasn't a typical shifter.

The detective was a wolf shifter, a wild, dangerous breed. And one who, instead of hunting humans, had taken a job protecting them.

Talk about screwed up. Gyth was fighting his heritage tooth and claw.

"Is it easy throwing your lover to the beast at the gate?"

He did turn at that, because the cop, as much as he might have a *very* small grudging respect for the guy, was starting to piss him off. "Don't concern yourself with Holly." A warning.

But Gyth just firmed his lips, then after a moment said, "It's not as easy to protect a woman you care about, Niol."

A woman you care about.

Niol's body tightened.

"You're always touching her," Gyth spoke quietly. "Brushing her arm, holding her wrist—*always* touching her."

Because he liked the feel of her against him.

"Watch that you don't give away too much of yourself, demon. You never know who is watching."

Niol glanced away and let his eyes drift back to Holly. Interviewing the human cop. Talking about a sadistic killer.

And broadcasting for the whole city to see.

You never know who is watching.

Yes, that was why Holly had wanted to go on air.

He rubbed his chest, aware of a dull ache below his heart. What the hell was that?

No way, no damn way could it be . . . fear.

I'll keep her safe.

No matter who was watching.

Fucking bitch.

Her face filled the television screen. Lying green eyes all intent and sorrowful as she talked with the idiot cop about the murders.

And about the *brutal* killer who was loose on the streets.

Like *he* was the one doing something wrong.

No, no, all he was doing was taking out the trash. Putting down the monsters.

She *knew* that. But, oh, no, Holly Storm carried on like he'd murdered people, humans who mattered.

Not just spawns of the devil.

Demons didn't deserve to live. They were evil, down to the core.

Survival of the fittest—and as far as he was concerned, the *fittest* was the human race.

Now the bitch was asking for information, for any tips on the crimes, and he couldn't help but tense. He'd tried to be careful, but during that first kill—and Holly was at the damn scene right then, so he *knew* the cops had found the whore's body—he'd been surprised by the fury that swept through him.

That demon whore shouldn't have tried to fight me. He'd just wanted to get more information on her boyfriend. He hadn't even realized she was a demon, until she'd attacked him and her blue eyes had flashed black.

No choice then, he'd needed to put her down.

"Police are encouraging people in the city to be extra vigilant. Pay attention to your surroundings—and stay on guard."

Holly was such a fucking nuisance. Back in the early days, it had been different, but now . . .

Now she was a problem that had to be eliminated.

As soon as fucking possible.

Chapter 10

When the camera turned off, he went to her. Niol took Holly's hand and pulled her away from the cops and into the shadows.

He wanted to kiss her so bad he ached, but the cop, the shifter jerk, had made him . . . worry. "Come home with me tonight." Sure, he had guards on her, but having her in his house, in his bed, that was different.

He could protect her then.

Better than he'd protected Gillian.

She blinked. Dammit, he loved her eyes, glamour or no. Because in her eyes, he could *see* what she felt. Fear. Anger. Lust. "We tried that," she said quietly, licking her lips, "we barely made it through the door before—"

Niol's mouth crashed down on hers. He was starving for her taste. The day had been so long and he'd found himself thinking about her, wanting her, too much.

Her lips were so soft and when those lips parted, he couldn't control the groan that rose in his throat. His tongue swept inside her mouth, tangled with hers and tasted the sweetness that was . . . Holly.

He pushed her against the brick wall, caging her with his body, and she kissed him—kissed him with the same wild hunger he felt. Her hands wrapped around his neck, the tips of her nails stinging his flesh.

His cock stretched toward her, stiffening with arousal. Too many clothes were between them, too many cops around.

A piss-poor place to get her naked.

But if he could just get Holly back to his place . . .

Niol tore his mouth from hers. "We wouldn't make it past the door this time."

Her breath caught. "That a promise?"

Absolute guarantee. Her breasts teased his chest, the nipples tight, and he could remember those sweet pink nipples so vividly. But he wanted to see them again. Suck them again.

Make her moan and come again.

Make those green eyes darken to sexy black.

And he'd show her this time, she'd see the change—

"Ah, Holly?" A cough, from too close by. "Are you, um, finished here?"

Niol's hold on Holly tightened. The cameraman. Ben or Bob or something.

"We . . . need to get back to the station. I got more footage—we can edit and record a segment to air for tomorrow morning, too . . ."

Niol turned his head very, very slowly and met the guy's stare. Human. Nervous, shifting from foot to foot.

Holly's hands fell away. "I'll be—right there, okay? Just give me a minute to . . . finish up."

A quick nod and the human scurried away.

A minute? Niol raised a brow and glanced down at Holly. "Love, I can be fast when the need arises, but what I have planned was going to take a lot longer than a minute."

She almost smiled. Almost. And he liked her smile. That slow curve of her lips. The wink of her dimple. The way her nostrils flared just a bit when her mouth lifted.

But the smile never fully matured and she shook her head, saying, "I've got to put the story to bed."

Um, and he wanted to put *her* to bed. "We need to talk, Holly."

"Talk?" Her brows rose. "I didn't think talking was what you wanted."

Not first, but after the hunger was slaked. "Last night . . . I want to make sure—"

"You were right." She breathed the words, looked stunned by her admission, and shook her head. "I don't know how it's even possible, but . . . you were right."

His confusion must have shown because the woman had been damn doubtful at his place *and* just as furious as he'd been.

Her shoulders moved in a little roll. "I went to see an expert earlier. She confirmed what you'd told me."

An expert. The only supernatural expert he knew in the city was most definitely a *she.*

The Monster Doctor. Emily Drake. "You went to see Emily?" He'd planned a little visit to the Monster Doctor himself. Now, it looked like that trip wouldn't be necessary.

He'd almost been looking forward to seeing Dr. Drake again. Once, Niol had thought about using the doctor—a woman with her special talents sure would have come in handy in his world.

But fate had intervened and Emily had slipped away from the demon world.

For the time being.

"You know Dr. Drake?" Holly seemed surprised.

"Well enough," was his reply. Emily. He'd met her years ago, when she'd stumbled into his club, drawn by the power of the *Other.* He'd watched as that dick Myles tried to control her and then watched her fry the demon to ashes.

Not a woman to be messed with, unless you were looking for a serious psychic burn.

And, now, well, you didn't screw with her unless you wanted an attack from her very jealous and protective wolf shifter lover.

He *still* didn't get that connection.

"She told me . . ." Holly glanced to the left, probably to make sure her cameraman wasn't around. "She told me she knew the first minute she saw me. How is that possible? How could she know, how could you . . . but I didn't?"

Damn good question—and one that Giles had better be finding an answer for.

She looked so worried that he wanted to kiss her—right between her furrowed brows.

Hell. What was the woman doing to him?

He was so not the comforting type.

The wild-sex type, yeah. The ass-kicking type, yeah. The fear-me type, yeah—all him.

Not the hold-a-woman-and-let-her-cry type.

She was screwing with his head and right then, he couldn't afford that distraction.

Not until the demon hunter was crossed off his list.

"Come with me to my place," he said again. "We'll talk. I'll tell you all I know about—"

"Demons."

She'd always been curious about his kind. Maybe too curious. Perhaps because deep down . . . she'd suspected?

Ben's shoes crunched gravel as he headed toward them, again, and Holly shook her head. "I-I have to go to the station."

"After." A demand.

Her lips firmed.

Maybe he should have made the demand softer but soft wasn't his style, either. But he tried now, for her. "I should have . . . handled things differently last night." He just hadn't counted on getting punched between the eyes. Or grabbed so hard by the balls, but *lust could do that.* "I thought you were playing me, I didn't realize—"

"That I didn't know what the hell was going on in my own life?" Shadows flickered in her eyes. "What can I say? That *is* the story of my life. Didn't know Zack was screwing around and the bastard was right in front of me—"

Who the hell was Zack?

"Didn't know my own brother was fighting for his life, until I walked in and found him dead on the floor of his bedroom."

Well, shit.

"So really, I guess this isn't that unusual, is it? Some reporter I am." She tried to shove past him.

He wasn't going to allow that. Not at all. She couldn't run from him, from what was between them, not yet. "You're a fucking fine reporter." A compliment he'd give . . . oh, no one else in her profession. "You care and you try to help other people." Not his way, but it worked for her.

"Niol . . ."

"As for being a demon, that doesn't change who you are. You're still the same. Your eyes change—big deal. You're still *you.*"

Crunch. The damn cameraman.

"Uh, Holly?" He inched closer. "I got to go . . . it's gettin' late."

What, did the forty-year-old have a curfew? Niol bit back his snarl. "Your place," he managed. A concession, one made to make her feel as if she had some of the control. "I'll be waiting for you." Getting inside wouldn't be a problem for him. He'd take care of his business, grill Giles, then take his lover.

Hesitation from Holly, enough to make him clench his back teeth, then . . . a slow nod.

He kissed her again, ignoring the human and taking his time with her mouth.

Yes, he'd wait, but he'd be damned if he waited long. Once she closed the door of her apartment, she'd be his.

"So . . . who the hell is Zack?" Niol demanded when he stormed into Giles's office.

Sure, it was after midnight, and the guy had only been on the case for less than twelve hours but for what Niol was paying the charmer, he expected some damn good results.

And Giles knew he didn't like disappointment.

The charmer looked up from his computer, brows beetled. "I know I locked that suite door."

Niol shrugged.

"Damn demon." Giles sighed and motioned him forward. "Zack . . . let me guess, you're referring to the esteemed Doctor Zachariah Nathaniel Hall? Otherwise known as the jackass of the MU biology department?"

Niol threw his body into the nearby chair. "Could be—what do you know about the jackass?"

Giles smiled, and it really wasn't a pretty sight. Too many teeth. "I know the jackass was engaged to your little reporter."

The lights over them flickered. "Run that by me again."

The investigator looked up and his smile dimmed a bit. "Holly . . . uh, Storm, she was engaged to the ivory tower guy."

The lady hadn't mentioned an ex-fiancé.

But then again, they hadn't exactly been exchanging secrets about old lovers.

Still . . . a *fiancé*? What the hell?

"The engagement ended two months later." Giles sniffed.

"Apparently, old Zachariah had a thing for one of his young students."

Fucking idiot. He'd screwed around on her?

Humans could be so stupid.

Whatever. The bastard's loss. His gain.

The lights steadied.

Giles looked at him. "He paid her a visit today."

And she hadn't mentioned that to him, either. "Why?"

Giles sighed. "Shit, man, how about a 'That's great—you work fast, charmer.' Or some kind of freaking praise? I haven't even been on this case for a whole *day* and—"

"Why did the asshole go to see her?"

No smile now. "I don't know yet."

Niol would find out. The human had better not be sniffing around Holly again. He'd had his chance and blown it to hell from the sound of things.

Niol wasn't the sharing type. Never had been. The human had better back off—or he'd get burned.

"Something I did find out though, you might find it interesting." Giles shoved a file across the table. "Holly had an older brother."

Didn't know my own brother was fighting for his life, until I walked in and found him dead on the floor of his bedroom.

He flipped open the file. Saw the old clippings from a Mississippi paper. *Overdose kills teen. Laurel youth loses battle with addiction. Body found by sister.*

Damn.

"Looks like the kid got hooked when he was young, maybe around thirteen. By seventeen, he was dead."

And Holly was finding his body.

"He was a year older than her. Newspapers say they were close."

Niol could still hear the echo of pain in her voice. Yes, they'd been close all right.

"A couple of the kid's friends were quoted as saying he took the drugs 'to quiet his demons.' "

Very slowly, Niol glanced up from the grainy photo of a boy with Holly's mouth and with eyes that were darkened by pain and fear.

"Your kind . . ." Giles licked his thick lips, "you guys can get hooked on the drugs fast, right?"

Some demons did. Because a demon's power, it could be a very, very dark thing.

Like Sam Miters. He'd gotten hooked fast and when he was young. Niol knew the poor bastard had heard the thoughts of killers. Slow, insidious whispers that had tried to drive him mad. For Sam, only the meth had quieted those voices.

The usual drugs wouldn't always work on a demon. If a demon went into a clinic, looking for help to stop voices and nightmare visions, usually he just got pumped up with antipsychotic drugs like chlorpromazine. And that didn't do shit for a demon, except make the voices louder and the visions clearer.

So the more desperate of his ilk tried their own drug mixes—and got addicted too fast to know they were sliding straight into hell.

Drugs weren't the way to treat demons. Mind shields, like the one he knew Emily Drake had created for herself, that was the way to keep the insanity out.

But it took years to perfect a shield like that and most demons, especially the young ones who'd just hit puberty and felt the full rush of their demon power for the first time, they didn't have that precious time.

They needed a fucking system in place to help the young ones so they didn't grow up to become like Sam.

And so they didn't die like—Niol glanced down. "Peter Storm." Had he been a demon? Odds were high that he had. Maybe he'd been stronger than Holly, had a greater power, and been scared to death of that unknown darkness.

"Have you found a demon link in Holly's family tree?" Had to be one. Demons didn't just randomly pop up as some kind of mutation in the general population. Vampires did that—those weird-ass Born Masters. They were born to humans. Seemed completely normal then—wham. Woke up one day with a wild hunger for blood and enough power to generally level a city block.

Maybe *they* were the cursed ones.

As for demons, his kind had been around forever. Since the first gasp of man, and before.

And they'd be around long after that last desperate breath, too.

"I'm working on the rest of the family now . . . give me more time, Niol." Almost pleading.

He grunted and pushed out of the vinyl chair. Great view, shitty chairs. "Call me." A glance at the round face of the clock on Giles's wall showed him that it was nearing midnight. Holly should be finishing up at the station soon.

And coming to meet him.

His cock swelled at the thought.

He'd meet her at the door.

Her house was dark when Holly pulled into the driveway just before one a.m.

The porch light glowed, but the interior of the house was pitch black.

She slammed her car door shut and stared up at the house and the darkness.

Maybe she should have been a bit nervous, walking up alone toward a house cloaked in shadows. A psycho was on the loose, one she'd deliberately baited on camera.

Maybe she should have been afraid.

But she wasn't.

Because Holly knew she wasn't *really* alone. She didn't glance over her shoulder and down the street to the left; she didn't need to look over to see the gray SUV that had been tailing her. She'd spotted the vehicle earlier, right after lunch, and recognized the two men inside from Paradise Found.

Niol's guards.

She'd been pissed for five minutes. Ready to call him and bawl his ass out for putting his goons on her tail.

Then reality had set in. *A killer was on the loose.* Holly knew that hit-and-run hadn't been pure coincidence, and if two really big, really strong demons wanted to watch her ass, who was she to argue?

Once the killer was caught, she knew they'd vanish.

So, no, she wasn't afraid of the darkness or of the monsters that waited under that cover—and she *knew* he was waiting for her.

Niol was inside her house. As promised.

Holly knew it, with every fiber of her being. She'd been thinking about Niol since she'd left him. He'd slipped into her thoughts almost constantly as she'd worked.

Not like the lovers she'd had in the past. Not even close.

Her fingers tightened around her keys.

She hurried toward the door. She wanted to get to him. To hold him. To strip and feel the hot slide of his body against hers.

For the last few hours, she'd been working on that damn demon killer story and she wanted to *forget*.

Niol would help her to forget.

Holly shoved the key into the lock and pushed open the door.

Silence.

Her heart slammed into her ribs. "Niol?" She crossed the threshold, kicking the door shut behind her. A quick punch of the alarm had her safe light shining steady again. "Niol, are you here?"

He was . . . She could almost feel him.

So dark. She reached for the nearby light switch—and warm, strong fingers curled around her wrist.

"Don't turn it on." His voice seemed to be part of the darkness, a growl that sent shivers skating over her.

He pulled her to him. His clothes rubbed against her, the hard strength of his body surrounded her.

"Niol—"

His mouth took hers, and, oh, yes, it was exactly what she'd been waiting for . . .

Lips. Tongue. Tasting. Taking.

Her sex clenched as a wave of lust had her shuddering.

Her hands found his shoulders in the dark. Tightened around that broad expanse. She wasn't going to pretend, not even for a moment, that this wasn't exactly what she wanted.

He was what she wanted.

His mouth lifted, slowly. "Come with me." He took her hand and tugged her through the house. The guy seemed to be able to see perfectly in the dark. She'd thought only shifters could do that. But he didn't stumble, not once. Didn't bang into her coffee table or walk into a couch.

No, he just glided quickly through the den and pulled her into the bedroom.

Candles flickered to life the minute they crossed the threshold—the tall, thick white candles she kept on her dresser and on her cherry chest of drawers. The sweet scent of vanilla filled the air and Holly's breath caught.

She expected him to pull her toward the bed. A soft mattress, silk sheets, and naked male flesh seemed like a perfect plan to her.

But Niol steered her toward the mirrored doors of her closet. He pushed her in front of him so that she stared into green eyes that looked smoky . . . and wild.

Niol stood behind her, his arms circling her body just below her breasts. His head bent toward her, his lips feathering over her neck.

His lips closed over her flesh and her own lips parted in hunger.

Then she felt the swipe of his tongue.

Her sex creamed.

She tried to turn, to catch his mouth and kiss him so that—

"Don't move." An order whispered in her ear. "Watch . . . in the mirror."

His hands snaked down her body. He caught her skirt and shoved it to the floor. Her skin looked so pale next to his tanned hands. Darkness and light.

His hands came back up, teased her stomach with a soft caress, then his fingers began to slowly unbutton her shirt. The edge of her bra peeked through the opening and Niol's fingertips smoothed under the light material, stroking the areola of one nipple.

Her legs stiffened. *The better to keep standing.*

The candlelight danced in the mirror, swelling higher, brighter.

The front of her shirt hung open now, clearly exposing her pale blue bra and the matching panties she'd chosen so carefully earlier that day.

Knowing what would come?

His thumb slid under the front clasp, popped it free and her breasts spilled forward, right into his hands.

He teased her nipples, plucking and stroking with his slightly callused fingertips. The friction was so freaking amazing and she began to twist against him as the tide of desire rose within her.

No teasing, dammit. She wanted the man.

"Watch." A seductive demand.

The eyes she didn't remember closing sprang open.

His hands cupped her breasts. His mouth hovered over her throat.

And his heavy cock pressed into her ass.

He wanted her, just as much as she wanted him.

In this, they were even.

His right hand slid down her stomach and eased under the elastic edge of her panties.

Yes . . . Did she say it? Or just think it?

Either way, Niol heard.

He stroked through her curls and found the core of her body. He slid those broad fingers over the button that was the center of her need.

A moan burst from her lips.

One finger found her hot, wet opening. Pushed inside. Not enough.

A second finger drove into her and his thumb pressed right over her clit.

Holly shot onto her toes.

Withdraw.

Thrust.

In and out his fingers moved in a maddening rhythm that didn't give relief, only made the fierce ache inside her grow even more desperate and consuming.

Her hands fisted at her sides. The nails dug into her palms.

"Do you want me?"

Oh, what, was the guy crazy? Hell, yeah, she wanted him—she was straining and twisting and moaning like a woman gone wild against him.

"Holly, tell me."

Withdraw.

Thrust.

She had to swallow twice before she could manage, "*Yes.*"

"Brace your hands on the mirror."

Her hands slapped against the cool surface.

The hiss of a zipper.

The rustle of a wrapper—condom.

Holly kicked away the skirt. Stood in her high heels, panties, bra, and open shirt. She waited—

He tore her panties away.

Finally.

Her stance widened.

Niol positioned himself behind her, arching her hips back to him, and—

His cock brushed against the plump folds of her sex.

His fingers trailed back down over the front of her body, finding that aching, quivering spot between her legs that she *needed* him to touch just as—

His shaft thrust into her sex, a hard, no-holding-back, balls-deep thrust.

"Watch."

Her gaze jerked up to the mirror. He was behind her, face set in tight lines of lust and hunger. Driving deep, the muscles of his chest rippling. Plunging, again and again—

And stroking with those fingers. Right over her clit. So good. So. Damn. Good.

Her body coiled. Tension mounted. She gasped his name, as the pleasure spun so close—

She saw herself in the mirror. Twisting and moaning. Body flushed. Nipples tight. Straining toward the mirror.

A woman with wild red hair. Cheeks stained pink. Gleaming lips.

Thrust.

Green eyes so dark, so—

Too dark.

The pleasure crested, slamming into her as Holly's climax erupted in a fury.

And her green eyes faded to black.

Shit, shit, that was—

Her sex spasmed.

Her body quivered.

So good.

"See what I see." The words rumbled against her as he kept driving into her. Again and again. His eyes blazed at her, a perfect black to match her own.

Demon.

Woman.

Man.

His cock swelled within her, filled every inch of her core. He shuddered. Then his hands dug into her hips and he jerked her up, higher, higher—

Withdraw.

Thrust.

"Beautiful . . ." He gasped out the word and came within her.

They made it to the bed. Somehow, someway. Holly didn't remember walking there, and she didn't remember him carrying her, either.

But the mattress felt good beneath her, and Niol's arms felt even better around her.

She inhaled the vanilla. The candles were burning down so quickly now. A wave of his hand would extinguish the light—hell, a stray thought probably would—she knew that, but Holly didn't want darkness, not yet.

"Tell me about your brother."

Not what she'd expected in the aftermath of that storm, and Holly stiffened. She'd blundered earlier when she'd spilled her painful secret about Peter. As a rule, she didn't talk about her brother, ever.

Niol's fingers trailed down the length of her arm. "Easy, love. I just want to know more about him . . . to understand you."

Her head turned, just a fraction, to meet his stare. "Is understanding me so important? I thought this—" Her hand fluttered between her sheet covered body and his naked chest. *One fine chest.* "I thought this was just about the pleasure."

His expression didn't alter. Niol, still using that mask that made her teeth grind together, even now. Surrounded by the scent of candles and sex, he hadn't let his guard down.

But then, neither had she.

My eyes flashed black. Holy Christ, she could still hardly believe that. Being told by Niol and Dr. Drake—that was one thing. Seeing it—

No more denial.

"It *is* about the pleasure," Niol told her in that voice that was seductive steel. "But I want to know you."

"You're already investigating me." A hunch, that, nothing more. Because she *did* know him. She'd done her own research after the first night she'd seen him, and been unable to get the demon out of her head.

She understood the way he operated. Understood the guards he'd locked onto her and understood that her demon heritage would be a mystery for him, one that he'd solve at all costs.

Maybe that was a good thing. She wanted to know the truth, too. All her life, she'd thought she was a human. She'd been surrounded by her "normal" friends, gone to St. Mary's Church every Sunday, gone to college—led a regular life.

Until now.

Niol didn't deny the investigation, just kept drifting his fingers up and down her arm in a slow, tempting caress.

"What are you hiding?" He asked quietly.

Pain. The instant answer. A hell of a lot of pain. "Why do you want to know about Peter?"

His hand stilled. "Because I think he may have been like you. Like me."

Not Peter. "Peter died of a drug overdose, okay?" The words ripped from her. "He was a kid, in too deep, he—"

"Demons fall prey to addictions much faster than humans, love." Soft, almost gentle. "The drugs—they're a temptation some can't resist. They quiet the voices and the visions of blood and death that just won't stop."

Ice poured over her. *"What?"* She shot up in the bed, clamping the sheet tight to her chest. "What voices? What visions of death? Peter didn't have—"

"Demons have different powers." He rose, too, but didn't bother pulling up the sheet to hide his body. "Some control the elements, almost like witches. Some can slip into a human's mind—"

Yes, she knew about that.

"Some have other, less . . . desirable powers." A pause. "Like your friend Sam."

Slashed to pieces. Holly licked her lips. "Wh-what do you know about Sam's power?" Sam had told her that he was a low-level demon, pretty average, pretty—

"Sam got the shit-end of the draw. He could read the thoughts of humans—across blocks, miles—without even trying."

That was the shit-end of the draw?

"But the only thoughts he could pick up were from killers. Rapists. Twisted pervs who wanted to hurt and maim. And Sam couldn't turn the voices off, no matter how hard he tried . . . until he found the meth."

Peter's voice drifted through her mind. *"You ever have nightmares, sis?"*

"We all have nightmares." They'd been in the kitchen, getting ready for school, and running late, as usual. She'd rolled her eyes and chugged her orange juice.

He'd been fourteen. She'd been thirteen.

"No. Not a snake's gonna bite me shit—"

"Shh! Don't let mom hear you say that—"

He'd grabbed her arm, knocking over the orange juice so that it poured over the tabletop and dripped onto the floor. "I'm talking about seeing people die. Getting ripped apart. Over and over—hearing some bastard laughing and—"

"Peter Marcus Storm!" Their mother's voice shrieked at them. *"What have I told you about . . ."*

"Cursing in my house," she whispered. Oh, shit. Oh, no. Peter had never talked about his nightmares to her after that. When they'd climbed onto the school bus, he'd stared at her, eyes sad and said simply, *"You don't have them."*

She hadn't understood.

Niol touched her cheek and she flinched away from him. "You remember, don't you, Holly?"

Peter had spiraled away from her so fast.

"When puberty hits, most demons come into the power, and for those with the Dark Touch—"

"The Dark Touch?" They had a name for it? Goose bumps covered her arms. Peter's face was so clear in her mind right then. Not the face after death—the bloated, pale face with the glassy eyes.

The youthful, worried face of her brother. Her nose, her mouth. His intense eyes and strong jaw.

"Those with the Touch pick up the negative energy and it can warp their minds. Demons have a well-deserved reputation for many reasons. The fact that those with the Touch fight insanity is one of 'em."

She wanted to scream. To yell that he was wrong about her brother, about every damn thing. But Niol knew demons far better than she did. "And what? Drugs are their only hope? Getting wasted? Overdosing and dying?"

"Mind shields." His jaw worked. "We have to find a way to screen the kids and get them suited with shielding to block out the energy. It can be done, it can—"

"Doctor Drake is teaching me how to shield." Said slowly.

Surprise flickered across his face.

"I won't be helpless again," she muttered.

"You never were." Niol's eyes held hers. "You never were."

So said the guy with enough power to fry his enemies from the inside out.

Her temples ached. There was so much to take in. "Niol, you-you really think my brother was one of those with that—power?"

"Can't know for sure. Not now."

Because her brother had been buried in Meadows Cemetery for so many long years now. She visited him every Christmas, every February seventeenth—the day of his birth—and every August third—the day she'd found his body.

"If he was like that . . ." And dammit, she was believing that he *could* have been. "Then why am I different?" Normal.

"You're a hybrid demon."

She knew the term. Someone with the mixed blood of a demon and . . . something else.

"Maybe a quarter demon, could be even less—I'm not done shaking your family tree."

Ah, okay.

"Power manifests differently for hybrids. Sometimes . . ." His jaw clenched. "Fucking powerful bastards are born. And sometimes . . ."

"You get me," she finished. "I don't have any powers, Niol. I can't make fire." She glanced at the candles, all but sputtering out. "Can't read minds. Can't do—"

"You don't know what you can do. Neither do I. Time will show us." He didn't sound particularly concerned. "What I *do* know about you—you can cloak your powers like no one I've ever seen."

Well, that was something.

"I should have sensed you from the beginning, but the glamour is too strong. I can only see through it when you—"

Climax.

What had Dr. Drake said? *Certain powerful instances or stressful situations may trigger the latent powers in you.*

Her climaxes with Niol sure fell under the "powerful instances" category.

"If it turns out you're a level-one—" Niol continued.

The weakest of the demons.

"Big deal." His fingers tangled in her hair and he brought her face toward his for a hard, long kiss. "I'll still want you like fucking hell on fire."

Darkness.

The candlelight was gone. A ball of tight need stirred within her again, but she held on to her control, needing to know . . . "Niol . . . do you have the Touch?"

Her hand lay on his chest. Touching the flesh so warm it almost seemed to burn her. Feeling the heart beneath her hand—and the hard lurch it gave at her question.

"You don't want to know all that I can do." Said with absolute certainty. "If you knew, you'd be running from me as fast as you could."

She didn't move her hand. Didn't move her body. "I've already seen what you can do—"

"Sweetheart, that was just the start." Light flashed in the room, but not from the candles. Flames hovered in the air, small balls of spinning fire. "What I can do . . . it'd scare you to death."

"Nice light show." Her hands lifted to his face. Felt the faint sting of a late-night shadow lining his jaw. "I don't scare easily, Niol." She dropped the sheet. Straddled his hips. Let the aroused length of his cock slide against her sex.

Flesh to flesh.

The way it had never been for them.

"I'm on the pill," she told him bluntly. "And I'm clean."

"I can't get any diseases that humans have—"

Her brow furrowed. "But I thought demons—"

"Lower-level demons can, weaker immunity. I'm not like them." He kissed her, hard and deep. She lifted her hips, rubbing along the length of that swollen flesh.

Inside.

She stared into his eyes. So black. So many secrets. "I don't scare easily," she repeated, and arched her hips.

The tip of his cock slid into her.

Face-to-face. Sex to sex.

Niol's hand eased between their bodies. Parted her folds. Stroked the bud that quivered for him.

Then shoved his cock deeper into her.

"Good," he growled. "Because you're not getting away from me."

She pushed up on her knees. Drove down. Up. Down. The rhythm grew faster, harder.

She wanted, *needed* the pleasure. The wild rush of release to cover the memories he'd stirred.

Screw it. She wanted him.

His cock was hot inside her. Long. Thick. Strong. Filling her. Stretching. Sliding in and out in deep thrusts that had her straining against him.

Her bed was big and sturdy. No squeaks. No moans from the mattress.

Just the deep slide of his cock.

The clench of her sex.

Deep.

Again and again.

She kissed him when she came.

When he released within her, his climax a long wave of heat that caressed her flesh, he said her name.

The spinning flames died away.

* * *

Kim Went crept down the hallway at News Flash Five. She knew the rotation of the guards, knew the exact movements of the anchored security cameras.

She'd studied the layout carefully before making her move.

Her lips were dry, her palms wet—and Holly's office door waited just a few feet away.

Her gaze skated up to the camera. Locked on the lens. The camera swept the hallway, and in five, four, three—

The lens shifted, giving her a perfect opportunity.

She moved in a flash, grabbing the doorknob, shoving open the door and nearly falling inside.

The envelope. Where was it? She had to find it.

Her big break was in that envelope. Her break—and her life.

Kim knew that Holly was sitting on one major story. Everyone at the station did. Holly kept going into private meetings with old Mac, and that guy knew what was hot in the news.

But he wasn't giving *her* a chance. No, Mac wouldn't let Kim on the air, he just sent her after his coffee.

Jerk.

She'd show him. She'd get this story, before Holly, and she'd get her spot on camera.

Kim hadn't worked her butt off the last four years at Mellrune University in order to be a freaking coffee fetcher. She had student loans that were choking her, and she wasn't going to be a gofer for the rest of her life, dammit!

She fumbled with the desk. Shoved papers out of her way. *Where was the envelope?*

Kim had seen Holly's face when she opened that delivery. Oh, yeah, pay dirt.

And then, when Holly had been so freaking desperate to find out who'd left the envelope—*a dead giveaway.*

Sometimes, news smelled like blood. Rich and tantalizing.

Kim loved the smell of blood. Always had. Maybe because her stepdad had been a vampire, a vamp who'd met an unfortunate decapitation end in a car accident. She'd tried to get him to transform her, once, but he'd looked at her like she was crazy.

"Shit." Her whisper was too loud. But she couldn't find the envelope. Kim jerked open another drawer. Then another.

The envelope had to be related to those murders. *Demon* murders. She knew the truth about those men and that lady the cops had just found.

She'd heard Ben and Holly talking about her, too.

Demons. All of them.

Old Mac probably thought she didn't know jack about the real world. She knew enough that she could probably give him nightmares.

Hell, yeah, this story was her big break . . . and it really *was* her life, too.

Because she wasn't about to let the killer come after—

The office door squeaked open.

Kim froze, crouched just over the desk.

A security guard? No, the patrol should have been on the other side and—

"*Hello, bitch.*"

Terror rose, choking her.

That voice—a low, sinister whisper. Evil.

Kim knew evil.

Knew when she was staring straight at it, even when it wore such a simple disguise.

She reached for the lamp—

And evil attacked.

Chapter 11

"I want to talk with Carl's friends."

Her voice was quiet. Her hands moved lazily across his chest.

Niol opened his eyes and turned his head.

Fuck. She was so beautiful.

Not a quick screw.

An addiction.

Her nails bit lightly into his flesh. "Did you hear me, Niol? I said—"

He caught her hand. Kissed her fingertips. Tasted her with his tongue. "I heard, love."

"He mentioned two names to me, Sean and Ted. Said they were close. If he was scared of someone, if somebody was after him, they'd know."

Yes, he rather thought they would.

"I think they're demons."

They were.

"You can set up the meeting with those guys. I know you can find them and—"

Ah, no rest for the wicked. "Meeting's in . . ." He glanced

over at the gleaming clock on her nightstand. "Forty minutes."

"What?"

He rose, stealing one last glance at the lady's gorgeous breasts. "The meeting's in forty minutes." Holly was right. The two demons might know something about the bastard who'd been after Carl. After a bit of tracking, he'd found the two guys and arranged a little get-together of sorts.

They hadn't exactly been eager to accept his initial invitation.

But they'd changed their minds, eventually.

"You weren't going to tell me about this?"

Niol jerked on his jeans. Rolled his shoulders. "If you asked, I was."

He heard a growl behind him, then a small palm curled around his shoulder and attempted to swing him around. He turned because he rather liked to see her flushed with anger.

"We're *partners* on this case. You're supposed to be my demon guide here! We're supposed to be working together—"

"I just told you about the meeting." A thank-you would have been nice.

Another growl.

He couldn't help it. Niol kissed her. Damn, but her lips were sweet. He savored the kiss for a moment, enjoying the soft press of her mouth against his, then . . . "Hurry, love, don't want to keep the young demons waiting."

Her teeth snapped together.

People were crammed into Paradise Found. As usual. So closely packed that walking a few feet was a serious effort. Niol sighed, swept his hand ahead of him, and nodded when a light breeze seemed to sweep the dancers back.

Business was good, and that was just fucking dandy, but the people got on his nerves some nights.

"Nice trick," Holly murmured from behind him.

Niol gave a nod and led the way to the far side of the bar. Two guards stood in front of the door, arms crossed over their chests. Demons. He'd always found it best to give these particular . . . types of jobs to his brethren.

When they saw him, they stepped to the side, clearing the access to the door. "They're waitin' on you, boss."

"Good." He jerked his thumb to the crowd. "Make sure no one disturbs us."

"Damn straight." From the guy on the left. Max. He'd been with Niol for about five years now, ever since the demon had gotten out of jail. The charge had been manslaughter, but Niol knew the asshole he'd killed had deserved to die.

He'd raped and killed Max's mother. It had just taken Max a few years to track the asshole. Niol had gotten Max a good lawyer, and he'd ended up only doing three years.

Easy time for a demon.

"Come on." He tugged Holly's hand. Saw the quick glance exchanged by the demons.

They knew to guard Holly just as carefully as they guarded him. *All* of his staff understood that now.

He'd made a point of educating every one of them earlier that night.

The door slammed closed behind them, muting the sounds of the bar. "Watch your step." The stairs were old, rickety, and the last thing he wanted was for her to take a header in those sexy shoes he loved.

But Holly's steps were sure, and in moments, they were at the foot of the stairs where—

"Oh, damn." Holly froze beside him.

He glanced at the two waiting men.

"Niol, why the hell are they bound and gagged?"

"Huh." The men stared at him with wide eyes, their arms bound to the chairs behind them. "Guess the guards were a little . . . overzealous."

"Overzealous, my ass." She flew across the room in seconds, snatching out the gags and fumbling with the ropes. "Jesus, Niol, this is kidnapping! Do you know how much trouble you could get into for something like this—"

Not much. The demons weren't going to rat him out. They were free now, but neither of the guys, who looked like they were about twenty-one or maybe twenty-two, were moving so much as an inch.

Smart fellows.

"Uh, are you guys okay?" Holly asked.

Their eyes were still on him.

Niol crossed his arms over his chest and waited. He could be patient when necessary.

It was the smaller guy who broke. The one with pale skin, a mop of blond hair, and a chin that looked a little weak. "You gonna kill us?"

Niol sighed. Why did he always get the drama queens? So the guys had been escorted in . . . maybe a little roughly, but seriously . . . "If I wanted you dead, you'd be ash by now."

The guy on the right—a big guy, long and lanky— gave a moan.

"Not. Helpful." A growl from Holly. She waved her hand in front of their faces. "Hi, there. I'm Holly. I, um, knew Carl."

Drama queen's gaze shot to her. "The reporter." He licked his lips. "Carl—he mentioned you."

"He mentioned you, too. Sean, right?"

A nod.

"And you're . . ."

"Ted." At least the guy wasn't moaning anymore.

"Right." Niol caught the flash of Holly's smile. Pretty smile, that. One he'd seen her use on camera to reassure dozens of witnesses.

Sean's shoulders began to relax.

Maybe it was a good thing he'd brought her along.

"I don't know what happened tonight—" She began.

"I do." Okay, now little Sean was starting to get an attitude. "*He*—" His bony index finger pointed right at Niol. "Sent his goons after us. We just wanted to get out of town, but he wouldn't let us leave. He made us come—"

Time to cut through the shit. "Why were you running?" Simple question. He knew they'd been fleeing, that was one of the reasons he'd had to pounce so hard on the men.

The two looked at each other. Didn't speak.

"Why. Were. You. Running?" Scared men ran. So did guilty men. He didn't think these guys were guilty of murder. They didn't have the look for it, but he'd been wrong before.

"S-someone's d-demon hunting, man." Ted. For his size, he seemed to scare easier. "You know th-this sh-shit." His watery eyes went to Holly. *"You know."*

She inclined her head.

"F-first Carl. *Shit.*" He shuddered and squeezed his eyes shut. The ropes were on the ground at his feet—feet that were moving back and forth in a fast tap.

"We heard—we heard what the bastard did to him," Sean said quietly. He swallowed, and the thick ball of his Adam's apple bounced. "Then we heard about Julia—"

"She never hurt nobody!" A snarl from Ted. Hmmm . . . hadn't quite expected that flash of fury.

"No." Niol pitched his voice low. "I don't imagine she did." The killer would pay particularly for Julia. Sweet girl. Sad smile.

"When we heard about her, we knew we could be

next." The words from Sean came fast, nearly tumbling over one another.

"How did you hear about Julia?" Holly's head was cocked, her gaze watchful. "Her body was just discovered by the cops."

"She's been gone for *days*." Sean nodded, that weak chin lifting. "Then we caught word tonight that the cops had found a woman all cut up, just like Carl—"

"Knew it-it had to be J-Julia . . ." Ted's hands knotted.

The smaller demon sniffed. "The people who were close to Carl, don't you see? We're gettin' picked off! That bastard knows *what* we are. He was watchin' just like Carl said and—"

"What did Carl say?" Holly's voice cut through the tumble of the demon's words.

Sean's mouth hung open for a moment.

Niol took a step forward. "Answer."

"He was being watched." Much slower now and hushed. "Saw a woman tailing him a few times."

"A woman? Did he say what she looked like?" Holly's voice vibrated with tension.

"She was pretty. Young. Short blond hair. Curly." He shook his head. "Said he caught a glimpse of her a few times, and didn't think anything of her at first . . ."

"Un-until the n-note appeared," Ted said, his breathing came harder, faster.

"The note?" Holly asked. Tension had her body strung tight. Her brows furrowed. Niol had the urge to reach for her, to stroke her shoulders and ease that terrible tension.

Not the time. Not the place.

"A note . . . and a picture arrived." Sean's lips pressed together and then he gritted, "A fuckin' threat, that's what it was. Some shit about getting rid of the impure—"

"We're the im-impure!" Ted erupted, shoving to his feet.

Niol locked a hand on the guy's shoulder and shoved

him back down. "The hell we are." He was so tired of that demons-are-evil crap. "The bastard out there slicing up demons—he's the impure one." The fucked-up one. "We're just the jerks who've gotten blamed for messed-up shit for centuries." And he was tired as all hell of being persecuted.

"Carl thought the woman left the note?" Holly's voice seemed too calm after Ted's furious intensity.

"Yeah." Sean nodded. "Her—or that guy Carl caught her with."

Now they were getting someplace. "Tell me about him," Niol ordered.

Another bounce of that Adam's apple. "Carl didn't see him well, and only caught a glimpse of the guy once, right before he found that damn note."

"What did he say about the guy?" Holly shifted from one foot to the other.

"He was tall. Had on a big coat." A helpless shrug. "That he'd kick the bastard's ass if he saw him again?"

Only he hadn't gotten to give the bastard that promised ass-kicking.

"W-we don't know any-anything else." Ted's voice was calmer now, but his eyes were pure black. Niol didn't take his hand off the guy's shoulder. Not yet. That demon was wrapped way too tight and ready to explode.

"Yeah, we do." Sean's eyes flickered between gray and black. "We know if we don't get our asses out of town, we're next."

"Why?" Holly's eyes narrowed. "Did you get one of those notes, too?"

The guy went even paler. "Not yet and shit, I'm not staying around to get one! Fucking death card. Found one at Julia's. She had one, Carl had one—you get that shit, you *die.*"

Holly turned her head and met Niol's stare. He could see the worry. The fear.

He released the demon. Caught Holly's shoulders. "Nothing's going to happen to me."

"Ah . . . shit." Sean's horror-filled whimper. "The guy's marked you, man? *You?*"

Niol glared at the punk. "I'm not scared of a human with a death wish."

"*I* am."

Yes, that was why the two had been breaking their necks to get out of town.

"Running isn't going to solve this problem." He didn't think the men were targets, at least not yet. Pity, he could have used some bait.

"It'll solve *my* problem," Sean snapped. "I ain't watch-in' them bury my friend. I ain't gonna sit there and watch 'em lower his coffin into the ground—"

"Hell, n-no." Ted seconded and looked like he might vomit. "Not Carl. He was my b-best friend since we were *s-six.* I won't w-watch him—"

"Niol." Holly's voice was so quiet he almost didn't hear her. Then he glanced back into her eyes. Saw the plea.

Aw, fuck.

Help them. Her lips moved, but she didn't speak.

Fuck.

His back teeth ground together. He'd planned to cut the demons loose, let them slink away as fast as they could, and get on with the hunting.

He'd put out the word to watch for the blond woman and see if anyone else had noticed her hanging around Carl.

But his money wasn't on the woman for the kills. Maybe she'd been a lookout. Maybe she'd been some kind of lure—

The killer Niol wanted was the man. He knew it. The way Carl and Sam had been taken down—and even poor

Julia—that much strength came from a man. The wounds had been too deep. Too hard.

Yes, it was the man he wanted and the man he'd find. Only a matter of time.

Especially since it looked like he was next on the bastard's list. Looked as if *he'd* be the bait.

"Niol." Holly's whisper. A sexy sound, really. Breathy. One that stroked over his skin and made his cock twitch. He remembered the feel of silk sheets against his flesh and warm, soft woman around his body.

He really didn't have time for this shit with the demon duo. Hell, what was he? The freaking guardian of the demons? He was looking for the asshole who was slicing and dicing them but—

Her hand pressed against his shoulder.

He clenched his teeth and gritted, "I'll put guards on you. They'll get you out of town and to someplace safe." But that was *all* that he was doing for them. Big green eyes or not.

Thank you. Her lips moved quickly.

Niol grunted.

The duo blinked at him.

"Are you—are you shitting us?" Sean asked suspiciously.

If only. Niol shook his head.

"I-I thought y-you were g-gonna k-kill us . . ." Ted's stark voice.

Holly sighed. "Oh, come on, what gave you that idea?"

Sean glanced at the ropes near his feet.

"Hmm . . . let's just call that even, shall we?" She said brightly. "No need to dwell on a bit of, ah, miscommunication."

"Miscommunication, my ass." Sean's eyes were on Niol.

He could almost like the little prick. Kinda reminded

him of Carl. Niol stared back at the demon, mouth shut. There'd been no miscommunication, but he didn't worry for a minute that these guys were going to go running to the cops. As a rule, demons didn't handle things that way.

"G-give us the g-guards . . ." Ted was still shaking. Despite his size, obviously he was the weaker of the two. "And I-I'll fuckin' f-forget everything!"

"Good plan," Niol murmured.

Holly's fingers tightened around him. *"Niol . . ."*

He caught her hand and pressed a quick kiss into the center of her soft flesh.

He heard the sharp inhalation of her breath, saw the flare of her pupils. He'd played the good guy for her. Hard, that. They'd just see how much she appreciated his efforts when they were alone and—

A heavy fist banged on the door upstairs.

"Niol! Problem!" Thomas's voice.

And Thomas didn't consider many things to be in the "problem" category.

He pointed to the male demons. "Stay here."

Their nods were instant.

His gaze slanted back to Holly. "And you—"

"No way." Her chin was up. "Whatever's happening up there, well, I'm gonna be by your side."

By your side.

When was the last time a woman had said that to him? Fucking never.

He kissed her. Hard and deep. Lips taking. Tongue thrusting.

This woman was more dangerous than he'd thought.

"Niol!" Another punch with a fist, this time, it was strong enough that the door groaned as if in agony.

He broke away from Holly and took the stairs three at a time, and he wondered just what hell was waiting for him in Paradise.

* * *

The man moved too fast. Holly hopped up the stairs as quickly as she could, but she was still six steps away from the top when Niol shoved open the door.

She caught a glimpse of Thomas's tense face.

Uh, oh. The guy looked nervous and when a demon as big as he was got nervous, that couldn't be a good thing.

She scampered up the steps.

"What the hell is going on?" Niol's hands were on his hips. His gaze scanned the crowd and so did hers. Other than the two vampires who were enjoying a quick drink—Christ, but that skeeved her out—things looked, um, normal. Normal for Paradise, anyway.

"Picked up a call on the police monitor." Thomas's voice had her glancing back at him, her eyes narrowed.

The guy was sweating a bit.

He glanced at her. "There's trouble at Flash Five."

Her heart lurched in her chest. "What kind of trouble?" It was the middle of the night. The place should have been all but deserted. Security guards, sure. A skeletal staff to monitor the phone lines but—

He pointed one beefy finger at her. "According to what I just heard, you were attacked."

"What?"

"Obviously, someone's wrong about the victim." His voice was a rumble. "But the body was found in *your* office. A female body and—"

The body was found . . . "Someone was killed at the station?" That wasn't possible. They'd stepped up security and—

In her office. Her face went numb as understanding dawned.

You were attacked.

No, no, she wasn't the one who'd been hurt, but it sure was a safe bet she'd been the intended target.

Only someone else had gotten caught in the killer's sights.

Holly took off for the door at a run.

All-too-familiar blue lights swirled in front of News Flash Five. Reporters were out en masse. Cameras rolling as the competition cashed in on another Flash Five tragedy.

Dammit. This was not—

"Easy, Holly." Niol's voice in her ear. He'd caught her just outside Paradise. Driven her here. Probably a good thing, that. Her hands had been shaking a bit too much for control of the steering wheel.

I have to find out who's been attacked.

In my office.

"There's Gyth," he continued quietly. "We'll figure out—"

Gyth looked up right then and zeroed in on her. Then he started stalking toward them, fast, and the cop sure didn't look happy.

Good. She wasn't feeling particularly happy, either.

Scared. Furious.

Not happy.

Gyth pushed past the line of cops and reporters. In seconds, he stood in front of them, arms crossed over his chest, a muscle jerking along his jaw. "When I got the call about a woman's body being found in Office B-12, I fucking thought you'd bought it, Storm."

A ripple of movement beside her as Niol slid forward. "Watch the tone, asshole, and just tell us what's happening here."

The cop's brows rose. "Don't know this time? And here I thought you were always one step ahead."

"*What happened?*" The fury in her voice surprised even her.

Gyth glanced at her again, and a line appeared on his forehead as he squinted, saying, "You look different—"

"What she looks is mighty fine for an attack victim." Brooks. She hadn't even seen the guy sidling up to them. He motioned with his hand, indicating they needed to step back and, "Away from the vultures."

She was one of those "vultures" and if she hadn't already had so much crap on her mind, she would have torn into him.

Later.

They stepped away from the crowd.

"Kim Went was found by one of the station's security guards. She was on the floor of your office—"

"Dead?" Niol's emotionless voice.

A shake of Gyth's head. "Alive."

Holly finally took a deep breath. *Thank God.* "I don't understand. What was she—"

"Someone hit her, hard, looks like with the lamp on your desk. Bashed the hell out of her head, but the EMTs say she should pull through. She's concussed, but after a few days in the hospital, they expect her to recover."

"We don't think the attacker was after Ms. Went." Brooks stared straight at Holly. "When the guards found her, the lights in your office were off." One shoulder lifted. "Kim is your rough height and size, and in the darkness—"

"She looked like me." Another blood mark on her soul. Another innocent hurt because of her. She was so tired of this. "Why? Why was Kim even in my office? She should've gone home hours ago."

"Looks like she was searching your files." Gyth tilted his head to the left. "Any idea just why she'd be doing that, Storm?"

Searching your files. Holly shook her head. "No." There hadn't been anything important in her desk files.

The only case she'd focused on lately was the demon hunter and—

Holly glanced at Niol. Kim had seemed like such a nice, *normal* girl. Smart. Pretty. Eager to please.

Too eager?

Holly remembered her own interning days at the station over in Birmingham. She'd spent too many hours fetching coffee and not enough chasing stories. She'd been about to go crazy when she'd literally stumbled into an armed robbery and made the evening news.

Her big break—one that had left her shaking.

In those early days, she'd been desperate to make her mark, though. Desperate to get the camera *on* her and to broadcast her stories.

Had Kim felt that same desperation? It would sure explain a little late-night snooping.

Maybe.

Or maybe there was more to the story.

Either way, Kim hadn't deserved to get her head bashed. Holly licked her lips. "I want to talk to her."

"I'm sure you do." Gyth offered a hint of fang. "But we get first crack at her, once she wakes up." He pinned Niol with his stare. "Anything I need to know about this attack? This woman?"

What did he think Niol knew?

Her lover just shrugged.

"Fucking thought so." Gyth shook his head and turned his attention back to Holly. "Be careful, Storm. Looks to me like you're starting to run out of lives."

Yeah, tell her something she hadn't already figured out. "Do you think this attack is connected to the other killings?" From what they'd said, it sure didn't fit the MO.

"I think *you're* connected to the killings," Brooks answered. "And I don't believe it was any coincidence that a woman in *your* office had her head smashed in the same night you went live with your story on the killer."

She'd never been big into coincidences, either. Her gut was in knots. *Shouldn't have been Kim. Shouldn't have been her.*

Should have been me.

"You're gonna need protection." Gyth made the announcement with his eyes on Holly.

"She's already got it," Niol responded quietly.

"I hope so—and I hope it's damn good." Gyth rubbed the bridge of his nose. "You wanted the bastard's attention. Well, no doubt, Storm, you've got it now."

Her gaze tracked back to the line of police cars. The swirl of blue lights danced before her eyes.

Yeah, she'd gotten the bastard's attention.

Now if she could just get *him,* before he hurt anyone else.

I'm so sorry, Kim.

Chapter 12

"Mom? Listen, it's Holly . . ." Like her mom wouldn't recognize her own daughter's voice. Holly juggled her purse, kept her cell phone to her ear with a raised shoulder, and fumbled with her car door. "You might see some stuff on the news—ah, damn—I'm *okay*." Talking with her mom's machine sucked, but, generally, it was the way they communicated.

Saying she and her mom were close, yeah, that would have been a flat-out lie. Her mom had all but closed her out emotionally since Peter's death.

"Mom, I need you to call me, all right? We have to talk." *Do you know I'm a demon? That Peter was? Why the hell didn't you tell me?* "It's really important." She rounded the front of the car. "And I need you to call me, all right?" *Please call me.*

The squeal of brakes.

She spun around.

A black sports car gleamed in the morning sunshine. The door shoved open and Zack jumped out.

Zack. *Dammit.*

One rotten start to the day.

"Call me," she finished in a whisper and managed to shove the phone back into her purse. Then she shook her head, aware that her mouth was hanging open a bit.

The last thing I need right now.

"Holly," he breathed her name and ran toward her, arms up.

As if he'd hug her.

She jerked back. "What are you doing here?"

His arms fell. "I saw the news this morning. Saw what happened at the station. I was . . . worried about you." His perfect features pinched with concern.

Holly pulled in a quick breath. "I-I'm okay. I wasn't there when—" When poor Kim had gotten slammed with the lamp.

"It could have been you, Holly." His hands fisted. "I told you before, working these stories—*it's not safe.*"

They'd had this argument more than a few times. "It's my job, Zack."

"Getting fucking targeted by a killer isn't your job!"

The fury caught her off guard. The roar of his rage. "I appreciate your concern," she managed evenly, "but what I do—that's no longer really your business." Carefully, she began to walk around him. "The work I do is important to me, and I'm *good* at what I do."

He caught her wrist in a grip that was a lot stronger than she remembered. "Don't walk away from me."

"Don't tell me to—"

"I'm worried about you."

His face was inches from hers, his eyes shooting blue and deeper sparks of gold fire at her. "There's a killer on the streets. Cutting people apart, and *you're* the reporter who is dogging him. You don't want that guy as your enemy. Hell, even I realize this is too hot." His hold gentled, just a bit. "That's too much of a risk. You need to back off."

Her eyes narrowed.

"Ah, Ms. Storm?" The voice was strangely muffled, a grating whisper.

Her head turned, titlted back, and she met the stare of a tall, muscled man with a buzz cut, green eyes, and a face hard as stone.

One of her bodyguards. She'd figured they'd stop hanging back after last night. Looked like they'd already stepped up their game.

The guard looked over at Zack. "This guy bothering you?"

"What?" Zack jerked his hand away. "Who the hell are you?" He puffed out his chest and took a step forward. Probably not a good idea, because the move just made the fact that he was a good seven inches shorter and hundred pounds lighter than the Hercules in front of them all that more obvious.

The guard rolled his shoulders and smiled, as if he were really looking forward to some action.

Or kicking Zack's ass.

Holly shook her head. *Not here.* The last thing she needed was this crap on her front lawn. "I'm fine." She glanced back at Zack. "And Dr. Hall was just leaving."

"What? No, we've got to talk, Holly—"

She stepped away from him. "No. We don't." She'd been polite, sickeningly so, in her mind. "I'm not hurt. Thanks for checking on me. But, Zack, you don't need to come over here again. My life—and what I do isn't your business." When was he going to get that?

"Because you're screwing that asshole Lapen?"

More rage. Flashing from his eyes and twisting his face. And she'd once thought the guy was so controlled.

"No, although, well, yeah, I am." She didn't stop the smile that curved her lips. "But mostly because we're over, and have been since *you* screwed Michelle." Her shoes tapped against the steps. "I want you to have a good life, Zack, I really do, but stay out of mine from now on, got it?"

A growl sounded. One that was very, very unlike the staid doctor she'd thought she knew.

Talk about having a close escape.

Marriage to that guy would have been the worst mistake she'd made in years.

Because if she'd stayed with him, she wouldn't have enjoyed the pleasure of . . .

Screwing that asshole Lapen.

Bruce Piler waited until Holly climbed into her car and the pissed-off doc stomped away. Then he pulled out his cell phone and called the boss.

"Thought you'd want to know," he muttered. "The jerkoff paid her a visit today. I'm thinking maybe he needs a little . . . intervention." And wouldn't he like to pound the shit out of the asshole who'd looked at him like he was some kind of trash? He'd gotten too many looks like that before and they always pissed him the hell off. "If you want, I'll be more than happy to—"

Bruce stopped, listening to his boss's reply. "Uh, figured you'd handle it yourself." He couldn't quite hide the disappointment, but he knew the boss liked to get his hands dirty every now and then.

The doc wouldn't know what hit him.

Niol waited for the esteemed Dr. Zachariah Hall in the third-floor lab of Brighton Hall.

No classes were in session. No students were in his way. Niol glanced around the classroom, vaguely curious. Sketches of the human body lined the walls. A skeleton dangled near the front of the room. Books were scattered.

Lab coats hung from hooks on the walls. The thick scent of bleach filled the air, stinging his nose.

The door creaked open. Zachariah strolled in, his head down, a book in his hands. He skirted around the chairs and lab tables automatically, never glancing up. Niol crossed his arms and waited.

The guy eased to a halt. He looked up—

Niol smiled. "Boo." He'd left his sunglasses in the car and his eyes were demon black.

"Shit!" The dick jumped and the book, anatomy judging by the bloody red pictures, tumbled to the floor. "How did you get in here? How did—"

"Easy there, Z." His smile faded. "I came in through the door. You know, that thing that opens."

The man's face bleached of color. "She sent you, didn't she? Hell, you think I don't know who you are? Everyone knows about you—you're—"

Niol straightened. "Oh? Just what am I?"

Blue eyes jerked toward the door, then back to Niol. "Criminal." A whisper. "Probably a killer. I've heard folks talk about you, Lapen. I *know.*"

The guy didn't know jack or shit. Niol pushed away from the counter he'd been lounging against and stalked toward the guy. Old Zack flinched back with every step he took. "You think you know me, huh?" *This* was the bastard who'd thought to marry Holly?

Too fucking tame. She would have been bored out of her mind with this jerk.

Holly needed fire. Passion. Not a dumbass in an ivory tower coat who'd been stupid enough to let a woman like her slip away.

"I-I know you're trouble." The guy's jaw jerked up. "And Holly doesn't need you in her—"

Niol moved in a flash, coming to stand toe-to-toe with the bastard. He didn't like the sound of Holly's name on his lips, not at all. The hot rush of his power filled him. It would be so easy to rip into this asshole's head. To make him forget he'd ever known Holly.

So easy.

"What Holly doesn't need," Niol gritted, holding on to his control, barely, "is a shithead like you trying to come back into her life."

Hall's lips twisted. "Because she's got you now? You think because you're screwing her—"

"Yes, I am—and enjoying the hell out of it," Niol drawled deliberately.

It was the shithead's control that snapped. In a blink. He attacked, screaming, coming at Niol with fingers fisted.

Humans.

Niol stepped aside, waving his hand to stir the air around his body. Hall missed him, but caught his psychic blast and hurtled into the side of a lab table, moaning at the impact.

Shaking his head, Niol stared down at the human. "I'm here as a courtesy, but if you want an ass-kicking . . ." He knew his smile was evil, because damn but he liked that thought, "I'll be more than happy to give you one." And he'd even do it old-school style. No power. Just brutal blows until one man fell.

He wouldn't be the one to fall.

Zachariah was already down—and making no move to get up.

"Huh. Kinda thought that'd be your response." He squatted before the jerk. "You had your chance with Holly. You fucked up. Now back the hell away *because she's mine now and I don't share.*" There was a push with those final words, one that he couldn't control.

Because *she is mine.*

The human blinked, then nodded slowly.

Satisfied, for now, Niol rose. He strolled toward the door, pushed it open, and ignored the slim brunette who stood on the other side, eyes wide.

He pulled out his cell phone, a new need rising in him.

Niol wanted to see Holly again. Just to make certain that she was all right. Just to . . .

Fuck, he wanted her.

"Bruce? Yes, that's done. Where is she?"

The response was one he'd expected, but his fingers still tightened around the phone. "Lay back. I'll be there soon and I'll take over."

Because lately, he didn't feel Holly was safe enough, not unless he had her in his sight.

Zachariah rose slowly after Lapen left. He knew his hands were shaking, but couldn't seem to stop the tremble.

"Zack?" Denise's worried voice squeaked from his right.

Denise. Hell. The girl had been giving him come-and-get-me signals for the last two months. She just wasn't getting that he wasn't interested. Not anymore. "Leave," he snarled. He couldn't deal with her now. Too many girls like her—he'd screwed up his life with them.

One mistake after the other.

He'd been so busy with them, he hadn't seen what was right in front of him. What was in his hands.

Until too late.

Now everything in his life seemed to be falling apart.

Falling apart.

"But I saw him—you need—"

"Leave!"

Her plump lips tightened, but after a moment, she turned and fled. Shit, but she was becoming a problem.

He'd have to deal with her soon.

Her . . . and Niol.

Zachariah closed his eyes, but he could still see *Niol's*

eyes, those black pools of nothingness staring at him.
Boring into him.

Holly had chosen that freak over me?

No, no, that wasn't even possible. Sure, she had a right
to be angry with him, but—*that freak?*

A criminal, a thug—and she'd let him touch her.

Zachariah pressed a hand to his side. The edge of the
table had stabbed into him and he knew the ache would
stay with him for days.

Holly had sicced her new lover on him. Let the guy
come and *threaten* him.

Fine. If that was the way she wanted it—

He'd tried to save her, but it looked like Holly wasn't
interested in a savior.

No, she just wanted her asshole lover.

Fuck her. And fuck Lapen, too.

Those black eyes . . .

A shiver slid over him. He'd never seen eyes quite like
that before. So empty one moment. So cold and dark,
then burning with fury in the next second. No, he'd never
seen eyes quite like that and he hoped he never did again.

Killer.

Kim was gone. Holly stared at the empty hospital bed,
her stomach tightening. *Not good.*

Holly stepped back and eyed the uniformed cop who
was stationed right in front of room four-oh-two at Reed
Infirmary.

"Uh, where is Kim?"

He blinked, that caught-in-the-headlights, surprised-
as-hell blink folks get when they don't know what's going
on. Then he swore and dashed inside the room.

"I went to the john for two damn minutes . . ."

Shaking her head, she eased back. Two minutes. More
than enough time for Kim to get out of there.

But why would Kim run?

Two reasons: Because she was scared. Or because she was hiding something. Holly just didn't know what reason motivated Kim.

The cop was on his radio now, talking fast, and she knew the real shit was about to hit the fan. A patient under police protection wasn't supposed to be able to just walk away.

But it sure looked like Kim had done exactly that.

Holly's eyes scanned the hospital corridor as she marched down the hallway. It was just past lunchtime, and the place swarmed with activity. Patients walked up and down the hall in their gowns, pulling IVs behind them. Busy nurses bustled into the rooms. A tired blonde answered phones at the nurses' station.

Too much activity. Made for the perfect cover. Easy to leave.

Or . . . easy to take someone? Holly couldn't ignore the dry fear in the back of her throat. Because there was a chance that Kim hadn't left on her own. And Holly hoped she was wrong about that.

After punching the button for the elevator, she glanced back over her shoulder. The cop stood outside Kim's room, eyes locked on her as he talked. She knew that look of suspicion pretty well. Shaking her head, she turned away just as the soft *ding* of the elevator sounded. The doors slid open with a quiet hiss and she came face-to-face with—

Niol.

"What are you—"

His gaze raked her and he stepped forward, throwing up a strong hand to hold the elevator door open. "Where's the girl?"

"Gone." She jerked her thumb over her shoulder. "The cop never saw her leave. I don't know if she left on her own or if she was—"

Niol caught her left hand and pulled her into the elevator. The doors closed behind her, blocking out the bustle of the nurses' station. "Taken?"

A grim nod.

The elevator began its slow descent. Three floors to go. Two. Then—

The elevator lurched to a stop.

Oh, no. She wasn't a good enclosed-spaces person. Hadn't been since she was six and she'd accidentally gotten locked in her mom's armoire during a game of hide-and-seek. By the time Peter found her, she'd been a shaking mess of tears and hoarse screams.

"Niol . . ." She inched closer to him. He could use his powers to—

He kissed her. Caught her chin in his palm, tipped her head back and kissed her with a deep, drugging hunger.

Well, damn.

Her fingers rose and curled around his shoulders.

His tongue pushed into her mouth, a warm, wet slide that had her nipples hardening. What the man could do with that mouth.

What I want him to do.

His head rose, slowly, and his eyes burned with heat. "I needed to taste you." Almost guttural.

Not words that a woman heard every day. Talk about making her feel sexy.

And making her forget the fear that had kept her up the few hours before dawn.

Holly licked her lips, tasted him, and managed, "Can you get the elevator moving again?"

A slight narrowing of those black eyes and the elevator kicked to life once more. "Sorry, love, I'm not good at waiting for what I want."

So he'd just stopped an elevator for her. She took a second, then managed to uncurl her fingers from those glorious shoulders of his. "I'm not so good . . . with tight spaces."

A smile that could only be termed wicked lifted his lips. "I am."

Oh, *damn*.

"Relax, Holly. You don't have to fear anything when you're with me."

Tempting words, but she couldn't let go of her control with him. Not yet. Her shoulders straightened. "I wasn't afraid." When he'd kissed her, she'd gotten too turned on, too fast, for fear.

A *ding*, then the doors slid open, revealing the bright walls of the hospital lobby. She hurried out of the elevator and into the area that was a good ten times busier than the fourth floor. *So easy to disappear.*

Niol followed right on her heels. A dark shadow following her and clearing her path.

"We've got to find Kim. Get her to talk to us about the attack."

Niol paused in front of the sliding glass entrance/exit doors. "Innocent people don't run." He slid his sunglasses onto his nose.

"They do if they're scared," she shot back and tried not to notice just how *good* the man looked. Pitch-black hair shoved back, chiseled jaw. Shoulders so wide they stretched the fabric of his shirt.

Down, girl.

Now wasn't the time for a sex overload.

"We need to find her," she continued doggedly. "She might've seen her attacker. She might know—"

"She ran from the cops." Niol shook his head. "That means she has something to hide." He stepped forward and the doors swished open.

I know.

"This Kim—maybe we're looking at her situation all wrong."

"What—what do you mean?"

"She might not just be an accidental victim in this mess." He glanced over his shoulder at her as she marched after him. "Maybe she *was* the target."

Holly hadn't thought so. At least, not until she'd seen that rumpled and very empty hospital bed. Because at that moment, she'd had the same suspicion. If the woman had stumbled onto a crime, wouldn't she *want* a cop's protection? "What would make her run?"

"I think she's going to have to tell us."

The sunlight was too bright. Too harsh. Holly squinted against the light, lifting her hands. "The cops will head straight for her place. If she's there, they'll find her and take her in for questioning."

"She won't go home." He stopped, hands lightly curled near his sides.

"Out of town?" On the first bus? In the first car she could find? Because she was scared? Or hiding something?

Maybe both?

"Come back to Paradise." His face was blank and those dark lenses only threw her reflection back at her. "I'll use my contacts and see what I can find out about her."

Demon contacts. It was why she'd sought him out in the beginning. Those contacts—Holly knew she'd never have as much pull in the *Other* world as he did. But . . . "Niol, do you think Kim's a demon?" Her voice was hushed now, because there were ambulance attendants close by and a bleeding teen who was being ushered inside by his frantic-looking mother.

His shoulders rolled. "Never met her. Hard to say."

Never met her. "It's true, then? Demons can recognize others on sight?"

He caught her hand and Holly really tried to ignore the hard skitter of her pulse. "Didn't recognize you."

As far as she knew, no one had. *Mom, call me, dammit.*

"Carl said he could see through the glamour other demons used."

An inclination of his head that could have been a nod. "Works like that for most." A pause. "Not for you." There was something in his voice that gave her pause. A curiosity. Puzzlement.

What am I to him? The stark thought had her freezing. In the beginning, the sexual attraction between them had been undeniable. But now . . .

Now, what was happening? What did Niol want from her?

"You're different. Your power doesn't reveal you to others. It works to conceal you. Perfect camouflage." Okay, now the guy was sounding—what, impressed? "Low-level power, but still one that would let you slip by the strongest of our kind."

Her nails dug into her palms. She was still not quite jumping on the I'm-a-demon bandwagon, but the low-level reference grated. Like she could help her power scale. "We're not all level-ten badasses."

Silence.

The light stroke of the wind against her cheek.

"You're right, and I'm very glad for that fact. Trust me on this, you don't ever want to know what it's like to have level-ten power."

The stench of ashes filled her nose. Not just ashes. Flesh. "No, no, I don't." That much power would push a person to the edge.

And the line between good and evil was, she knew, all too thin already for most.

Having the kind of power that would let you kill and control others at will—too darkly tempting and terrifying.

"How do you do it?" The words came out, tumbling from the reporter's curiosity and the woman's helpless fascination. And from her concern.

Living every day with his powers—that was a dangerous weight that she knew not many could handle.

A weight that would make some break and slide head-
long into the waiting darkness.

His mouth tightened. "You don't want to fucking
know."

"Yeah, yeah, I do."

The hands that had rested so easily at his sides fisted.
"My mother ran out on me when she learned just how
strong I was. Her latest dumb-ass boyfriend made the
mistake of trying to hit her when I was in the room." A
muscle flexed along his jaw. "I looked at the bastard, just
looked, and threw him through the window of our house.
We were on the second floor."

Oh, God.

"I'd never done anything like that before, didn't know I
could. Demon power kicks in with puberty, and it kicks in
hard. Don't know what the hell you'll get until then. My
mother stared at me like I was a fucking monster, *and she
was a demon, too.*"

Holly didn't speak. For the first time in her life, she
wasn't sure what to say.

"The bastard was okay. Lucky for me, he'd landed on
the neighbor's bushes. Broken arm. Bruised ribs. Scared
to death. He ran, never looked back." A rough sigh. Almost, broken. "Then she did, too. Dropped me off at my
grandmother's and never fucking looked back." He took a
step closer to her. "Because *she* couldn't handle me. She
saw into my soul that day. She saw what I could do, and I
terrified her." His voice shook with fury.

And pain. Pain that cut deep.

When had she ever thought the guy was cold? Emotionless? He burned with feeling. So much feeling.

She wanted to touch him. To soothe him. Stupid, but—
hell. Her hand lifted and brushed against his cheek.

"If you knew all I'd done, you wouldn't touch me." A

growl of rage but one that held a ring of truth. A tone that told her Niol believed exactly what he was saying. "Wouldn't let me touch you."

She swallowed. Where they were, who was around them didn't matter anymore. This, *this* mattered. She was seeing the man now, hearing him. "I know some of the things—"

A laugh, bitter and cold. "If you knew everything, you wouldn't be able to sleep at night."

Maybe she should turn away. Maybe she should run from him as fast as she could.

The sun seemed to burn her skin. The wind tousled her hair. No sweet touch anymore. A painful brush of air.

Maybe she should run.

And then maybe, *maybe* she should stay. Because when she looked at Niol, she didn't see evil.

She saw only him. "You've killed." Holly knew that. "More than—than once." She only had proof of the one killing, but her gut told her there were more deaths.

"Yes." A hiss like a snake from the mouth of a man.

So much power. What would it do? To know that you could kill with a thought. Control with a whisper.

She'd gone to church every Sunday when she'd been a kid. Sat in the pews and listened to the priest talk about temptation and walking the devil's road.

"It's so easy to walk that road." She could still hear his voice, the tang of a southern accent rolling the vowels and softening the consonants. *"The darkness is strong and strength—it is temptin' . . ."*

How tempting?

"You don't want to know." His voice, gravel rough.

Her lips parted. He hadn't—

"You don't want to know the things I've seen, the things I've done," he said. "Not really. Deep down, you want to pretend that I'm not bad. That I'm good." A grim shake of his head. "Love, I'll never be good."

But he wasn't evil, either. Her instincts screamed this to her. Niol, though, he was trying to make her afraid.

Of him.

Now why the hell would he be doing that?

"I never said you were a white knight, Niol." She would have been blind to have made that mistake. "I know what you are. I knew exactly what, *who,* I was taking into my bed." His past, no, she didn't know all of his secrets, but one day, she would.

"You didn't—"

"I wanted you." Her chin rose. "Still do. Sins of your past and all."

His nostrils flared and he turned his head to the left, then the right, searching the parking lot. "Too many humans here."

Yeah, this was the last place they should be talking about secrets.

"Come with me to Paradise," he said again and the words were low, whispered.

And Holly really, *really* felt like a tempted Eve right then.

Strength—it is temptin' . . .

Screw it. She'd always loved taking a bite of forbidden fruit. Her head moved in quick agreement.

Finally. Kim Went exhaled and unclenched her fists. Holly and her demon lover were *finally* heading toward their cars. Talk about having a lovers' quarrel at the *worst* place and time.

She hunched her shoulders, feeling the harsh rub of the scrubs she'd snatched chafe against her skin. But her only choice of clothing had been the garish green scrubs or her paper-thin hospital gown, complete with ass-exposing window. So she'd chosen the scrubs. She'd grabbed them, then hightailed it out of the hospital while the oversexed cop had stopped to flirt with the nurses.

Her gaze shot across the lot. A busy intersection waited on the other side of the street. A few taxis idled near the far corner. She could get over there, jump in one and figure out how to pay the cabbie later.

Priority one—get the hell out of this town.

Her head pounded like a bitch, but Kim knew she'd been lucky. That crazy-ass woman who'd attacked her had meant to kill, not just bruise.

Talk about one lucky break.

But if she didn't get out of there, *right then,* she might not be so lucky again.

The nutjob's voice screeched in her mind. *"I'll fucking kill you, demon! Fucking kill you!"*

How the woman knew Kim's secrets, damn, she didn't know. She'd always been so careful about using her glamour. Her powers were practically nonexistent, so she'd been blending in with humans, knowing they fit her more than demons, since she'd been thirteen.

But that screaming bitch had known.

How?

Many of the other demons she met didn't even know what she was. Something she'd learned early on—the weaker demons were sometimes able to slip right past the radar of those on the more powerful end of the spectrum. Maybe that was just old Mother Nature's way of balancing the system. *You couldn't hurt what you couldn't see.*

There were days when she thought her ability to blend in *was* her power.

And she'd be using that talent real soon. As soon as she got out of this city, she'd blend in and disappear.

I'll be safe. Soon.

The minute Holly's taillights left the lot, Kim ran, fast and hard, for the cabs.

Talking to Holly wasn't an option. The chick would be pissed because Kim had broken into her office. Not like she'd go out of her way to help her, now.

And Niol—that demon wasn't exactly known to be the helping sort.

Two cabs pulled away from the curb.

No.

One left. So close. Shiny yellow coat of paint. So damn close.

Kim reached out—

And saw the whirl of a long, black skirt from the corner of her eye.

She jerked her head to the left and met the bright stare of a smiling woman. "Oh, sorry!" The woman murmured, smile dimming. "Was this your cab?"

Kim's throat dried up. She stared at those too-sweet features. Into the eyes that seemed to sparkle with good will.

No. Dammit, *no.*

She *knew* that face. The lighting last night had been dim, just a bit of a glow from the parking area trickling through the blinds, but no way would she ever forget that face.

"T-take it." Kim stumbled back. The pavement bit into her bare feet. *Hadn't been able to find shoes to steal.*

The woman glanced down at her toes, a frown pulling her brows low. "Are you all right?"

Get away.

"Hey!" The call came from the cabbie as he stuck his head out of the driver's side window. "You ladies want a ride?"

Kim's gaze shot to him. *Help.* Her lips parted.

The woman stepped closer to her and raised her hand as if she were going to hug Kim—

The hard prick of a needle shot into her arm.

"My friend's not feeling so well," the woman said, turning her head toward the man. "I think we're going to sit out here for a bit. Thanks, though."

The bright sunlight seemed to weaken. Kim shook her head and tried to speak. *Help.* Her tongue was huge in her mouth, swollen and twisted. She couldn't talk. Could only stare—no, try to stare. *Too dark.*

The drumming of her heart filled her ears.

No.

"If she's sick, I can help, I can—"

Help.

She barely heard his words over the slamming drumbeat.

"We've got a ride coming, don't worry about us." Sharper, now. "You can leave. He's—he's right there."

No, don't leave.

Please don't leave me.

Maybe Holly was still around. Surely she wouldn't let this crazy bitch take her.

Kim's knees buckled.

Or Niol. She'd take him over this—

The woman's arms caught her, held her tight. "It's okay, I've got you."

I've got you.

Tears slid from Kim's eyes.

The cab rolled away. She heard the squeak of the tires.

No, no, she wasn't going to be lucky again.

Darkness.

Chapter 13

"We've got a problem," Colin announced as he stormed into McNeal's office. "Our vic—uh, captain?"

Danny McNeal was standing close, *too* close, to Smith. And his hands were on her shoulders. And—

Sonofabitch. Had those two been making out? In the station?

Smith straightened her shoulders and pulled away from McNeal. "Right. That should be all you need to know about the Jamison case."

The who?

McNeal nodded, the light gleaming on his completely bald head. "We'll finish the briefing later."

Aw, shit.

Did they think he was buying this crap?

Smith marched past him, held his gaze, and then gave him a quick wink.

His own eyes widened. Smith? Winking at him? For a very tense while there, the woman had all but ran whenever she saw him.

Maybe her visits with Emily were paying off.

Maybe she wasn't so afraid of monsters anymore. Not that he blamed her, after the hell she'd lived through.

"Detective."

Colin realized he was staring after Smith and that McNeal sounded pissed.

What else was new?

"Shut the door and tell me what the hell is goin' on."

Colin kicked the door closed with his heel. "Kim Went disappeared from her hospital room about twenty minutes ago."

"Fuck." McNeal dropped into his chair. "Willingly or—"

"Don't know." For her sake, he sure hoped the escape had been her idea.

The captain's dark brows rose. "The press know?"

"Holly Storm was there when the cop on duty . . . ah . . . discovered Kim's absence."

"Of course she was." A hard sigh. "Storm's every-damn-where these days. If there's a murder, her pretty face is right on the scene and she's shoving a microphone at my cops."

Yes, that was the general status quo for her.

"Get a team out. Start canvassing the area and get your ass over to Went's house."

A nod. Colin turned to go—

"Gyth, do me a favor." McNeal's voice. Quieter than he'd ever heard before.

Colin glanced back at him.

"Forget what you *think* you saw in this office, got me? Smith's a lady, and I won't have her being gossiped about by the cops in my division."

The bastard cared about her. Colin wouldn't have been more surprised if McNeal had shifted in front of him right then. "Ah, right captain."

"I mean it, Gyth. Not one fuckin' word. Or you—and your pretty-boy partner—will find your asses sitting desk duty for the next month."

Colin rolled his shoulders. He really wasn't the threat-taking type. "Smith's not the kind of woman you can play around with." No, Smith wasn't about *play*. He knew because the lady reminded him a lot of his Doc. Same quick intelligence, same core of steel that had let both women survive nightmares.

"I'm not playin'." Dead quiet. *Deadly* quiet. "Forget what you saw."

"Don't worry, captain. I've never been much for station gossip." Not exactly big into fraternizing with the others. Brooks was close to him, but that was all. He couldn't risk the other cops finding out his secret.

He reached for the doorknob.

"We both know Went won't be at her house."

Damn right, but checking was protocol.

"When you're done, head over to Paradise. She's one of Niol's. He might have a lead on where you can find her."

One of Niol's? Now just how did the captain *know* that?

Colin wrenched the door open.

A low chuckle sounded behind him. "Storm's not the only one with sources in this town."

Niol met with three demons at Paradise. A woman with brown hair and gorgeous blond highlights, a man with tattoos over most of his body, and another guy in a perfectly pressed three-piece suit. Holly listened to Niol give them orders about Kim and she hoped they'd find the woman.

Alive.

When the demons cleared out, after sparing her more than a few curious glances, the silence in Paradise seemed deafening.

Alone with Niol.

If you knew the things I'd done, you wouldn't let me touch you.

Holly figured they should probably talk. Try to clear the air more between them. There were too many secrets, on both sides. But as she stood there, her hands at her sides, her eyes on him, talking, well, that really wasn't her priority.

"They'll check back within the hour and let me know what they find." He walked behind the bar. Poured a shot of whiskey.

He downed the liquid in one gulp. "Patience has an in with most of the demons in Atlanta. They all owe her or they want to fuck her. So if any of them know anything about your missing girl, they'll tell her."

They all owe her or they want to fuck her.

"Do you?" She asked quietly as her heels clicked across the floor. Being in Paradise now, it seemed surreal. No vampires. No witches.

Just them.

"Do I what?" His fingers were clenched tight around the glass.

"Want to fuck her?" That bitter taste in the back of her mouth was jealousy. Patience James was a looker. Could have passed for a succubus. Tall. Ballerina thin. Model pretty.

And a demon. A strong one, just like Niol.

"I already did."

Her eyes narrowed. The glass in his hand shattered.

Niol blinked and looked down. "Damn, love, didn't know you had that in you."

Neither did she. Hell, *had* she really done that?

And *how* had she done it?

He shook his hand and shards of glass littered the bar top. "Guess this is the part where I say she meant nothing to me or some shit like that, huh?"

"Did she?"

A shrug. "I like Patience, always have. The woman's cutthroat, but loyal."

Not exactly a description of a one-night stand. "Then why aren't you with her now?" *Why are you with me?*

He pressed his hands into the marble top, ignoring the broken glass. "Why aren't you with that prick PhD?"

"Because the *prick* screwed around on me with some blonde looking for an easy A." Her own hands fisted on her hips. "And while I'm not *cutthroat,* I *am* real big into loyalty."

A grunt. "So you don't want the asshole back?"

"No. *No.* I want—" Her lips pressed together. Maybe she'd better bite back that answer for the time being.

"What? What do you want?" He jumped over the counter. Jumped over it in one wild leap.

Okay. That was impressive.

Niol grabbed her arms and jerked her close. "What do you want?"

Too close. She could feel his breath brush over her face. Feel the hard edge of his flesh against her. The straining ridge of his arousal jutting against her hip.

And his eyes . . . she could see herself in those eyes. A desperate reflection.

But she wasn't the only desperate one. She could see that in his eyes, too.

"Who do you want?"

"You." Asshole. Demon. Niol.

The devil with the heart he fought to keep hidden. But she was learning the truth about him. One slow moment at a time.

"And I fucking want you." He kissed her. With lips and tongue. With hands stroking and taking. With body pressing and yearning.

The same way she kissed him.

"Not Patience." The words were growled against her mouth. "She isn't you."

Holly raised her lashes. She caught his jaw. "She better not be in your bed again, either, demon. I'm not into sharing." Zack could tell him that. The jerk had actually looked afraid when she'd torn into him that morning so long ago. He'd stumbled away from her, eyes wide, sputtering an apology.

"Good. Because if you look at another man, if you *touch* him, you'll find out just how dangerous I can be."

"Idiot." The word tumbled out. "Who would compare to you?"

He smiled at her. Smiled and nearly broke her heart because that curve of his lips—it was real.

I'm falling for him.

He caught her waist in his hands. Lifted her. Spun and set her on the edge of the bar.

The smile turned reckless. Wild.

Her Niol.

Not falling. She'd already fallen. Headfirst. For a man who she knew wasn't looking for happily ever after. Niol would run screaming from a picket fence.

Holly swallowed. *Now. Focus on now.*

His fingers pushed under the edge of her skirt and the *now,* oh, yeah, it picked up a whole lot of importance.

"I want you. Right here. In my Paradise."

A shiver had her tensing. Here? They were alone—she sure hoped they were, anyway. But a bar? Okay, she'd had her share of sexual encounters. Even made love on a beach once, but a bar . . .

"Trust me." He leaned forward. Kissed her neck. Right under her left ear, in the spot that made her close her eyes and moan.

Yes.

"There's no one here to see you come . . . but me."

Trust.

He licked her neck. Niol eased his fingers up a bit higher, skimming the sensitive tops of her thighs. The bar's edge cut into the back of her legs, but she didn't care. Holly was too focused on Niol.

And his mouth and tongue.

Such a skilled mouth.

The edge of his teeth scored her flesh.

"Are you wet for me, love?"

Her panties were getting soaked.

"Because I'm hard for you. So hard and ready to feel the warm, creamy clasp of your sex all around me."

Her hand slid between them. Found the long length of his cock through his jeans. Oh, yeah, he was ready.

And she was *more* than ready to have him inside.

His fingers brushed the crotch of her panties. A rumble sounded in his throat. "Just the way I like."

He stroked his index finger along the crevice of her sex. A long, slow swipe that pushed the cotton against her flesh and made her want—

So much more.

Not nice and slow. Hell, no. Fast and wild.

In the bar.

This time, the thought sent a shudder through her. Not fear.

"You're so wet."

That finger was under her panties. Pushing between her folds and into her core.

And he was so—so *damn*. She fumbled with the snap of his jeans, hunching her shoulders so that she could reach him better. Holly managed to jerk down his zipper and she heard his hard hiss of breath.

Then the length of his cock spilled into her hands. Long and hard. Warm. Strong.

His touch on her sex, in her, wasn't enough.

Her breasts ached. The nipples pebbled against her blouse.

The bar top felt cold against her, while he was burning hot. "Niol . . ."

He yanked the panties away.

Finally.

But this wasn't going to work. She was a bit too high and—

Niol grabbed her and twisted, sitting her on top of the nearby bar stool and coming flush between her thighs.

This'll work.

He guided his cock into her sex, one hard inch at a time.

No condom.

Flesh on flesh.

So good.

His teeth clenched and sweat beaded his brow. Hell. The man was trying to be easy with her.

When had she ever asked for easy?

Her legs wrapped around him, squeezed tight. If he wasn't gonna take, then she sure would.

Her hips slammed forward and that thick wonderful flesh filled her, so deep and full and so—

Niol growled. Those black eyes shot with fire and he withdrew. Drove deep.

Not easy anymore.

She smiled and wondered if her own eyes reflected the same dark flames.

"Fucking beautiful . . ."

Then she just held on for the ride.

And what a ride it was.

The scent of passion filled the air. The stool chafed her thighs but she didn't care. His fingers dug into her hips. Big deal.

His cock—oh, but he was so far inside her—

She rose toward him, balancing with her hands on his shoulders and the new position sent the length of his arousal sliding right over her straining clit with every fast thrust.

Holly realized she was calling his name and that she

was all but tearing the flesh from his shoulders as her nails dug through the soft fabric of his shirt.

He was nearly fully dressed.

She was naked from the waist down.

Being bad could feel so good.

"Come for me." A whisper of temptation right before his mouth took hers and his tongue thrust past her lips. Thrust just as his cock thrust into her sex.

Holly clamped her inner muscles around him. *Come for me.* The silent order was hers, to him.

Niol's erection swelled within her and she kissed him with a frantic hunger. Loving his taste. The slam and drive of his body.

Loving—

She came with a firestorm of release, a passion that rocketed up her body and shot through every cell—and he was with her. The jet of his semen filled her and he trembled against her as he pumped into her body.

Pleasure. So much pleasure. Hers, his. Didn't matter. It was *so* good.

Sex with a demon. The. Best. Ever.

She didn't want the pleasure to end. No. Not now. Not ever.

His lips rose. His breath heaved out. Just like hers.

No barriers between them. As she stared up at him, Holly could *see* him. Not the mask. Not the dark image he portrayed. Him.

Niol.

I see you now.

She was in so much trouble.

Because he was already pulling back. The mask sliding into place. The fire in his eyes faded as he withdrew his flesh from her body.

Holly bit back her cry of protest and tensed at the slow glide of his cock retreating from her sex.

Then he stepped back and she pushed her legs closed.

She had to push them with her hands because her thighs felt like jelly.

Her sex throbbed with remembered pleasure.

He jerked up his jeans. Zipped and fastened them with a blur of movement. *Too quick. Don't end it so fast.* She wanted more.

Niol stared down at her and she waited, waited for something, *something.* She just wasn't sure *what*—

"I thought I loved a woman once."

What? Okay, that was sure as all fire damn *not* what she'd been waiting for.

The man had the most piss-poor timing in the world. Holly shot off the stool and her legs nearly gave way. Niol caught her, steadying her with a fierce grip. "Look at me."

If she did, she might slug him. The guy needed some serious post-sex manners knocked into him. *I loved a woman once.*

Way to shatter her ego. "I-I don't think now is the time for this-this conversation—" Oh, that sounded dignified. Nothing like the scream building inside her.

"She died." His hand fell away from her.

The fire of their sensual encounter faded in an instant and goose bumps rose on her flesh.

"Didn't just die," he muttered. "She was murdered."

Her breath caught. There was pain there, a *lot* of pain, enough to wrench her heart. Was this woman the succubus she'd heard others whisper about?

I loved a woman once.

"I did things when she became lost to me." His lips thinned and Niol shook his head. "Until then, there was a line that I tried not to cross because I knew, *I knew* just how strong I was. And I knew my mother was right about the monster she saw in me."

"Niol . . ." *If you knew the things I'd done, you wouldn't let me touch you.* But she could still feel his imprint on every inch of her flesh.

"But when Nina passed, I lost control and I killed." Flat. Cold. "It was so easy for me." His hand fell away from her.

Yes, she could imagine that it had been. Holly swallowed. "You wanted revenge against her killer?"

"I got my revenge." Same flat voice.

That voice scared her. So she lifted her chin and put her hand on his chest. Right over the heart that thundered in a mad rhythm that belied his sinister cool.

Niol jerked at her touch. "Don't, Holly."

"Don't what? Don't touch you? I want to touch you. I'm not going to back off." *Because there was more to him than darkness and death.*

Once upon a time, she'd brought home every stray in the neighborhood and set up "Holly's Home" for animals. Peter had shaken his head at her and told her she couldn't save the world.

Her mom had only let her keep one cat. She'd cried for days when she'd lost the others.

And learned that she couldn't save the world.

No, no, she *hadn't* learned that. Because she went on the news every night, a secret part of her hoping to make a difference.

Just as she hoped to make a difference with Niol.

Not saving the world but maybe saving *him*.

"You don't know what you're doing." Now his hands grasped her upper arms and he lifted her onto her toes, staring down at her with an almost desperate rage. "Don't make me—" He stopped, and a muscle flexed along the rock-hard length of his jaw. "Don't make me care about you, Holly. Because if I did and if anything ever happened to you—"

She could see the promise of hell in his eyes.

"Whatever you do, *don't* make me love you." His eyes bored into hers. "I don't love well, but I kill perfectly."

Not the heartfelt confession every girl dreamed of hearing.

A threat she'd never hoped to get.

Her mouth had gone so dry her throat ached. She swallowed over the lump of dust and said, "Niol—"

His head jerked to the right. Toward the long line of windows on the far side of the building. Windows always covered by thick black curtains. "What the—"

Glass shattered as circles of fire—no, *bottles* with burning rags in them—shot through the curtains.

The bottles crashed into the floor, into the tables, into the bar, and flames exploded in a burst of white-hot heat all around them.

Holly opened her mouth to scream.

Niol roared and lifted his hands, and the flames died in an instant, with only the faint wisps of smoke drifting in the bar.

Her scream choked out in a gasp.

Niol ran for the door.

She grabbed her shoes. *When had I lost them?* She spared a brief glance for the scorched tables and bar, then she thundered after him.

He nearly ripped the front door from its hinges. *Fast and strong.* She knew that, but she'd never seen him quite like this.

The slam of car doors.

The screech of tires.

Holly's gaze flew to the right. A black van shot down the street in a fog of exhaust and the stench of burnt rubber. *Getting away.* The bastards who had just tried to *torch* them were fleeing.

And they'd get away. They were too fast.

The tag. She could get the tag number and—

Another roar from Niol. One that seemed to shake the street itself. He lifted his hands up high and then slammed them down at his sides.

She watched, stunned, horrified, as the van flipped into

the air, rolled, once, twice, then hit the black pavement and rolled again, finally stopping when it crashed into a wooden light post.

Wow.

"Niol . . ." She tried to grab his arm, but he was already storming down the road, heading for the broken van that swayed so slowly now, back and forth. Smoke or steam, Holly couldn't tell which, rose from its exposed belly, spewing into the air.

The driver's-side door flew off and crashed ten feet away.

That's one pissed-off demon.

Not that she blamed him. Those assholes had just tried to kill them.

Screw the shoes. Running in heels wasn't an option. So Holly kicked 'em off and took off after him.

The whine of a siren reached her ears just as she skidded to a halt next to Niol. He had the driver out. He was a young guy with coal-black hair, matted red near his forehead. Watery green eyes. Busted lip.

"Who the hell are you?" Niol's fingers were white as he held up the kid. No, not really a kid. The guy had to be in his early twenties.

Holly bent down, craning her neck to see into the demolished vehicle. Two more guys. One starting to move in the backseat—very, very slowly. The blond in the front was out cold.

"J-Jon D-Douglas . . ." Blood dripped from the guy's busted lip and stained his rounded chin.

"Do you know who I am?" Niol snarled. The guy's booted feet dangled over the ground. "Do you know just what the fuck you've done?"

The wail of the approaching siren was silenced by the sudden rush of wind that shook the van.

Holly reached for Niol. "Find out why, Niol." She

knew Niol had enemies. She would have been an idiot not
to have known that a demon as strong as Niol didn't always play nice with the other paranormals in town.

But with all the twisted crap going on with the demon-
hunter case . . . they needed to find out *why*.

"I-I don't kn-know you, m-man . . ." Bleary eyes started
to clear, a bit. "Y-you got th-this wrong. M-my friends—
we're h-hurt, n-need h-help . . ."

Niol's lips peeled away from his teeth. "Do I look like
I give a shit that you're hurt? Asshole, if you don't start
talking, fast, you'll be *dead* in the next five seconds."

Jon choked. Niol dropped him and the guy retched on
the ground.

"Human." Niol shook his head. "A human came after
me? The idiot must want to die."

A whimper from the backseat.

Holly's palms were slick with sweat. The setup was
wrong. Any paranormal in town would have known that
using fire against Niol wasn't exactly the smartest option.
The guy could manipulate the elements pretty much at
will.

Carefully, so as to avoid the, ahem, mess on the ground,
Holly knelt beside the guy. He was shaking and rocking
back and forth and the wind had quieted enough for Holly
to hear the siren again.

The cops were closing in. Not much time.

She had to find out what was going on before Niol carried through with his rage. "Who sent you to Paradise
Found?"

Jon looked up, wiping the back of his hand over his
mouth. His eyes changed as he stared at her, she could see
it. The bravado came back. *Doesn't think I'm a threat.*
She knew what the punk was going to say even before he
snarled—

"F-fuck off, bitch, you—"

His words ended in a gasp and his face began to turn purple.

His hands clawed at his throat as he fought for breath.

"Don't *ever* talk to her like that, asshole."

Holly glanced up at Niol. Lines bracketed his mouth. Fury covered his face. "Give him a breath," she ordered softly, her stomach so knotted she ached.

One black brow rose, but she heard Jon take a wrenching breath. "Good." She held Niol's stare a moment longer, then glanced back at the punk. "If you want to keep breathing, answer my questions."

What was this? Holly wondered. *Good demon, bad demon?* Whatever worked. Time was running out.

A frantic nod.

"Let him keep breathing." Her hands were clenched, her nails digging into her palms. The pavement bit into her knees as she knelt before Jon. "You don't know what you've gotten into, do you?"

"H-how is-is h-he—" Jon broke off, shaking his head. "N-not p-possible—"

"Trust me, it's possible." Lambs to the slaughter. Niol was right. The odds were sure looking good that ol' Jon was human and way out of his league. "Someone sent you to torch Paradise." To rouse the beast. "Who." Not a question, and if the guy truly wanted to draw another strong breath, he'd better answer.

Holly wasn't particularly in the most caring mood. The guy had just tried to burn down the building *she'd* been inside. If Niol hadn't been there—

No. Not going to think about that.

Sometimes it definitely paid to have the big, psychic badass as your lover.

And as your muscle—because Jon started talking, fast, the stutter all but leaving his voice as he said. "Woman. Found us at M-Myer's."

Myer's. She knew that place. A run-down bar near MU. Frequented most often by freshmen with false IDs.

"Offered us a g-grand apiece, *cash,* to burn the bar—"

And the guys had what—jumped at the chance to become pyros? "You didn't know who owned Paradise?" She had a suspicion but—

"Hell, no, why would that matter?"

Why, indeed?

"T-told us to go in the day, when no-no one was t-there."

But she and Niol had been there. Chance?

Lust.

Such a deadly sin.

"Weren't g-gonna hurt anybody."

Just burn down the bar.

"Give me a name." Niol's voice was still thick with barely banked fury, but at least he was letting the guy breathe okay now. That was an improvement.

So the punks hadn't meant to kill them. Just destroy Paradise.

Better, but not the most reassuring thing she'd ever heard.

"I-I didn't get her name." More blood shot from his mouth. Hmm . . . the guy might have lost a tooth somewhere. "Just her money."

Great.

"Tell me exactly what the woman looked—"

The screech of tires. The slam of doors.

Holly didn't need to look over her shoulder to know that the cops had arrived. The siren shrieking full-on in her ears told her that time had run out.

Chapter 14

Fury was a red haze that colored his vision. Niol tasted the ashes of rage on his tongue and knew that his control was razor thin.

Holly could have been killed.

If the assholes had attacked while he hadn't been around—

I knew she'd be dangerous to me. Fuck me, I knew.

He couldn't afford this kind of weakness.

Not now. Not ever.

A slim black casket, gleaming in the afternoon light. Nina had been inside. Her laughter gone, her spirit stolen.

Niol swallowed.

Gillian. His half sister. He hadn't even known about her, not until just a few months before her death. Seemed his mother had started a whole new life after she'd ditched his ass.

But, Gillian had come looking for *him.* Wanted him.

Then he'd found her that cold dawn . . .

In her red dress. The dress I'd bought for her. Blood soaking the dress and pooling all around her slender body.

He hadn't been able to keep her safe, either.

All his so-called power and two women he'd cared for were dead.

His gaze locked on Holly.

Not three. Not fucking three.

"You'll destroy everything, every damn body! I don't want you near me, got it? I don't want you near me!" His mother's last words to him. Screamed in her fury.

"Niol, pull it back." The clipped man's voice caught him off guard. He flinched. He knew that voice.

Detective Colin Gyth.

The shifter. He'd killed the murdering bastard who'd attacked his Gillian. For all their differences, and there were a hell of a lot of 'em, Niol owed the wolf a debt.

"Pull. It. Back."

It took Niol a moment to understand. He tore his eyes away from Holly and glanced up at the sky. Toward the swirling clouds of red and black. The howl of the wind reached him and lightning crackled across the sky.

Too much power. His curse.

He inhaled slowly. *She's alive.* Not like the others.

But she could have been dead, *because she'd been with me.*

So damn arrogant. He'd thought he could keep her safe from everything out there.

He should have known. He hadn't saved the others, and now, *he* was causing the threat to her.

A cool hand against his. Soft. Feminine. "They didn't get us." Holly's voice. Strong.

But she wasn't strong.

A demon, but as weak as a human.

Gillian had been a low-level demon, too. Fragile.

So easy to destroy.

Not her blood. I won't have Holly's blood on my hands,

too. The stains on his hands had already soaked through the skin.

Another deep breath.

She stroked the flesh on his arm.

His eyes stayed locked on those clouds. *Control*. He wouldn't lose it now. Not in front of the cops who'd fire at him if his power went wild.

Fire and maybe hit Holly.

A long, thick arc of lightning, a blast of thunder, followed by a heavy stench in the air—fire and fury.

Can't. Love. Her.

Deep breath.

Won't.

Her fingers on him.

Niol squeezed his eyes shut. "Get the bastards away from me if you want them to keep livin'."

"We need to get the Jaws of Life out here!" Brooks. The one Cara mistakenly had taken to mate.

Cara. So like her sister Nina.

A succubus who loved.

Dangerous, that.

Niol grunted and metal screeched.

"Not anymore we don't," Gyth muttered and there was a clatter as the broken side door hit the ground.

He could hear someone babbling, pleading. The asshole kid.

His eyes opened. Narrowed on his victim. "I see you again, you're dead."

"Ah, Niol, you can't threaten someone in front of cops—"

Slowly, he turned his attention to the human. What did Cara see in him?

"These jerks just tried to kill us!" Holly's fierce voice. She stepped in front of him.

In front of him.

Niol blinked.

"They made molotov cocktails and threw 'em into the bar. Their van crashed when they were hightailing it out of—"

"Lucky coincidence," Gyth said, face straight.

"—here, but this guy—" Holly charged right on, pointing her finger at Mr. Sobbing, "Confessed and right before you came up with sirens blazing—"

Niol finally glanced around at the scene. Fury was settling, for now, and he could think past the immediate need to destroy.

For the moment.

Two patrol cars had braked nearby. Their lights still blazed, doors hung open, and uniformed cops stood on alert, guns drawn.

Then there was Gyth's black Jeep. Right in front of them.

"—he was going to tell us about the woman who hired him to torch the bar."

"Was he?" Gyth, who'd had his own gun drawn, holstered the weapon and jerked the kid to his feet. "Then he can tell us all."

The kid stared at him, at the hint of fang Gyth had let slip loose. Then he looked back at Niol. His eyes widened and then rolled back into his head.

He sagged in the wolf shifter's arms, out cold.

Lucky bastard.

Niol started walking away from the cops, fast.

Because he couldn't be around the fools in that van a minute longer.

And he had new prey to hunt because he'd slipped into that punk's mind in that one precious instant, gone in hard and fast and deep. His probe had been so brutal *he'd* made the jerk pass out.

Lucky. It would have been nice if the kid had suffered

more from his psychic push, but he'd get that blood punishment later.

For now, Niol had gotten exactly what he wanted.

He'd seen the woman. A perfect image.

Tall and slender. Hair bundled under a long black scarf. Golden skin. Dark sunglasses perched on high cheekbones. Rounded jaw. Thin lips. A small black mole on the side of her neck.

New prey.

I'm coming.

He'd find out just why the bitch had targeted him.

The cops got out of Niol's way. No one moved to stop him. Hell, no one seemed to *move* at all until Niol was gone.

Holly crossed her arms over her chest, feeling chilled, and, well, abandoned.

Niol hadn't even glanced back at her when he'd marched across the street.

"Storm, you just keep turning up in bad places." Gyth stepped closer to her as he shook his head. Behind him, Brooks and the uniforms checked out the wounded pyros.

One of the cops had his radio out as he called for an ambulance.

Oh, yeah, they'd need that ambulance.

"I was in the bar, minding my own business." *Just finishing up some great sex.* "Then these jerkoffs decided to get fire crazy."

He crept even closer. So close that when he spoke again, she knew the others couldn't hear his faint words. "Real stupid to go after Niol with fire."

It was. "They're humans, aren't they?"

His nostrils flared. "Smell that way." His gaze trapped hers. "But then, so do you."

There was a definite question there, one she was going to ignore. "I don't think they know exactly *who* . . ." What. "They're dealing with."

"I'd say that's shit straight." One brow rose. Those blue eyes were brilliant with intensity. "And I'd say it's a good thing we arrived when we did. Otherwise, I think our torchers would be dust."

It was hard not to flinch at that. No denying that Niol had been enraged, but he'd held on to his control.

She'd *seen* him fight to hold it.

She'd also seen him walk away from her without a backward glance and that had hurt.

"Why—" Holly stopped and cleared her throat. Because she'd sounded hoarse, from the wind, of course. It had been blowing like a mini-tornado moments before. Had to be from the wind. "Why were you in the area, detective?"

He scratched the bridge of his nose. There was a groan from the man still in the front seat of the van. Holly glanced over at him. Brooks had his index finger in front of the guy's eyes and the cop was getting him to track the movement.

That one seemed to be coming around, finally.

"I was coming to see Niol."

Her attention turned back to Gyth.

"Had a few questions for your lover," he continued in that same near-whisper voice.

"What kind of questions?" Surely he wasn't back to suspecting Niol—

"Questions about Kim Went and about the fact that I'm pretty sure she's a demon."

Her breath came out, fast. "What?"

"Didn't you know?"

She would have been blind and deaf to have missed the suspicion from the good detective. "How do *you* know?"

Holly asked instead. Niol had said he didn't know, how had—

His lip curled. "Sources, Storm. Sources."

Well, well.

"And I have it from one of the best sources in the city that Kim Went is a demon."

"So you came to ask Niol—"

"If he knew she was one of his brethren . . . and if the attack at News Flash Five was really aimed at you—"

No way to stop the flinch that time.

"Or at her. Because we all know we've got a demon-hunter on the streets."

And a missing demon now. One already weakened, who could so easily stumble into the hunter's grasp.

His heart thudded in his ears. A hard, blasting beat. Niol yanked open the door of Paradise and stormed inside. The stench of burnt wood and plastic had his nose twitching and a snarl rising to his lips.

Should have ripped the fools apart.

But she'd stopped him. She'd—

The floor creaked behind him.

Tired of this shit.

Niol moved in a blur and grabbed the idiot behind him, locking his fingers around a thick neck. He shoved the guy—yeah, it was a man—up against the closest wall and held him pinned with his steely grip.

"I'm not in the fucking mood for visitors," he snarled. The rage was still too close to the surface. His control too thin. And this dumbass had just picked the wrong moment to stumble into Paradise—

"G-girl . . . y-you . . . w-want . . ." The man, some guy with a receding hairline and bulging eyes, struggled to speak as his face began to redden. Hazel eyes shot to black.

Demon. He'd known that from the first glance.

But the fellow's words had him pausing and his grip eased, just a bit. "What girl?"

The demon sucked in a sharp pull of air. His feet dangled off the floor by a good ten inches. Niol wasn't even straining.

Sometimes, it was so good to be a level-ten ass-kicker.

Gillian's stark face flashed before his eyes.

His teeth clenched. "What. Girl?"

"H-heard P-Patience talking d-down at th-the Gin—"

Gin Easy. A seedy bar where those *Other* cast out of Paradise usually wound up.

"S-she was ta-talking about a-a demon m-missing . . ."

His own patience was just about gone. "What about her?" Were the cops still outside? Was Holly?

"S-saw her . . . hour ago."

Niol dropped him. The fellow's legs slipped out from under him and he fell to the floor.

The door to Paradise opened with a groan. "Thanks a lot for deserting me out there—" Holly began.

His gaze shot to her.

He saw her take in the fallen man and she stumbled to a halt. "Ah, Niol? What's going on?" Her nose was wrinkled in a little scrunch that shouldn't have been cute.

But it was.

Don't care. He couldn't be weak, not with her.

"This guy," Niol stepped back a foot, two. "Says he knows where Kim is."

"What?" Her jaw dropped.

"He's just about to tell us everything he knows." A threat.

The demon pushed up onto his knees. "Not—not unless you meet my terms." Seemed braver now.

Shit. Why the hell did everyone want to bargain? Did he look like he wanted to make a deal?

Another stupid demon myth and this jerkoff should know that. Demons *hated* deals. Mostly because no one in demonkind ever stuck by their word.

But because some jackass long ago had gone around scamming the humans . . . that myth about making a deal with the devil still circulated.

"I don't make deals."

Holly grunted at that.

His lips twisted. Okay, so she was the exception. And look where that particular exception had gotten him. Tied up in knots and so hard and horny he could barely think half the time.

A slow rise to his feet. The demon lifted his chin. "Then *you* don't find the g-girl—"

Oh, *definitely* seemed to be getting his balls back. Really poor timing that. Niol motioned with his hand and one of the charred tables flew across the room and slammed into the demon's chest.

And right back down to the floor he went.

"Dammit, Niol, the cops are right outside!" Holly hurried forward, then stopped, frowning down at the groaning demon. "Ah, sir? What's your name?"

Because acting all sugar-and-sweet nice was going to work with the guy. "Stay away from him, Holly." Not a gentle order. More of a fierce growl.

She shot him a pissed look. So what? He wasn't about to risk her safety again. When the woman didn't move, Niol grabbed her wrist and jerked her to his side.

After a moment, the demon shoved the table off and rose, much slower this time, to his feet. "N-name's S-Sylas K-King."

"Where. Is. The. Girl?" He'd never met Sylas King before, never so much as even caught a glimpse of him in the city.

Sylas balled his hands into big, hamlike fists. "Need your help."

Right. He'd agreed to help one woman, one determined reporter, and now everyone wanted a handout. "It'll work this way, Sylas. Tell me where the girl is and I'll let you walk out of Paradise in one piece or you can—"

"Why do you need his help?" Holly. Sounding curious and all reporter-girl again.

"Got me a son." The fearful pause was gone from the man's voice, but the fear lingered in his gaze. Good. He might not be as dumb as Niol had originally thought. "He's thirteen—starting to show his power."

Niol felt a punch in his gut. He knew where this was going. He *knew.*

"I don't got me much power." He shook his head. "Can barely control fire, but he—he's different."

Niol's eyes closed for a moment, then opened just as Sylas said—

"My boy's going dark on me. Gettin' the Touch."

He saw the tremble that shook Holly's body.

"I don't want to lose him." The words came faster, rushing out. "Don't want him to slip to the drugs or kill himself. Shit, he's already tried razoring his wrists once. You've got to help me, you've got to—"

"He will." Holly sounded absolutely certain. Niol glanced fully at her. Saw the pain on her face. *Remembering her brother.*

"I will." Niol repeated, his voice hard. *Who are you kidding? You know you'd do just about anything to take that look off her face.*

Weak.

He'd have to stop this before it was too late.

Pity had stirred in him at the man's confession. *Not another one.* Not another lost demon forced into the darkness.

Maybe he *could* help this one.

Or maybe the Monster Doctor could.

Could be time to start executing his plans. He nodded. "Tell me about the girl and I'll see what I can do for your boy."

Sylas opened his mouth, then hesitated. "You give me your word?"

For what it was worth. "Yes."

"Tell us," Holly urged. "We don't have much time."

"Saw two women in front of Reed Infirmary. Your girl—she got sick or something and her friend had to help her."

Every cell in Niol's body seemed to freeze. "Her friend?"

"Yeah, a blonde. She had her hair pulled back, a scarf around it, but it blew loose. She had on sunglasses—"

Like the bitch who'd sent the pyros after him.

"She said she'd take care of-of the other one. Said they had a ride waitin'—"

"And you just drove off and left them?" Holly's voice was hushed but Niol heard the vibration of anger.

"I did." Admitted with his chin up. "At first, I did. Then I got worried. Didn't . . . seem right. And that other girl—" His eyes were on Niol. "She was one of *ours*. I saw her eyes flash black and I saw fear in 'em. I don't like seeing fear in a demon woman's eyes."

Join the club.

"There wasn't any car coming to meet them. When I circled back, I saw the blonde shoving the demon into the back of *her* car. I followed 'em." He wet his lips.

"The address."

Kim could be dead by now. Cut up like the others and left to bleed out . . . with parts of her body gone missing.

Holly's fingers dug into his arm. He knew she was thinking the same thing.

No time to lose.

Sylas rattled off a shaky address.

Niol and Holly rushed for the door.

"Don't forget my boy! You gave your word! Don't you forget my—"

This was the side of the city most folks stayed away from, if they were smart.

Holly's nails bit into the leather that covered Niol's passenger seat. They'd all but flown out of the parking lot of Paradise, and the two detectives, Gyth and Brooks, were right on their tail. A good thing, Holly figured, because she sure didn't know what they'd find waiting for them. Niol took the curve hard and Holly slammed into the passenger-side door.

He stopped a distance away from the house, away from the small, run-down house that almost seemed to be tipping over onto the railroad tracks.

"Stay here," Niol ordered, his jaw clenched as he killed the engine. His gaze was on the house and the air in the vehicle had thickened with tension.

And fear. Hers, not his. The guy just looked pissed off while she was so nervous her stomach twisted.

Be alive. A plea. She didn't want Kim to be dead. Not Kim with her quick smile and her slow laugh.

Not Kim.

Niol opened his door.

"I'm coming with you." The words sounded tougher than she'd thought they would.

He looked at her, one of those you-can't-be-serious expressions on his face.

But she was serious. "I *know* her, Niol. If she's in there—" Dead or alive, "I have to go in." She couldn't stand back on the sidelines, not for this.

The Jeep pulled in behind them, wheels almost soundless on the pavement. The cavalry had arrived.

Niol turned away from her and Holly hurriedly jumped out of the SUV.

"What the fuck is goin' on, demon?" Brooks demanded, but kept his voice low.

Niol didn't answer, so Holly cleared her throat and jerked her thumb toward the house. "We got a tip. Kim could be inside—"

Brooks pulled out his weapon.

"Stay here."

Did all men love to give that order or what?

Brooks turned to his partner. "No warrant, but I'm sure not gonna stand around here with my thumb up my ass if that girl's inside—"

"I don't need a warrant." From Niol. Then he was gone. Turning, running, and heading straight for the house.

"*Sonofa—*"

The detectives ran after him.

So did Holly. Crap, she'd put her heels back on. They were gonna slow her down and—

Be alive.

The door of the house flew off as Niol bounded up the rickety steps.

"Blood." The growl came from Gyth. "Too much—"

She didn't smell it, not yet, but she'd trust that shifter's nose anytime, anywhere.

Kim.

Niol disappeared into the house and the shifter bounded right after him.

Brooks turned around and caught Holly, stopping her just when she was about to enter the house—

His face was stark white. And she could smell the blood now. Clogging her nostrils. Choking her.

A muscle jerked along his jaw as he said, "I don't think you want to see—"

"Holly! Holly, get in here—she's alive!" Niol's voice seemed to shake the house.

The cop's eyes widened and he dropped his hold. "Is it clear?" He barked to his partner.

"Bastard's gone, for now."

Brooks went in before her.

Holly stumbled inside, her breath rattling in her chest.

"Looks like playtime was interrupted," Gyth muttered.

Holly peered around the detective's broad shoulders. Understanding sank in at once.

A table—some kind of folding exam table—was set up in the middle of the room, and Kim was stretched out on that table, strapped down.

Bleeding. Too pale.

Niol bent over her, his fingers around her throat.

Kim was nude, except for the blood covering her. So much blood.

"Oh, my God—"

"We need an ambulance, *fucking now*—" Gyth yelled into his cell phone.

"He left her to bleed out," Brooks said and he put his hand over the gaping wound high on the left of Kim's abdomen. "Asshole just left her—"

Holly's skin was icy cold. Bruises lined Kim's face and she looked *so young*.

And then, those still lashes tried to lift.

Still alive. Niol had said it, but when she'd seen the body, she hadn't believed—

Holly was beside her in an instant. "Kim? Kim, you're safe, now, okay? You're safe—"

Her eyes didn't open.

Holly took her hand, a hand even colder than her own. "No one's going to hurt you anymore. We're going to get you help, okay?" Brooks and Gyth were working on her now, applying pressure to her wounds and—

"Bastard sliced her open—" Gyth's snarl.

"That's not all he did . . ." Niol, a rage banking his voice and sending a tremor down her spine.

She glanced up at him. "What are you—"

Kim's body jerked. Once. Twice. Again and again and blood poured from her lips. "*No!* Kim, Kim, stay with me!"

Her body fell back against the plastic.

Her black eyes were wide open now, staring sightlessly ahead.

No.

Chapter 15

"**B**astard took out her spleen." Smith paced in front of McNeal's desk, her hands trembling. "Gave her some kind of drug, some shit I've never seen before and the docs on duty in the ER hadn't seen either, and he just cut her wide open." Faster now, she turned and marched straight back. "She's a kid, just a—"

McNeal caught her. Pulled her against his chest and held her. Kim Went had been discovered by his detectives just over five hours ago. As soon as he'd gotten the word about the girl, he'd sent Smith to the hospital with a police escort to get her past the red tape that would have otherwise kept the ME out of the operating room.

But, dammit, he'd wanted one of his own in there with that girl. Someone who could understand what the hell had happened to her and someone who could look for evidence.

Not that any evidence had been found so far.

"The last person seen with Went was a blond woman." He'd dealt with his share of female killers before, and he knew that when you were talking about the *Other* world, the usual rules didn't apply. So, sure, a female supernatural would easily have the physical strength to overpower the two males who'd been killed.

Could be the hunter was a woman . . .

They had the demon taxi driver in the interrogation room. He was giving them as much of a description of the woman as he could.

The only lead they had so far.

Well, him . . . and those idiots who'd tried to torch Niol's bar. Gyth had alerted him to the guys, and he'd been waiting for 'em. They'd gotten patched up, then they'd come to him.

It had taken ten minutes to get them to tell everything they knew about the woman who hired them. Unfortunately, they knew damn little.

But McNeal didn't believe in coincidences, and he couldn't wait to compare their description with King's.

"She knew what she was doing." Smith looked up at him with those big, dark eyes that always made his stomach clench. He'd taken a look in those eyes long ago and known that he was lost. "This wasn't the work of an amateur." Her lips trembled, but she kept talking and she kept her chin up. *My Smith.* "This woman knows how to use a scalpel—"

Damn. "Am I looking for a doctor, Nathalia?" His hands smoothed up her chilled arms and he didn't give a shit that the blinds were up in his office. If one of his cops saw them, screw it. Nathalia needed him.

And he sure needed her.

"Could be." A hard pull of breath. "This person didn't make any mistakes. No hesitation marks were around the wounds, just straight cuts. Quick and cold."

An amateur would have hacked the girl to pieces.

The other bodies *had* been carved like hell gone bad, but the organ removal—he'd read the reports—had all been done a bit too well. Maybe the carving job had been deliberate, a way to hide the other surgical precision.

"Is she gonna make it?" He asked. He'd voiced the same question to the docs in the ER. They hadn't answered, just stared at him like he was crazy for asking.

But they'd been human. They didn't understand and that's why he'd brought in Nathalia.

Kim Went had a much stronger healing system in place than a human. There was a chance, slim, but a chance she would recover—

"Niol said she would."

Niol. He blinked. Since when was Nathalia on a first-name basis with that guy?

"He was at the hospital. Him and the reporter. They stayed in the waiting room the whole time Kim was in surgery." She swallowed. "They *care* about that girl."

News to him.

"The reporter, Storm, was crying." That he could believe. He'd caught a few of Storm's stories. Seen enough to know that she wasn't the usual fluff reporter. "They didn't leave, not until—"

She stopped, breaking off abruptly. Like he was gonna let her end there. "Until what?"

A sigh. "Until Niol got to see the girl. He stared at her a few minutes after surgery, just watched her, then I heard him tell Storm that Went would be all right."

If the devil had said so . . .

The tension in his shoulders eased, just a bit. He knew Niol's reputation. If the demon had said that Kim would live, she would.

"Another half hour, hell, another fifteen minutes, and Kim would have died." She pulled away from him and started her pacing again. She looked tired. Dark shadows lined her eyes. Her arms hung limply and the sexy stride he so enjoyed watching was gone. "That bitch just left that girl to die."

After she'd taken a little souvenir. What kind of freak job was he dealing with here? "Niol told Gyth we were after a human." A human who'd taken to carving up the demons in his city and stealing body parts? Shit, what would he have to deal with next?

Sometimes, he could still remember the good old days. When humans killed humans and supernaturals kept to the shadows.

Not anymore.

Nathalia paused near his one window. "Guess we can all be monsters deep down, huh?"

His hands clenched. This was a sore point for him. Nathalia was freaking beautiful and perfect and . . . *human*. For a time, he hadn't believed she'd want him, not if she knew the truth about him.

He sure wasn't beautiful. More like scary. He'd been called that a few times. Perfect—uh, that was another word that would never fit him and the shit that was his life.

As for human . . . not quite.

Even when he held Nathalia late at night, when she was beside him in bed and he could feel the soft beat of her heart, he worried he'd lose her.

Because he was a monster, too. And no matter what that crap in storybooks said, Beauty didn't want to spend her life shacked up with the Beast.

She wasn't looking at him now. Just staring out the window with her shoulders slumped. "When I . . . first found out about the *Other*—"

He winced. That had been a brutal introduction, and just thinking about the attack she'd suffered made him want to *kill*.

"—I thought all supernaturals were evil. Even though Gyth saved my ass, my head—" She glanced back at him and McNeal *thought* he managed to wipe the desperation from his face. "—it was all messed up."

An attack by a psycho could do that to a woman.

"It's okay." His voice sounded gruff. He hadn't planned

that. He'd wanted to sound soft and comforting, but his voice was always like gravel. "You don't have to—"

"That girl—Kim. When I saw her, I didn't think about her being human or *Other*. I just saw a victim."

Because that's what the girl was.

"Monsters, humans—we're all a tangled mess, just trying to survive." Her eyes held his. "And I'm not afraid anymore, Danny. *I'm not afraid.*"

That cracking was his heart. Breaking—no, bursting, because dammit, he *loved* her. A woman who'd walked through hell, but could still understand the monsters.

He walked to her, slowly, even though he knew she wouldn't frighten off. "You don't need to be afraid anymore." He'd never let her be in danger. Never.

"But others do. Kim. Holly Storm. They have to be careful." She turned fully to face him. "This killer is smart and she's good."

She'd sure managed to clear out of that house fast. Gyth and the crime scene guys had been poring over that place and they'd found jack shit. A guy with a nose like Gyth's wouldn't miss anything.

Which meant there was nothing to find.

And it meant they had three dead bodies.

And one live victim.

Thanks to the demon king of the city. Owing that guy stuck in McNeal's throat, but he'd make sure he paid his debt.

McNeal always paid his debts.

After the killer was caught, and he would catch the slicer, he'd handle Niol.

Her eyes were grainy from crying. Because, yeah, she'd cried like a baby when she'd been in that ambulance with Kim. Cried and prayed—prayed like she hadn't prayed in *years*—and used every bit of her strength to will Kim to live.

And so far, she had.

So far.

Holly climbed from Niol's SUV, her knees shaking and her calves trembling. Her stomach was one hard knot. She couldn't remember the last time she'd eaten and she just wanted to crawl inside and wash away the blood staining her fingers.

Just wash it away.

"Holly . . ."

Niol's voice. Tense.

She didn't stop walking. She didn't know what to say to him then. The guy confused her too much. She wanted him. She needed him and—

And if she wasn't careful, she'd lose her heart to him.

Because she knew Niol wasn't the staying kind. Or the loving kind. He'd warned her of that, himself.

Her steps were heavy on the sidewalk. She wasn't paying attention to—

"Holly?" Not Niol's voice. Feminine. High. Screech-level.

Her head lifted. Her gaze searched the darkness and saw the figure standing on her porch.

Mom?

Oh, damn.

"Tried to tell you." Now Niol was talking. Quiet. Whisper-like. "We aren't alone."

Her mom was there. Since when did her mom pay her late-night visits? Or any visits?

Click. Click. Click. Her mother's shoes on the steps. "I've been waiting here for *hours*, Holly Ann Storm. Hours. I called your cell at least a dozen times and you couldn't be bothered to answer."

She'd had to turn the cell off in the hospital. Frowning,

she dug around in her purse and, after a moment, felt the cool touch of the phone. *Forgot to turn it back on.*

Holly continued walking, one foot in front of the other. She passed her mom and pulled out the house keys. "Sorry, Mom, I was—"

"Out. With a man." A sniff. "You sounded like you needed me, Holly Ann. I came all the way from Birmingham and you weren't even—"

Holly shoved open her front door. The alarm beeped as she flipped on the lights and punched in the security code and—

"*Oh. My. God.* Is that blood?"

Yeah, and a lot of it. She'd scrubbed as hard as she could in the hospital, but her fingernails were still stained red and her shirt, though dry now, had Kim's blood coated on the front. "It's really been one hell of a night, Mom."

Her mother had followed her inside. The lights flickered off the red of her hair, a shade softer than Holly's own, one that had a bit of professional help. Her mom was in her early fifties, but could easily have passed for a woman just hitting her mid-forties.

Holly dropped her bag onto the sofa and thought long and hard about collapsing next to it. Her mom seemed stunned, staring at her with wide eyes—a perfect shade match there—and parted lips.

Niol loomed in the doorway behind her. Holly wasn't sure her mom had even seen him yet. "Uh, it's not my blood, Mom."

"You take these dangerous stories. You stay out all hours with strange men—" She finally glanced back over her shoulder at Niol as she snapped, "It could be your—*No!*"

The last was gasped. And that horrified gasp was full of recognition. Recognition that a human who'd spent the last seven years living in Birmingham, Alabama, shouldn't have for a demon in Atlanta.

Holly got a really, really bad feeling in her gut.

No, no she wouldn't have kept this from me. Not all of these years. Not after Peter—

Her mother still had her eyes glued to Niol. He lifted a brow and his own black eyes stayed locked on her.

"S-send him away." Hoarse.

Holly blinked. "What?"

Her mother's head turned toward her. Very slowly, as if she were afraid to take her gaze off Niol. *Her mother had always been smart.* "Send him away." Stronger now.

Holly glanced over at Niol. No expression there. She took a deep breath and said simply, "No." Then she motioned to Niol. "Shut the door so the alarm will kick in." And she walked away.

Silence behind her. Then a hand caught her arm. She swung around and met her mom's wild eyes. *Used to be so calm. Not anymore.* "You don't know what you're doing! This—this *man*, he's not for you! Go back to that nice doctor you were seeing. He was a good man, safe. He was—"

"Screwing around on me." Which her mother already knew. "Thanks, but no thanks."

Niol walked past them. Made himself comfortable on her couch.

Her mother's nails dug into her skin. "You don't know what you're doing."

But her mother obviously knew Niol. Holly kicked off her pumps and heard the whisper of relief from her feet. "Niol, you didn't tell me that you knew my mother."

His gaze swept over her mother's figure. Kelly Storm kept herself trim from a vicious workout routine. She'd been working out every day, for at least an hour a day, since her husband had passed away from a heart attack just over two years ago.

"Never met before." He offered a smile, one that didn't look reassuring.

"I *know* who you are." Kelly's voice was arctic. "And I want you to stay away from my daughter. She's not your kind. She's—"

Holly's heart slammed into her ribs. She gazed at her mother and just felt . . . sad. "Why didn't you tell me?" Enough crap. Enough tension.

Kelly blinked. "I don't know what—"

Her hand waved toward Niol. "You *know* exactly what I'm talking about." Lies. "Are you a demon, too, Mom?"

"No!"

Such a fast denial. "Who, then? It has to be someone in the family. Dad? Was he—"

"I will *not* talk about this." Her hand fell away and her thin shoulders straightened. "This is nonsense. Ridiculous. There are no—"

"I'm a demon." The first time she'd confessed. Made her feel . . . strange. Right. "Peter was, too. But you *knew* that, didn't you? When he started talking about the voices and the things he'd seen, you knew what he was and you said *nothing!*" Rage bubbled up, hard and too fast. *Rage.* All those years when her mother had been so distant with her. Those years when she'd watched her brother slipping away.

Wasted years.

When she'd known.

A tear slipped from the corner of her mother's eye.

Holly had seen her mother cry three times in her life. Peter's funeral. Her father's hospital bed and now.

"Easy, Holly." She jumped. When had Niol moved to her side? He wrapped an arm around her and pulled her close. "Easy, love."

Shit, she was crying, too.

One hell of a night.

"You should have told me." The rage was gone. Now she just felt tired. "I could have helped Peter, I could have—"

"You were a little girl." Whispered. "There wasn't anything you could do. I-I didn't know, not until it was too late . . ."

Peter's face flashed before her.

No.

Kelly licked her lips. "I-I don't guess I need to ask how you—how you found out." Her eyes darted to Niol.

"Holly's not a half-breed." He spoke with cold certainty, but his hold on her was warm. "Not you. Not her father—"

"Her grandmother." She looked so frail then. So small. "George's mother was a-a demon." Her gaze turned back to Holly. "I swear, baby, I didn't *know* what she was. She died before I married your father and he seemed so *normal.* I-I thought he was. Until Peter . . ."

A swallow. Loud in the quiet room. "George thought you were both just like him, that the demon trait or gene—or whatever the hell it is—had just passed you by. God, baby, I prayed it had passed you by."

Her head pounded. "You knew and you let Peter—"

"I did everything I could for Peter! I *loved* him! He was my son! *Mine*! Demon, human—it didn't matter!"

She'd never heard such passion in her mother's voice.

"I sent him to doctors. One after the other. For days. Months. They tried every treatment, every therapy but nothing worked. He slipped away from me while I watched because *nothing worked.*"

My boy's goin' into the dark.

And it was happening again.

"Then he left me and I was so scared you'd leave me, too."

So she'd started to shut me out. "You weren't ever going to tell me, were you?"

A shake of her mother's head. "I just prayed you weren't—"

Like him.

A fist squeezed her heart. A cold, clammy fist that just tightened and tightened.

"Peter had a . . . sickness." Niol, his voice softer, pitched with sadness. "We call it the Dark Touch in the demon world."

Kelly's lips trembled. "Could you—could you have helped my son?" A pause, so brief, then. "You're strong. Some say maybe the strongest born this century."

Well, that was a new one for Holly.

"Could you have helped him?"

Her mother's words twisted with Jon's. *You got to help my boy.*

Holly looked up at him, saw the clench of his jaw. "Not then. No, I couldn't."

Brutal honesty.

"But I'm sure as hell working to make sure no more kids go Dark."

The fist eased its hold. Niol glanced down at her with eyes cloaked in so many shadows.

He looked worried. For her.

Niol pressed a kiss to her lips. "Talk to your mother. Get past this. It can't eat you up anymore."

He would know all about being destroyed from the inside.

His head inclined toward her mother. "Interesting meeting you, Mrs. Storm."

Her mouth parted.

Then he walked away. Calm, slow steps. In moments, the door clicked closed behind him.

Holly stared at her mother. Two feet between them, but it sure seemed like so much more.

Do you hear the voices, Hol?

"He . . . he's not what I expected."

A cold-blooded killer. She knew that was what most people expected. "There's more to Niol than just—" His reputation for death. "What you see and hear."

Her mother crept forward, hesitated.

Holly couldn't move.

"I didn't know how to tell you. There weren't any signs, I thought it had skipped you—"

It. There was no *it.* She was a demon. Blood, bones, and soul.

"You're afraid of Niol." Her voice sounded rusty. Of course, most folks were rightly afraid of Niol. "Are you— are you afraid of me, too?" *Because of what I am.*

Another inch forward. Her mother's hands lifted, then fisted. "No."

Holly wanted to believe that.

"I'm not afraid of you, baby. *I love you.*"

Holly couldn't remember the last time she'd heard those words.

One more inch. "But I understand just how dangerous this world is, especially for you." An inhalation of air that sounded too loud in the room. "I just want you to be safe."

With a demon-hunter on the streets, that wasn't going to be an easy order.

Her mother's gaze searched hers. "You . . . care for him, don't you?"

That damn fist was back, but Holly managed to nod.

"I saw it, in your eyes."

Had Niol seen it, too?

"I always wanted you to be safe, with a man who'd pro- tect you." Her mouth lifted into the ghost of a smile. "Guess Niol knows how to protect what's his, doesn't he?"

Holly opened her mouth to answer and—

"He'd better," her mother continued, that smile vanish- ing, "because if that demon lets anything happen to you, I'll kill him."

Then her mom threw her arms around her, squeezing so tightly that Holly struggled for breath.

* * *

Dr. Emily Drake sat behind her desk. Her gaze darted to her watch. Nine twenty-eight a.m. Her first appointment would be checking in soon. A charmer.

She liked the charmers. They were the most easygoing of the *Other.* Actually, most of their trouble usually came from their creature companions. Communication issues.

She tapped her pen against the top of the desk. Yes, her patient would be here any minute and she was glad for that fact because she needed a distraction.

She couldn't get the demon-hunter case out of her head.

Colin had come to her just before dawn. Eyes stark, the scent of blood on his body. He'd told her about the young demon they'd found and the horror she'd endured. McNeal had already sent orders that as soon as the girl woke up, he wanted Emily in that hospital room with her.

But Emily didn't think Kim would be in the mood for talking right away. No, the rage and the fear would be too strong at first.

She'd survived. Barely.

The first victim to live through an attack by the hunter. She was lucky, but Emily wasn't certain Kim would feel that way when her eyes finally opened. She didn't know if—

Her office door swung open. Emily glanced up, pasting a smile on her face.

"I *said* you can't go in there!" Vanessa's voice, reaching shriek level.

But the man in her doorway didn't flinch. His legs were braced apart, his arms loosely at his sides, and his black eyes zeroed in on her.

Niol.

Well, damn.

Her palms started to sweat. She hadn't seen Niol in months. She'd stayed out of Paradise and he'd stayed out of her way. Fair enough arrangement.

She and Niol didn't exactly have a good history between them.

And she knew that her wolf shifter lover really wanted to kick the demon's ass.

"Tell the witch to back off."

She wasn't the least bit surprised that Niol knew about her assistant's *Other* powers. The guy always seemed to know everything.

But he'd never come to her office before.

Emily rose to her feet and cast a glance at Vanessa. The woman was pale, with wide eyes—*she knew about Niol's reputation*—but she wasn't backing down.

"It's okay. I can talk to Mr. Lapen for a few moments." A glance at her watch, a deliberate and fake one this time. "My appointment will be here soon—"

A grunt. "Shaughnessy won't be here today." A smile that made the hair on her nape rise. "He had a . . . change of plans."

Niol knew *too* much.

He glanced over his shoulder. "Treat my friends well, witch."

His friends?

Oh, this couldn't be good.

Vanessa gazed back at her and Emily managed a nod. Her glasses felt too tight, as if they were pinching her nose and a dull ache had begun behind her left eye.

Always happened around Niol. His power was so strong it seemed to lap at her.

The door closed with a soft click. Emily didn't sit down and Niol just kept staring at her.

When he finally moved, stalking across the room toward her, she braced her hands on the desk. "Why are you here?"

His head tilted. "I came to collect a debt."

"What?" She didn't owe that bastard anything. She

knew how he operated and she'd made absolutely sure
that she didn't—

"Come now, Emily, don't look so surprised. You had to
know I'd come calling one day." He glanced over at her
black leather couch. "Interesting. Bet the wolf likes that."

Her cheeks heated. *Yeah, Colin did.*

Control. "I don't know what debt you're talking about—
" She wasn't going to touch the couch reference, "but I've
got clients who *need* my help. I don't have time—"

"I need you, too, Emily."

He said her name as if they were close. Friends.
Lovers.

They'd never been either.

After a moment, he headed for the couch. Didn't lay
down, just sat, with his legs sprawled before him. "You're
such a smart lady. Surely you've wondered . . ."

His eyes were so dark. Humans could get lost in those
eyes. She knew that—she'd seen it happen.

And Holly was dating him? Sleeping with him?

"I remember the first time you walked into my Paradise. You were shaking because you were afraid—"

Terrified might be a better word.

"And because you were so hungry."

Slowly, she sat back down into her chair. The leather
creaked beneath her.

"You needed my world, didn't you? Needed to touch it,
to feel it in order to keep surviving."

She'd always suspected Niol's mind was razor sharp
and that his instincts for people were dead-on. No wonder
the guy was such a fine predator. "Where is this going?"
Her voice was cool and perfectly calm. She was good at
that, good at pretending. She'd had so much practice over
the years.

Niol's gaze said he knew that and his slow smile had
her stiffening.

"I let you into my Paradise. Gave you free rein in my world."

Okay, yes, she'd always wondered about that, but— "You also introduced me to the asshole who tried to shove his way into my mind." Myles. Demon bastard. He hadn't been expecting her to fight back.

His mistake.

The faint lines around Niol's mouth tightened. "When I realized what was happening with Myles . . . it was too late." His brows lifted. "You took care of the problem before I could intervene."

Lie. Emily didn't buy that one for a minute. "Bullshit—"

"Doctor—*language.*"

Emily growled.

"Myles was a mistake." A shrug. "But I think he certainly paid for his crime, don't you? You blasted every bit of his power away. Wouldn't have thought it was possible, if I hadn't seen it for myself."

For a moment, she was back in Paradise. The roar of the laughing crowd around her. Smoke in the air. And a demon at her feet. Dizzy, lost, she'd fallen facefirst into the gleaming bar—

And woken in a hospital.

"I've always wondered . . ." A couple of things. She drew in a deep gulp of air. The whole conversation was surreal, but she'd wanted answers for years.

Answers. She'd always craved them.

And never found them all.

Some mysteries just couldn't be solved.

"Who got me out of Paradise?" She asked him quietly.

One black brow rose.

Damn.

"I couldn't very well leave you bleeding on my floor, now could I? Not good for business."

Like his clientele would have cared that an unconscious and bleeding woman was on the floor.

He eased back a bit on the couch. "I took you out,
made certain there were no . . . uncomfortable questions
at the hospital, and I stayed—"

Now *that* surprised her.

"—with you until you were awake again."

What? Niol had been there, when she'd been at her
weakest? *Very* scary thought.

His bottomless gaze held hers. "Myles had friends.
Shit-scum, but powerful. The eye-for-an-eye type. They
would have just loved to get their hands on you."

She'd worried about them. Had some nightmares after
she'd gotten out of the hospital. But then the fear about
retaliation had just seemed to vanish from her mind.

"I . . . eliminated the threat to you." He spoke easily.
Calmly. As if he were talking about getting rid of trash.
And for him, maybe he was. Emily had never understood
him. His mind had been closed to her. Always closed. Not
like the others. She could pick her way so easily into the
thoughts of most paranormals.

Not Niol.

Not that she'd ever really wanted to try.

Because Emily knew, deep down, that if Niol wanted
to go after her, the way Myles had, well, she wouldn't be
knocked out.

She'd be killed.

Niol was just too strong. She'd heard rumors once
about level-tens. The talk was that they could live for
freaking ever. They could heal so fast that their bodies
were in a constant state of perfect health.

But the longer they lived, the more their . . . demon
selves emerged.

The rumors were that some demons out there, some
level-tens were so old they had cloven feet and tails.

Rumors, of course; she'd never found any information to substantiate that, but—

But level-tens couldn't be killed by any weapon of man—that much was true.

And Niol, since he more than tipped the power scale, she sure didn't want to tangle with him.

"Since I took care of that little problem for you, I'd say that puts you in my debt."

Her eyes narrowed. "What do you want?"

He held up his hands. "Don't look so worried, Emily. I'm not the threat you think."

She snorted.

"I just need that wonderful mind of yours. So interesting, so strong."

Emily's stomach knotted. "I always thought you were testing me," she murmured, deliberately throwing the words out as her own test to see how Niol would respond.

He nodded. "Yes, I was."

Sonofabitch. He'd let her into Paradise to test her like a lab rat, and he had the gall to sit there and say she owed *him*?

"Had to make sure you were capable, that you could handle the darkness."

She'd been handling darkness for years. She didn't need some arrogant ass of a demon to—

"If you weren't strong enough, then you wouldn't have been of any use to me."

Cold and hard. Just like she would have expected.

But—

But his eyes weren't cold. The darkness was lit with a fire she'd never seen before.

I want in his mind.

Because Emily had the feeling that the puppet master was hiding too many secrets of his own.

He leaned forward, dropping the easy pose. "You tell no one about the work I want you to do—"

Niol wanted therapy?

"*No one,* and you—"

Her office door flew open and banged into the wall.

Her breath choked out in surprise. Niol didn't even blink.

"*What the fuck are you doing here, demon?*"

Her very much enraged wolf shifter lover stood in the doorway. Not in cop mode, definitely not. More like jealous fury mode.

And it was sweet, kind of, anyway.

Emily shoved to her feet and hurried to his side. "I'm all right, Colin. I don't need—"

He kicked the door closed. Hard enough to have her windows rattling. "You don't need this jerkoff giving you a hard time. I want you to stay away from Emily, got me, demon? We both know you're trouble and—"

Niol rose slowly to his feet and despite the fact that Colin's claws were out and his teeth were lengthening into fangs, the demon didn't look worried. "I'm not staying away from her."

A growl.

"I need her." His head tilted. "And I'd hate to have to hurt you, seeing as how I know Emily has become uncomfortably fond of you, but *I need her.*"

Colin sprang forward.

Emily grabbed his arm, pulling back at once. "Colin, let him talk." Something was happening here, something important.

Colin's body vibrated beneath her touch. "Fine." Barely human. "But if he pisses me off, I'm taking his head."

A real threat, that.

She turned to Niol. "Why me?"

"You can build the best mental shielding I've ever seen in my life." Admiring. "I need that talent."

Like a level-ten needed help keeping his mind secure from others. "Bullshit." Sometimes, Emily just had to call 'em like she saw 'em.

"A debt, doctor, remember?"

"You're not gettin' in Em's mind! You're not—"

Niol shook his head, interrupting Colin's snarl. "I don't want in her head. I want *her* to use her talent to get into the minds of demons—and to teach them to shield."

Her mouth was open, but Emily didn't know what to say. Demons had their own, instinctive shielding. It came with the psychic power. Why would—

"Sometimes what nature gives isn't enough," Niol said, as if reading her mind.

And the guy probably could.

He strode toward them. Stood toe-to-toe with Colin. "You're in my way, wolf."

Colin's jaw clenched, but after a moment, he stepped to the side.

Niol kept walking. Grabbed the doorknob and wrenched open the door, heading into her waiting room.

"Vanessa called you, didn't she?" Emily whispered. And the man had made amazing time. She craned her neck, watching Niol.

"Hell, yeah, she—"

Niol strode to the left. He stopped and bent toward a dark-haired man and a thin, pale teen.

Then he glanced back at her.

"Who are they?" Colin whispered.

Demons. She saw right through their glamour.

And now they were heading right toward her.

"Colin . . . give me a minute with them, okay?"

The fangs weren't showing now, but the wolf was in his eyes. "You sure?"

Niol answered. "Yes, she's sure."

Colin didn't move.

Emily smiled. "I'm sure." She didn't sense any kind of threat from them, but she did see desperation.

Niol led the other demons into her office. Emily followed at a slower pace, her mind whirling.

The teen sat on the edge of her couch, his hands clenched before him. The older demon—had to be his father, they looked just alike—stood by his shoulder, rocking nervously back and forth on his heels.

Niol didn't sit this time. "Tell me, Doctor Drake . . ."

Now he was being formal?

"Have you ever heard of a demon getting the Dark Touch?"

Her heart slammed into her ribs. *The Dark Touch.*

A demon with the Touch was cursed to only pick up the psychic touch of the evil in the world. Killers, rapists—they all called to the dark demons.

They called and insanity and death followed.

"It first hits at puberty," Niol said. "When a demon's powers begin to develop."

She'd heard that.

"It gets worse as the demon ages. The voices get louder—"

The teen flinched. His eyes were down, boring a hole into the floor.

"Some drugs quiet 'em, for a time. Others just make them scream louder."

The father had his lips pressed together. His eyes stayed up, on her.

Help him. It was in the man's eyes.

She glanced at Niol. And in his.

A bead of sweat trickled down between her shoulder blades. She wouldn't give false hope. The kid would deserve better than that. "Niol, I'm not sure—"

"I am." Absolutely certain. "You can keep a level-ten demon out of your head, you can—"

"Myles was a level-nine," she told him. Niol should know that. He didn't make mistakes—

"I'm not." Black eyes held her. "And you can keep me out without even trying these days."

These days.

It had been a test. One long-ass test.

"Teach him how to block, Dr. Drake. Teach Ken how to keep the voices out and the darkness at bay."

The boy looked up, blinking.

Emily stared at him. His eyes . . . demon black, but familiar.

Because she'd seen that stark fear before. The wild horror that insanity was close.

She'd looked like that, years ago. Every time she'd glanced in a mirror, she'd seen the *same thing*.

A firm nod. "Right." She reached for her pad and motioned for the door. No audience was allowed. Niol knew the rules, of that she had no doubt. "Ken, my name is Emily Drake, and I-I'm going to help you." She *would* help him.

And the others she suspected Niol would be bringing her way.

Niol inclined his head and walked quietly toward the door.

When the door shut, Emily forgot him and turned her attention to Ken.

And the darkness around him. A darkness that was very different from that she sensed around Niol. Because this darkness, maybe she *could* fight it.

Chapter 16

Two car wrecks. A bank robbery. And a shooting in the suburbs.

It had really been one bitch of a day. Holly rolled her shoulders, more than ready to leave the station and head home.

Or to Niol's—because she *needed* to see him.

How bad was that?

A knock sounded on her door. Her *new* door. She'd demanded a new office and gotten one. Granted, it was small and she knew it had been the storage closet until oh—about six hours ago, but she wouldn't complain.

Holly glanced up and found Mac standing in her doorway. "What's up?" She asked cautiously, half afraid the guy would send her out to cover another story.

Not tonight.

His eyes narrowed. "We need to talk, Storm."

Great.

She motioned to the one chair across from her desk. No room for more.

He shut the door and marched over.

He didn't take the seat. "How long you known about 'em?"

She blinked. The lines on Mac's face looked deeper tonight. His hair a bit grayer. "What are you talking about?" With Mac, it could be any—

"The damn fucking demons, Storm. How. Long?"

Her jaw dropped.

"It was that asshole who got torched in the alley, wasn't it?" He shot at her. "Always knew there was more to the case. Figured you had to know after that, especially when you hooked up with Niol." Mac shook his head. "*Christ, Niol?* Were you just looking for the toughest asshole you could find?"

In a way, yeah, she had been.

Holly considered her options, fast.

Okay, she didn't have many and Mac was glaring at her like—

"Knew Niol was a demon the first time I saw him."

How?

"Are . . . you a demon?" That would make sense, but—

"Hell, no." His shoulders stiffened. "Human. One hundred percent human."

She couldn't say the same. "Then how did you—"

"I saw my first demon back in 'Nam. He'd taken a hit, dead center in his chest." His chin lifted. "Knew there wasn't anything I could do. I was a medic with piss little training and I was in a fucking jungle with gunfire all around me." He sucked in a breath. "Told the kid he wasn't alone, thought it would help him. Then he turned his head and looked at me—"

She knew where this was going. At a time like that, the glamour—

"His eyes were *black*. Never seen anything like it before." A pause. Thick. "But I sure as hell have since."

She didn't look away from him. Did he know her own secret?

"More people than you realize know about the demons." His hands were fisted. Big fists, now that she noticed them. "And not all humans are happy about the paranormals."

Not a newsflash.

The small office felt even, well, smaller. The desk separated them, but Mac's gaze seemed to bore into her.

"Some folks think demons should be wiped off the earth."

She'd always liked Mac and his no-nonsense attitude. Always thought he was smart. Tough as nails.

But, dammit, had that just been a threat? "Some folks don't understand this world we live in very well." Her voice was even. Impressive, that. "Demons aren't evil—"

"They're not *all* evil."

"Just like humans!" She fired back.

He nodded. "Thought that would be the case with you. 'Specially after I heard about your new boyfriend."

What in the hell was happening?

He leaned over her desk. Stabbed a finger toward her. "Stay on your guard, Storm. You might be safe, but Niol will always attract trouble."

Then he turned around and stalked out and Holly stared after him, still not sure . . .

Had Mac been threatening her, or trying to warn her?

The storm that had loomed since noon finally unleashed its pounding fury just as Holly ran for Niol's front door. She'd gone to him, headed straight for his house, when she'd finally slipped out of the station just after the last broadcast.

Her skin was soaked in seconds as she ran and—

"Holly."

Niol stood before her. Raindrops slid down his cheeks. His dark T-shirt clung to him, molding to his chest as the rain pounded against him.

He'd been waiting for me?

She stumbled to a halt, caught by his stare and the roar of thunder.

The rain was a cold touch on her skin. Stinging.

And Niol seemed just out of reach.

Then he moved toward her.

Maybe she should have called first. Maybe she was presuming one hell of a lot by showing up on his doorstep, but she'd—

Wanted him. "Niol, I—"

He kissed her. An openmouthed, knee-shaking kiss that screamed possession and lust the way the storm screamed its fury.

His hands locked on her hips. Slid down and caught the curve of her ass. He jerked her against him, right against the bulge of arousal that couldn't be hidden with the wet clothing.

The cold wasn't affecting him.

And it sure wasn't slowing her down any.

His mouth lifted and he stared at her, those secrets still in his eyes. "I was going to stay away."

What?

"Fucking can't."

His head bent and his mouth pressed against her neck. *Oh, yes.* She'd always loved it when—

The swirl of his tongue.

The faintest press of his teeth.

Her nails dug into his shoulders and her head tipped back. If the man wanted access . . .

Her thighs parted and he slid one muscled leg against her core. She rocked against him. Not enough.

Not nearly.

"If we don't get inside in the next thirty seconds . . ." Growled against her throat. Holly shivered. "I'll take you here."

Tempting. She'd never made love in a rainstorm and it sounded wild and sexy and—

And her guards were out there somewhere. Waiting. Watching.

Her eyes opened, blinking against the raindrops. "In . . . side." Okay, yeah, that was her sounding all hoarse. Couldn't help it.

A nip of those teeth.

Heat pooled in her sex.

He grabbed her hand and ran with her toward the brightly lit house. Water splashed around them. Thunder rumbled close by.

The thick wooden door opened just as they reached the steps. Handy trick, that.

Warmth hit her, battling against the chill she'd all but stopped feeling.

The door slammed.

She pushed wet hair out of her eyes. Jeez, she probably looked like hell. Serious drowned-rat syndrome while he—

He looked *good* wet. Hair dripping. Muscles flexing beneath the shirt that clung like a second skin.

Holly swallowed. Oh, damn.

Niol reached for her—

But Holly shook her head. "I'm taking you this time, demon."

He blinked.

She smiled and sank to her knees before him.

"Holly, you don't have to—"

Removing wet jeans was a very tricky business. "I want to." She wanted to taste him so badly that her mouth had gone dry.

The snap popped loose. The zipper hissed down.

His arousal sprang into her hands. Full and long and thick and—

And she wanted him.

Holly bent her head and took the tip of his erection into her mouth.

"Fuck."

Not now, but soon.

She licked him, learning his shape slowly, using her lips and her tongue to tease and take.

As he'd taken her.

A drop of his essence leaked out and she tasted him. Salty, but strangely sweet. He tasted different from a human—better.

She wanted more.

Another inch. Two. His length slid into her mouth as his hands sank into her hair.

"Love, that's good. *So damn good.*"

It was sure good for her. Holly's sex clenched as she took him. More, now, deeper.

His hold on her became harder and her mouth moved faster. Her cheeks pulled in as she took him. Her fingers dug into his ass—*great* ass—and her nipples ached as the need and lust tangled within her.

Her gaze lifted to his face. Flushed cheeks. Shining eyes.

"Dark," he whispered and she knew that her own eyes had changed. His jaw clenched. "No . . . more."

But she wanted more.

His hands pulled her back. "With you, love, or not at all."

Well, she sure wasn't taking the "not at all" option.

Holly rose, knees trembling. She yanked off her shirt, heard the slap of the wet material hitting the floor. With a tug, her bra came loose and her breasts were bared to him, nipples pebbled and hungry.

His lips closed over her nipple and he sucked. A deep, hard pull that was exactly what she'd wanted. His left hand took her other breast. Fondling and squeezing and her hunger built even more.

Getting out of her pants was hard. They clung. They twisted. But after one wild shimmy, she'd ditched them, her shoes, and her panties.

The bed was close. The couch was closer.

Niol had her on the cushions, her legs up and spread, his cock against her eager opening, in a blink.

"Now." A snarl from Niol.

"Now." She growled the word right back at him.

He drove deep.

Yes. What she'd wanted all day.

What she'd needed.

The rhythm was fast and hard. Almost . . . desperate.

Pleasure built and tempted.

Withdraw. Thrust. His fingers marked her flesh, digging deep, just like hers did.

Their eyes locked. Holly's drumming heartbeat filled her ears. She strained against him, needing to be even closer.

The climax slammed into her.

Him.

She lost her breath and could only hold on as the release blasted her. Niol was with her every second. She heard the gasp of his breath, felt the hot pulse of his release, and saw the satisfaction fill his face.

When her heartbeat slowed and the little convulsions in her sex finally eased, Holly realized her legs were around his hips, her heels digging into him. She also realized she didn't want to move.

Her lips curved. Having sex with Niol was damn fine.

"Can't fucking stay away."

A frown pulled her brows low. He'd said something like that before—

Niol kissed her. Hard. Angry. With the edge of desperation she'd felt earlier.

His mouth tore from hers. "Can't."

She didn't understand, but Holly just shook her head, needing to soothe him. "You don't have to—I *want* you with me."

Niol didn't speak. Just kissed her once more.

He had an addiction. A drug of choice that was in his blood, twisting and turning in his veins.

Demons had a problem with addiction. All the paranormals knew that.

He'd been so careful over the years. *So careful.*

Niol turned in the bed and let his gaze fall on Holly's face. Her hair was dry now and curling just a bit. He brushed a lock back from her cheek.

His addiction.

One he'd lie for. Kill for.

And quite possibly even fucking die for.

After seeing the Monster Doctor, he'd thought of Holly. Of her life with him and without him. Niol didn't doubt for even a moment that her life would be a whole lot easier without him.

But I can't stay away.

When he'd seen her car pull into his drive, his cock had hardened instantly and his heart had raced. He hadn't been able to get to her fast enough. To see her. That slow smile that stretched across her face, the wink of that dimple.

Holly had been beautiful in the rain.

No, he hadn't been able to wait to see her—or to take her.

Yet she'd stopped him. Gone to her knees before him and parted those sweet lips.

She'd nearly driven him to *his* knees then.

Sexy, smart, and strong.

His addiction.

His fingers traced the curve of her cheek. *One that I won't give up.*

The conscience that had tried to raise its head was quiet now, hushed by his need and hunger.

He just needed her too fucking much to do the honorable shit and walk away.

Don't make me love you.

Maybe he should have given her the warning sooner.

Too late now, for both of them.

Fucking incompetence. The demon bitch was still alive and guarded by half the police force.

There would be no getting to her now. No slipping inside and finishing up the job, the job that should never have been screwed up in the beginning.

A spleen. *Jesus Christ*—that was useless. A heart would have been something. A brain, oh, yeah, a good, clean brain. The addict's brain hadn't been an option, too screwed up by the chemicals, but the girl—*she would have worked*.

Gloved fingers curved into fists. Not the way the deal should have gone down.

And now there were witnesses. At least that was the story on the news. *Witnesses*. Some nosy bastards who were working with the police on a sketch.

Dammit.

More problems.

If the girl lived, there was no telling what she'd remember. Demons had different responses to the drug she'd been given. Every single time, the response shifted.

No prediction there. Just fear.

Fear.

Fucking demons—they were ruining the world. They

all needed to be killed. Sliced open and drained dry. Only then would the world be a safe place. Only then.

"Have to clean up the mess." Always. No one else could do it right.

The story on the news blared. The anchor cut to an earlier shoot and there was Holly. Going on and on about that freaking sketch.

Lying, evil Holly. Just as twisted as the others. She was another loose end. Too many of those were lying around. Time to cut them all and wipe away the blood.

Mac was sending her ass all over the city. Holly glanced down at her watch. Four fifty-eight p.m. She'd been running with her cameraman since she'd arrived at the station a little after ten that morning.

She'd woken in Niol's arms. A pretty great place to be. But before she'd even had the chance to give him a good-morning kiss, her cell phone had started ringing.

Mac. Telling her to drag her butt into the station because they were short a reporter. Leo Dodge, the police beat reporter, had been involved in a car accident. The guy wasn't hurt too seriously, but he'd broken a leg and sprained his wrist—

And she was the cover for the day.

At first, Sue Patrick had said she'd cover. The blond special-interest reporter had been pushing for more hard-hitting stories. But then she'd backed out, claiming she'd come down with food poisoning.

Highly possible, considering the woman investigated restaurants with health violations every week.

Holly rolled her shoulders. She didn't want to be covering follow-ups on home break-ins and stolen cars. She wanted to be working the Hunter case. Wanted to be at the hospital, by Kim's side.

She might wake up today. Might. The doctors hadn't

seemed too optimistic, but Niol had said that Kim would survive. He knew a lot more about the demon psyche and healing powers than those MDs.

Ben braked the news van in front of a small brick house. Boards covered the front windows. Weeds hid the sidewalk. He pushed back his cap as he leaned forward to get a better view of the place.

Holly frowned. "Uh, we're supposed to be meeting someone *here*?" Creep city. Great. The house looked abandoned. Sitting at the dead end of the small neighborhood, it was separated from the other houses, other *inhabited* houses, by an overgrown lot.

"Mac said we were."

Holly pulled out her notebook. "Vandals," she said. "Twenty-eight-oh-nine Nemoy Road." Mac had told her this house had been targeted three times in the last month by vandals. The place appeared scary as hell, so why vandals would want to break in and spray paint the walls—

"Guess the owner's gonna meet us here?" Ben asked, not looking too confident.

Holly's gaze tracked back to the house. She didn't see anyone. No cars were in the broken driveway. "We'll see." Her thumb jerked toward the sloping porch. "Let's just get some shots. I'll check my notes again and then be ready for a take." If the owner didn't show up, they'd still have material and they could finally wrap up this too-tiring day.

Ben's door squeaked when he shoved it open. He uncoiled his body and stretched. Holly exited on her side, aware of a tension between her shoulder blades. Odd that, when she—

"Shit, I swear I've seen that SUV before."

She rounded the hood and came to his side. His gaze was on the gray SUV near the neighborhood's entrance. Holly forced a smile. "You probably have. SUVs like that are *everywhere* these days."

He grunted, then shook his head as he opened the side

door of the van and grabbed his camera. "Guess you're right."

Her gaze darted back to the SUV. Her guards had been with them all day, and after seeing Kim's injuries, she was real glad of that fact.

While Ben set up, Holly reviewed her notes. Some teens had been arrested two weeks ago, charged with vandalism. Seemed like a pretty straightforward story.

"Help me . . ."

The hair on Holly's nape rose.

Her gaze lifted from the notes and zeroed in on the house. "Uh . . . Ben?"

Another grunt.

Then a curse as he banged his knee on the van.

"Did you hear that?" She asked quietly, turning to stare at him.

His brows bunched together. "Hear what?" His cap cast a shadow over his face.

Great. "Nothing."

But . . .

"Help."

Holly jumped. Okay, that was a woman's voice. Weak, but definitely a voice and it was coming from inside the house.

"What the fuck?" Ben shoved his camera back into the van and took off toward the house.

"Ben, wait!" She ran after him, managing to catch him near the steps and grab his arm.

"Somebody needs help, Hol! We've got to get inside—"

Her stomach knotted. Something felt *wrong*.

It is wrong. Someone is inside, probably hurt, and you're dawdling your ass out front. Get moving! She swallowed. "Right, let's—"

He was gone. For a big guy, he sure could move fast.

God, please, don't let me find another broken body.

She hurried after him, yanking her cell phone out.

He kicked the door open and ran inside, calling out, "Hey! Hey, we're here! Where are you? Where are—" He bounded down the hall.

"Nine-one-one operator. Please state your emergency." A polite female voice said in her ear.

"Ben, wait! Ah—I'm at 2809 Nemoy Road. Someone's hurt—"

"What's the nature of the injury?"

"It's a—"

Thud.

Her fingers squeezed the phone. "Hold on," she whispered. Then, louder, "Ben?" He'd gone into the room up toward the right, but she didn't hear him anymore. "Did you find someone? Ben?"

Oh, shit, this wasn't *good*.

"Help me."

Not Ben's voice. The woman's. But coming from the room Ben had just entered, she was sure of it.

Why wasn't Ben talking?

What the hell was going on?

Run. Her instincts screamed at her but she couldn't leave Ben behind.

"Send the cops." Her voice was so soft she was afraid the operator wouldn't hear her. Holly stepped back, slowly.

I can't leave him.

She needed a weapon. Something, anything, but the house was empty. No furniture anywhere.

Just red-paint-stained walls.

The paint reminded her way too much of blood right then.

She kept her phone on, just in case. She'd done a report once on tracking cell phones. Help could find her that way.

The operator kept talking. Asked how many people were hurt, but responding back to the woman right then was probably not the best idea ever.

The guards are outside. I can run out and get them—
And Ben could be dead before she got back.

Holly had seen how fast killers could work.

Fumbling, she slid the phone into her purse and managed to pull out her can of mace. Not much of a weapon. Damn little, but there was no choice.

The door to that room squeaked as it swung inward.

"Ben?" She raised her voice. Tried to sound in control. *Answer me.*

No answer.

Holly lifted the mace and her death grip tightened on it.

"The police are coming! They'll be here any second—" More like in ten or fifteen minutes, but what the hell. She wasn't—

A growl. A deep, inhuman sound of fury. Then a figure in black shot out of the room and ran toward her, with something glinting in his hand.

Holy shit—a knife!

Her finger jerked on the mace and a stream of liquid shot right toward the guy in the black ski mask.

A high-pitched scream.

The flash of the knife.

Holly jerked back and felt a burn on her side—*No, no, no.* The mace fell from her fingers as she kicked out. A long-delayed response that she still thanked God that her Tae Bo instructor had taught her years ago. Her foot caught the attacker's stomach and shoved him back.

Then Holly ran as fast as she could. Because her Tae Bo skills were pretty poor.

The guards. Get to the guards. "Help!" Her scream was deafening. She was proud of that. And scared because her side throbbed with a burning pain.

The guards would have more acute senses than a human's. Even as far away as they were, they'd be able to hear her—

"Holly! Holly Storm!"

She loved her some demons.

Two men stormed in the front door.

"Watch out! He's got a knife—" Holly glanced back over her shoulder.

No one was there.

What?

One of the men, a big, burly, linebacker, I'll-Break-You type shoved past her.

Wincing, Holly grabbed her side and wasn't the least bit surprised to feel something wet and sticky touch her fingers.

Not now.

"My cameraman's missing!" She yelled to the other guy, pressing down hard with her hand. "We have to find him and make sure he's all right—" And they needed to find the psycho in black.

Oh, damn, but when had she ever been this glad to see a demon?

The guy—Burns something—hurried toward her. "*You're* hurt—"

A door slammed. Had to be the back door. The linebacker was giving chase. Good.

"I'm okay—no, stop, I'm all right!" He was trying to pull her hand away, but she didn't want to look at the wound then. Holly wrestled out of his hold and ran toward the end of the house.

I'm running, can't be hurt too bad.

The demon reached the door before her. She took a deep breath, but could only smell her own blood. "Ben?"

Her guard went in first. Holly tailed right after him.

Ben was pushing himself up from the floor. An old board, looked like a two-by-four that had fallen from the ceiling, lay beside him. He blinked up at her. "Hol? Wh-what's goin' on?"

She could have kissed him then. "Take it easy, Ben."

He lifted his hand and touched the back of his head. "What the hell hit me?" His baseball cap lay on the stained floor beside him.

They already knew the *what*. Now they had to figure out *who*.

The thud of footsteps. Holly glanced over her shoulder, aware of a faint prickling in her face.

The linebacker shook his head. "Long gone."

Hell.

"Did we . . . stumble onto the v-vandals?" Ben's voice drew her gaze back to him. He was on his feet now, swaying just a bit.

"I don't . . . think so." No, not vandals. There was no spray paint around. The guy who'd come after her had been sporting a knife. He'd meant some serious business.

He'd been waiting for them. Hiding in the house and waiting for them to come inside.

How had he known they'd be there? Only Mac knew.

Mac.

"We are in such fucking trouble." The linebacker's eyes were on her fingers—her *bloody* fingers.

"Hol?" Ben paled. "We've got to get you to a hospital, we've got—"

On perfect cue, the wail of a siren cut through the air.

Holly hoped, really hoped, that the dispatch lady had sent an ambulance because the world around her was starting to dim.

When Holly opened her eyes, a bright light shone right in her face. She winced and tried to turn away.

"Coming back, are you?" A woman's voice. Dry.

Holly blinked and attempted to focus past the light.

"Hi, there." A face appeared before her. A woman with faint laugh lines around her eyes and a green hospital cap over her hair. A white mask was pulled low, dangling from her throat. "You're all stitched up, hon. Should be good as new."

Stitched up? What was she—

The house.

The psycho with the knife.

Holly shot up, nearly slamming her head into the doctor.

"Easy . . ."

"Did you put me out?"

A quick smile. "No, hon, you were out when the EMTs brought you here." She pushed an instrument tray away. Holly glanced at that tray and tried not to think about Kim.

Failed.

"You needed eleven stitches. You were really lucky—"

Wasn't that the truth.

"The blade dug across your skin, but you managed to deflect the brunt of the hit."

Her shirt was gone. She wore a hospital gown, one gaping open in the front. Perfect. Holly jerked it closed and winced when she felt the pull of the stitches.

"You've got a crowd outside." One blond brow rose. "Lot of folks must care about you."

"*I want to see her—now.*" The roar penetrated right through the walls.

"Yep, sure must care."

That familiar roar—Niol's voice.

"Think you can walk out under your own steam?"

Fifty-fifty shot of that.

"Usually, we're supposed to keep folks in for observation, but . . ." A delicate pause and the cheerful gray eyes suddenly darkened to black. "You're not most folks, are you?"

Her breath caught. "How did you—"

A wink. "I knew your grandmother." She handed Holly her shirt. "Take care, little demon." Then the doctor turned around and walked away.

At the first opportunity, Niol was going to nail demon ass to the walls of his bar. Niol glared at the two ex-guards, his body vibrating with fury. "Where the hell were you two while Holly was getting attacked?"

They looked at each other.

Niol's back teeth locked. He'd thought she was safe—

Like Gillian.

—and she'd nearly been killed.

On his watch.

That bitter taste in his throat, he knew it was fear. Not a damn thing he could do about it.

The air in the waiting room was thick and hot. From him. The rage inside screamed for release.

His control held only by the thinnest thread.

Need to see Holly. Have to touch her.

"Ease up, Niol."

That jackass human detective again. Niol tightened his fingers into fists. It would be so easy to send him through the window. He'd tell Cara it had been an accident. No big deal.

"It was just a flesh wound. I saw her myself—she's fine."

She'd better be.

Too many times. Holly had nearly been killed *again.*

What the fuck?

Niol had thought, after the attack at the club, that the hunter was coming for him.

But he'd been wrong and Holly had paid for his mistake.

The impure will die.

The message had been loud and clear, but the picture had been of him *and* Holly.

The bastard knew her secret, knew even when she hadn't, and his lady was on the hunter's list.

Time to kill the asshole and incinerate his soul.

"Get on the streets," he ordered the demons. "Find him." They knew damn sure who he was talking about. "I don't care who you have to bribe or who you have to hurt—"

"Ah, Niol—" Brooks's eyes widened.

"Find him."

They nodded.

He stabbed a finger toward Brooks even as he heard the crack of glass behind him. *There go the windows. Can't stop it.* "Tell your partner *we're* hunting again, and this time, *I'll* find the prey before he does."

The shifter would know exactly what he was talking about. Gyth had beaten him to the last kill they'd competed for, but not this time.

This time, he'd be the one to send the sick bastard to hell.

No one touched Holly. No one made her bleed.

No fucking one.

"Niol, calm down."

He spun at the female voice. Quiet and soothing.

Cara.

The succubus stood just inside the doorway, her blond hair a halo around her. Absolute perfection—from the top of her perfect hair to the tips of her dainty, fire-engine-red-painted toenails—and she didn't do a thing for him.

Not with her powers, not with her body.

Because he was a demon long gone.

Shit. *Shit.*

"He's trying to kill her."

He heard a gasp from the right. Holly's mother. She'd arrived a few minutes ago, her nervous hands fluttering as she eyed the ER doors. She hadn't spoken to him, and he hadn't been sure of what to say to her.

Probably not the best thing to say in front of Holly's mother, but—

He was scared.

Time was running out, he could feel it.

I won't lose her.

Cara stepped forward. "Brooks isn't going to let that happen."

"No, *I'm* not," Niol snapped. Cara knew better, she *knew* what he had done in the past. He wasn't one to stand by and let another—

"Niol, don't go down this path again." She was right in front of him, her voice was soft, and he knew she didn't want the others to hear.

He didn't really care about them.

But he sucked in a breath and fought for calm.

"Let the police take care of this," she whispered, and her hand caught his arm. "I don't want—Niol, you have to be careful."

She knew what he'd done, and Niol also knew that Cara had kept his secret. When Nina had been murdered, he'd gone after her killer. It hadn't been pretty and the death hadn't been easy.

Vengeance never was.

"You lose a bit of yourself every time you cross the line." Her gaze held his. "If you keep going this way, one day, there won't be anything left."

Niol shook his head. "He went after her." No choice. He couldn't risk another attack. Hell, how many more attacks could Holly survive? "He's killing demons in my city, doing things you don't want to know about." He'd bet the cop hadn't told her about the hunter's organ-snatching. "He has to be stopped."

But first, he had to be found.

The faint scent of lavender.

Niol's head jerked up. Holly, pale, with wide eyes, stood in the doorway. The same spot Cara had held moments before, but—

So different.

Not built for temptation like the succubus. Her hair was a wild curtain of fire around her face. Her lips were still, all color gone from them. Borrowed scrubs covered her, and her slim hands twisted in front of her.

The most beautiful thing he'd ever seen.

Niol went to her. Pulled her tight against him, felt the thud of her heart and the fragile strength of her bones.

He wanted her then. Wanted to kiss her and take her and make sure she was *all right*.

And he wanted to just . . . hold her. To keep feeling the soft vibration of her heart. To know that she was safe.

"You've got to stop doing this to me," he grated, and pressed a kiss to her forehead.

"I'll try," was her response, so quiet and calm, just like Holly. *Just like his Holly.*

His lips tried to curve.

Lost. So very lost in her.

He caught her chin. Lifted her head. And kissed her.

It should have been an easy kiss. Gentle. Delicate. She deserved that now.

But he wasn't a gentle man and he needed to taste her too much.

Wild and hard—it was his way.

And hers—because she kissed him right back with the same fierce need.

The silence in the room behind them thickened.

His hold tightened on her and she made a soft sound in the back of her throat. A moan, a sigh and he wanted her even more.

When he lifted his head, Niol had no idea how much time had passed. Didn't really care. Color was back in

Holly's face, staining her cheeks, and her eyes sparkled with life again.

Better. So much better.

A cough behind him.

Niol turned but kept Holly in his arms.

"Baby, are you all right?" Her mother asked.

"Yeah, Mom, I'm fine." Her smile didn't look too convincing.

Kelly's gaze turned to him. "You'll stop him?" There was knowledge there, and Niol realized that Holly and her mother must have had one big revelations night.

"I will."

"The police will—" Brooks began.

But Niol cut him off. "Find him first," he challenged.

Kelly gave a nod. "Good. Good." Then she pushed Niol's arms aside and hugged her daughter.

"So she's why." Cara. Soft and almost sad. "Be careful, Niol. You know your weakness."

His weakness stood right beside him. Yes, he knew.

The succubus turned to her lover with a shrug. "You'd better find him first."

"Damn."

And Niol knew the cop had brought Cara in to calm him down. Pity he wasn't in the calming mood.

But he *was* in the killing mood.

Let the games begin.

Niol took Holly home. He wanted her by his side, where he could be certain that she was safe.

But he also needed to be on the streets. Because no one could put the fear of the devil into the lowlifes he needed to talk to quite like, well, he could.

But being with Holly—that came first.

He took her to his house and up to his bed. He stripped her, being careful not to touch her wound.

She watched him with her emerald eyes. So quiet and close, but seeming so far away.

"You . . . never slept with Cara, did you?"

Not the question he'd expected.

Holly rubbed a hand over her face. "Ugh! I can't believe I just asked that! Don't tell me, it doesn't matter, I—"

"No. I never did." It mattered or she wouldn't have asked. "I was involved with her sister, but I think you know that."

And she knew the way that story ended.

A hard exhale. "I do, *I know.* But when I came in there and saw the two of you . . ."

"What?"

Her head fell back against the pillows. "I was jealous, okay?"

More than okay with him. "Good."

"What? No, not 'good.' Good isn't wanting to yank another woman's hair out right after you've had a doctor shoving stitches in your side."

The woman could make him smile.

"Hell of a day." She covered her eyes with the side of her arm. "And it's only gonna get worse from here on out, isn't it?"

Yes, it was.

"I have to . . . go out." He couldn't delay any longer. She'd be completely safe in his house. He'd doubled her guards, but in the house, she wouldn't need them. No one could get past his security.

Her arm slowly lowered. "What are you going to do?"

So far, he'd played this game by human rules. For her. He'd tried to be good, tried to rein in the monster inside.

And all he'd gotten for his trouble was her pain.

"Whatever I have to do." If he had to rip into minds—human or *Other*—to find the bastard out there, he would.

This shit ended tonight.

"Niol . . ."

He put his fingers to her lips. Such soft lips. "I don't have a choice anymore. He's come too close." *To you.*

He wouldn't tell her any more. She didn't need his plans on her conscience.

"Stay here. You'll be safe." He kissed her because he had to. "I'll be back before you know it." Niol started to rise.

Holly caught his arm. "I heard what Cara told you."

Cara was like family to him, but right then, he could have easily kicked her curvy ass from the city.

"Don't do this for me. Don't hurt innocents for me. I don't want that—dammit, Niol, that's not who you are—"

"Isn't it?" Maybe it was time they both stopped pretending. Nice little fantasy, but here's ugly reality. "You need to see me, Holly. All of me." Before it was too late for her.

Maybe it already was. He stared into her eyes and saw straight to her soul.

I don't deserve her.

But he'd fight like hell on fire for her. "Stay here, Holly—"

"While you go out and fight the monster in the dark?"

He *was* the monster in the dark. "You can't come with me this time."

She pushed up on her elbows. "I thought we were partners on this case, remember? The whole point was that you were supposed to give me access to your world."

Not this part. "Is that what we are now?" He asked softly. "Partners, just working on the case?"

Her pupils flared at that. "You tell me."

Stubborn woman. He even liked *that.* "I agreed to help you because I wanted you in my bed." Couldn't get more stark and honest than that.

She wet her lips. "I came to you because I wanted your help . . . and because I wanted you in *my* bed." Her chin was up. "After the shit hit the fan—"

Not delicate, his Holly. He didn't want delicate.

"I stayed around because I wanted *you*."

Good that, he liked—

"But we're still partners, Niol, and partners don't abandon each other."

He stiffened. "I'm not abandoning you."

"Let me come with you then, let me—"

His gaze fell away from hers. Because when he admitted this, he couldn't stare into her eyes. "You make me weak."

Silence.

"I think of you too much, worry about you. I-I can't do that when I hunt." When he used his powers, like he planned tonight, when he went into the darkness so far, there was no room for inattention.

"Niol . . ."

His stare returned to her. "You're hurt, Holly. You have to heal, and I can't hunt tonight with you." No more to say. She might be pissed at him, but there was no choice.

He wouldn't risk her.

Niol headed for the door.

"Don't hurt an innocent, Niol."

Glancing back over his shoulder, he forced a smile. "Love, there aren't any of those left anymore."

Not true.

He was staring straight into the soul of an innocent right then. One who'd never touched evil, well, not until she'd touched him.

Sleeping wasn't an option for her. After Niol left, Holly paced the floor of his house. Upstairs, downstairs, as she went *crazy*.

She called the hospital to check on Kim. Of course, they told her *nothing*. Not that she blamed the staff, really.

She knew Kim was being protected and information on her had to be kept close to the vest.

Before she and Niol had left the hospital, they'd stopped with Brooks to check on Kim.

Still unconscious and the doctors had no idea when or *if* she'd wake up.

Holly rubbed her eyes. They were so grainy at this point that they hurt, but she couldn't stop thinking about Niol or about the bastard who'd attacked her.

A man. Tall, broad-shouldered.

But she'd heard a woman's voice calling for help, and Kim had been attacked by a woman.

Holly didn't think for even a moment that the two incidents weren't related. Coincidence—hell, no, she wasn't buying that anymore. So that meant—

Either the woman had hired another guy to do her dirty work for her, a distinct possibility . . .

Or maybe . . . just maybe she wasn't looking at a single killer.

Her breath hitched.

A team. She'd seen this before. In her last big murder case, a woman had been helping the killer lure in his victims. They'd been a bloodthirsty team, right until the end—when the male had decided it was time to ditch his partner in crime.

He'd ditched her the nice, old-fashioned way. He'd left her broken body for the police to find.

A team. The more she thought about the idea, the harder her heart pounded.

The shrill ring of her cell phone had Holly jumping. She whirled around and saw her bag on the nearby countertop.

Holly answered on the fifth ring.

"Dammit, Storm, where the hell are you?" Mac's voice.

Her blood chilled. She didn't trust him, not anymore. "I'm resting because it's the middle of the night. Where the hell are you?"

"At Kent Towers downtown. We've got a bomb threat and I need your ass down here to get this story! The idiots from Channel Seven are already on the scene. Ben's on his way but I *need* you here, Holly."

"Get someone else." *Don't trust him.* He'd sent her to the house on Nemoy. He'd warned her. Okay, she was pretty sure he'd threatened her, too.

"*There is nobody else.* You're the best damned reporter at the station and you know it! Christ, look, I'm sorry for stepping on your toes, earlier, okay? You wanna date the king of all demons—fine, date the king of all demons. Just get your ass down here!" The scream of a siren sounded in the background. "Fuck, bomb squad is here. *I need you.*"

He sounded just like the old Mac. Not dark and threatening. Just . . . Mac.

This is my job.

"They're gonna scoop me, Holly. Come on . . ."

But I can't take a chance with my life. "I'll be there, but I'm not coming alone." She'd take the guards and they'd better stay *close* this time.

"Fine—bring a damn entourage, I don't care! Just get your ass over here!"

Click.

Sure didn't sound like a man bent on her death.

Holly grabbed her keys and rushed for the door.

"This is Holly Storm, reporting live from Kent Towers, where bomb squad members have just wrapped up an intensive four-hour search of the building. No bombs were found . . ." A good thing in her mind. "But investigators aren't closing the case yet. Now their attention will turn to tracking the person who made the false claim." And throwing his ass in jail. "I'll be back with more live news later in the day." When most of the folks would actually be *awake.* "Back to you in the newsroom, Steve . . ."

She waited a beat until she got the clear from Ben, then her shoulders dropped.

For the last two hours, she'd been running on fumes. Those fumes were gone now and she'd be crashing in the next half hour.

Where was Niol?

Maybe he'd be back home when she got there.

As long as he's safe.

Mac was gone. He'd cleared out when word had first come down about the hoax. The guy had been assured that he wouldn't be scooped, and, satisfied, he'd taken off.

And left her and Ben to carry the story.

Poor Ben looked like he'd been beat, hard.

But, then again, he had.

"Get some sleep, Holly," he said and she realized she probably looked the same way.

Her side throbbed.

"I'll see you tonight at the station." He dragged his camera away.

Her guards stepped forward.

"Holly!"

She winced at the call, recognizing the voice instantly. *Not what I need.*

She turned and caught sight of Zack. His face was flushed as he hurried toward her.

"Your mother called and told me what happened—"

Her mother had done *what?*

"When I found out you were here, I had to come—"

"Give me a minute," she told the guards. Just seeing the man made her head throb.

Some of the other reporters were still around and she sure didn't want them hearing *this* conversation. The entrance to a parking garage was just a few feet away. She maneuvered Zack that way. The guards could still see her there, but the reporters wouldn't be able to overhear this little talk.

The sun had just begun its ascent and the pink colors from the sky spilled a few steps inside the cavelike entrance of the garage.

He grabbed her shoulders and pulled her close. "You could have been killed."

"But I wasn't." She pushed him away. "Zack, stop doing this, okay? I am not your concern anymore."

A muscle flexed in his jaw. "I want you to be."

The guy was thick. "I'm with someone else now, Zack, and I'm happy with him." True, and that realization stopped her. They were neck-high in trouble, but when she was with Niol, she was . . . happy.

Well, damn.

"I've met your 'someone else.' He's not right for you." His lips thinned. "He's dead wrong."

"Not your call to make." Holly took a deep breath. "You came. You saw that I was all right. There's no reason for you to stay here anymore."

"Holly, I—"

"We're *over,* Zack." Couldn't get clearer than that. Her voice was calm as she said, "Stay away from now on, okay?"

He stared at her. Eyes so intense. "If that's what you really want . . ."

It was.

"I'm sorry for what happened. Sorrier than I can ever say." He swallowed. "I fucked up, but I guess—I guess there are some things that can't ever be changed, huh?"

For a second, he was the guy she'd first met. The nice guy. Smart. With the kind eyes.

"Good luck, Holly. I mean that. Have a good life." He snapped his mouth closed, as if he wanted to say something else, but he was stopping himself. Then he spun on his heel. Strode to the row of cars parked on the far right side of the garage.

Holly blinked. Well, okay, that had gone much better than she'd hoped.

Now, time to get out of there before the exhaustion had her falling on her face. She needed to—

Holly froze. Then her gaze very slowly backtracked to the row of cars on the right side of the garage. Zack was sliding into his Corvette, his back to her, but two cars over—

A white van sat parked in the semidarkness.

There had to be hundreds of white vans in the city. *Doesn't mean that was the one that nearly ran me over.*

But . . .

But she'd already stopped believing in coincidence.

Her guards. Holly spun around. They were talking to someone. Who was that? Mac?

"Hey! *Hey,* I—"Something slammed into the side of her head and Holly hit the concrete.

Chapter 17

She *hurt*. Holly didn't want to open her eyes because the pain was so intense.

And because she was afraid.

A grinding teased her ears. Grinding, grinding . . .

No, not a grinding, the sound of a car moving.

The van.

Her eyes flew open, but she could see only darkness. *What the hell?*

She shook her head, twisting—*oh, God, what happened to me?* Her eyes—no, not blind, *a blindfold.* The fabric slipped just a bit. Holly tried to wrench her hands up but couldn't move.

She was tied, her hands bound behind her, her feet strapped together.

No! Someone had lodged a thick cloth in her mouth, so she couldn't cry out. Holly could only lay there, and wait for whatever the hell would come next.

Kim, strapped to that table, blood all around her.

No.

* * *

Niol stared at the vampire before him, the stench of decay filling his nose. The bastard was smiling, long, thin fangs glinting.

"You think I'm scared of you, demon? I'm fucking immortal! Nothing scares me!"

Idiot. Had to be newly turned. Niol smiled. "Just because you *can* live forever, asshole, doesn't mean you *will*." He focused his power, felt that sweet rush of dark heat, and threw the vamp across the room.

The guy smashed into a table. Niol moved fast, grabbed a broken piece of wood, and shoved it right over the vampire's heart. "Now, for the last time, what do you know about the woman at Myer's who hired those idiots to torch my bar?" Because it was all connected. *Dots.* Little fucking dots. All he had to do was follow the trail and find his killer.

"S-she w-wasn't into v-vamps . . ." Gasped out.

Better. At least the asshole wasn't denying he'd seen the woman anymore. Niol had gone through three demons and one shifter to get to this asshole. *Connecting the fucking dots.* Everybody remembered something. Remembered seeing someone, somewhere.

This guy—Lane Mims—he was the link Niol needed.

"Who was she interested in?"

"D-demons. Only w-wanted to w-watch d-demons . . ."

Niol's muscles tightened. "Why?"

"L-let me go!"

"Tell me what I want and maybe I will." He shoved the weapon a good half-inch into the vampire's chest. "Tell me nothing and I'll kill you."

Blood coated the vamp's shirt. "D-don't know wh-why. She-she just watched d-demons."

Because she wanted to slice them to bits?

"What else do you know about her?"

"She-she was a student at MU."

Mellrune University. Niol's blood heated. *What were the odds?*

Lines of pain etched onto the vamp's face. "F-followed her one n-night."

Yes, he knew that. Knew that old Lane made a habit of following human women—and sometimes doing more. When he'd been human, the guy had landed in jail twice for rape. Becoming a vampire sure hadn't changed the guy for the better, and Niol knew his human habits hadn't faded. "And?"

"W-went to some lab at the u-university." The vamp's breath blew into his face. Rancid.

"You mean to tell me you followed the blonde back to the university one quiet night . . ." Lane only hunted at night. "She went into a deserted lab, and you didn't take a bite?" Niol shook his head. "Lane, I'm disappointed." *By your bullshit.*

The vampire's eyes narrowed and the evil inside showed its face. "B-bitch wasn't . . . alone."

Niol eased up the pressure on the vampire's chest, just a bit. "Really?"

"Some ass-asshole with her. S-started m-making out w-with h-him the minute . . . she w-went inside—place smelled l-like f-fucking bleach—"

Niol bet the lab had smelled better than the vamp. He clenched his back teeth and ordered, "Tell me what the man looked like."

The vamp's head shook. "C-couldn't . . . s-see much—"

Niol smiled. "I know you, Lane. I know you like to watch." Watching and hurting. That was the way Lane got off with his prey.

A smile, trembling with pain but wide with memories. "N-never know h-how close . . . to-to d-death they are—"

His fingers tightened around the wood. No, some people never knew.

He's not an innocent. After the jerk finishes telling me what I want, no reason I can't stake his ass.

Holly's face flashed before him.

"What. Did. He. Look. Like?"

"T-tall. B-blond."

Every damn dot connected. *Fuck.*

"B-big d-dick—"

His cell phone rang.

The call that saved the asshole's life.

"Hold him," he snarled to the demon on his right.

Thomas gave a grimace but took over vamp duty.

Niol glanced down at the phone and felt his gut tighten. *Holly's guards.* But, no, it wasn't them.

It was a number he'd never seen before. His eyes on the squirming vampire, he punched the button to take the call. "Who the hell is this?"

Laughter. Cold and high.

"Got somethin' of yours." The voice was female. Mocking.

"Do you?" He'd never sounded calmer or been more afraid. Not Holly. Not her—

A lamb among wolves. And she hadn't even known it.

"I'm going to slice her open, from groin to neck." More laughter.

Niol fought not to incinerate everyone and everything around him. *"Don't touch her."* The demons around him stilled at his fury.

They knew his moods well and he saw their eyes jerk to the exits.

"Try and stop me." A taunting whisper.

The vampire whimpered.

"If you really want to save the demon reporter, then come and get her."

A trap—one meant to catch and kill him. Niol didn't care. The crazy bitch had the perfect bait. "Where?"

More laughter. "You come alone—*and you tell no one*—or you'll find Storm in pieces."

The woman had just asked for her own death. "Agreed."

A sound that could have been a purr. Then she rattled off the address and said, "Can't wait to see you, *love.*"

The call ended and the rage exploded.

She was bait. Holly curled against the floor of the van. Bait to lure Niol to his death.

"You're awake, aren't you, demon?" That voice seemed familiar.

Holly didn't move.

"I know you are." Screamed.

Not even a flinch. She wasn't about to let her body betray her.

Where had she heard that voice?

"Your lover's coming, and I'm going to have so much fun playing with him."

The van jerked to a stop. Holly let her body roll forward. Her head rammed into some kind of bag.

"Dammit, she's still out."

Not alone. Holly forced herself to keep breathing slowly. The psycho woman was talking to someone else. Holly had only heard the woman speak. She'd woken just before the bitch called Niol.

"You think he'll really come after her?" The woman asked, her voice high and shaking with excitement.

One of the van's doors squeaked open. A second door opened immediately after.

Definitely not alone.

Christ. *Where have I heard that voice before?*

She could have told the woman that, yes, Niol would come after her. Holly didn't doubt it for a minute. He'd come after her and bring hell's fury in his wake.

She'd seen the fury before and knew that she'd see it again.

Provided, of course, she could stay alive until he came for her.

The doors slammed shut. One, then the other.

Breathe. Breathe.

Squeaks and groans as the van's back doors opened.

Then hands closed around her ankles and yanked her toward the killer.

"Come on, Holly, you're not fucking fooling me." A man's voice.

And this voice—she knew it instantly.

No.

He jerked her up and ripped away the blindfold.

Holly blinked and stared up at the face she knew too well.

Zack.

She shook her head. *This isn't happening.* Why would Zack want to hurt her? Or Sam? Or—

"Fucking demon." He turned his head toward the woman. "See her eyes, Michelle? I told you she was just like the rest of them."

Michelle. Blond grad student Michelle. Ms. I'll-Do-Anything-for-that-A Michelle.

Michelle smiled at her, smiled with her perfect capped teeth, and said, "This is really going to hurt you."

Holly almost choked on the gag.

"Let's get her inside and on the table. We'll keep her alive until he gets here." Zack licked his lips. "I can't wait to cut him open. Those other demon bastards said he was the strongest—"

They'd probably been willing to say anything before they died.

"I'll find the secret with him, I know I will."

The secret?

I was engaged to this freak?

She shook her head again. No, Zack couldn't be in front of her, he couldn't be planning to kill her, to slice her up and—

And Zack made his living dissecting specimens and studying them.

He held up a syringe. "For old times' sake, I can make this easy on you." He reached for the gag and wrenched it out of her mouth.

Holly licked her lips and tasted blood. Probably from that nice smack she'd taken into the concrete.

"What do you say, Holly? You don't have to feel the pain. One little stick and you'll slide right into the darkness."

The darkness. "Fuck you, asshole." She wouldn't make this easy on him. *Not Zack. This couldn't be happening.*

His lips tightened. "Then, demon whore, get ready to scream."

And she did. A loud, long desperate scream that she really hoped someone would hear.

Come on, just let one shifter be within a five-mile radius . . .

Zack's fist came right at her face.

When she opened her eyes the next time, Holly was strapped to a table. *An operating table.* Oh, damn—not a nightmare.

Michelle's smiling face popped over her. "Wakey again, huh?"

Yeah, it *was* a nightmare. Holly growled and jerked against the restraints that held her.

Michelle leaned closer and whispered in her ear. "You should have taken the drugs. Zack likes to play."

Bile rose.

The blonde pulled back and glanced over her shoulder. Then she reached for the instrument tray and picked up a scalpel. The light glinted off the sharp edge. Another sweet smile. "He likes to play," she said again, "and so do I."

And then the crazy bitch took the scalpel and sliced down Holly's left arm.

She screamed, her head jerking off the table.

"No one's going to help you, Holly." Zack. Twisted, *insane* Zack. Zack the Demon-Hunter. His footsteps slapped against the floor and then he was beside Michelle. "Things like you," he continued, "don't deserve to live."

Her arm burned with a fiery pain and the blood flowed out, fast and hard. "And you think sadistic killers like you do?" Had he always been crazy? How could she have missed this?

Shit—she was a reporter! She should have been able to see crazy staring her right in the face.

But he'd hid so well from her.

Zack frowned, his perfect brow lining. "I'm not a killer. I'm a scientist."

"You're fucking insane!" If she got loose, she was going right for his throat.

The lines faded from his forehead. "You would think that, I suppose. Being what you are." His fingers reached out and smoothed back her hair.

Michelle's grip on the scalpel tightened.

"I should thank you, Holly." His fingers lingered on her cheek.

She jerked her head away from him.

"If it hadn't been for you, I never would have even known about the *monsters* who live in this world. I didn't realize what was right in front of me." His lip curled in disgust. "The impure, trying to desecrate the human race with their taint—"

She wouldn't listen to his bullshit. "You're the only

monster I've seen, Zack. You've *killed*. Carl. Sam. Julia. Those weren't specimens in your lab, they were people. People with families and lives and—"

His fingers clamped over her mouth. "They weren't people. They were demons."

The pressure of his hand was almost enough to break her jaw.

"Demons . . . like you." He glanced at Michelle. "I can still remember when I first really saw *you*. You'd been lying to me, tricking me—"

"I told you she wasn't good enough for you," Michelle muttered, glaring. "Right from the beginning, I told you!"

His fingers lifted and he wiped them on his shirt.

As if he were cleaning himself off.

Asshole.

"Then when you surprised me that day at my office—"

You mean when I caught you with your head between her—

"Your eyes changed. Flashed to black."

Her chest ached worse than her arm and her head. She'd unknowingly revealed too much to him, and so many had paid the price for her mistake.

"At first I thought I'd imagined it."

"But I saw it, too," Michelle piped up with a nod. "And I'd seen it before . . ."

"Michelle knew what you were."

And she knew exactly *what* Michelle was, too.

"So I started watching you and you lead me to the others."

Something was squeezing her heart. Too tight. "You didn't have to kill them."

He blinked and actually looked confused. "Of course, I did. How else could I study them? I had to look inside—"

Oh, God.

"—to see if I could find the source of their power."

Michelle tossed her scalpel back onto the tray. "It's all genetics. I've told you that from the beginning."

"I think there are differences in the brain. There have to be in order to account for the psychic surges in the demon population."

"But genetics are—"

They were arguing like they were in a damn lecture hall. They'd killed, terrorized, all for—"Some kind of sick experiment!"

They shut up, finally, and turned their stares back to her.

Zack nodded. "You do understand."

Hell, no, she didn't. "You cut them up, sliced them apart to—"

"Ah . . . now, I *had* to do a bit of work with my knife, bloody things up, you know—couldn't have it looking like a professional just went right in and extracted an organ or two."

Bloody things up.

"If I hadn't used the knife to hide most of my scalpel incisions, the cops would have known that a . . . professional was working."

Working? Working! Professional, her ass. *Psychotic.*

"Your lover will be the perfect specimen," Zack said with a nod. "All his strength . . . I know I'll find the secret with him."

Once he cut Niol open.

Not going to happen.

"You don't know what you're dealing with. You should get the hell out of here while you can."

"The demon's not going to hurt me." A twist of his lips. "Come on, you know better."

"I-I've seen him kill. He'll destroy you."

"I've seen him kill, too," Michelle said. "For *you.*"

We started watching.

Zack tapped his chin. "I think the demon will do just about anything for you."

"No, you're wrong!"

"He won't leave you here to die. He'll come for you. Come alone, and when he does . . ."

Michelle lifted a syringe. "I'll be ready."

Her eyes narrowed on that syringe. "What is that?" Fear hushed her voice because sure, she knew Niol was kick-ass strong and she'd been trying to scare the psychopaths around her, *but* . . .

But they were acting too confident. They knew full well just how dangerous Niol was—that was obvious. They *wanted* him because he was dangerous.

"You knew that I had a master's degree in pharmacology, didn't you, Holly?" Zack took the syringe from Holly. "This is a little brew I'm pretty proud of, I've got to say. Sure, it doesn't work perfectly. I haven't quite figured out the demon system, but it can knock a demon out in five seconds."

"But sometimes the demons wake up before they're supposed to," Michelle said. "Like a patient in the middle of an operation when the anesthesia wears off."

They were both insane.

"Sure you don't want a taste?" Zack brought the needle close to her arm. "You'll be out so fast—"

And what? Wake up when they were cutting her open? "Keep that thing away from me!" There had to be a way for her to escape.

Why—why couldn't she have been born with stronger demon powers? She would have loved to be able to toss the freak duo across the room with just a thought.

He leaned toward her. "Are you scared, Holly?"

Hell, yes, but she'd never admit it to him.

An expression of sadness drifted over his face. "I had plans for you, back at the beginning. I was going to spend my life with you—"

"You were screwing *her*!" Bad enough he was threatening to kill her, now she had to listen to this crap again.

His nostrils flared. "Michelle understood me."

Uh, yeah, that was obvious. Who else would have joined in to help him torture and kill?

Michelle's fingers curled over his shoulder. "Of course, I do. You just want to make the world a better place."

His shoulders fell and blessedly, that needle dropped away from her arm. "That's all I want. To rid the Earth of those who don't belong, the mutations who should never have been born."

So now she was a mutation?

"I've got to check outside," Zack murmured, placing the syringe on the instrument tray. "Got to make sure I see the demon coming."

Because if he didn't, Niol would kill him before Zack ever had a chance to scream.

He turned away, hurrying from the room.

And leaving her with Ms. Cut Happy.

Michelle tilted her head, seeming to listen to Zack's footsteps as they faded away.

Holly glanced around the room, trying to figure out where she was. The walls were bare, old, yellow. No furniture was in the room.

Another abandoned house? An old office building? *Where?*

"What can you do?" Michelle asked and Holly's gaze turned back to her. The woman studied her with narrowed blue eyes. "Can you make fires? Move objects?"

Why did she want to know?

"I don't think you can," she continued. "You would have tried something by now."

True.

"Carl tried." She lifted her hand and brushed back the long fall of blond hair that partially hid her forehead.

The move revealed a slanting red gash. Still healing. "He got me—"

Good for Carl. She was glad he'd gone out fighting. He'd always been a fighter.

"But he couldn't stop Zack."

Holly swallowed.

"What can you do?" Michelle asked again.

Nothing. But she'd be damned if she admitted her weakness. Instead, Holly narrowed her own eyes and growled, "You really don't want to find out."

Michelle jerked away, her elbow ramming into the table. "The p-power is *wasted* on you! You don't deserve it, just like you didn't deserve him."

Now that didn't sound like a woman who thought demons were a terrible mutation who needed to be stopped. Holly's lips parted. "You don't want to destroy the demons—you want to find out where their strength comes from!" Because she wanted the same power. Twisted bitch.

Michelle just smiled her cold, perfect smile.

Holly jerked against the restraints. "Get me out of here, and I'll tell you everything you want to know." A lie, but so what?

The smile dimmed a bit.

"I didn't start out as a demon," Holly continued, voice low. "I *became* one." Ah, but she could bullshit with the best of them. "You can change, too. Let me go and I'll tell you *everything.*"

Michelle's fingers fluttered in the air. She glanced toward the open door.

Come on. Come on . . .

Then she looked back at Holly. "I—"

"He's here!" Zack's bellow.

Holly's heart seemed to stop.

Zack ran into the room, face flushed. "Get ready! Grab the g—"

The wall behind him exploded.

When the dust cleared, Niol was there—looking tall and dark and very pissed.

And Zack, bleeding and shaking, was at Holly's side, the scalpel pressed to her throat. "You so much as blink, demon, and I'll cut her from ear to ear."

The blade already *was* cutting her. Digging into her skin and sending a rivulet of blood sliding over her flesh.

Niol's black eyes were on Zack. *So much fury.* The air in the room boiled with his rage.

Holly wasn't breathing anymore.

Then Niol laughed and she'd never heard a colder sound. "Dr. Hall, you don't know who the fuck you're dealing with—"

The floor trembled, rolled, and when Zack cried out, Niol raised his hand. The scalpel jerked free of Zack's fingers and flew right to Niol's waiting palm.

The restraints holding Holly broke free. *Love demon power.* She heaved up, twisted, and shoved both of her feet right into Zack's chest. He stumbled back, arms waving as he tried to catch himself.

The bastard hit the floor, hard, and Holly jumped to her feet.

"My kill." Niol's voice was guttural.

She hesitated and glanced up into his eyes.

Niol stalked forward. Zack flew up into the air as if jerked by a puppet string. "You took what was *mine*, asshole." *The puppet master.* Niol threw him across the room.

Zack thudded into the far wall, landing close to a slowly rising and bleeding Michelle.

The floor rolled again.

Niol is out of control. She knew it, could feel it in the fierce rush of air all around her.

"Now I'm going to take everything that's yours."

Zack's fingers shot up and he began clawing at his throat, as if fighting against unseen hands. His face mottled and his eyes bulged.

Niol was killing him, with just a thought.

"Niol—"

The roar of a gun.

No.

Holly jerked at the sound. Michelle was on her feet, a wide grin on her bloody lips, and a gun in her hand.

One that was aimed right at Niol.

One that she'd already shot.

"Again!" A scream from Zack. A Zack who was breathing again.

Holly's gaze flew to Niol. A red circle, ever widening, bloomed in the middle of his chest. The bitch had fired straight at him, right into his heart.

Niol fell to his knees.

"No!" This time, the roar was Holly's.

Chapter 18

The bitch had shot him. Niol's legs sagged beneath him and his knees hit the floor with bruising force.

Fuck. Should have made sure she was out.

His chest burned while a cold numbness eased into his fingertips.

"Again!" Zack screamed.

Niol lifted his head and locked eyes on the woman. He'd take the hit, then take them both down because there was no damn way he'd ever let them hurt Holly.

Shaking, he tried to rise—

Holly stepped in front of him.

The heart that the first bullet had barely missed stopped.

A laugh from the crazy blonde.

"No, Holly, *move!*" She wasn't like him. She couldn't take a shot and survive.

"Not in a vital organ!" The soon-to-be dead man's scream. "She won't live, he will—*not in a vital or—*"

Niol grabbed Holly. *No damn way.*

He shoved her to the floor.

The second bullet tore through his shoulder.

Fuck! Fuck! Fuck!

These humans were pissing him off.

His feet slipped on the tile as he fought to rise. Too much blood, dripping everywhere. Too much—

The psycho bitch had the gun aimed at him again. Time to end this shit.

His eyes narrowed. He blocked the pain—

Her fingers squeezed the trigger—

Focus. He'd get her to turn the gun back on herself—

"You're not hurting him!" A scream of fury.

Then the gun jerked from the blonde's fingers—and flew right through the air and into Holly's hand.

Sonofabitch.

His little demon still had a few surprises for him.

Her face was stunned.

So was the blonde's.

Niol sucked in a sharp breath. His woman was something else.

"No! No, you fucking bitch! It's not going to end like this!" The bastard ex-fiancé screamed and lunged forward, kicking a surgical tray out of his way. He reached out, swiped something up with his right hand—

A scalpel already red with blood. *Holly's blood.* The same scalpel he'd had to her throat. Niol had dropped the scapel when the first bullet hit him.

Zack snarled and lifted the weapon high with his hand and jumped right at Holly.

Time to die. Niol blocked the pain and sent out a burst of raw power.

He saw the sudden terror on the human's face.

I'm stopping your heart, bastard, and it'll never start again.

Understanding in those blue eyes.

See you in hell.

Holly fired her gun, sending the bullet blasting into Zack's chest.

He fell to the floor, body twitching, then—

Still.

One down.

A shriek.

One to go.

Niol glanced over at the woman. Her eyes were on Zack's still body and her mouth was open as she screamed. Again and again.

Wincing, he managed to rise to his feet.

"Niol . . ." So soft when the screams were so loud.

His gaze went back to the only one who mattered. Her lips trembled as tears leaked from her eyes. "Oh, God, Niol, your chest . . ."

He forced a smile. For her. "Love, it's not as bad as it looks." Yes, it was, but he'd heal. He lifted the arms that felt leaden.

The blonde let out another wild cry, then streaked behind them, running for the door.

Holly's breath caught and she took a step after her.

"No." Niol snagged her hand. *Alive. Safe.* He'd been so worried and—

Afraid.

He hadn't been able to manage finesse when he'd arrived at the run-down house. He'd gone in, fury engulfing him, and the rage had blasted right into the wall.

"My men are outside. She won't get away." She'd never hurt another demon again.

Holly turned back toward him. She reached up with her right hand, touching his chest. His blood soaked her fingers. "Don't do something stupid and die on me." The words were tough but her lips still shook.

He kissed her. Tasted her, and knew that he'd just come seconds away from truly losing his soul.

If she'd been dead on that table when I arrived . . .

Her body brushed his.

Don't think about it.

The salt of her tears brushed his mouth.

Crying, for him.

When had a woman ever done that?

When had he ever deserved tears?

Niol lifted his head. "Don't be scared. It takes more than bullets to kill me." To knock him on his ass, or rather, his knees, yeah. Bullets would do that, for a while. "No weapon of man can take out a level-ten, love. A gun can't kill me." A lot more would be required to rip him out of this world.

Her gaze flickered to the body. Niol stiffened. "It wasn't your kill." He didn't want that knowledge on her. Holly's soul was clean and would stay that way. "Before you fired, I—"

She shook her head. "*I* killed him. That's what we tell the police and anybody else who asks."

Her eyes met his once more.

She knew, he realized. Maybe she'd known the instant he sent out his power.

Smart. Tough.

His.

Her chin lifted. "Zack—he was messed up. What he wanted to do—" Holly broke off and shook her head. "He had to be stopped."

Niol wiped away the blood on her throat. Pressed his fingers against the cut to try and stop the bleeding and—

"You saved my life tonight, Niol. For what now? The third time?"

She saved me. "Who's counting?" He pushed her toward the door. He wanted her out of that room, away from the blood and the death and back someplace safe.

"I am." Soft.

He realized his hands were trembling. From the blood loss.

From the fear of losing her.

She was safe now. The hunter was gone. No more danger. No more case.

His little reporter wouldn't need him to walk on the wild side anymore.

He'd saved her, but Niol was very afraid that now, he'd lose her . . .

And there wasn't a single thing he could do about that.

"Police!" He didn't stop walking at the yell. Didn't even flinch. Holly glanced up, her brows pulling together as they crept into the hallway and found half a dozen uniformed officers waiting with guns drawn.

Michelle stood trapped between two of the cops. Tears streamed down her face. Her hands were cuffed in front of her. Niol's demons were behind the police line. The demons had fury stamped on their faces, and their gazes were locked dead center on the blonde.

Payback. They want it so badly they can taste it.

Some demons were damn territorial. You didn't hurt one of theirs and walk away.

His eyes lingered on Michelle. *No, you didn't walk away.*

Payback would be coming soon for her. The cops had better watch her closely and keep her far away from any demon inmates.

That would be a hard job because the cops wouldn't be able to see the demons until it was too late.

"Lapen? *Shit!* We need a stretcher in here, ASAP!" Brooks shoved past the uniforms, lowering his weapon as he rushed forward.

His wounds were already closing. Niol knew that by the time he made it to the hospital, the bullet would have worked out of his chest and the wound would have closed.

The bullet in his shoulder had gone straight through—that hole was nearly healed now.

"Not necessary," he said, tightening his grip on Holly. He had the feeling she was about to slip right through his fingers.

"Is all that your blood?" Brooks demanded, lips tightening. "How are you even on your feet?"

For a guy who spent his nights with a succubus, the man should really know more about demons.

A shot in the chest, no matter how close the range, wouldn't stop a level-ten for long.

Niol caught sight of the wolf shifter cop, pushing his way through the crowd.

A gun wouldn't kill him, but that one—though he'd sure never let on to the detective—*he* could give Niol a good run at death.

A wolf shifter's claws, if they got a lucky swipe at his throat, would be able to end his days. Not a mortal weapon, so one deadly to him.

Not that he'd ever be telling the cop . . .

There was a reason level-ten demons didn't get along with wolf shifters. Self-preservation.

Gyth reached for him, as if he'd *help*. "Get the hell away from me," Niol growled, straightening his shoulders. The day he needed help from a wolf would be the day he—

"Humans are here," Gyth whispered. *"You were shot in the heart, asshole. Let me help."*

Not the heart. The woman's aim hadn't been that good.

But Holly's shot at the male had been perfect. The lady sure knew how to handle a gun. He'd have to ask her about that one day.

One day. But for now . . .

Niol gave a grim nod, then, though it grated, he wrapped an arm around the wolf shifter's shoulders and let Gyth lead him from the house. He kept his right hand locked on Holly. No way would he leave her behind in that shack that smelled of death.

"He's going to kill me! You have to protect me! I need help!" The bitch's screams rose, making his temples

throb. He spared a glance for the blonde as he passed her and watched with satisfaction as she jerked back against the cop near her.

"We'll take care of her, don't worry," Gyth said. The words, Niol knew, were a warning. Because when Gyth turned his head, just a fraction, and met Niol's stare, he saw very clearly what the cop was thinking. *My job. Don't even think of going after her.*

Ah, but the wolf knew he liked to hunt.

Niol tossed one more glance at the woman. Then he lifted his eyes to the cop who held her with one hand clenching around her shoulder. A middle-aged cop, with black hair already going gray, a strong jaw, and lips that were pressed into a firm line. Niol met his warm brown gaze—and looked straight through his glamour.

Brown eyes flashed black.

Told his partner before. Demons are a third of the force. "Don't worry, detective," he said, keeping his voice calm, but making sure he was heard by the ones that mattered. "I'll leave this case in the hands of the police. I'm sure it will be handled just right."

The cop on the other side of the blonde stepped forward. Niol recognized him. *Another one of mine.*

A slight inclination of the cop's head.

"Don't worry, love," he told Holly as they left the woman's cries behind them, "she won't hurt anyone else."

That was a guarantee.

They stepped onto an old porch. One with rotting wood and loose boards. Police cruisers surrounded the house. Two ambulances waited near the drive, and there was even a fire truck braking at the side of the broken street.

Niol glanced over at Gyth.

The wolf gave a slow smile. "I put a tail on you. Figured after the fire, you wouldn't be taking shit much longer."

No, he wouldn't.

"Didn't expect a grab on Storm." The smile dimmed. "Thought you were the target, not her."

"So did I." For a time.

"I didn't expect a grab, either," Holly muttered.

Gyth shook his head. "When you came in here and I heard the explosion—"

The shifter would have heard the wall collapse from miles away.

"—I knew the shit had hit the fan. I called for backup and got to the house just when the shots were fired."

Gyth exhaled on a heavy sigh. "That blonde came running out—don't know where the hell she thought she was going, but I had to hold your men back when they saw her."

Yes, Niol bet he'd had to hold them—hard.

EMTs rushed toward him with a stretcher. Dammit. Niol felt the eyes on him. He heard the screech of tires and saw the news vans jerking to a stop in a cloud of dirt.

"Sir?" A young guy, clean shaven, wearing a perfectly pressed uniform.

"Go with them, Niol," Holly said, her voice stroking over him.

His teeth clenched, but he climbed on the stretcher. He'd disappear long before the ambulance pulled up at the hospital and the ride would keep him away from prying eyes.

Least I'm finally away from the shifter.

Though he'd admit the bastard wasn't as bad as he'd thought. Emily could have done worse.

Course she could have done better.

Holly leaned over him. Her eyes were wide and stark and the dried blood on her neck made him want to kill that asshole all over again.

"Thank you." Her mouth lifted into a half-smile.

He didn't want her fucking thanks.

He just wanted her.

The EMT moved to strap him down.

"Don't even think about it!"

The guy backed up, fast.

"Kiss me, Holly." One more kiss, before the world that was waiting with cameras and microphones stole her.

"Storm! *Storm!*" Niol didn't look away from her as he heard the yell.

Holly bent over him and brushed her lips against his. *Not nearly enough.*

His fingers tangled in her hair. He pulled her closer and thrust his tongue into her sweet mouth.

Still not enough.

"Storm! Storm, get a mike! *You're* the damn story! *This is the best story of your life!* Get. A. Mike!"

Her head lifted. The EMTs waited to wheel him away. And the cameras waited for her.

His heart ached, and not because of the bullet slowly making its way back up through his chest.

She'd stepped in front of a bullet for him. Been willing to die. *For him.*

Don't deserve her. Never will. Need to walk away.

Maybe for once, he should do the right thing.

"Good-bye, love." His fingers slipped down her cheek. Brushed over her lips.

Then the EMTs rolled him away from her. She looked so fragile, with the blood on her clothes and the shadows under her eyes. So breakable.

But today, faced with hell, she hadn't broken.

She'd fired back. Tried to kill a man she'd nearly married. *Protected me.*

They pushed him into the back of the ambulance. The instant the doors slammed, Niol jerked upright. One of the EMTs, the woman, was a shifter. She'd come to Paradise a few times. A real fox.

He pointed to the brunette. "The vehicle makes a pit stop before the hospital."

She smiled. She knew the way things worked in this city.

Unable to stop himself, Niol turned his head and watched through the back window. Two men stood on either side of Holly. Ben, the cameraman he'd seen a few times. His head was bandaged, and he had his camera hoisted up on his shoulder.

The other guy was older, with silver-streaked hair. He shoved a microphone toward Holly.

Her gaze lifted. Met his.

Do the right thing.

The siren wailed to life.

The ambulance pulled away.

Doing the right thing—fucking hard. But for her, he'd do just about anything.

Even if that meant leaving her.

He'd left her. The red lights from the ambulance lit up the street and Holly watched those lights, spellbound.

He'd left. And she'd seen his eyes—seen the good-bye in them. This wasn't an I'll-See-You-Later leave.

This was the end.

The hunters had been stopped. The demons were safe again, and Holly had never felt more alone.

"*For Christ's sake,* Storm, take the microphone!"

The bellow had her lifting the gaze she'd dropped and looking into Mac's glittering eyes. The guy's face was crimson and he seriously looked like he would be bursting a blood vessel any minute.

"Take the mike." Her cameraman's whisper.

She blinked and realized that bright lights and cameras were all around her. She heard other reporters talking, running with the story they'd no doubt picked up on the police radio.

It was *the* story. One she knew more about than any other. But she didn't want to tell it. She wanted to go after Niol.

It can't end this way.

It didn't matter why they had come together in the beginning. She didn't care about his past. She just wanted his future.

She wanted him.

"I'm begging you—take the microphone!" Mac. His knuckles whitened around the microphone. Had she really thought he might be the killer?

She'd sure never thought Zack was . . .

A red hole in his chest. Eyes wide with terror.

No. *Don't go there.*

The fingers that were shaking fisted.

The ambulance was gone now. The sudden wind on her cheeks stung, bringing tears to her eyes.

Holly swallowed and slowly straightened her shoulders.

This wasn't the way things would end for her. Saved, but alone. No damn way.

This wasn't her ending. Wasn't *their ending.*

Her eyes narrowed. "I know where to find you."

"Maybe we should get a doctor to look at her," Ben mumbled. "Could be she's in shock."

Probably was. Holly figured that would account for the trembling. But, as always, a breakdown really wasn't an option for her.

There was a story to cover, and after that, there was a demon to catch. A demon who wouldn't be getting away from her so easily.

No, not so easily.

Holly reached for the microphone. "How do I look?"

She knew the answer, though, even before Mac helpfully supplied—

"Like shit, sweetheart, shit." A whistle. "We're gonna blow those other bastards right out of the water!"

As usual, his tact was absent.

Such was Mac.

"Zoom in on her neck—and her side—some blood's there, too," he ordered.

But Ben hesitated. "Hol—you sure you don't want a doctor to look at you?"

The bleeding had stopped. Luckily, her wounds were shallow. She'd be fine. "Start rolling." This was *her* story. Hers, Sam's, Carl's—she owed it to them. And to Kim and Julia.

The other reporters on the scene, they scented there was more to the story than met the eye. Once upon a time, she would have been like them. Desperate to reveal the *real* truth about the killings.

But there was something more important at stake tonight. Justice had been served. *Would* be served to Michelle. Now there were others to think about. Others to protect.

All of the demons in the shadows.

The many monsters who feared humans would come hunting them, too. If their secrets were revealed.

Niol didn't fear discovery, but the others did. So she'd keep their secrets safe.

She'd also get her story, and maybe a freaking Peabody Award to boot. Hell, she *deserved* one.

Ben turned on the camera and a light spilled onto her. Holly lifted the microphone, aware that the lens would pick up her trembling. Nothing she could do about that.

Or about the fact that she probably really did look like shit.

Holly took a deep breath and looked right into the lens. "Justice was served tonight, here on this quiet street where a vicious murderer" *You never can trust some people* "was killed, and his co-conspirator . . ." *Probably should be using the word "alleged" but screw that* "was captured by police."

Her left hand lifted and brushed over the cut on her throat. "The killer was delusional, seeing demons everywhere, and in the end, his insanity pushed him over the edge" *and sent him to hell,* "and his life ended with the shot of a gun."

Holly heard Gyth swear behind her. She would've recognized that voice anywhere. She knew the guy wanted to yank her off the air and she also knew that he wouldn't. She'd bled for this story. *It was hers.*

She'd give the cops a statement later.

"I'm Holly Storm for News Flash Five, and I'm live on the scene of what could have been my own murder . . ."

The lens rotated as Ben moved in for a close-up.

"Damn, but she's something else." Brooks shook his head as Holly delivered her story, voice cool and calm, face bruised and bloody. He sucked in a sharp breath. "Should we be worried about what she's going to say?" One word about demon-hunters and they'd be screwed.

Holly Storm had them by the balls.

All she had to do was direct the cameraman's attention to Michelle—that woman would spill everything about the demons. *We need to get her loaded into the truck, fast.*

Gyth shook his head. "Storm won't talk about the *Other.*" The guy sounded completely confident.

Brooks didn't exactly share that confidence. "Maybe we should pull her off the air. We've got a dead body on the scene, man, and—"

"I shot my attacker . . ." Still cool and calm.

Brooks closed his eyes. *Fuck.*

"She didn't kill him." Brooks cracked open his eyes

and saw that Gyth was still watching Holly Storm, his head cocked to the left as he said, "But she'd take the fall in a heartbeat for that kill."

For him.

Brooks felt his temples throb. "Niol got to him first?"

Gyth didn't answer, but then, he didn't really have to. Brooks knew just what Niol was capable of doing with his mind. "Should've given us a statement first," he muttered, rubbing the bridge of his nose.

"I don't think Storm makes a habit out of doing the things she *should* do."

He was getting that.

"Niol's not gonna make it to the hospital, is he?"

"No, but we know where to find him."

True. The guy had never been one to hide. Brooks figured they'd get his statement soon enough. One thing he'd learned, the *Other* cases didn't always go by the book.

Five minutes later, the camera finally lowered.

They headed for Storm.

She dressed with care. Sexy two-inch heels. Short black skirt. Low neck, cleavage-showing, bloodred shirt.

Her side ached and her arm still stung, but, all things considered, Holly figured she was doing pretty damn well.

For a woman who'd almost been sliced open.

She took a deep breath.

Over. Zack wouldn't hurt anyone else, not ever again.

Holly stared into her mirror and watched her eyes fade to black. She could control the change now. It felt . . . natural.

At this point, she rather liked those eyes.

Not impure. Not a mistake.

Me.

The cops had kept her for hours. So many questions. So many eyes on her.

Then there had been more cameras. Other reporters wanting her to talk.

When she'd finally managed to escape, her first instinct had been to run straight to Paradise.

But she hadn't wanted to see Niol still covered in blood.

Besides, she'd known that the police were going for him—*his* turn to answer questions.

So she'd waited and let the darkness fall.

Holly glanced at the clock. Close to ten p.m. now.

Things should just be getting started at Paradise.

Time for her to hunt a demon . . .

And to lay her soul bare before him.

Chapter 19

Demons and vampires packed the floors of Paradise. Holly walked right past them, her chin up, her shoulders back, her heels clicking on the floor.

Music blared in her ears. A loud, drumming beat that heated her blood.

So many bodies. So much power.

But she wanted only one man.

There. At the bar. Head back, strong fingers wrapped around his glass of amber liquid.

A whisper went through the crowd and she knew she'd been spotted.

News traveled even faster in the demon world than it did in the human one.

Niol's head lowered and his eyes locked on her. No surprise showed on his face.

He knew I was here the minute I stepped inside Paradise.

He watched her, his face still, expressionless. The mask was back. The demon who felt nothing.

Holly didn't stop walking.

She could see right through the mask. She could see the emotion in his eyes. Burning black fire.

More whispers as she drew closer to him.

They'd have an audience for this. Not her style, but his.

Holly stopped two feet away from him. The guy looked good. No, gorgeous. Not even a hint of pale skin. Apparently two gunshot wounds didn't slow the man down long at all.

Though they'd sure scared some years off her life.

His gaze swept over her, lingering not on the exposed skin of her breasts, but on the faint cut on her throat, the bandage on her arm, and the wound on her side that was covered by her silk shirt.

"You shouldn't be here." A rumble of sound.

Her brows rose. "I thought I was welcome here." If he wanted to tell her to fuck off, he could do it. But this wasn't going to be some quiet ending. She was coming clean with Niol.

Time to tell the demon just how she felt.

"You're an asshole, Niol. You saved my life, but then you left me and didn't look back."

His eyelids flickered at that.

Had he looked back?

The glass in his hand cracked. Slowly, carefully, Niol sat the drink down on the bar top. "Why are you here, Holly? The case is over."

And so are we.

No, not yet.

"There are only two reasons humans come here . . ." This came from the bartender.

I'm not human. Those rules didn't apply to her. They never had.

"Are you here to play?" Niol asked.

Holly shook her head. "Game time's over, demon."

His lips tightened and Niol stood, the barstool scraping on the floor behind him. *"Why are you here?"*

For you. She knew her eyes said the answer for her.

He shook his head.

She closed the distance between them, rose up, and kissed him. Kissed him with her hunger, with the lust that was always so close, and with the love that had stirred slowly within her.

A gust of wind tossed her hair and teased her flesh.

Niol lifted his head.

The blaring music quieted.

"Come with me."

To hell and back if she had to. *Oh, wait, been there.*

Niol caught her wrist and led her toward his office. The door slammed behind them and he wrapped his arms around her, caging her body tightly against his.

"I'm trying to do what's right," he gritted, and his fingers dug into her arms. "Don't you see, love? For once, I want to do what's right."

The demon wasn't nearly as dark inside as most people thought.

Not dark at all, really.

She finally saw him clearly. Her demon. Her Niol. Just . . . hers.

He stared into her eyes and his jaw clenched. "Fuck, no Holly—I warned you! It's too dangerous! You can't make me love—"

"I love you, Niol." Good, bad. Everything.

He swallowed. "You shouldn't. I-I'm not . . . what you need."

"You're the only man I need and the *only* one I want." There was really just one thing he could say to make her leave. Just one. "You saved me. And I'm not just talking about tonight." Though she'd never forget her first sight of him in that horrible room. One look, and she'd known that he would keep her safe.

Maybe she'd always known that.

"You showed me who I really am. You got me to stop hiding from myself."

He didn't speak.

Final shot. Holly licked her lips. "Do you want me to stay with you?"

"What I want doesn't matter." His fingers were steel strong around her. "What *you* need—"

"Do you love me?"

Don't make me love you.

The only answer that would matter for her. If he said no, she'd walk away, and drag her pride with her.

She'd walk away, but dammit, she'd miss him.

"Do you?" She pressed and the mask on his face cracked.

Niol's lips took hers. Wild and hard and hot and oh, just what she wanted.

"Hell, yes," he growled against her mouth. *"Yes."* The words seemed torn from him.

Probably because they were.

But he shook his head and shoved back from her. "I can't let you stay, this isn't the world you want—"

A world of demons and shifters and dark shadows that would always hide some of the light. "Yes, it is."

"I'm trying to do the *right* thing here, Holly!"

"Screw right," she said, and felt the happiness swell inside her. "I just want you." She knew life with him wouldn't be easy. The guy wasn't an easy man.

Demon.

But with Niol by her side and in her bed, she'd be a happy woman.

He caught her face in his hands. "You love me?" Niol seemed a bit stunned.

"More than any damn thing." He didn't think he deserved love, she knew that. Tough. The man was going to get all the love she had to give.

"I'll want forever—if you make me think—*I'll want forever.*"

Ah, now that sounded like the demanding demon she knew and loved. "I wouldn't expect anything else." And forever for him, if the stories were true, would be a very long time.

Maybe she wouldn't have as many years as he would, but she'd enjoy the time they had. Every. Single. Day.

And night.

The nights—she'd enjoy them the most.

The lock clicked behind them. Niol's warm hands slid under her shirt and crept up to her breasts. *What I want.* Holly arched toward her demon lover.

Forever.

In darkness and in light.

Detective Colin Gyth headed toward the holding cell. There were a few questions he still had for Michelle Ridgeway, questions that he wanted answered before he went home and crawled in bed with Emily.

No guards were around when he approached. Colin tensed. *Not right.*

He ran forward—

And found Michelle in her cell. Her body lay sprawled on the floor, a bedsheet tied around her neck.

Fuck.

His gaze scanned the area, noting the placement of the sheet. One end wrapped around the woman's throat. The other knotted high in the bars.

Looked like a suicide.

Looked like one . . .

His teeth snapped together.

But it sure as hell isn't. I'd stake my badge on it. Too many demons around. Too many with powers that would let them slip right into a human's mind.

But he'd never be able to prove it.

Sonofabitch.

It looked like the demon-hunter case was closed.

The next night, Niol sat at the bar and waited for his reporter. She'd promised to meet him after her last broadcast.

She chose me. That fact still managed to shock him, and little shocked him.

He'd take it slow with her, make sure she understood just what his life entailed. Then, when she was ready, he'd let her know that when he said *forever,* well, he meant it.

No way would he spend any days without her. There were ways to extend a life—ways he'd share with Holly.

As he'd share everything with her.

A young blond woman walked into his bar. He watched her, vaguely curious. *Not demon.* Human.

Not there to play.

Interesting.

He glanced at his watch. Holly would be there soon. Five minutes, ten tops.

He'd have her naked in his office three minutes after that.

"I'm looking for a vampire."

Niol blinked and found the blonde in front of him. Terrible haircut. Short and shaggy.

He motioned to the bar. "Take your pick."

Her hands balled on her hips. "His name's Lane. Lane Mims. Asshole with a habit of hurting women."

Niol stared back at her. "Haven't seen him." Who the hell was this woman?

Holly walked into the bar. He caught a glimpse of her over the blonde's shoulder, caught her scent—sweet lavender. Niol rose.

The human put her hand on his chest. A hand that

pushed a small business card against him. "Yeah, you have."

When her hand moved, he caught the card. *Bounty hunter.*

Behind her, Holly cut her way through the crowd.

"If he's dead, I'm wasting my time here." Blunt.

Holly saw him and a smile lit up her face. Her dimple winked.

My life.

So fucking simple.

The card turned to ash in his fingers. He stepped to the side and reached out a hand to Holly. "Guess you'd better head back to—" What address had been on the card? "Louisiana, then. Because that vamp isn't around here." Well, pieces of him could be.

Lane had made another attack. Barely left a teenage girl alive.

The cops hadn't caught him, but the demons had.

The woman's lips thinned.

Holly took his hand and glanced at the other woman.

But the bounty hunter just turned and walked away.

"Who is she?" Holly asked.

To her, he wouldn't lie. Ever. He'd told her all his secrets in the hours before dawn. Every black deed, and she'd stayed with him. "Bounty hunter. Looking for a vamp—"

"Lane."

He hadn't given her the name, but if there was one thing he'd realized about his Holly—the woman had some damn good sources.

"I saw the girl. *Kennedy.* I talked to her when I went to the hospital to check on Kim."

"Kim's awake?" He hadn't heard that—

"Yeah—yeah, she's awake. Doesn't remember anything about the attack. The doctors don't understand how she's survived, but they think she's going to make a full recovery."

Good.

"Kennedy—she wasn't doing as well."

Because she was a human.

"I-I called Dr. Drake. Asked her to stop by and talk to her."

Smart. Emily would help the girl. All the other doctors would just think she was crazy when Kennedy started talking about men with fangs and claws. Emily would understand.

Yes, the Monster Doctor would help her.

Just like she was helping the King boy.

"Lane—he's been stopped, hasn't he?" Not a question, too much certainty there.

"Yes."

"Good." A dark understanding was in her eyes, the kind one only got after living in the *Other* world. "Prisons just can't hold some people."

They sure couldn't hold vamps. But in this case, it didn't matter. Lane wouldn't be a problem for anyone, not anymore.

He'd have to check on the girl. He'd ended the vamp's attacks, but—too late. Kennedy's assault was on his shoulders. He'd left the vamp in such a hurry to find Holly. There hadn't been enough time then to—

Holly nodded. "You did what you had to do . . ."

And he'd do it again.

"I saw what he did," she continued. *"I saw."*

No judgment against him. No fury. Understanding.

The woman had his heart in her fist.

"You don't have to fight alone anymore, Niol. You've got me now."

Holly didn't look at him with fear or revulsion or disgust.

She just looked at him as if he were—a man.

Every dark secret. Every black spot on his soul. *She knew*.

Fuck if she didn't make him want to be—hell, *better*.

Maybe he could be, for her.

Her slow smile spread over her face. The smile that made his cock jerk and his control weaken.

His woman.

One that wouldn't run away, one that wouldn't fear him.

One that wouldn't break, no matter how fierce the danger flowed around her.

She'd shot her ex-lover for him. Put herself in front of death, for him.

A woman like her, if she offered herself, a smart man held as tight as he could.

"I love you," Holly whispered.

Niol knew he was staring at his weakness and his strength.

His heart . . . *held in her fist*.

Screw doing what was right. Holly wanted him, he wanted her, and he'd make sure he gave her every single thing she desired in this life. He'd love her every night. He'd give her as much pleasure and passion as she could stand, until she screamed for him to stop, then screamed for him to start again. He'd protect her. And he'd fucking destroy anyone who ever tried to hurt her.

Fate could be a cruel bitch, but sometimes, *sometimes*, she could take pity on a demon.

She'd sure given him a real taste of Paradise.

Need some INSTANT GRATIFICATION?
Jill Shalvis's new book is just the thing . . .

This was new for him. And oddly . . . stimulating. "I think I'm going to be okay."

Emma arched a brow. Daring him to admit the truth. "Annie told you," he said with a sigh.

"That you're on a volunteer search and rescue team and you were called out to save a guy who'd gone off a cliff on his rock climb? That said guy panicked once you had him halfway up the cliff to safety, knocking you down about fifty feet? Yeah, she told me. *You* might have told me."

Stone looked at Annie, who was suddenly very busy at the stove.

"Oh, and given the redness I see around some of your cuts and bruises, you do need the antibiotics."

"You said I looked good."

"That was a few days ago. You don't look good now."

She let him start sweating over that one for a beat, before she shook her head. "You fell off a cliff and you're scared of me?"

"Hell, yes."

She stood up and headed toward him, and he stumbled back a step, smacking right into the door.

Spencer winced.

Annie cackled.

"Careful," Emma said, still coming at him. "Your ribs." She reached her hand into her bag.

Oh, Christ. He pictured another needle and felt his skin go clammy. His stomach went queasy. This wasn't working for him, not one little bit. Not unless she was going to strip down for him again. "I don't need—"

Still looking at him, she pulled out . . . a prescription bottle. "Are you afraid of pills, too?" she asked innocently, when he was beginning to suspect there was nothing innocent about her at all.

Annie snickered again.

"I swear to God," he muttered in her direction.

Emma lightly smacked the bottle against his pecs, a fact he found interesting—was it his imagination, or did she touch him a lot?

More importantly, did she do it on purpose? It was worth finding out, and testing, he leaned into her, just a little.

Her pupils dilated.

Check.

Her nostrils flared.

Check, check.

If they'd been wild animals, their foreplay had just been conducted. Still testing, he lifted his hand and covered hers, still against his chest.

She stared down at their now entangled fingers around the pill bottle, then lifted her gaze to his. Her breathing had changed.

Quickened.

Test over, he decided, his own breathing changing as well. Because oh hell yeah, she was aware of him, every bit as much as he.

Which meant she was all bark and no bite.

That was *very* good to know.

The saga continues in Beth Williamson's
THE REDEMPTION OF MICAH,
out now from Brava . . .

Two hours later, Micah sat in the parlor and listened to the sounds from the bathing room upstairs. Miracle was singing at the top of her lungs while Candice hummed along. There was splashing, giggles and fun going on, yet he didn't join them. He couldn't.

He ran his hands down his face and looked around at the opulent furniture left behind when Madeline moved to Denver. The room reminded him of his mother's house and how they'd lived their lives in oblivious ignorance. Taking whatever they wanted without ever giving back.

Perhaps having Eppie but losing her inch by inch was his penance for such a childhood. Or perhaps it was punishment for his other multitudinous sins. No matter, it was his life and he'd come to accept it, but he couldn't enjoy it. Miracle was everything sweet and good in his life, and he treasured her beyond words. Just thinking about her soft hugs made his throat tighten.

God, he loved that little girl more than life.

With a sigh, he stood and headed toward the stairs. Each night he sat with Miracle as she visited her Mama before bed. Her childish voice would detail every second of her day to an unresponsive Eppie. One day perhaps, it would be more than a one-sided conversation.

Micah knew exactly how many breaths she took each hour. He watched the rise and fall of her chest, waiting and hoping. The hell of it was, he wasn't sure what he was hoping for. Micah wasn't ready to let her go but seeing her trapped between two worlds was killing him. He missed her, he loved her and dammit all, he wanted to see her open her eyes again.

It had been a true blue miracle the baby survived the trauma to its mother's body, even more amazing was that the child was born healthy and perfect. When she was pregnant, watching Eppie had become a habit because he could watch his child. *Their* child. The baby made from a love that shouldn't be, but was. Miracle had been active, sometimes for hours at a time. During that six month period, Micah never got tired of sitting by Eppie's bedside and watching, placing his hand on her belly, telling them both he loved them.

Micah wanted so many things, but the two that burned down deep in his gut was the fact he wanted to convince Eppie to marry him and he wanted to tell her he loved her. He'd been hesitant of revealing his feelings before, afraid of being rejected, of losing what he could have.

Regret was something he knew well, ate it for breakfast, lunch, and dinner each day. It brought him nothing but misery yet it was still his constant companion.

He entered Eppie's bedroom and was immediately awash in her scent, that unique smell that always made her heart beat faster. A gas lamp burned on the side table, bathing her in a golden glow. Just being in the room with her made him feel better.

She still looked beautiful, even if she'd survived for nearly three years on broth, milk, and water. Micah knew every inch of her body from the adorably crooked little toe to the sweet spot behind her right ear. He ran his fingers down her cocoa colored cheek, the skin as smooth as her daughter's.

"Hey there, Eppie girl." He sat down in his usual chair and put her hand in his. Squeezing the limp fingers, he started talking of Daisy and Miracle's antics. "That crazy dog actually came back and started digging when I was fixing the damn hole. Miracle wasn't happy about tying her up but she did it anyway. She's a good girl."

"Who's a good girl?"

Eppie's voice, long since unheard, made the hairs on the back of his neck stand up.

"Jesus Christ." He jumped out of the chair, knocking it backward a good three feet, along with his stomach. Micah looked down into the eyes of the woman who held his heart. "Eppie?"

She blinked and glanced down at herself, then back at him. "Why am I lying in bed? Have I been ill?"

"Are you really talking to me, honey?" His heart slammed into his throat as it pounded so hard, even his bones vibrated. "Eppie, oh my God, tell me I'm not dreaming."

"I'm not sure who you are or why you're in the bedroom with me, but I'm fairly sure you shouldn't be calling me honey." Eppie cocked her head and narrowed her gaze. "Who are you?"

And keep an eye out for the latest from
Shannon McKenna, TASTING FEAR,
coming next month from Brava . . .

"What's wrong now, Nancy?"

Liam sounded exhausted. Fed up. She didn't blame him a bit. She was a piece of work. Her mind raced, to come up with a plausible lie. Letting him see how small she felt would just embarrass them both.

She shook her head. "Nothing," she whispered.

He let out a sigh, and leaned back, leaning his head against the back of the couch. Covering his eyes with his hands.

That was when she noticed the condition of his hand. His knuckles were torn and raw, encrusted with blood. God, she hadn't even given a thought for his injuries, his trauma, his shock. She'd just zoned out, floated in her bubble, leaned on him. As if he were an oak.

But he wasn't an oak. He was a man. He'd fought like a demon for her, and risked his life, and gotten hurt, and she was so freaked out and self-absorbed, she hadn't even noticed. She was mortified.

"Liam. Your hand," she fussed, getting up. "Let me get some disinfectant, and some—"

It's OK," he muttered. "Forget about it."

"Like hell! You're bleeding!" She bustled around, muttering and scolding to hide her own discomfiture, gathering gauze and cotton balls and antibiotic ointment. He let her fuss, a martyred look on his face. After she'd finished taping his hand, she looked at his battered face and grabbed a handful of his polo. "What about the rest of you?"

"Just some bruises," he hedged.

"Where?" she persisted, tugging at his shirt. "Show me."

He wrenched the fabric out of her hand. "If I take off my clothes now, it's not going to be to show you my bruises," he said.

She blinked, swallowed, tried to breathe. Reorganized her mind. There it was. Finally verbalized. No more glossing over it, running away.

"After all this?" Her voice was timid. "You still want to . . . now?"

"Fuck, yes." His tone was savage. "I've wanted it since I laid eyes on you. It's gotten worse ever since. And combat adrenaline gives a guy a hard-on like a railroad spike, even if there weren't a beautiful woman in my face, driving me fucking nuts. Which puts me in a bad place, Nancy. I know the timing sucks for you. The timing's been piss poor since we met, but it never gets any better. It just keeps getting worse."

"Hey. It's OK." She patted his back with a shy, nervous hand. He was usually so calm, so controlled. It unnerved her to see him agitated.

He didn't seem to hear her. "And the worse it gets, the worse I want it," he went on, his voice harsh. "Which makes me feel like a jerk, and a user, and an asshole. Promising to protect you—"

"You did protect me," she reminded him.

"Yeah, and I told you it wasn't an exchange. You don't owe me sex. You don't owe me anything. And that really fucks me up. Because I can't even remove myself from the situation. I'm scared to death to leave you alone. And that puts me between a rock and a hard place."

She put her finger over his mouth. "Wow," she murmured. "I had no idea you could get worked into such a state. Mr. Super-mellow Liam let's-contemplate-the-beauty-of-the-flower Knightly."

His explosive snort of derision cut her off. She shushed him again, enjoying the feel of his lips beneath her finger. "You're not a jerk or a user," she said gently. "You were magnificent. Thank you. Again."

He looked away. There was a brief, embarrassed pause. "That's very generous of you," he said, trying to flex the wounded hand. "But I'm not fishing for compliments."

"I never thought that you were." She placed her own hand below his, and rested them both gently on his thigh. Her fingers dug into the thick muscle of his quadriceps, through the dirty, bloodstained denim of his jeans. Beneath the fabric, he was so hot. So strong and solid.

She moved her hand up, slowly but surely, stroking higher towards his groin. His breath caught, and then stopped entirely as her fingers brushed the turgid bulge of his penis beneath the fabric.

Here went nothing. "I think I know what you mean, about the hard place," she whispered, swirling her fingertips over it. Wow. A lot of him. That thick broad, hard stalk just went on and on. "Or was this what you meant when you were referring to the rock?"

His face was a mask of tension, neck muscles clenched, tendons standing out. "You don't have to do this," he said, his voice strangled.

Aw. So sweet. Her fingers closed around him, squeezing. He groaned, and a shudder jarred his body. "I can't seem to stop," she said.

"Watch out, Nancy," he said hoarsely. "If you start something now, there's no stopping it."

She stroked him again, deeper, tighter, a slow caress

that wrung a keening gasp from his throat. "I know," she said. "I know."

He reached out, a little awkwardly, clasping his arms around her shoulders, staring into her eyes as if expecting her to bolt.

He pulled her close, enfolding her in his warmth, his power.

Suddenly, they were kissing. She had no idea who had kissed who. The kiss was desperate, achingly sweet. Not a power struggle, not a matter of talent or skill, just a hunger to get as close as two humans could be. He held her like he was afraid she'd be torn away from him.